Dedication:
Jemima Parry-Jones MBE
Director - International Centre for Birds of Prey
Newent, Gloucestershire, GL18 1JJ.
www.icbp.org
++44(0)1531820286 (option 5 for a human if you are lucky!)
Charity Number 1159749

MERCEDES LACKEY

A VALDEMAR NOVEL

SPY, SPY AGAIN

FAMILY SPIES BOOK III

TITAN BOOKS

Spy, Spy Again
Print edition ISBN: 9781785653483
E-book edition ISBN: 9781785653490

Published by Titan Books
A division of Titan Publishing Group Ltd
144 Southwark Street, London SE1 0UP
www.titanbooks.com

First Titan edition: August 2020
10 9 8 7 6 5 4 3 2 1

A CIP catalogue record for this title is available from the British Library.

Printed and bound by CPI Group Ltd, Croydon CR0 4YY.

I

Tory and his best friend, Prince Kyril—Kee, to him—finished their long trudge across Companion's Field and paused at the high stone wall surrounding the entire Palace complex just as the last of the sun disappeared in the west. The last rays gilded the very top of the wall and turned the Guard just above them into an odd silhouette, half in light, half in darkness. He took a breath of the balmy summer air with deep appreciation; some of the Companions began drifting their way across the lush, green field with anticipation, even though he and Kee wouldn't be doing anything until twilight had settled in. The Companions all took great interest in their nightly race. So much so that he suspected them of secretly placing bets.

I wouldn't put it past them. Though what would a Companion use as a wager? Extra apples? Pocket pies? They get everything they could ever want or need. Maybe bragging rights are enough.

Not on who would win . . . it was a very off day for Tory when he *didn't* win. But whether or not he or Kee would finish without any penalty marks against them.

"Right, or left?" asked Kee, looking up, not at the formidable barrier of the wall but at the supple birch trees they'd be using to reach the top of it. The birches weren't nearly as old as many of the trees in the field; sadly, for all their grace and beauty, birches didn't live nearly as long as goldenoaks or beeches. But birches had one virtue that none of the other trees here had: flexibility.

The Guard glanced down at them. From where Tory stood, his amused expression was easy to read. The Guards enjoyed this nightly contest too, and even their commander encouraged their participation in it. Tory began warming up exercises, and Kee followed suit. Though . . . sometimes he only *pretended* to warm up; there were tricks you could use when you had to move desperately fast without getting a chance to warm up first, and from time to time he needed to practice those tricks as well.

"I'll take left, I took right last time," Tory said, and he snickered as he stretched his legs. "It won't matter, you know. I'm going to beat you anyway."

"You think," Kee retorted, making a face at him. Kee was the one of the six royal siblings who looked the least like either his father or his mother; he was shorter, slender, black-haired and had eyes of a peculiar shade that looked silver. His mother often teased him, saying she was sure a Hawkbrother had slipped in and left one of their own in the cradle, taking away her "real" baby. Kee found this hilariously funny, in no small part because his minor Gift of Empathy (just enough to be useful, not so much as to be a bother) always let him know she was just joking.

"Care to make a bet of it?" Tory challenged.

Kee shook his head. "You'd cheat."

Tory just snorted. Of all of his siblings, he was by far and away the most agile, and that was saying something. He'd been climbing and swinging on things since he was old enough to walk. Fortunately, by that time his mother had become used to seeing her children swarm over high places like tree-hares and took it all in stride. He'd been taking lessons from professional acrobats since he was nine. There was not one single structure on the Hill that he hadn't been to the top of multiple times—ideally without the owners even having a clue that he'd been there. Kee knew about some of that, but not all of it. Tory knew that there were things you just didn't talk about in his family, and whose manor house you'd been atop of—or inside—without the owner's knowledge or permission was one of those things you didn't talk about, even to your best friend. "Plausible deniability" was a way to keep those friends from getting into trouble. If there was one thing that Herald Mags' children could do, it was keep secrets.

Especially harmless ones. It didn't do Kee any harm to be blissfully ignorant of at least half of what Tory had done in his life. It also didn't do Kee any harm to think he could beat Tory on their nightly run around the walls, and the illusion that he had a chance would keep him trying.

It's about close to time. The sun should be well down by now. Up on the wall, the Guard bent over for a few moments, then straightened with a now-lit torch in one hand.

Tory was very much in favor of keeping his friend on his toes by encouraging this rivalry every night. *He,* at least, had some notion of what he was going to do with the rest of his life. He'd be his father Mags' agent, just as his older brother and sister were—though his sister Abi had an entirely separate career as a Master Artificer and Architect. Mags was in charge of the King's intelligence network, as his father-in-law had been before him, and being a Herald was no hindrance to that. In fact, it was an advantage, since people saw the white uniform and assumed, without ever bothering to *think* about it, that absolutely everything a Herald did was going to be above board and out in the open. That assumption made Mags a very good spy indeed, even when he wasn't in disguise. Mags was assumed to be the forgettable Herald-husband to the King's Own, "good old reliable Mags," former Kirball champion, plodding to and from his duties at the courts down in Haven. He was considered a minor Herald, useful mostly because he had the most powerful Gift of Mindspeech in Haven as well as the ability to impose coercive Truth Spell on command. And, of course, because he was the husband of the King's Own Herald. Very few people had any idea he was a lot more intelligent than he looked. Even fewer had a notion of a tenth of what he did for King and country. Tory had been brought up from the beginning—as had Abi and Perry— knowing that at the very least, he was expected to be able to defend himself, help his parents, and, above all, never, ever become a victim or a hostage. As Mags himself had once grumbled, "Me'n Amily did quite 'nuff uv thet on our own."

But Kee was not-quite-middlemost in the family of six Royal children. His oldest brother was first in line for the Crown, and a Herald. His second brother was second in line for the Crown, and a Herald. His older sister was third in line for the Crown, and a Herald. So the succession for the Crown was secure, barring an utter catastrophe wiping out the entire Royal Family, and if that happened, there would be a lot more to worry about than who was going to wear the Royal chunk of gold on his or her head. But Kee had not been Chosen . . . and so far nobody had found anything for him to do. So Tory had taken it upon himself to give his friend all the challenges he could handle.

Like egging him into taking every single course at all the Collegia that wasn't directly associated with being a Herald. And mastering every weapon the Weaponsmaster could shove into their hands. And, of course, his own little inventions, like this one.

Now the only light in Companion's Field came from that torch the Guard had in his hand. "You ready?" the man called down to them.

"Count us down!" Kee called back.

The Guard moved close to the big iron torch-basket that would illuminate the ground around this section of the wall. "Ready," he said, moving his torch close to the oil-soaked wood. "Steady. Go!"

And as he touched the fire to the basket, sending a column of flame up that all the Guards on the wall would be able to see, Kee and Tory raced up the two birch trees they had chosen for themselves. Reaching the tops within a breath of each other, they let go with their legs and bent the supple trunks down until their feet almost touched the top of the wall, let go of the branches, and hit the walkway running, going in opposite directions.

This wasn't *just* a race. That signal light had told the other Guards that the boys were coming. It was the Guards' job to try to stop them or, at least, tag them. And Tory's first opponent loomed right up ahead of him, a black silhouette against the light from his own ward-basket.

Ha. He's new to this. The Guard had made the fundamental mistake of thinking that because he was big, he'd be able to stop Tory just by blocking him. Tory allowed him to go right on thinking that—until the very last moment, as he leaped up onto the battlement on the outer face of the wall and, leaping from merlon to merlon on the crenellated battlement, raced past him.

He jumped down, not losing much speed in the process, faked to the right, then the left, and then, when the next Guard made a lunge for where the man *thought* Tory would be, he made a diving roll past, jumped to his feet, and was gone before the man could lay a fingertip on him.

As he ran, dodged, evaded, and, at one point, leaped *over* one of the Guards, he kept an eye on the other wall. And as he had more or less expected, twice one of the great basket-torches flared green. The Guards at those stations had tossed in a handful of copper salts to indicate that Kee had been "tagged."

One more Guard. The man lunged at the same time that Tory jumped —he planted one foot on the top of the man's helm and shoved him facedown into the walkway as he himself kept right on going.

Fortunately the Guard's helm kept him from injury, but—*that had to sting.*

He grinned and hurled himself from the top of the wall to the ground beneath. His feet barely touched the grounds of Healers' Collegium as he tucked and rolled, somersaulting twice, propelling himself back up onto his feet and into a run, heading for the wall of the building of the Collegium itself. This was a tricky part—not because he didn't know every handhold on the wall by heart, but because he had to make sure no one inside heard him scrambling up. He had to make no more sound than an errant branch tapping on the stone, or perhaps a small, nocturnal animal scrambling across it. A roof rat, maybe.

He reached the roof not even winded. This part was easy; the slates were dry and clean, and the rough rawhide soles of his climbing boots gave him plenty of grip. His goal was in sight— the top of the tallest tower of the Palace—which, providentially, was a square tower with another battlement around the flat top and access via a panel in the floor to the inside of the tower itself. That easy access to the inside was going to be very handy when he got there, because at this point, despite being in excellent shape, his sides had started to ache, and his breath burned a little in his throat and lungs. As it always did on this part of the run. Being in good shape could buy you only so much, and it wasn't the ability to sprint at your top speed indefinitely.

Which is so unfair. Companions can. Why can't humans?

He reached the Palace and the battlements on the roof. The Palace itself was four stories tall; it had four towers that reached an additional three stories high, one on each corner and a fifth, square one in the middle of the front that reached five. That middle one was his goal, but he had to elude the Guards on the battlements first.

It'd be a lot easier if I could kill them, he thought, wryly.

But the battlements here had the slanting slate roof of the Palace itself behind them, and he was able to slither his way past the Guard on the roof side without the Guard spotting him until it was too late, and he was past. Now was the most harrowing part of the run: the lizard-climb up to the top of the tower. Well, harrowing for someone who didn't do this every night it wasn't raining or snowing—and some nights when it was. Whoever had built this thing certainly hadn't done so with people like him in mind.

Then again, if the Guards had been allowed to shoot him, he'd be a pincushion by now.

It would be fairer to them to give them chalk-bags they could shoot at me with a sling. Do I want to be fairer and mention that?

Nope.

With his breath rasping in his lungs and his fingers and toes on fire with the strain, he hauled himself over the battlements at the top of the tower and tumbled to the feet of the amused Guard there. And no more than two breaths later, Kee did the same. "Gods *damn* it!" Kee rasped, pushing himself up into a sitting position, while Tory just sprawled over the wooden floor. "You beat me again!"

"Even—if I hadn't—" Tory gasped, trying not to laugh, "You got—tagged twice."

Kee swore. "So I did. Damnit."

The Guard gave both of them a sketchy salute and went back to his proper business of being on watch.

When they had gotten their breath back, Tory pulled the handle on the trap door at the rear of the tower, and they both clambered down a wooden ladder to the next floor down, which was actually a big iron grate strong enough to take the weight of several armed men. Tory went first, and Kee followed, closing the trap behind himself.

Now they were in a very familiar little room with several narrow windows on each of the four sides. The windows had been arrow slits, originally, though now the entire structure acted as a windcatcher, cooling the rooms of the Palace below it during the worst of the summer months. That was why the floor of this room was an iron grate instead of a solid floor, and their hair blew almost straight up to a comical effect. But that effect was exactly what they both needed right now, given that they were both sweating like a couple of racehorses. Heavily shielded lanterns going all the way down to the ground floor gave more than adequate light to see by— safety was paramount, given that Guards used the ladders in here three times a day to get to their post on the top of the tower. *Can't have our Guards breaking their necks on a regular basis. They're hard to replace.*

They plopped down on the grate at almost the same time and just enjoyed feeling cool—and then, actually *cold*—for the first time that day, although earlier in the day the uprush of air had felt merely pleasantly cooling. He and Kee had been up here after weapons practice to take advantage of the artificially created wind.

That had been just a bit naughty. Technically you weren't *supposed* to be up here to cool off; in fact, most people in the Palace didn't even know about this room, assuming it was some sort of Guardroom, so they didn't know the potential for cooling you off on a hot day. Tory was always of the opinion that it was better to apologize than to ask permission, so on blistering days like today, he and his sibs and the Royals could often be found up here when they were done with weapons practice or the heat was unbearable.

In winter, of course, the last thing you wanted was anything stealing the heat out of the building, so in winter the slits were sealed with tight-fitting wooden plugs and wax seals, not to be opened again until late in the spring. Even then, given the howling winds outside and the fact that the tower was cold stone, the inside of the tower was anything but pleasant in the winter, and the guards that used the ladder to get to their post had to beware of ice on the rungs. Not a place to linger.

When Tory finally felt up to anything besides breathing, he nudged Kee's knee with a toe. "Shall we do our nightly nursemaiding now?" he asked.

"I'm up to it," Kee agreed. And as one, the two of them closed their eyes and fell into a unique rapport with each other.

Unique, because although neither of them was Chosen, they had a rather major Gift. Unique, because that Gift was shared and didn't operate unless the two of them were together. Together, they could "look in" on any member of the extended families of either of them, as if they were Farseeing, no matter how distant that member was. And since those members were indeed scattered across the landscape of Valdemar, it was a very useful and comforting Gift indeed.

Well, "Gifts." So far as the Heralds had been able to tell, Tory was the actual Farseer, or at least the stronger and most reliable of the two. Kee was able to boost his range to . . . well, certainly anything within the borders of Valdemar. And together they could both See what Tory could reach. That was useful, because that meant there were *two* sets of eyes on whatever Tory was looking at and two minds analyzing the scene.

They located and dismissed King's Own Herald Amily, Tory's mother, and Herald Mags, his father. Both were in attendance at a social gathering of the Court out in the Pleasure Gardens that neither of the two boys had any interest in at all. The Crown

Prince, Trey, was with them, and he didn't look bored only because he and his wife seemed to be having some private game going; they kept whispering to each other and occasionally smiling with a conspiratorial air.

They also located and dismissed Rafi and Sofi, Kee's younger siblings, both of them in the Royal Suite, sharing a table with a tutor, their heads bent over lessons. Perry was next—in a tavern, somewhere down in Haven, outwardly gaming, actually intent on overhearing the conversation of a couple of men two tables over. They paused there for a moment, but it didn't look to Tory as though Perry was in any danger at all of being found out. And anyway, his kyree was "sleeping" in the shadows just outside the tavern, pretending to be a wolfhound. Anything that monster couldn't battle his way past to get to Perry's side was—well, it wasn't something that would be found in a tavern in Haven. And the ruckus would bring the local constables or the Guard long before an expert dirty fighter like Perry got into any difficulties.

Next, they checked on Niko, who was on a mission from the King to Duke Farleigh's Court. Also nothing to be concerned about; the Duke was a fervent loyalist, and Niko appeared to be having a fine time at a late dinner with the Duke and Duchess. Niko would, without a doubt, return not only triumphant but with some pretty thing for the young lady he was slowly courting. Neither Niko nor his lady seemed to be in any hurry to wed, even though it was clear to everyone Niko had met his match in her. She wasn't a Herald, but that scarcely mattered; she obviously understood the bond between Herald and Companion and wasn't in the least jealous of it. That was a rarity in anyone who wasn't themselves a Herald.

Kat, as Tory would have predicted, was eyes deep in some wrangling. Kat was the King's "problem solver." Whenever there was something going on that distant negotiation couldn't resolve, Herald-Princess Kat went there in person and applied whatever was most effective—reason, persuasion, negotiation, or browbeating. She usually didn't have to resort to the last, and from everything Tory saw, she wasn't doing any browbeating tonight. No, this was more like some spirited bargaining with what looked like a Lord Mayor and several Guild Heads.

And last of all, they searched for and found Abi, Tory's sister, the Master Artificer. Of all the members of their joint families, she was the only one who looked worried. She bent over a table scattered with sketches of walls and towers and tables of figures, weighted down with many samples of small slabs of stone that were broken in half. By that, Tory surmised that the construction of the walls and guard towers to replace the wooden palisades around the distant northern town of Westmark was not going well. Abi would probably be there a while. They could probably expect a message from her in the next fortnight, complaining about the lamentable weakness of local materials.

Tory heard Kee chuckling and looked up to see his friend grinning. At that point, of course, their concentration was broken, but they'd completed the nightly familial survey, and all appeared to be well.

"Poor Abi!" Kee said. "What's she going to do?"

"Think of something," Tory replied. "Like she always does. Oh, and probably yell at stonecutters for passing off inferior merchandise as adequate to the job." He thought for a while. "If it's the worst case, she'll just build a double wall with rammed earth between the walls. It's a lot more labor, but she's not going to build anything inferior. She'll build them a proper defensive wall even if she has to drag everyone in town up onto the walls to ram the earth herself."

"If she has to do that, won't she be there until maybe next spring?" Kee asked.

Tory just shrugged. "I don't know. She'll probably tell us in the letter she will, *without a doubt,* be sending us to vent her ire."

Kee laughed, his eyes sparkling with mirth. "Let's get downstairs. We've done our duty for the night. I'd like some wine."

"So would I after that run," Tory agreed.

With their hair still flying around their faces, they took the metal ladder down the inside of the tower until they reached the door at the base, standing open, with a Guard to make sure no one went up there who shouldn't, although that had never stopped Tory and the Royals. Adventurous pages and squires were the ones to be deterred mostly. Tory was pretty sure most of the highborn, even if they had known what purpose the tower served, wouldn't be caught dead climbing a ladder up so many stories and chance ruining their expensive clothing. *I have to wonder, though, how many fellows have tricked girls down this corridor to open the door and watch their skirts fly up?*

They made their way to the suite of rooms still used by Mags and Amily, though two thirds of their children were living elsewhere. They both knew that if they went to the Royal Suite, the two youngest children would see their presence as an excuse to stop studying and would try to tease them into a game of cards or double-draughts, and trying to wrangle those two back into studying would be futile. Then they'd get a tongue lashing later when the tutor complained about their effect on discipline.

Besides, this was better. The two of them would have the King's Own's suite all to themselves.

When they entered, it was dim, with only two candles illuminating it. That suited Tory just fine. It had been a long day of physical training, capped by his run against Kee. *This is a good life,* he thought to himself with great content. *Mind, I don't mind change, as long as it's for the better, but this is a damn good life.* Half of the room was taken up by the big table that served not only for meals taken away from Court and Collegium, but also for games, planning sessions, and even the occasional architectural planning session when Abi was here. The other half was a jumble of rugs, cushions, padded chairs, and settles.

As Tory had hoped, there was a bottle of wine chilling in the porous pottery cooler on the mantelpiece at the "jumble" end; he appropriated it and put in another. By the time his parents got away from all their Court nonsense, the new one would be cool. Kee got a couple of cups from beside it, and Tory popped the cork and poured for both of them.

They sprawled out on the floor in the main room, with cushions behind their backs and rugs under them. They left the door open for more breeze. "What are we going to do with the rest of the summer?" Kee asked, sipping his wine in the dim light.

"Same thing that we do every summer, Kee. Train. Run the usual watch for agents and troublemakers at Midsummer Fair. Train some more. Do anything that my father or yours asks us to. Hope for something exciting to happen." He waggled his eyebrows roguishly, although the effect was probably lost in the dark. "Flirt with the ladies."

"The ladies think you and I are *shaych,*" Kee said sourly.

Tory snickered. He knew that, of course. It had probably been inevitable, given how close the two of them were. He chose to find it funny. "That rumor has whiskers a league long. Besides, that makes it all the better. They think we are safe to flirt with. We can get away with *anything.*"

"Only when there ain't Companions 'round t'tell on ye," said his father Mags, just coming in the door. Amily was right behind him. "What're you two sittin' around i' the dark like conspirators for?"

"Conspiring," Kee replied promptly. "Where Companions can't hear us. Good evening Heralds. You will be pleased to hear that all is quiet on all fronts."

"Except Abi's tearing her hair out about something involving her walls," Tory added.

"I'm sure we'll be hearing about it in a fifteen-page letter soon, then," Amily replied, as she and Mags divested themselves of all their hidden weapons. Which was . . . quite a lot. Almost as many as Tory carried. The various knives and instruments of mayhem made soft *thuds* as they laid them out on the table. "Did you drink all the cooled wine?"

"We put a new bottle in the cooler," Tory replied. "I knew you'd skin us both if we didn't."

Amily went around the room lighting a few more candles as Mags opened the second bottle of wine and sniffed it. "Rosehip summerwine. Good choice. I f'rgive ye for drinkin' the first one."

Amily ended her rounds by slipping into the bedroom and emerging in loose white trews and a shirt, barefoot. "What *were* you two doing, lurking up here anyway?"

"Escaping being made the babies' excuse for not studying." Tory took an appreciative gulp of his own wine as his mother settled on her favorite chair by the cold fireplace. The fireplace served very nicely as a windcatcher itself during hot weather, and the good breeze stirring everyone's clothing proved that. "Other than that, taking our well-earned rest after our nightly wall-run."

Mags returned from the bedroom wearing roughly the same as Amily. "Ye know the hazard they never warn ye 'bout as a Herald playin' Royal bodyguard?" he asked, settling down next to Amily with a cup of his own. "Half-drunk nobles stumblin' 'bout sloshin' overfilled wine cups."

Amily giggled. "I *really* thought Lord Bannin was going to tip a whole cup over you at least three times, the sot."

"Well, 'e don' care. Niver seen 'im less'n half soused. An' wi' 'im wearin' half th' clothes in 'is wardrobe, if 'e spills on hisself, 'e just needs t' peel off the top layer an' toss it t' a page t'be set t' rights agin," Mags replied, with a smirk.

"Maybe that's why he dresses that way," Kee offered.

"Maybe it's because he's always afraid the King will get tired of his nonsense and toss him out, and wearing half his clothing will save time in packing," Tory snickered. Lord Bannin was *not* a favorite among the Heralds; his utter selfishness combined with an appalling attitude toward anyone who didn't look, think, and act *exactly* like him and his inner circle made the most xenophobic Holderkin look like a welcoming innkeeper. He fancied himself an intellectual, but his ideas, so Tory had been told by several acerbic scholars, were like summer thunderstorms—all flash and noise and nothing productive.

And he treated Heralds as if they were something he'd just scraped off his boot, probably because even the densest of them could see through him to what he really was.

"It's not fair to make fun of Lord Bannin," Kee deadpanned. "He can't help it. He's suffering from a terrible condition. His face looks so much like his ass that his bowels don't know which way to push."

Amily nearly spilled her wine all over herself, she started laughing so hard. And Mags almost choked.

"All right," she said finally, "On that note, I am off to bed. If I drink any more, I'll be tipsy, and that never ends well in the morning." Suiting her actions to her words, she did just that, after making sure all the windows on the outer wall of the suite were flung wide open, regardless of the moths that came flitting in, attracted by the candles. At least the fireplaces at both ends of the suite gave the bats that followed a good, safe way to exit.

After a long interval of silence, enlivened only by the antics of the bats chasing the moths, Mags cleared his throat gently.

"So, did we innerupt anythin'?" he asked.

"Nothing of any importance," Kee admitted, pouring the last of their wine into his cup, collecting Mags' bottle, and placing both in the basket by the door for empties. "We were just wondering what we'd do this summer."

Mags nodded, with an expression of sympathy on his face. But he didn't say anything, which was actually a lot better than if he'd made some remark. Instead, he let things sit for a moment, then his expression changed to one of deep thought.

"I got a notion," he said, finally. "But if you two don' like it, we won't pursue it no futher."

Well, Tory had to admit that sounded promising.

"What's the notion?" asked Kee, perking up with interest and combing his hair back over his forehead with one hand.

"Likely yer father wouldn' much care fer it," Mags said to the Prince. But the sly look Mags got only made both of them want to hear it even more.

"What the King doesn't know isn't going to hurt him in this case," Kee pointed out. "If we can't trust you, we can't trust anyone."

"I got me a head full'o assassin-stuff put there by th' Sleepgivers," Mags said. Tory nodded; he certainly knew the story, and so did Kee—how Mags was the lost son of the heir to the leadership of a very large clan or very small nation of professional assassins known as the Sleepgivers. How in the course of doing work in Valdemar on behalf of the Karsites, they had discovered their missing heir. How subsequently they had attempted to kidnap him and convert him to their ways by magically overlaying his mind with the minds and personalities of dozens of Sleepgivers past. . . .

How thanks to his Companion, Dallen, that hadn't worked. At all.

But this was the first time that Tory had heard that some of those memories and skills had *stuck*. If that was what his father was implying—

"Lots'o assassinn-tricks. Not partic'ly useful on account of I don't act'lly need to kill anyone that often, but . . . inneresting. Some I passed on t' Perry, but not most uv it. Seems a shame to waste it though. Reckon you two'd like to learn some uv it?"

Kee licked his lips with anticipation. "You're right. Father'd be appalled. I love it."

Tory nodded. "Me too. Thing is, I bet we can make a lot of that stuff less than lethal if we want. Even things like poisons, because surely you've got the antidotes in your memory?"

"Fer th' most part, aye," Mags agreed. "But a lot uv it's gonna mean some real serious new trainin' on yer parts. I got the direct mem'ry of how t'do the tricks straight from th' source, muscle-memory an' all. I kin do most uv it jest by thinkin' 'bout it. Ye're gonna haveta learn 'em the hard way."

"Like what kind of tricks?" Kee wanted to know.

Instead of answering directly, Mags put down his cup, got up, and went over to a corner of the room, studying the crown molding around the intersection of wall and ceiling. And before Tory could ask what he was doing, suddenly his father was no longer standing in the corner, he was *right up* in the corner, back to the ceiling, somehow braced up there. Looking down at them with just a bit of a smirk.

Then he dropped straight down with a muffled *thud*—much quieter than Tory would have thought possible—landing in a crouch with knees flexed.

He stood up again, facing them. "Little tricks like thet," he said, casually. " 'Twill take a deal of trainin'. Lots uv hard work an' practice when ye could be lazin' about an' flirtin' wi' ladies. Still want to?"

Kee and Tory exchanged a look; Tory saw Kee's face change expression from incredulous to avaricious, and he expected his had done the same. Did he *want* to learn that sort of thing?

Was a pine tree green?

"Yes, please!" they chorused together.

2

A cool night breeze stirred in the grass and rattled in the branches of the scrub. Siratai crouched in what should have been cover too scant to hide a housecat--just a low bush and a scattering of weeds, really, a bit of scrub next to a desert shepherd's hut. There was a full moon, and she should have been completely visible to anyone looking at all closely.

She wasn't even remotely visible, of course. She was a Sleepgiver, and between her training and clothing designed *specifically* to hide someone in the moonlight, only another Sleepgiver could have spotted her.

And perhaps she would not be seen even by them. There was no point in false modesty; she was the best of the best. She had to be. Not only was she the daughter of Beshat, the acknowledged leader of all Sleepgivers, she was the Sleepgiver tasked with ridding the Nation of the cursed Karsites. The plaguey Karsites had been a thorn in the Nation's side since the Sleepgivers had canceled the contract with them to interfere with the Kingdom of Valdemar. And that had happened before Sira had been born.

The Karsites, it seemed, did not believe that such contracts could be canceled except by themselves. They had responded to the cancellation in the most strenuous and bloody terms they could manage. The Sleepgivers had, of course, taught them an even bloodier lesson.

One, it seems, the fanatics refused to learn. If there was one thing that a Karsite could hold, it was a grudge. *Not exactly shocking for a lot of fanatics, I suppose.* They had been sending their priests across Ruvan to exact revenge on the Sleepgivers ever since the Sleepgivers had bloodied their noses for them and sent them packing with their own demons in hot pursuit. She'd heard about that story, the one that involved Cousin Mags, from the ones directly involved. Oh, that had been a tale!

Mind, the Sleepgivers had not done all that well out of that situation themselves; they'd lost the heir to the Banner Bearer of the Nation, that same Cousin Mags. But she knew the rest of that story too, and the result of all of the adventures in the strange land of Valdemar and the dogged pursuit of the one known as Mags had been that her father Beshat became the leader of all the People, so for her, it was an untarnished tale of triumph.

And now, well, it was time to add to that tale, with another mark in the tally of dead Karsite priests.

Sira lay flat to the ground, so still even an owl would not have been able to see her breathing, within easy reach of the hut door and just inside an invisible perimeter she had watched the wretched priest mark out this afternoon.

The idiots truly never learned.

They *always* trusted the first guide to approach them—and the only guides in Ruvan who knew exactly where the Sleepgiver Nation lay were, of course, Sleepgivers themselves.

They never questioned why a guide would even be willing to take them within shouting distance of the Nation's rough border, here in the heart of Ruvan.

They never wondered why Ruvan tolerated a Nation of paid assassins in their midst in the first place.

And the first thing they did when they saw this "deserted shepherd hut" that was supposedly a day's ride from the border of the Nation was to dismiss the guide and take up residence in the hut. They just could not resist the prospect of getting to camp within four walls and a roof, and they never once suspected the hut was a honeytrap.

And they always, *always*, assumed that because they were a day's ride away, they were somehow safe and "invisible."

They never suspected that when they began their preparations to send their demons into the Nation, they were anything but unobserved, for Sira was already here and watching them.

And this scenario proceeded exactly in this manner. Every. Single. Time.

This time was no exception. The Sleepgiver playing guide had quickly sent word to her father of another idiot at the Ruvan Border. Bey sent Sira out. She'd waited in the hills above the hut until the "guide" and his idiot appeared on the flat desert plain, trudging along it without the least attempt to disguise their presence. The idiot didn't even insist on traveling at night so he'd have had a *little* chance of getting to his destination without being spotted.

I suppose I should be grateful they make my job so easy . . . but really, I'd like a challenge once in a while!

Maybe she ought to suggest to her father that from now on the Sleepgiver "guide" just kill them quickly as soon as they were out of view of any witnesses. And if that didn't work . . .

Maybe we should start chucking the heads over the Border into Karse.

But her father would probably object to that. He preferred that the priests just cross the Border and vanish.

She'd gotten into place once twilight had deepened enough that, in her mottled gray-and-darker-gray clothing, with soot smeared across her face under the masking cloth, only another Sleepgiver would have seen her patient, slow creep across the landscape. And now, as predictable that scattered grain would bring pigeons, with the rising of the moon, the idiot came out of the *well-lit* hut into the darkness *carrying a lantern in one hand.* Thus ensuring he wouldn't see her unless he actually stepped on her.

Does demon-summoning destroy one's mind, or do only the mindless go into demon-summoning? It was a valid question, she thought.

He began his own labors, trickling some powder or other from his hand into the little trench he'd marked in the dirt. This probably marked the perimeter of the circle with some protective magic that would keep his demons from attacking *him* once he'd summoned them. And she was greatly tempted to change her plans, use the narcotic powder she also carried, render him unconscious once he'd conjured them, and go break the circle.

That would be stupid, Sira, she chided herself. *There'd be nothing stopping them from attacking you. His hubris may be contagious.*

She set the idea aside with regret. But it certainly would be highly amusing to watch the priest's own minions ripping him to bloody shreds.

She waited patiently until his movements put the hut between himself and her. And then she moved, swiftly and surely, gliding noiselessly in through the open door. It was dark in there, of course, because he had the lamp. But she didn't need to see to get into the rafters as silently as a spider. She knew every inch of this hut as well as she knew her own bedroom.

Once wedged in place, her little *vadar* tube loaded with a dart and in her mouth, she *quieted*. All Sleepgivers had to learn how to do this to one extent or another, because so much of what Sleepgivers did was waiting. But she was especially good at *quieting*. Again, her breath slowed, her mind stilled, and if there had been a Mindspeaker about, he'd have been hard put to tell that there was more than one person in this immediate area. Waiting was easy in this mental state, and nothing bothered her. Insects, even mice and rats, could run over her and not even make her twitch. She was neither cold nor hot, no matter the conditions. She simply *was*, a trap waiting to be sprung.

Light preceded the priest in through the door. He entered muttering what were probably incantations but what might also have been grumbled complaints about having to march on foot all this distance and live in a primitive hut for days at a time. He didn't *look* like the kind of fattened, lazy magician who would find such a thing a hardship, but you never knew. The demon-summoning priests of Vkandis were a minority of the priests of the Karsites, and they enjoyed a great deal of prestige within the religion. With that prestige might well come a privileged and luxurious life.

He was not, of course, wearing the uniform of his calling; the robes of any priest of Vkandis, red *or* black, would mark him as a great plague to be eliminated at all cost once he crossed the border with Ruvan. The Karsites were not good neighbors to anyone, and Ruvan made absolutely no objections to people slaughtering Karsites wholesale, much less assassinating their priests, if they were found inside the Ruvan borders.

No, he was wearing the wrapped headgear and loose robes sported by just about any commoner of Ruvan. Nothing threadbare or patched but not of silk or fine linen either. Modest ornamentation in the form of a touch of embroidery at the neck. Hard to tell the exact color in this light but probably beige or sand. At least he'd had the sense to dress as someone who would neither be shunned or abused for his poverty nor attract attention for his wealth.

The first bit of good sense he had displayed. And the last.

Information was always valuable, and this might apply to the inevitable next Karsite idiot who came ahunting. Sira took all this in without effort, and instantly, as she waited.

Waited for him to put down the lantern. The scent of hot oil rose to reach her nostrils. Old oil. He hadn't even changed what had still been in the lantern.

Waited for him to pick up whatever it was he was going to need for the summoning. A book—hadn't he at least memorized his spell? Cretin. And a stick. Might be an object of power. Might not. Treat it with caution.

Waited for him to get . . . right . . . directly . . . under . . . her . . . and . . . bend . . . slightly.

She inhaled swiftly and completely through her nose and blew all the air out in a fast, strong *puff* through the *vadar* tube. The tiny dart that had been in the tube shot out and embedded to the feather right in his spine, between the shoulder-blades, in the hollow where it would slip between the vertebrae and deliver its load of toxin straight into the great spinal nerve.

He yelped and swatted, probably assuming he'd been stung by an insect or a spider. He swatted again as the prick began to burn, and then he collapsed in a boneless heap as the *sechel* toxin went to work.

And again, she waited.

Only when she smelled his bowels voiding did she drop down to the ground beside the twitching body. His eyes were open, he convulsed a little, and he struggled to breathe. He was dead; he just didn't know it yet.

He could have been saved at this point if she had given him the antidote, but he would have been paralyzed for the rest of his short life.

Not that she had any intention of saving him. The antidote she carried was in case of an accident to herself.

His minor convulsions jerked his head around so that he suddenly looked up into her eyes. His eyes were fully dilated and his expression slack; he had lost control of his facial muscles. But he could still think, and she saw the horror in his eyes.

Was there something else in there? Did some distant priest of greater talent watch through his eyes?

Well, if so, her father had a message for her to deliver.

She bent over him, and said, slowly and in excellent Karsite, "If there is anyone in there *listening*, I beg you, for the sake of your dwindling number of priests, stop plaguing the Sleepgivers. You cannot breed priests faster than we can kill them."

Then she slit his throat and embedded his own dagger in his heart. Yes, he had been nine-tenths dead, and rapidly dying. Still, a Sleepgiver took no chances.

She plucked the dart from between the dead man's shoulderblades with great care for the point and put it back in a protective sheath. The sheath went into an envelope of similar sheathes, the *vadar* tube beside them. The envelope went into the breast of her tunic, under the camouflaging wrappings. Then she blew out the lantern, waited in the darkness for her eyes to adjust, and slipped out.

Good. Nothing out there waiting.

She went back in and dragged the body as far as a little hollow that still held ashes and bone fragments from the other Karsite priests she'd killed here. She went back for the book and the stick, using silk from her body wrappings to pick up each one, then took them out and dropped them on the body. Last of all she uncorked a very special flask of very special oil, decanted it on the body and book, and bent to light his clothing with her firestriker. The oil-soaked clothing caught immediately, and soon the body burned with an unnaturally bright, white, hot flame.

There were no manifestations of any sort as book, stick, body, and whatever other magic items he was carrying went up in the conflagration. And never mind how curious the Mages of the Mountain were about Karsite magic. Not that she would have given in to their pleas that she bring back items of magic—she was under orders to bring absolutely nothing back from any of these kills. There was no telling what might be coming along to the Mountain if she were to do so. And at the very least, she knew that

Sleepgiver magicians could find the location of anything they had enchanted, so it was reasonable the Karsites could find the actual site of the Mountain that way as well. She sat beside the body, faced away from it to conserve as much of her night-vision as she could, and waited for the flames to die down. When she was sure they would burn out safely, she stood up.

Time to be gone.

She arranged her possessions for travel and set her face to the west, taking a pace best suited to moonlight.

———

Five leagues and some small part of the night later, she was secure in her own camp. Which was *not* in an exposed hut surrounded by scrub but halfway up an escarpment, in a little sandstone cave exactly like the many other sandstone caves all around it. She liked this one; it was one of several that had a little hollow at the back of it that exactly fitted her body. For the moment, she was not in that hollow; she lay belly-down on the floor of the cave, surveying the valley below and the cliffs above.

The desert was cold at night, and a chill wind passed by the face of the escarpment. It carried with it few scents besides that of *cresete* bush and sage. Off in the far, far distance, a tiny speck of yellow flickered. The corpse still burned.

Anything that moved at all out there got her immediate scrutiny, but the only things moving in the moonlight tonight were a small herd of desert deer, a few rodents that she identified by their characteristic scuttling, and one lone hare. And bats. There were a lot of bats here—bats by night, swallows and a desert falcon or two by day. It was peaceful here and much to her liking. She sometimes came out here for peace and pleasure when she wasn't hunting those idiot priests.

Satisfied that she would sleep undisturbed, she inched her way to the back of the cave and unfolded a silk-lined woolen blanket. It smelled a little of horse and sage. This would keep her comfortable even in the coldest of desert nights. She wound it around herself, made sure all her weapons were immediately to hand, and dropped off into instant sleep.

She woke just as instantly as the swallows nesting in the cave above her head began to twitter sleepily. Once again she inched her way to the front of the cave, moving so slowly she didn't even alarm the birds, and surveyed the landscape below her. It was clear of anything, and there was not even a thin skein of smoke on the horizon to mark where the dead priest had burned last night.

A turn of the glass or so later, she was on the move. Her face was scrubbed of soot with her face-wrap, and all the silk camouflage was stripped away and stowed in her bedroll secured to her back; her short hair was neatly tucked into her headscarf, her dart case was inside the breast of her tunic, water bottle at her side, provisions in a pouch on her hip beside her fighting-knife, quiver on the opposite hip, short-bow in her hand. She had other weapons on her person, of course, but those were hidden.

The sun wasn't even up yet, but she wanted to get to her horse before the heat became intolerable. To that end, she ate one of her meat biscuits on the move, eyes everywhere, on the alert for anyone who might be able to spot her. This close to the border of the Nation, this deeply into the kingdom of Ruvan, she didn't really think that there would be anyone stupid enough to try to ambush someone dressed as she was . . . but a Sleepgiver who assumed anything generally was not a Sleepgiver who prospered.

By noon she was on her horse, a scrubby, pony-sized, rough-coated specimen of a breed the Sleepgivers had been cultivating for centuries, if not millennia. You didn't *train* this breed of horse, you *taught* it. Aku had been an "old" horse when she got him, but his kind were long-lived.

The old horse teaches the young rider. The old rider teaches the young horse. They were as clever, as smart, and as bloody-minded as their riders. If she needed to, Sira knew she could have tied herself to Aku's back, passed out, and he would bring her home safely. She also knew that if she ever offended him, he'd plant all four feet and refuse to move, even to the point of needing as many as six more horses to drag him away. But he could go at a trot for three days straight from predawn to twilight and still fight a skirmish at the end of it. He could smell out water all on his own, and he had the good sense not to drink himself sick when he found it. He could even—unheard of in any breed of horse other than the Shin'a'in war steeds—be left with a full bag of grain and eat only as much as he needed for as long as the grain lasted. And then he would untie himself and go back to his stable.

Not in search of her. Aku was a horse, after all, not a dog, and not some fabled creature like the White Beasts of Valdemar. Given the nonappearance of his rider when the food ran out, he would simply go home, not in search of a mere human. He could only be reasonably expected to look out for himself and any mares and foals he happened to be with. The people of the Nation did not expect miracles of their horses.

His gait was *terrible*, like all of his kind; the one for distance was a very rough, hard trot. Sleepgivers who rode his kind quickly learned not to *sit* in the saddle unless the horse was walking. Not even at a gallop. You put all your weight in the stirrups, and by the time you'd been riding for six months, you had calves as hard as stone and thighs that could crack a walnut.

Or, conveniently enough, a neck.

And you, yourself, could run for leagues.

It was *excellent* conditioning for the sorts of things a Sleepgiver had to do. And not so bad for the sorts of things the more ordinary members of the Nation might find themselves faced with.

Aku was pleased to be heading homeward, so his trot was as smooth as he could make it right now. Which was not very.

But Sira was used to it, and she allowed part of her mind to wander while the rest of her mind was on the lookout for the least hint of trouble, be it weather, wild beasts, or humans who should not be in the lands of the Nation.

It was said that in the days before the Sleepgivers became a Nation and made the Mountain their home, they had been the silent, deadly guards for a great Wizard in the west and north. It was said that there was a great war of Wizards and that when it was clear that their master had lost this war, he had sent those of his guards on duty to protect his lesser kin as they fled. It was said that this had been no natural way of travel but that he had sent his people fleeing through gates in the air, to seek shelter wherever they landed, before he destroyed his stronghold and his enemy with it.

This Sira believed, because she had seen the lesser versions of these gates in the air, linking the southern and northern Mage Schools of Amber Moon.

But the gates of those far-off times had been much, much bigger and could send people to where there were no other such gates, needing no anchor. This she also believed, though it was hard. She was enough of a Mage herself to understand just how much power such things represented. And there had been *dozens* of them.

It was said—*said,* because in those long-ago days the not-yet-Sleepgivers could neither read nor write—that those guards not on duty had gathered their herds and their families and the few Mages that were with them at the time and fled through the gate apportioned to them, as the lesser wizards had fled through their own. And that no one knew where they would end up, because that way the enemy could not anticipate where they would go and ambush them.

And that was how they came to be in the least hospitable land in all of Ruvan. Which was not yet Ruvan in those days. It was an empty land of high plains and mountains, dry but not inhospitable. And it was very lightly inhabited. Except, fortunately, where the guards and their families and herds had landed, which was empty.

She wondered what they had felt, those people, when they found themselves in that valley long ago. At least there had been water and grass, and the mountains themselves had given protection and shelter from storms.

They were hard people, and she suspected that finding themselves in desert mountains dismayed them not at all. They found more water and more grassy valleys, they carved the mountains to suit themselves, they learned to grow crops that would sustain them and their horses, and if they did not precisely prosper, then neither did they fade. They kept their ways and their training, and they learned to be even more deadly than they had been in the past, so that, should they seek to serve another, they would *never* lose a master to an enemy again.

But, so she had been taught, as time passed and their numbers grew, it became very clear that the Mountain could not sustain all their numbers. And when they ventured out of the range they called home, they found themselves in the heart of a land of people much softer than they were, as the land that sustained them was softer than the lands wherein the Sleepgivers dwelt. For while the Nation had been carving a life for themselves, others had been coming to inhabit the land around them, and they called that land their own without ever knowing of the presence of the Nation.

Sira told all this to herself as she rode, as every Sleepgiver who was not also inhabited by an Ancestor must do, now and again, to remind herself of what she was and where she had come from.

Those who had once been ridden by the Ancestors in the Talismans, of course, did not have to tell themselves these things, for the Ancestors dreamed the tale as a waking dream, day in, night out. But she did not have that kind of Talisman. And thanks to her father, neither did any other Sleepgiver of these days.

And so, she recited to herself, in rhythm with Aku's bone-jarring trot, *it came to pass that the Elders gathered and said to themselves, 'There is no lack of murder and warfare among the nations, even after the lesson of the Mage War. So let us sell our skills not as the guards against death but as the givers of Eternal Sleep. Guards are paid well, but not as much as one who can eliminate an enemy by removing his head and slipping away into the night unseen.' And so they did. And so the Sleepgivers came to be.*

Not every person in the Nation was a Sleepgiver. Not even most. Only some, but that "some" was enough to keep the rest of the

Nation in the sustenance they needed. In these days, the Sleepgivers were very, very highly paid. The best of them cost a king's ransom. *But*, she thought, without hubris, *we are worth it.*

The King of what had come to be called Ruvan—he, the First of that Name—very, very quickly saw the value of what the Sleepgivers had to offer and made the First Contract. He would grant the Mountain and all the land around it in perpetuity to the Nation. He would see to it that no one in all of Ruvan harmed so much as a hair on a goat belonging to the Nation. And he would interfere in no way with any contracts they should make, even if it be against one of his allies, so long as they took no contracts against the Royal House of Ruvan itself.

And very wise of him, too, she thought with amusement. He very carefully protected himself and his line, effectively making it impossible for anyone *in* Ruvan not in the Royal House to prosecute a Sleepgiver for murder and opening up the possibility of contracts against anyone else in Ruvan.

The contracts from those days were still in the archives in the Mountain, as were all contracts that had been made from that day forward, for the People were at last literate, and Sira had read some of them. They read like the contracts only an apprentice would take now—merchant against merchant, petty lord against petty lord, and almost nothing outside the borders of Ruvan itself. But over the years, that had changed . . . oh, how it had changed. Though most contracts were made with those in the south, the west, and a little to the north. The Karsites held themselves aloof from such things, probably preferring their own ways of treachery and murder, the Shin'a'in took care of their own need for vengeance, and very handily too, and anything north of Karse, north of Menmellith, was unknown. There was no interest from the Nation in places where there was no money to be had.

Until the Heir to the Banner of the People went missing, and with him, his beloved.

The Heir had been an only son, soft of heart, empathic of mind, most probably a Healer born, and with a great revulsion against killing, and had there been other siblings, he could have been passed over in favor of someone more suited to ruling the Nation. There was no dishonor in being a Healer; they were as vital to the Nation as Sleepgivers. But there were no other children of his father, neither male nor female, and so he was not to be excused by a Banner Bearer who had no interest in passing the Banner to a collateral line, however much he valued his own brother. And so this Heir had defied the will of his father; he had taken his beloved and fled.

Probably because if he hadn't, that old flint-hearted tyrant was going to force a Talisman on him. Heirs were not usually required to take a Talisman; such were known to dull the mind to original thinking, and the Banner Bearer had to be a man (or woman!) who could solve problems great and small. But Sira had no doubt that her great-uncle was the sort who would have let pride overrule good sense. She had not known her father's uncle, but from all descriptions, he had not been the sort of man who would have sacrificed his pride for the happiness of his son.

"Horses are often smarter than people, aren't they, Aku?" she asked, and Aku's ears flipped back in acknowledgement that he had heard her, though his pace didn't falter.

The oppressive heat of the desert was a little lessened in the valleys she and Aku traversed. There was sparse grass here and often water, though you had to dig to find it or take it from the pads of the pear-cactus. Above, yellow and red mountains and flat-topped mesas kept the valleys in shade for most of the day. It was a hard land, and she wasn't surprised it had spawned as hard a man as her own great-uncle.

So the Heir ran, and ran in an unexpected direction. North and west. And so he and his beloved vanished. And the Nation sent out hunters to no avail, until it became too expensive to mount the hunts. The Nation above all was adept at conserving its resources, and after a time even the Banner Bearer had to admit that the cost was not worth the reward, when his brother could be Heir and had a fine son of his own who could be Heir after that.

But that changed when the Karsites, casting aside every custom of the last centuries, came to the Sleepgivers with a contract to destroy the Royal House of Valdemar. That being the last direction the Heir had been heard of, the Lord of the Banner decreed that they would take that contract, and use the money from the Karsites to pay for the search for the lost Heir.

I would have given a very great deal to have seen my great-uncle's face when he discovered the son of his son was a Herald of Valdemar.

Well, for a man who would have forced a Sleepgiver Talisman on a Healer, his own son, whom he knew and presumably cared for at least a little, it was of no matter whatsoever to decree that a Talisman must be forced upon Mags of Valdemar, a young man he knew not at all, in order to bring him back to take his proper place at his grandfather's side. And he broke the contract with the Karsites.

"My great-uncle," she said to Aku's ears, "was an idiot."

But if he had not been an idiot, my father would not now be the Bearer of the Banner of the Lammergeyer. And I would. . . . well, I would not be getting a great deal of practice in how to eliminate demon-summoners, so there's that.

It was the lammergeyers themselves, circling over the Mountain in long, lazy glides, that told anyone who did not know the way that they were very near the stronghold of the Sleepgivers. Lammergeyers had been chosen as the emblem of the spirit of the Nation before the Sleepgivers themselves even existed. What better emblem? The Lammergeyer not only lived on death—being a scavenger—it lived on the remains of death that nothing else could. They ate bone. Literally. They lived and thrived where no one could ever expect a bird of their size to live and thrive. And, as Sira knew from visiting the roosts where the falconers of the Nation tenderly nurtured the giant birds and their young, they were as great-hearted, clever, and personable as any eagle. More, in fact. They made friends of their falconers and of a few like Sira who chose to visit them regularly. Sira was fond of them, and they of her, and she knew all of them by name.

They liked her brother, the Healer, even better. She didn't begrudge him this. It was rare that he had anything to care for that didn't in some way have blood on its hands. She often wondered if that runaway Heir, the father of Mags of Valdemar, had been like her brother. If so . . . it was too bad he could not have had Bey as his father.

Too bad for him, that is. For herself, she very much liked things the way they were.

The lammergeyers saw her and dipped their wings in greeting, but the sentries on the cliffs had long ago signaled that she was coming back—triumphant, of course, because the only way she would have come back without killing the Karsite would have been if for some reason she had needed to spare his life, and then he would have been most uncomfortably thrown over Aku's haunches. The path she took, the *only* path to the Mountain, led through valleys that held many hiding places for herds and flocks and those who tended them, and at the first echo of hoofbeats approaching, those flocks would be whisked out of sight. And it didn't matter that the rider was one of the Nation; that was the way things were done. That was how the Nation had survived, like the lammergeyers, where others could not. And, of course, the sentries were Sleepgiver-trained, if not apprentices; unless she had taken a considerable amount of time to look for them, she would never have seen them.

But the Mountain . . . oh, the Mountain . . . that was a different matter altogether.

It stood in a valley of three springs, surrounded on three sides by lush (for the area) meadows full of horses, and, where the land had been rotated to grow crops, gardens. There were trees—most of them fruit- or nut-bearing, the rest, incense trees whose resin was worth more than gold. And above it all rose the Mountain, the Home of the Nation, the training ground of the Sleepgivers, the hall of the Healers, the Archive of the Records and Contracts, and the Place of the Lammergeyer Banner. Carved by the patient hands of generation upon generation of the Nation, every vertical thumb length held green terraces and stone houses, and the fabric of the Mountain itself had been carved into spacious halls and home upon home upon home.

And in the very top—her home, just below the aeries of the lammergeyers.

She could not see it soon enough.

Neither could Aku, who increased his pace to a spine-shattering gallop.

She rose a little in her stirrups, leaned over his neck, and endured.

3

She dismounted at the base of the Mountain and did not even need to give Aku a swat to his haunches to send him on his way. He probably would have been affronted if she had. He trotted off straight to his stable, reins lax on his neck, where he would go on his own to his stall, drink the water waiting for him there, eat a bit of hay, and wait with the patience of a Sleepgiver for someone to come unsaddle him and rub him down. Not that he would have to wait long, if at all. Since her coming had been noted, the grooms were most likely waiting for him.

As for her greeting, well . . . that would be some time in coming. First she would have to climb to the top.

There was *some* help in that, at least: ingenious rope-lifts from terrace to terrace, operated by a boy or a girl. You turned up at the lift, pulled the string beside it that rang a bell at the top, and put one foot in the sling at the bottom of the loop of rope. At the top, the boy or girl would drop rocks into a metal basket until it equaled your weight, and you could pull yourself up the face of the rock with ease. A lock on the rope at the top enabled you to step off and be on your way, and the boy or girl at the bottom would unload rocks until the two children could lift the weight back up themselves. The rest of the rocks would go up in a second load, and the lift was ready for the next person.

It was excellent strength training.

But there were a great many of those lifts to get from the bottom of the Mountain to the top, and it was nearly sunset when she reached the terrace of her home.

Sunset, and time for the evening meal. The smell of cooking coming up the Mountain on the updrafts from thousands of busy kitchens would have driven her mad if she had not been a Sleepgiver. But it did make her just a trifle impatient.

When the Nation first came to this place, they had made use of natural caves at the base, and since there seemed to be no other people about, had not troubled with a defensive wall. As their numbers had grown, they had first created terraces from which to sculpt more rooms into the flesh of the Mountain itself; then they had expanded the terraces to build gardens onto them, then created staircases to make new terraces dug into the Mountain, then built gardens . . . until at last they had reached the peak. After that, those who were so inclined had moved themselves and their herds or farms into the surrounding land, the entire bottom section had been given over to the dormitories and training rooms for Sleepgivers and Mages and trades, and the top was reserved for the Banner Bearer and his (or her!) family.

This was . . . an interesting reversal of advantage. The farther up

the Mountain you were, the harder it was to get water—the harder
it was to get *anything*—up to your home, and the more inconvenient
it was to dispose of waste. In summer, yes, Sira's home was the most
comfortable . . . but summer was only half the year, and the winter
winds could be bitter in the extreme. So although the Banner Bearer
was literally as well as figuratively atop the Nation, that came at a
cost to comfort—thus literally and figuratively reminding the Bearer
at nearly every moment how dependent he was on the Nation.

But it was a lovely home.

The warm, cream-and-red banded stone had been sculpted not
with the angles and peaks of conventional architecture that Sira had
seen elsewhere in Ruvan, but in sweeps and curves and folds, as if the
wind had done most of the work. The terrace garden, watered by the
cisterns also carved into the rock above, had a sculpted, round-topped
battlement along the edge that stood as tall as Sira's collarbone—a
must, given that there could be children romping about—identical
to the battlements of every terrace, with one not-so-small exception.
Lammergeyers in every imaginable pose had been sculpted in bas-
relief all around it, and statues of lammergeyers as well as the birds
themselves were perched upon it. There were many entrances onto
this terrace, which, like all the others, held a functional, rather than
an ornamental, garden. But Sira took the first, and most imposing,
just off the staircase from the terrace below. This entrance had a
lammergeyer with wings spread carved above it.

It led into a single large room. Within that room was a table cut
from the living rock of the mountain with bench seats likewise cut
all around it. More rock benches had been cut out of the walls,
and niches for lanterns cut into them, and at the back of the room

was a single entrance into the living quarters of the Banner Bearer. The great embroidered Banner itself hung on the back wall, and before it was a stone bench softened by a cushion. The moment she entered the room, she felt a great weight dropping from her shoulders. At last she was home.

By all rights and custom, Sira's father, Beshat, the Banner Bearer of the Nation, should have been sitting on that cushion waiting for her to come to him.

But he was far too impatient and far too loving a father to do that. As soon as she stepped into the room, she was caught up in a hug; her father picked her right up off the ground and swung her around in a circle before putting her down again and stepping a pace back. She broke out into a rare grin of delight, then sobered.

"I see you lived," he deadpanned.

"You don't get rid of me that easily, father," she said just as dryly. "Would you like my report?"

"We eat first. You won't have had anything other than meat biscuits and water. I don't want to miss any details because your stomach is growling too loudly for me to hear them," he replied with a lifted eyebrow.

He waved at the entrance to the living quarters, and they passed through the cloth door.

The rooms on the other side were very much like the Banner Hall behind them; most of the furniture had been cut out of the stone when the rooms were chiseled out. Every home on the Mountain was like this; wood was saved for important things. Fires were fed with carefully dried dung made into charcoal. Even the beds were niches cut into the stone, with featherbeds to soften them. Feathers there were here in abundance; most households had pigeons and chickens, there were plenty of edible birds in these mountains, and the Nation wasted nothing. The notion of wasting as much as a single feather on a bird meant to be eaten by singeing it off rather than taking care to pluck it would have invoked strong disapproval. Every bed niche had a featherbed and a feather comforter or two for winter, and winter clothing was stuffed with feathers for warmth. Metal, bones, and horns were used in place of wood for most small things, and many large, so Sira hung her laminated sinew-and-horn bow on a bone bow rack, and slung her blanket roll and some of the belts and pouches beside it, once she was on the other side of the hemp door curtain.

Each room commonly used by the family had a door and large windows facing the terrace. The windows were open now; in winter they would be covered inside and out with two panes of laminated horn and copper, and the copper door would be closed where it now stood open. The first room was a small one, to entertain guests. The second, which lay beyond that, was the room in which nearly everything else was done—cooking, eating, socializing, studying. There was a room beyond that one where Hakal, her Healer brother, and Jeshan, her brother who specialized in poisons and antidotes, worked with their herbs, minerals, and other things, making both potions that cured and potions that killed. Hakal and Jeshan were responsible for the toxin on her darts, derived from a species of toad. Hakal also made the antidote, though to her knowledge, no Sleepgiver had ever troubled to use it.

The entire family aside from her father was waiting for her around the stone table; the food was in its metal and ceramic pots on the table, ceramic plates awaited the meal, but nothing had been served. Even Nalad, her younger sister, who was in training, was there, along with Rayakh, who trained tracking and attack dogs. As she and Bey entered, she was met with broad smiles from dark faces that looked very like her own. There was a strong resemblance to their father in all of Bey's children.

"I see you survived," said Anhita, her mother.

"And yet, I am perishing before you," she replied. "My stomach is much too closely acquainted with my spine."

"Did you lose my dart?" demanded Jeshan.

"Not even the point, dear brother," she said in mock indignation.

"Then you may eat," he told her graciously.

She took her usual place at the table, between her eldest brother Teychik, the Heir to the Banner, and Hakal; her father sat at the foot. Her mother was already in her place at the head, and she began to send the pots around.

There was pepper-lentil stew tonight, with cleaned and chopped chicken-innards in it. Flatbread, of course, as there was with every meal. Curds of goat-cheese mixed with honey and herbs, boiled barley with lamb and herbs, stewed nettle and stewed fireweed with herbs, a dish of goat butter, and, in honor of her return, roast chicken. A lammergeyer landed on the wall of the terrace with a great thunder of wings, then hopped to the windowsill, waiting with infinite patience for his plate of bones. Sira would have known without the red and black band on his right leg that this was Windhover, the special pet of the family, older than she was, and probably as dear. Since it was dinner time, the lammergeyers of the aerie and from nests around the Mountain were circling down to land on the terraces all over the Mountain in anticipation of their evening meal. If the owner of the terrace a bird landed on didn't happen to be serving meat tonight, he would send the bird off by showing him an empty plate, and the lammergeyer would simply flap off to another terrace for a helping of fresh bones full of nutritious marrow.

By custom and common consent, no business was spoken of over a meal, whether or not there was a Sleepgiver at the table.

That had been true even when the Sleepgivers had renounced and lived apart from their families, in the time when they all wore Talismans that dulled their own personalities and left only room for their skills and their duties. Now, though, at Bey's order, Sleepgivers could go back to their families—or start families of their own— once training was complete. Still, for now, most of them chose life apart, with their brothers and sisters in death. For most families, while there was great pride that one of them had passed the trials of strength and cleverness, and passed the training, there was a certain . . . well, it was not unease, precisely, but perhaps *uncertainty* was a better word. People who do not practice the trade of death generally found it difficult to converse normally with those who did.

As she ate, Sira felt herself relaxing. There were six Sleepgivers in the family, though only three of them were active at it. Her father and mother—Anhita had been *legendary*, even before she had set her eyes on Bey and decided that he needed her as a wife—and Teychik, Siratai, Nalad, and Ahkhan. As good as Sira was, her mother was better, and she had handled most of Sira's training herself—instructing Sira as she demonstrated moves with Teychik, serenely coping with the demands of young Ahkhan and baby Hakal at the same time.

Teychik looked very distracted tonight, and Sira had a good guess why. There was an orphaned girl named Lalanash, a rescued slave brought into the Nation as a foundling, who was just finishing her own Sleepgiver training. He had been giving frequent lessons to her—lessons that Sira suspected were, more often than not, things that had nothing whatsoever to do with his own specialty of sniping from cover, single-shot kills.

That suspicion was exploded into full-blown certainty by Anhita's not-at-all subtle question as the raisins were passed around to finish the dinner. "Tey, when are you finally going to take that girl to wife and move out? I'd like your bed niche. It's not too late for me to have another baby."

Tey spluttered. Bey roared with laughter. Sira nearly choked. "That's my 'Hita," Bey said. "She misses the challenge of practicing knife strikes with a baby on one hip."

Anhita looked both sly and demure, and she tucked one long strand of her black hair behind her ear. "I do. It's good for balance."

"You could borrow a baby," Ahkhan suggested helpfully. "Or use a bag of barley."

"No one will let me borrow a baby, and a bag of grain is not the same," her mother mock-pouted.

It was very true that Anhita was one of those women who very much enjoyed every aspect of raising and training children with the same relish she had given to her Sleepgiver duties, and Sira's father always claimed the only reason she'd *stopped* having babies was that their home had run out of bed niches. That was probably not true. It wouldn't have taken much effort or time to bring in stonecutters to lengthen the bed corridor and add another niche to the end. But it *was* clear that Anhita had made up her mind that her eldest was being too slow about choosing a mate and settling down as the *full* Heir, and had decided this was as good a stick as any to prod him into moving faster and getting *on* with the job.

Poor Tey! Sira almost felt sorry for him. Almost.

With their mother and father's obvious approval and participation, that gave everyone a ripe topic of teasing and ribaldry while they finished the meal. As the rest cleared the dishes to the dry sink to be scoured with sand, Sira took Windhover his plate of bones from the kitchen. Her mother had, of course, stripped all but the tiniest scraps of meat from every bone before she cooked it. Lammergeyers ate bone, but it had to be raw.

Windhover gazed with approval at the plate heaped with lamb- and chicken-bones, and his red eyes pinned with anticipation and pleasure. Sira hand fed him the smallest ones, the little wing and rib bones that looked like tiny splinters in his huge beak. After that, all she needed to do was hold the plate; he was surprisingly dainty as he picked out the bones one by one. He swallowed the next-smallest ones quickly, a whole chicken leg bone going down like a few raisins for a human, then took his time swallowing the fist-sized chunks of lamb bones that had been prepared for him. In the wild, lammergeyers lifted entire pelvic bones as big as they were high into the air and dropped them on the rocks below, to shatter into pieces of a size they could eat. It took young lammergeyers as long as seven years to master the trick, and that was where the Nation assured the survival of a healthy population around the Mountain. Young or old, the lammergeyers here could supplement their scavenging, and a day when no carcass could be found, or a day in which a youngster simply could not hit the rocks, no longer meant a day that ended with an empty belly for them.

When Windhover was done, he bent his handsome head down for Sira to scratch, closing crimson eyes in bliss. Unlike vultures, to which they were related, lammergeyers had fully feathered necks and heads, and Sira thought they were every bit as beautiful as falcons. As she scratched him, she watched her family continue to tease Tey, who by this point was bright red under his deeply tanned skin. She wondered if she ought to rescue him and decided against it. This was, after all, one more thing he needed to learn to be able to deal with and not betray a hint of how he felt. One day he would be the Bearer, not merely the Heir to the Banner. He would need to know how to accept flattery, insult, and innuendo without turning a hair. The Nation might be united and one great family—but even in families, there were those who caused trouble.

Hakal left the others and came out to the terrace to join her. "Is the dart case in your blanket roll?" he asked, reaching a hand under Windhover's chin to scratch him. The bird nearly melted with pleasure. "I need to clean the toxin off the darts and get them ready for the next time you need them." Hakal might only be thirteen, but he was as poised and focused as a Healer twice his age.

"No, here it is. And I only needed one dart. These idiot priests of the Karsites are almost *too* easy to kill." She frowned. "I wonder if they are sending us the ones that are stupid, unreliable, or troublemakers for us to weed them out for them."

"It's a theory," Hakal agreed, then changed the subject. "The Mages have been asking when we expected you back. It seems they found some *really old* Talismans that aren't like the others." He waited for her to respond. She didn't, so he prompted,

"What do they mean, not like the others?"

This . . . was a potential mire. For years the family had tried not to talk about the Talismans around Hakal, but they had all known he was going to start asking about them eventually. It appeared that now was that "eventually."

"Did you ask the Mages?" she asked, finally.

"They said to ask you," Hakal persisted. "Or father, but he's busy, and you're not. You can all stop dancing around the subject now. I want to hear about them. I got the feeling this was going to be a long explanation."

Windhover finally had his fill of scratches, lifted his head away from their hands, and then lifted his wings. Since that was the signal to get out of his way, they both backed up. His wings were huge, powerful, and getting hit with one would certainly end in a bruise and possibly a broken bone. When they were far enough away to avoid injury, the lammergeyer pushed off from the battlement and half fell, half flew off to the side. He dropped out of view for a moment, then rose back into sight, laboring up to the aerie (and possibly a second meal) with the assistance of updrafts.

"You've never liked the old Talismans," she temporized.

"I _hate_ the old Talismans," he corrected, flushing. "And I don't know why. They felt wrong. I don't want them near me."

"Well, if the Mages said you were to ask me about them, I guess they feel you're ready to hear about them without throwing a fit," she said. "Again."

They were both quiet for a moment as they recalled the very memorable scene when Hakal was being tested for training and had been too young to know better than to make a scene over something he didn't care for in public. Everything had been fine until he had encountered one of the last of the Sleepgivers still wearing the old-style Talismans. No one then had known he was a Healer. All they had known was that the moment the Sleepgiver got within touching distance of the boy, Hakal had turned into a screaming, biting, fighting whirlwind, insisting that the man not come near him. And since that made it obvious he was never going to be a Sleepgiver, no matter what else he *would* grow into, and most of the Talismans had already been replaced with the "new" versions, it had been decided that the situation was moot.

And then, of course, his Healing powers manifested, and it didn't matter anymore. And no one talked about the Talismans at all around him or showed theirs to him.

Hakal looked over the edge of the parapet, staring down at the terrace below. "I promise not to pitch a fit," he said.

"Sleepgivers all wear them. Everyone in the family does except you. Even me," she said, and pulled hers out. "See?"

He started. "But—how can—why don't—"

"Because these are the kind all the Sleepgivers wear *now*, and that all of them *used* to wear; but for a couple of centuries until just recently, they were wearing something else. This one is just magically stored memories, and very specific ones. Memories of how to do things. Here—put it on. I promise it's safe. It won't upset you at all." She slipped the cord over her neck and handed it to him. He took it very gingerly, and spent a long time staring at it. Then he looked at her, frowning fiercely.

"You'd better not be trying anything—"

"You idiot," she said without rancor. "Why would I do that?

You're a Healer. You're valuable. If I spoiled you somehow, I'd be cleaning the aerie for the rest of my natural life. They're *Mother's* memories, you dolt. Put it on."

He slipped the cord over his head. "I—don't feel anything." He looked at her again, expression uncertain. "So what—"

"All right. Now think very hard about how you'd get from this battlement to the aerie *without* using the stairs. Climbing the wall outside."

"But I—" he protested, and then his eyes glazed over for a moment, and when he came back to himself again, he stared at her in open-mouthed shock, the updraft from below teasing bits of hair out of his braid.

She nodded. "See? Memory, but not just memory like pictures in your head. *Every* kind of memory. Exactly where you'd put your hands and feet and how it should feel if it's right or wrong, down to the least little muscle movement. And now if you needed to do that, you could."

He pulled her Talisman off and handed it to her with a shudder. "No, I couldn't. Not in a million years. That's crazy."

"You could if you really had to. And that's what most of the Sleepgiver training is—assimilating memories and then practicing them until we're as good as the original person who imprinted those memories. I've got Mother's. Tey and Ahkhan have Father's, and Father has *his* father's. But those Talismans take . . . months to imprint. The person doing the imprinting has to wear them while *doing* all those things. Think about all the things Mother knows how to do as a Sleepgiver! Just *doing* them takes a lot of time, and she has to wear the new Talisman *and* have a Mage working with her the whole time. Sure, they work for everyone, and when Father dies, Tey will inherit his and give it to a new, young Sleepgiver he wants to honor. But there was a while when we had a lot more new Sleepgivers than we had Talismans for them, and most of the working Sleepgivers were out on missions for money to support the Nation. So that was when things changed. The Mages would imprint a *lot* of Talismans on a Sleepgiver when he was dying, and the way they did it was like taking a little bit of his spirit and putting it in the Talisman. So . . . "

She stopped, because now Hakal was open-mouthed in horror. "*That* was what I felt!" he choked. "It was—something *imprisoned*, but in control of the Sleepgiver!"

"Exactly," she said, matter-of-factly, because she figured that was the easiest way to get Hakal to calm down. "When he got back from Valdemar, Father and the Mages started going backward through the old records, and we found the place where that became the way things were done *all the time*, and the old kind of Talismans went into storage. And the reason the spirit-trapped Talismans became the only ones was because the Bearer at that point was a right bastard and wanted to completely control the Sleepgivers. The spirit-trap ones dull your mind and make you more obedient. So that was why he ordered the old ones put away. That way he had Sleepgivers that were just as good as the ones in the past but who would never question anything and always obey orders. He kept spies on the Mages so they'd never tell what was happening, and within a generation, it just became 'that's how we do things.' And when Grandfather died, Father decided we weren't going to do that anymore."

"Sometimes I regret that decision," said her father, who had left the table and was now within earshot. He grinned at Sira, who knew exactly what he meant, and at Hakal, who stared at his father as if he couldn't believe his ears. "Oh, come now, don't act so shocked. You've heard some of my screaming matches in the Council Chamber. It would be a lot easier if everyone knew I was in complete command of a small army of absolutely obedient, ruthless murderers now, wouldn't it?"

Hakal closed his mouth with a snap. "I—guess so?"

Sira laughed, and her father punched her shoulder—or rather, punched where her shoulder had been until she moved it *just* out of reach. He nodded a little in approval.

"Your mother and I decided that we were going to reverse this 'tradition,'" Bey continued. "And believe it or not, there were those who put up a fight, until we pointed out that the Talismans had essentially created slaves."

Sira and Hakal both nodded; slavery was a hot subject within the Nation. *No one* approved of slavery; this was a pragmatic as well as an emotional issue. The Nation had no problem with adopting foundlings into their midst, and not infrequently those foundlings came out of slave trains that were injudicious enough to attempt to evade Ruvan authority by passing through Nation lands. The enslavement of children infuriated the people of the Nation, great and small. It infuriated them even more that children had been torn from the arms of dead or living parents to be made into slaves. Such foundlings were always brought into the Nation when there was no chance they could be returned to their own families, which was almost always.

Not the adults, though. Children adapted easily; the adult slaves, raised in slavery, did not, and were generally almost more trouble than their grudging labor was worth. Being slaves had taught them that only doing *just enough* to avoid being punished was the way to survive, and their understandable greed when presented with food freely available, meant they cost more in food than they produced in labor. Adults were usually freed with whatever food and water had been with the slave train once they were guided to the vicinity of some town outside the Nation. Then they were told to make their way on their own.

"We compromised; we went through the stores of Talismans and found the *old* ones, the ones that were just memories, and offered to exchange them with the Talismans of a dozen volunteers." Bey grinned again. "When those volunteers felt the results, they did all the work of persuading the rest of the Sleepgivers for us."

The horror and unease on Hakal's face had finally faded, and Sira was pleased to see that he had regained his curiosity. "Then why was that Sleepgiver still wearing a bad one when I saw him?" he asked.

"Because there were not enough of the old Talismans that we trusted to replace all the bad ones," his father told him. "Some were *too* old and the memories had faded and needed to be renewed with someone else's. And, it seems," he glanced at Sira, "some we could not recognize what was in them at all. In the old records it is suggested that there were experiments with the earliest Talismans, and it didn't seem worth the risk to give one of those to someone who was already damaged by having been enslaved by those spirit-fragments. The Talismans with just memories actually proved to be healing in spirit to the ones who had been under the thrall of the bad sort."

"Satisfied?" Sira asked her little brother. He nodded. "How long did it take that accursed priest to succumb?" he asked her, his mind already turning back to his own work, and hers.

"About as long as it took him to slap at the place twice, thinking he'd been stung by an insect," she told him. He considered this, then smiled with satisfaction.

"I don't think it's worth going for anything faster," he said to his father. "There's a limit to how much I can concentrate the toad toxin. So, it's ready for the Sleepgivers' general use."

The three of them spoke about trivialities then for a little until Hakal drifted off to his workroom to clean the dart, and Sira was left alone with her father as the sun began to set spectacularly, painting the landscape with fire. Huge shadows wafted over them as the lammergeyers headed for their nightly roost in their aerie.

"Routine?" asked Bey, and he didn't have to say anything more for Sira to know that he meant her mission.

"Routine. I delivered your message, but I honestly could not tell if he was being mind-ridden or not. Hakal's toad toxin is very effective. What are these Talismans that the Mages have found?"

Bey shrugged. "I have no idea. I'm not half a Mage the way you are. I gather they are something they found while you were gone, something very different from anything they've seen before. They're actually afraid to meddle with them, which is something I don't ever recall one of our Mages saying."

Mages, so Sira was given to understand, were even rarer among the Nation than they were in the lands around the Mountain. She often wondered whether it was because her people were so intent on uncovering potential Sleepgivers and Healers that they overlooked Mage-potential in favor of any sign that a child could fit into Sleepgiver or Healer ranks. Certainly no one had been more surprised than she and her parents when, in the middle of her Sleepgiver training, she had jokingly tried to ignite the kitchen fire with a fire spell—and succeeded. After that, she had divided her time between the training halls and the little Mage-enclave down in the safest part of the caverns, where everything not in immediate use was kept, and where all those old Talismans had been found.

Just as no one ever wasted anything, the Nation as a whole never threw away anything.

And because she was half a Mage and half a Sleepgiver, she was the one the Mages had asked to start destroying the bad Talismans, on her father's order.

"I never got a chance to tell you before I left what occurred to me about those Talismans I'm clearing," she said abruptly. "I think . . . I think they were more than merely spirit reflections. I think some of them, the most powerful, were actually haunted. I think that's why a kind of stupid and powerful half-personality took over their wearers and dulled their own minds."

Her father cast her a quizzical look. "What do you mean, *haunted?*" he asked. "As in a spirit or a ghost?"

"Spirit, no. Ghost . . . maybe," she temporized. "You know that the Mages all say that at least some ghosts are not actually spirits bound to a place or object. Instead, they are the full *image* of someone's spirit at the moment of trauma and death. A kind of reflection that persists over time. More than just memories, less than a person or a person's spirit. Dimly aware that they exist, stubbornly determined to continue what they were doing when they died. Desperately determined to persist, in fact—after all, the Talismans were imprinted at the moment of a Sleepgiver's death, when they were desperate to keep living." She paused. "Am I making sense?"

"Quite a lot of it." Her father crossed his arms thoughtfully over his chest. "Much as I hate to bring this up . . . could these Talismans actually *be* the fractured spirits of the dead Sleepgiver?"

"I don't think I would be able to answer that definitively unless I had *all* the Talismans imprinted at once from a particular dying Sleepgiver and broke them at the same time," she told him honestly. "I don't *think* they are chained, fractured spirits . . . but I don't know for certain."

"All the more reason to keep breaking them, then." Bey's mouth narrowed into a tight line. "I cannot think of anything worse than that--fractured spirits in slavery to a Talisman . . . *our people*, and we have done that to them!"

"It's not a certainty, Father, it's only a possibility, and I'm inclined to think that it is unlikely." She actually *didn't* think that, but she wanted her father to feel better. It wasn't *his* fault, not any of it, and he was making it right.

Finally Bey sighed, uncrossed his arms, and turned and leaned on the battlement, looking out over the valley. By this time the sun was down, and the stars had started to fill the sky. "Be glad you are not the Heir, Sira. The responsibilities to our people weigh as heavily as the Mountain."

"And you are strong enough to carry them," she said confidently. He reached out and patted her shoulder.

"I am glad you think so, my daughter," he replied. "And well done on your mission."

And with that, he went inside. She stayed out for a while before retiring to the long hall that held the bed niches, and her own soft featherbed.

It was certainly far superior to the hollow in the rock she'd slept in last night.

4

Harvest Fair at night was very different from Midsummer Fair at night. For one thing, dense fog tended to form on the big open commons where the Fair took place. The weather changed every night a couple of candlemarks after sundown, bringing a fog so dense it even penetrated into the lanes behind the tents. For another, sundown came a lot earlier; that alone meant that younglings had to leave around suppertime or before, shooed out by the fair wardens. Haven younglings that is; plenty of younglings who had come with their farming or trading parents remained here in the fairgrounds. But they were usually eating, getting ready to sleep, standing first watch on their livestock, or taking a turn behind the counter of their stall at sunset so their parents could eat. They weren't roaming the aisles either; if they had to go anywhere, they used the lanes behind the tents.

So any younglings out in the aisles between the stalls would be questioned by the fair wardens, and they'd better have a good reason for being there. Night was for adults, and a whole different crowd than you found at night at Midsummer Fair.

Midsummer Fair evenings brought lots of people from Haven down to enjoy a balmy night full of entertainment and excitement. Harvest Fair . . . not so much. It was colder, and there were fewer entertainers out in the open, in no small part because the sorts of flimsy costumes that attracted the most money were ill-suited to the damp chill and fog. As for "free" entertainment that relied on coins dropped in a hat . . . there was none of that. Musicians would work only in tents. Instruments went out of tune quickly, and cold, stiff fingers fumbled to create the right notes. There were a few fire-eaters and jugglers, but not many, and they only performed a trick or two before going back into their tents. Tents were warmer—and if you were performing in a tent, and there was an audience, you knew you'd already gotten your pay.

Night at Harvest Fair meant crowded cooktents, surprisingly so given that the majority of people who were at the fair were farmers. One would assume they'd cook for themselves, but although on paper it *would* be cheaper to cook for yourself over a fire, in actuality there were many reasons why it wasn't, in practice. The cost of firewood was artificially inflated at the Fair, you would have to take up precious cargo space in your wagon with food for the entire week, and you would have been up since sunrise, so by the time suppertime rolled around, you generally didn't have the energy to cook.

And the cooktents knew their clientele well after so many centuries of Harvest Fairs. Suppertime meant huge kettles full of hearty soups that had been cooking all day, good beer that looked dark and was not too strong, and trays of heavy, equally hearty breads. This was what a farmer was used to; his biggest meal of the day was breakfast, not supper, and what he wanted before he went to bed was something warm and filling, but not so filling he'd get indigestion in the middle of the night. In the morning, the cooktents would be ready with pocket pies—meat pies, fruit pies, vegetable pies, egg pies. And to help fill in the corners there would more bread with plenty of butter or drippings, barrels of apples, and several kinds of cheese.

As soon as the farmers and their younglings cleared out, the cooktents prepared for a slower crowd, and one that wanted only two things: strong beer or wine and salty snacks, preferably hot.

That would be when Tory, Kee, Kat, and Perry would make the rounds of the cooktents. Anyone in there now was most probably a farmer—or a fair warden or Constable, keeping a sharp eye out for pickpockets and sharpsters. With rare exceptions, pickpockets were not the concern of their little intelligence network. Right now, their job was to idle around the aisles, becoming invisible as possible.

For Perry and Kat, that meant blending in with the thin crowds, figuring out what parts of their outfits to change to look absolutely inconspicuous. *They* were the visible parts of the team. Larral the *kyree* and Kee and Tory were the invisible part. And Herald Mags was set up in the rear of the Guard tent, shared with the Constables, coordinating all of them.

Kee was somewhere over on the east side of the Fair; Tory had a vague sense of where he was and probably could have found the Prince within a quarter-candlemark if he'd had to, even without his father's help. He and Kee were putting into practice all those

Sleepgiver tricks they'd been learning from Mags over the summer.

Well, to be fair, the learning part was the easiest. Thanks to Mags' extremely powerful Gift of Mindspeaking, Mags could just *plant* "memories" of those tricks into their heads over the course of an evening. The memories came complete with exactly how it felt to do them right, too. So most of the learning was actually practice to get those moves so ingrained into their bodies that they were second nature and required no thought at all.

They certainly hadn't been bored this summer, that was certain. As soon as Mags reckoned they'd mastered a trick or a move, he started them on a new one. And it was a little daunting to realize they'd been at this all summer and well into fall, and he *still* hadn't taught them everything that was in his head.

It helped that Perry had learned a lot of these same things years ago, so when he came back to Haven between jobs, he helped them train.

Right now Tory had fitted himself in between two darkened tent stalls; one was, by the scent that permeated even the canvas of the tent, a spice-and-herb seller, the other a seller of herb seeds. Neither of them were going to get any customers by night; farmers who wanted such things would get away for a candlemark or so and come by daylight, so they could see what they were purchasing.

Tory crouched low between the two tents so that a casual glance by a passerby had little chance of finding him, and he had fitted himself exactly into the darkest part of the shadows between the tents. He was so quiet and so still that not even the proprietors sleeping at the back of the tents were aware that he was there.

He was waiting for a particular tent stall across the way to open up again.

One of the things he had learned from Mags' memories was the concept of being quiet. Not just "quiet," but *quiet;* silent even inside your own head, which was a real trick indeed. His father said that if it had not been for the fact that his own Gift was so very strong, when he and Kee and Perry went *quiet,* even he wouldn't be able to tell they were there. It was curiously restful to do this. He was just a relaxed body holding a pair of eyes and ears that observed everything that passed him without actually thinking about any of those things.

The spice seller always tossed restlessly, probably wishing he were back in his own bed at home, until he found a comfortable position and dropped off, breathing slowly and deeply. The seed seller snored. Gently, almost musically, and nothing anyone would notice unless they were right next to him. Both sounds told him he was doing his job right, which was to remain unnoticed.

There was enough traffic in the aisle to keep the air moving and the fog dispersed, though not so much that Tory's view of the stall was in any way impeded. Behind him, though . . . the fog crept in and deepened in the lanes behind the tents, chilling everything and giving that peculiar quality to sound that only comes in a fog. Sounds seemed simultaneously muffled and echoing, and his back and shoulders felt clammy as the damp penetrated his clothing.

That was fine; there was nothing back there that he needed other than an avenue to travel noiselessly and without anyone spotting him, and a little cold and damp was not going to harm him.

He did feel sorry for people trying to sleep tonight without adequate coverings or a little charcoal heater or a banked fire. Ideally, their beds should be a canvas cloth over a nice bed of hay, then a feather-stuffed canvas blanket, or pure wool. That damp chill would penetrate nearly anything else, making waking up pure misery for anyone old enough to get an aching joint.

As that wisp of a thought drifted across the back of his mind, he alerted like a guard dog and tensed all over. Movement across the aisle.

The stall lit up from within as the proprietor lit lanterns; then the front of the stall slowly rolled up as he raised the canvas flap.

There it was, in all its peculiar glory, slanting display racks of the oddest mix of wares in the entire Fair.

Rutolf, owner and sole proprietor, sold what he referred to as "curiosities." They could be anything from the fang of some unidentifiable (but undoubtedly large) creature drilled to be suspended, perhaps as part of a barbaric necklace, to tiny mother-of-pearl figures carved in a strange and sinuous style that looked nothing like the trinkets produced on the shores of Lake Evendim. He had piles of small, white, silken-furred skins of some sort of weasel. He had dyes from the plants in the Pelagir Hills that could produce colors you couldn't get any other way. He had horns alleged to be the cure for an aging gentleman's fading sexual prowess.

And Mags was fairly certain the man was a go-between for several known agents working in Valdemar. The problem was, so Tory's father had told him, the merchant had one of the most effective natural Mindspeech blocks Mags had ever seen.

Because of course he does. That would be the first thing that was wanted if you were sending spies into a country full of Mindspeakers.

Tory was here tonight to confirm that and to discover how the agents were identifying themselves. Mags had planted the images of all of the known agents in Haven in Tory's mind, so recognizing them was not going to be a problem as long as they didn't try to disguise themselves too heavily.

Of course, it might have been asked—and Tory was sure that more than one of the King's Councilors had—why Mags didn't simply have these agents rounded up, if they were known to be spying for other countries.

The answer was absurdly simple. If Mags had done that, another agent would be inserted, and he'd have to go to the trouble of identifying the new one. And the new one might be better at remaining undetected and certainly would be more cautious than the one who had been caught.

Even more important, Mags could control every bit of information that a known agent learned. Truth to be told, he had most of them *buying* information from him, in his persona of Willie the Weasel who owned a pawn shop down in Haven!

And to be honest, at least half of them were working for allies of Valdemar who were just verifying that what they were told by Valdemaran officials and diplomats was actually true. Everyone did that; Mags had his own network of agents in Menmellith, Rethwellan, Hardorn, and Kata'shin'a'in. There was no point in even trying to get an agent placed among the Shin'a'in; you had to be raised among them to be accepted by them. But it only made sense to have intelligence agents among your allies, so if things started to go wrong within the ruling government, *your* country had warning of it, and you'd be able to take steps to ensure your own country's safety. Revolutions sometimes spilled over borders, though in Valdemar's case that generally meant refugees spilling over the border rather than the revolution itself causing unrest among the people.

Tory watched and waited as people drifted up to the stall,

perused the wares, mostly left, sometimes bought. Based on the number of actual customers Tory had counted so far, the price of the items they bought, and his likely traffic during the day, Rutolf was making a very tidy profit. With what he was probably being paid by at least four other countries, he would probably be able to retire from traveling a rich man. As long as he didn't end up a dead one first. Espionage was not a forgiving business.

He was beginning to think this would be a dead end, when he suddenly recognized the profile of one of the Rethwellan agents his father had planted in his mind. He held his breath until the man approached Rutolf's stall. They talked together for a few moments, Rutolf offered him one of the white weasel furs, the man shook his head, and Rutolf reached beneath the counter and produced a tree-hare pelt instead. They exchanged some coins, and the man went on his way.

Well, there were several places where they could have exchanged information. I think I need to wait and see if this was a fluke or an ordinary transaction.

As it happened, he didn't have to wait very long. The aisles weren't exactly *filling up,* but there were more people in them as the farmers and their offspring left the cook tents and did a little browsing before bed. And this time the agent was from Hardorn, and a woman.

She made apparently the same conversation and the same transaction. So it wasn't a fluke, and it wasn't an ordinary purchase. Rutolf was keeping those tree-hare pelts under his display for no other purpose than to give a screen for passing information and possibly orders or money.

He was going to have to get much closer.

A Sleepgiver is never in a hurry, he reminded himself. And so he took all the time he needed to ease himself back into the lane behind the stall tents, moving so slowly that not even a leaf rustled as he moved. Once there, he stood up with the same care, flexed all his muscles so he'd be moving normally, and set out at a slow walk to the end of the lane.

He had a knitted hood over his head and shoulders, something not uncommon around Haven at this time of year. His leather tunic, knitted hood, shirt, and trews were all a heathered charcoal—the natural result of knitting with yarn blended from the wool of a white and a black sheep. This was almost the perfect color to blend into a shadow under circumstances like these. And the color wasn't even, which was also a plus. There were only two things he needed to do before he got closer.

He reached the end of the lane, exited through a larger-than-usual gap between two stalls, crossed the aisle, and entered the foggy bounds of the lane behind Rutolf's tent. Once he was deeply into the shadows there, he reached into a pouch under his tunic and pulled out a little wooden box that contained a mixture of grease and finely ground soot. He smeared this liberally around his eyes, then pulled the top of the hood down to his eyebrows, and the bottom up to the bridge of his nose.

Now he eased his way toward Rutolf's tent one slow, deliberate step at a time, toe-walking and rolling his feet to avoid making any sound at all, not even that of a displaced pebble. Fog eddied and swirled around him as he listened carefully between each step. The curious acoustics of the fog made it seem as if every sound of bargaining, of conversations within the little tent stalls, or of sleeping was coming from right next to him. Few of the stalls in this section were open because most of them sold things most late-night buyers would not be interested in, so few of them were brightly lit. Once he reached the tent, easily identifiable by Rutolf's shadow flung by the lantern light against the back wall, he got down on his hands and knees, positioned himself at the gap between Rutolf's tent and the next one to the left, and then got even farther down, onto his belly.

This was one of the Sleepgiver tricks: crawling on your stomach like a snake as you were easing yourself into an observation point. It took incredible muscle control and was not for the impatient, since progress was measured in terms of distances half the width of a thumb.

And gods, it was cold. Even through gloves and well knitted wool, it was cold. The ground just sucked all the heat right out of him.

Finally he was in position, and he heard every word Rutolf was saying to a customer. Not one he was interested in; this one was buying one of those "virility horns."

He rolled over a tiny bit at a time until he could just see Rutolf from below, reaching over his display to give the customer his package. Rutolf was right-handed; he probably would not look in this direction, and even if he did, his eyes were used to the lantern light, not the shadows hiding Tory. And Tory would have to be having a very bad day indeed if Rutolf happened to catch the shine of his eyes in the dark.

Now it was time to wait again. It was still awfully cold down there on the ground, and the smell of damp, cold earth and crushed grass just made him feel colder.

At least it's not raining. At least I'm not in mud.

Then—finally—

A face looked at Rutolf's across the display counter that Tory recognized. "I understand you have flea furs," said the second Hardornen agent.

"I do, very fine, very soft, a pleasure to wear," said Rutolf, and handed the man one of the white weasel pelts. But from where Tory was, he clearly saw a folded paper packet, which could hold orders or money or both, under the pelt.

The agent took the tiny fur and the packet under it in both hands, sliding the paper out from beneath the pelt and into his pocket. He made a show of examining the pelt at great length once he had safely stowed what he actually came for. "It is very fine," he said. "How much?"

"Two silver, and a bargain at the price," declared Rutolf. "These are the finest of ermine pelts from the barbarian North. Very rare! Very fine!"

"And too fine for my pocket," said the agent, handing it back. "I heard you had pelts for four coppers."

"Oh, my friend, you disappoint me," Rutolf sighed, putting the ermine pelt down and reaching under the counter. His eyes never left his customer's face. The agent's gaze was just as locked on Rutolf's. "I have tree-hare. Also fine, but common. No one will think you are a gentleman wearing such as this."

I could be hosting a Bardic quartet down here for all that they'd look at me.

The agent slipped a much more substantial paper packet out of the front of his tunic and slid it under the fur as he took it from Rutolf. They both put their hands down near the display trays, well out of sight of anyone but Tory, and Rutolf took the packet and slipped it under the displays. "Yes, this is more to my taste," said the agent. "I am not concerned with being taken for a gentleman."

Rutolf made disapproving sounds but accepted the four coppers. "If you change your mind, I will not take it back!" he warned. "You will have to buy the ermine at full price!"

"I will not change my mind," said the agent, and he moved off, just in time to make way for a farmer, his wife, and three older children, who all crowded around to goggle at Rutolf's odd wares. That gave Tory all the time he needed to ease his way back to the lane again, crawl a little way away from Rutolf's stall before he stood up, then pull back his hood, wipe the soot from his face, and replace his hood again.

No point in trying to be stealthy now, and every reason to act like anyone else who would be back here. He sauntered along behind the tents, some lit, some not, no longer making any attempt to be quiet.

Not that he needed to, since he wasn't running into anyone—and even when he wasn't being stealthy, he was still pretty quiet.

At least now that he was off the ground and moving, he could warm up a bit.

The fog crept around back here like some sort of living thing. It was pretty unnerving, even if you weren't superstitious.

With no particular need to move quickly, he took his time about making his way to the Guard tent, pausing long enough to get himself first a mug of good hot mulled wine to chase the cold out of his body, then a snack of beer and hot cheese-stuffed bread before cutting back into another lane and entering the Guard tent from the rear.

The tiny canvas-walled room had a few chairs, a quarter-cask of beer, a box full of mugs, and a lantern hanging from a support overhead. Mags was there, in one of the chairs, with a *listening* look on his face that told Tory he was probably Mindspeaking with one of the others—or at least listening to them. So he dropped a second cheese roll into Mags' hand, sat down on a stool in the darkened rear of the tent, and waited.

"Thankee," Mags said, after an interval that Tory enjoyed very much for its quality of not involving him lying flat on the cold, hard ground.

"Rutolf's your man. Agent's recognition sign is 'I understand you have flea-furs.' Rutolf says yes and passes him a white weasel fur that he calls 'ermine' and under it's a packet. Agent looks at it and says he can't afford it and only has four coppers. Rutolf takes it back and gets a tree-hare pelt from under the counter; they both hold the pelt near the display for a moment and make an exchange under it, the agent pays for the pelt and leaves."

Mags considered this. "It sounds t'me like 'e knows these agents on sight."

"Aye. Otherwise how would he know what packet to give to who? He passed stuff off to two from Hardorn and one from Menmellith while I was watching."

Mags sighed. "No luck passing you or Perry off as an agent then. Well, we'll just have t' do this the hard way." He closed his eyes for a moment. "All right, Perry's takin' first watch, an' he'll wait to see if Rutolf passes anythin' along to anyone we're actually worried about. You'll take second watch. By then, Fair'll be closed."

Tory nodded. The unspoken part of this would be that if one of the actual enemy agents here took a delivery from Rutolf, he or Perry would have to follow him and figure out where he was staying now. And once they had that information, Mags would set a watch on the agent until they were able either to get their hands on those orders, to learn from subordinates or deduce from his actions what the orders were.

It would, of course, be *much* easier to waylay the man and get their hands on that paper, but that would just open up a world of bad consequences.

If they knocked him out in an attempt to make him think that he had just been the victim of a robbery, they'd barely have time to search him for the paper and glance at it before taking obvious valuables and leaving him in a dark corner to recover. The paper was probably in code, and they'd have no way of memorizing what was on it in the short time they'd have before the agent regained consciousness. And even if they made the ambush look like a robbery, the agent would rightly be alarmed and alerted and would have to assume his identity was known. Then he'd probably bolt, and then would come the problem of figuring out who his replacement was. Haven was a large city, the borders with Valdemar's allies were open, and people came and went all the time.

The best outcome would be if Rutolf was just servicing "friendlies." Mags already had people in those networks, and he'd know soon enough what the orders were.

"Go on out and just do a gen'ral watch in the entertainment tents. I'll have Perry send Larral for ye when we need ye, if'n I don't talk t'ye m'self." Mags went back to that "listening" look, and Tory nodded and left, not at all loath to be turned loose to drift around the Fair.

All of the big entertainment tents were on the outskirts of the Fair, but there were plenty of small ones mingled in with the stalls and food vendors, and most of them were the sort of thing that Kat would look *very* out-of-place perusing. There were not as many of these at Harvest as there were at Midsummer, mostly because the working farmers generally came with wives or older children and these were definitely not something a child should watch or a wife would be happy about. And if the farmer did sneak off for a bit of salacious fun and titillation, things would be very uncomfortable if their spouses found out later.

Because the girls who worked these shows generally wore just enough to keep the Fair wardens from booting them out when they performed the little dances to drum up interest in the full show, putting them out on a box in front of the tent in this weather risked them getting pneumonia. So the callers relied on larger-than-life-sized paintings on canvas to advertise. Some of these paintings were surprisingly good. Mind, since the paintings were meant to last decades and were often traded from show to show, it was vanishingly unlikely that any of the girls who performed inside the tent would *look* like the girls on the paintings, but Tory was pretty certain most of the customers were not at all bothered about hair and eye color.

The first of these shows he encountered seemed to have gotten just enough of an audience that the caller was ready to shut the tent flap and start the show, so Tory paid his coin and ducked inside at the last minute. Some of the fog followed him inside, but it quickly dispersed in the somewhat warmer air within the tent.

The show was a new variation on "dropping clothing to music," at least to him. All the girls were up on hoops suspended over the heads of the audience, and they did remarkably agile poses to the music of a single gittern player and a drummer while the hoops slowly rotated. The caller stood under each one as she did her turn, catching the dropped articles and stowing them behind the canvas backcloth, until the show was done. There were ropes and a pulley for each of the hoops, which was obviously how the girls got up there. Once Tory's initial interest in the mechanics of the show had been satisfied, he did his job, which was to watch for people passing messages to each other. Venues like this were ideal for passing messages, since by all rights, there wouldn't be an eye in the place that wasn't on the girls.

When the show was over, the caller hustled the customers all out quickly, chivvying them like a housewife shooing hens. Probably because those girls were pretty impatient to get down off the hoops, get their scarves back on, and perhaps bundle up in a nice blanket.

Tory spent the next couple of candlemarks going from girl show to girl show without seeing anything more suspicious than a pickpocket. Since the thief in question was youngish, looked starving, and Tory just had a feeling about him, instead of alerting a constable, he intercepted the lad just before he went for a beltpouch by the simple expedient of grabbing the offending wrist in an iron grip and pulling the thief away from his intended target.

"Don't," he whispered harshly, as the lad froze after a couple of steps. "I'm not the only set of eyes in these tents. Go hire yourself out as a horse watcher if you need money."

The fellow did not even bother to protest; as soon as Tory let go of his wrist, he bolted. Would the warning keep him from trying again elsewhere? Well, that wasn't Tory's problem. He'd stopped the theft and scared the thief, and what happened after that was out of his control.

He stopped and got another cup of mulled wine, but it was beginning to look as if the fog and cold were taking their toll, and people were heading to bed early. You could no longer call the people in the aisles a "crowd." It was more like a trickle. And more and more of the shows and vendors of hot drinks and snacks were cutting their losses and shutting down.

Just as he got a last cup of mulled wine—this one in an edible cup of something like a very hard, crisp cookie!—Mags came to that conclusion too.

:Target closed down for the night, and no reason to stay down here. See you back home.:

That Mindsent message had the feeling of something that had been sent to all four of them, himself, Perry, Kee, and Kat. He decided to take his time walking back since he still had some wine, and he strolled down to the livestock section of the Fair, just to be sure things were quiet there as well.

Everything seemed to be in order there, though the fog was thickening to the point where he was going to have to be careful walking home—and he found Kee waiting for him at the horses.

Also holding an edible cup of mulled wine.

Kee lifted his cup to him. "Remember the first time we came to Harvest Fair and Kat brought us? We never did get all the horses we wanted."

"Man can only ride one horse at a time," Tory observed, looking out at the same corral full of drowsy beasts that Kee was.

"Well, now, that's true enough." Kee sipped, then nibbled. "On a night like this it's tempting to just grab a couple of rooms at the best inn we can find and rejoin everyone when the fog clears."

"And if we were anyone else but us, I'd go along with that idea. And while I wouldn't be in trouble, there'd be no end of fuss if *you* weren't in your proper bed at daybreak. Did you get anything tonight?" Mags hadn't said anything, but, then, the man had been busy.

"The only message passing was between people planning on going to bed with someone they weren't married to," Kee said, with such chagrin in his voice that Tory figured he must have discovered this himself, in a particularly awkward way. "At least, they found excuses to meet at an empty hay tent. I didn't stick around to discover anything else."

"Wise. Person could end up with a broken nose otherwise." The wine was gone, but the spicy cup was still edible, so he finished it. "Don't ask me how I found that out."

"I don't have to, because I know," Kee teased. One of the horses ambled over to them, looking interested. "Think this'd hurt a horse?"

"It's a cookie. I wouldn't feed these things to a horse on a regular basis, but it can't be worse for him than a lump of sugar."

Kee held out the remains of the cup on the flat of his hand. The horse sniffed it over, appeared satisfied, and lipped it off gently, then wandered away, making crunching sounds.

"Well. The walk isn't getting any shorter by waiting," Tory said finally.

And then *something* practically drove him to his knees, hitting his mind with bruising force.

Rage! Pain. Focusfocusfocus . . .

"*What* the——" Tory gasped, clutching the top railing of the corral in an attempt to stay upright.

"You're getting it too?" Kee choked.

RAGE! He went down to one knee.

Then——as abruptly as it had come——nothing.

"What in the *hell* was that? Never mind," Tory amended. "We've got to check on the others, *now!*"

They clasped wrists, because when they were dropping into their "Farsight" trance unexpectedly, that seemed to help. Tory braced himself against the wood of the corral, and opened his mind.

Sofia and Rafi—

In bed. Sofia was asleep, Rafi was sneaking in some bedtime reading by the night candle.

Mags— Strolling up the High Street with Kat, Perry, and Larral.

Mother— In conference with the King.

He sensed Kee checking on his brothers and they both satisfied themselves that they were safe; he sent his own mind questing after Abi, and found her sound asleep in her far-off bed, with a "scholar's mistress" of books and papers piled on the side she wasn't in and the covers pulled over her head.

He let go of Kee's wrist and shook his head to clear it. "I checked on our grandfathers and they're telling old stories over wine with my grandmother," the Prince said. He sounded utterly bewildered.

"We need to catch up with Father and the others," Tory replied. "That's all I can think right now."

Kee nodded, and they both turned to sprint around—not through—the Fair. It was much faster to go around the sprawl of tents. Not to mention that anyone running through the aisles right now would bring the attention of Constables, Fair wardens, or both.

They stopped once to make sure of the route the others were taking back, then sprinted again. They caught the group about halfway through Haven, in a neighborhood of middling prosperity and mingled shops and homes.

At that point, the two of them slowed to a fast walk, so as not to alarm the others by running at them—which would certainly be the signal for a display of weapons from all four. Fog like this brought out thugs and footpads who took advantage of it to knock their victims unconscious before robbing them right there in the street.

"Father!" Tory called out, as soon as they were within earshot.

The shadows in the fog ahead of them stopped and turned as one.

They were still panting as they caught up, and Mags' keen ears caught it before Tory could say anything. "You two all right?" the Herald asked with concern.

"We were just standing there, and we got—hit with something. Not a vision, for me at least it was all emotion and a little thought. Mostly anger. But it was out of the blue, and it hit us both like a cudgel." Tory looked over at Kee.

"I got flashes of fighting," Kee added. "Then it all just cut off. We checked on everyone in the family, and they're all fine. But— what could it have been?"

"That—" Mags replied, his voice colored with astonishment. "— is a very good question!"

5

Fall and spring were the two best seasons on the Mountain: neither blistering hot nor freezing cold. And morning, for the household of the Banner Bearer, meant going down to the nearest market to buy perishables. Since it was her turn to shop, Sira returned from the midlevel Mountain market with four string bags of pots of jam she could not resist, plus meat for tonight and produce for the next couple of days packed into a bundle on her back.

The beehive on their terrace still had some activity, but her mother had taken the honey harvest from it a fortnight ago, leaving plenty for the hive to use in the spring to get themselves started. Almost everyone had hives; honey was the main source of sweet things besides fruit.

She unloaded her bags into the kitchen, where the cook, one of the three servants they had, took it from her. Not many people on the Mountain had servants; those were more common out on the farms. All three of the family servants had been liberated from slave trains as children and had elected to stay with the Nation, but they had not been suitable for Sleepgiver training. At that point, being Foundlings and without a place and family of their own, their choices had been to learn a trade and serve a seven-year unpaid apprenticeship, move out to the farms and work as servants, laborers, or herders there, or become servants to one of the families on the Mountain that could afford to pay a servant's wages. There was enough prosperity that some families had servants, mostly the craftspeople and Elders, and the designation of "servant" did not have quite the same negative connation among those of the Nation that it did in other lands.

"Thank you, Nilda," Sira said politely to the cook, who had been with the family for as long as Sira could remember. For that matter, so had Seteen and Lharosh, who shared the household duties that Sira or one of her siblings didn't do. Shopping was one of the duties that the siblings took turns with; Bey might be respected and the (so far) unchallenged Banner Bearer—but he ruled over a people who were the best assassins in the world, and all it would take would be for one disgruntled soul to decided he didn't want to take the traditional way of challenging the Banner Bearer, and . . . well, all Sleepgivers had access to poisons and knew how to use them. So all shopping was done by the seven children. All cooking was done by Nilda under Anhita's strict supervision, and all food was tested before anyone ate it.

I'm sure everything about us would seem odd to anyone outside the Nation, but one of the oddest is probably that my father is essentially a King and has only three servants and no guards.

Then again . . . Bey didn't *need* guards, and neither did his wife and children. Sleepgivers didn't have ranks as such, but everyone knew that the entire family was certainly in the top tenth—and they knew how to fight as a team. It would be suicide to go up against them. Plus, they had a Healer. No . . . a direct confrontation was never going to happen, so there was no need of guards.

And as for the normal servants, when you lived in a simple dwelling like theirs, where even most of the furniture was stone, there wasn't a great deal of cleaning to be done. None of them had elaborate wardrobes, and the only people in the entire family who had the sort of luxurious clothing one would associate with a ruler were Bey, his wife, and his eldest—that was just two outfits apiece, one for warm weather, and one for cold.

Besides . . . that wasn't how the Nation worked.

The Nation had been born under austerity, and even if these days things were no longer "austere," no one ever forgot that, and simplicity was part of their culture.

So was sharing, for one of the tenets of life in the Nation was, "For the Nation to be strong, *all* must prosper." The fees the Sleepgivers got for their missions belonged to the Nation, after a deduction of what the Elders decided was the proper amount went to the individual Sleepgiver who had taken the mission. The shared monies went to purchase all the things the Nation could not produce itself, and these were held in common stores. Farmers and herdsmen could determine whether to trade their surpluses for stores or sell or trade them at a market—for that matter, so could anyone who had extra from their terrace gardens. It was a little complicated, but not much, and the system meant that although no one got rich, no one starved either. And although food was simple, these days it was abundant and varied.

She had brought up some bones from the butcher for Windhover as well, and she put them in storage for his evening visit. Then she went out to the terrace garden to harvest whatever late produce was still ripening. There were still love apples, and a squash was ready, and there was always kala leaf, right up until the frost and sometimes past it. Gathering it didn't take long.

The Karsites had been suspiciously quiet in these last few fortnights, which, while giving Sira a twinge of unease, at least allowed her to spend her time looking at those strange Talismans the Mages had found.

And once she brought her harvest to the kitchen, that was what she intended to go back to doing.

The Mages had been right; these Talismans were very different from the ones that had held the memories of Sleepgivers, and very much different from the ones that had held fragmented personalities of Sleepgivers. They didn't even *look* the same. All of *these* Talismans were bronze disks, cast, she thought, but probably lost wax rather than a multiuse mold. They were no bigger than her thumbnail, where the Talisman she wore that held her mother's memories was a quarter of the size of her palm and carved from the fire agate found here in the Mountain. All the Talismans she had ever seen before were carved from fire agate and roughly that size. There were, in fact, three craftsmen who did nothing but carve them.

There seemed to be . . . something living in these odd bronze pieces. Not merely memories. Not personality fragments. Some sort of spirit.

Were they the souls of dead Sleepgivers? Earlier today her delicate probing had convinced her that no, whatever was in there, it wasn't ghosts. The other Mages hadn't managed to muster up the courage to look as deeply as she had, but they tentatively agreed with her.

She retired to her bed niche to ponder them further. It was warmer back there—the family hadn't yet gotten around to putting up the horn windowplates and doors on the home itself, though they were already on the Great Chamber.

The bed niches—in her parents' case, an entire small room—were all along a narrow stone hall entered through the kitchen so that the sleeping areas were in the deepest part of their home. There was a niche for each member of the family and each of the servants. Each niche had a sliding three-panel "door" made of a frame of metal covered in padded fabric that could be pulled tightly shut for privacy. Each niche was much longer than the platform for the bed, with a storage area at the foot, mostly used for clothing, and shelves cut into the stone of the rear for storing things you wanted immediately at hand. There was a lamp holder set into the stone at the head of the bed; in that lamp was a copper ball with a spell on it. When you opened the lamp, the ball glowed, making enough light to read by. When you closed it, the spell stopped—spells being *processes*, as Sira's teachers had told her, repeatedly, not *things*. And if you set them correctly, you could stop and start them at a signal even a non-Mage could use. When the copper ball was consumed, that ended the spell. These lamps might have seemed a waste of magic . . . but this actually was nothing of the sort. Within the Nation, wood was a precious resource, and you used it only where nothing else would serve. Oil, fat, and wax for lanterns, lamps, and candles were also precious resources. And there was the question of safety—within the bed niches, having an oil lamp or any source of open flame was an invitation to disaster, burns, or even a painful death if you overset it while it was lit.

The Mages of the Nation used their abilities in the most practical ways possible, and for the benefit of the most people. Which was one reason why the only magical object a Sleepgiver ever had on his or her person was the Talisman. Employing magic to do what a Sleepgiver could be *trained* to do naturally was a terrible waste of resources.

It occurred to Sira—as it had, more than once—that if there was any principle the Nation was built on, it was "Waste nothing, and do nothing wastefully."

She jumped up into her niche and closed the panels, opening the lamp without needing to see where it was. Once she had plenty of light, she pulled the pouch of Talismans off her belt and poured them out onto the bed; she picked one up at random and held it so that any markings on it would cast a good shadow.

As before, she noted the hole, so they were definitely meant to be strung on a cord or a chain and worn on the person. They were all so old and worn that their markings were blurred and hard to make out, so while she had been shopping, she had decided to try the shadow technique to see if she could make anything out. She held one face up and flat so that the worn marks on it cast the longest possible shadows, and she frowned with concentration as she tried to make something out.

On one side . . . well, it was definitely a pattern, rather than an object or a face. Waves? Possibly. Regularly spaced wavy lines, at any rate. And on the other side . . . definitely script and completely illegible even if it *was* a script anyone here would have been able to read. She picked up the next; it was like the first, so she put them both to the side, together, in their own little depression that she punched into the feather comforter with a finger. The third had wavy lines, but they ended in curls. The fourth had wavy triangles. The fifth and sixth, straight triangles. The seventh was like the third.

It occurred to her that these could represent something very simple, like elements. *Water, wind, fire, and mountains? Earth, maybe?*

So if these represented the four elements, *what* was bound to them? There were definitely binding spells there, but nothing coercive. No, the bindings seemed to be more like an anchor to the Talisman itself. Which would make sense, if you were somehow binding some form of the elements to the Talisman, but how in the name of the Bright and Dark would element-based magic help a Sleepgiver? Plus . . . there definitely was a different presence associated with each of these things.

Could these Talismans date all the way back to the Beginning? To when the Nation had first settled on the Mountain? Or maybe even before?

Could they even be Talismans as *she* understood the term?

We never waste anything, she reminded herself. *We never throw anything away. This might represent some form of magic that dates to before the escape, to the Mages we were sworn to protect, rather than our own!*

In which case . . . these probably were *not* meant to infuse a new Sleepgiver with memories of an experienced one, but for something else entirely.

This was both exciting and alarming.

By all rights, she ought to give them right back to the Mages who lived on the lowest level of the Mountain, deep in the labyrinthine passages that led to storerooms and libraries and workrooms, all protected from the vagaries of wind and weather. She should do that . . .

Except they had no more idea what these things were for than she had. And all *she* had was a theory.

No, I want to hang on to these for a while. If those cursed Karsites ever stop sending their cursed priests, perhaps I can persuade Father to let me go talk to the White Winds or Amber Moon Mages and see if they have any ideas what these things could be. The Nation had a mutually beneficial and amicable relationship with both magic schools, based on certain favors exchanged in the past and a recent contract to supply them with guards and guard trainers who elected not to become Sleepgivers.

The Mages of the Mountain were reclusive souls; it was difficult enough to persuade them to come out as far as the outer caves to get a little sun, and they really preferred not to have to speak to anyone who wasn't also a Mage. The suggestion that one of them should *travel* somewhere would probably be enough of a shock to send half of them to their beds for a week. So if anyone went to talk to other Mages, it would have to be her.

She rummaged in her mending supplies for some waxed sinew, and it didn't take too long before she had in her hands a neat little braided necklace with each of the bronze Talismans spaced evenly across the front. She held it onto her neck for several long moments— just to be certain that skin-to-bronze contact for a prolonged period wasn't going to trigger something. But nothing happened, and she tied it on so that it hung at the level of her collarbone, just above the leather thong that held her own Talisman.

Once again, she waited, alert to any changes, but the only thing that happened was that the seven bronze disks warmed to the temperature of her skin. Finally, she nodded. *If I go on a mission, I'll take them off if I need to, but right now they're safer where they are. And all anyone will think is that I've got a new necklace. Good thing they look nothing at all like our Talismans.* She fingered one, finding the soft, well-worn bronze pleasing to the touch. *Interesting. I wonder if these were actually worn as jewelry for a while after people forgot what they were for? Ah, no, the Mages had them in storage, so probably not.*

She pulled back the panels of the screen, closed the lantern, and decided to go talk to her father about that possible trip, assuming he was alone.

He was, which was not extraordinary. He was considered one of the best Banner Bearers of recent generations, if all of Sira's information sources were telling the truth (and they had no reason to lie). There had been some skepticism about whether or not he was going to have the stomach for the job, especially when he started talking about parting Sleepgivers from their Talismans, but by this point, because his assertions had been proven to be correct and because he was not inclined to issue edicts unless he absolutely had to and there was no other way to solve a situation, people respected him, respected his authority, and didn't bring him problems they knew he would only tell them to sort out among themselves.

So he was all alone in the Great Council room, which was a bit gloomy, what with two layers of horn between him and the outside sunlight.

"I should have thought you'd have opened the lanterns, Father," she said, peering at the Banner Bearer's chair through the shadows. "You're sitting back there like an old Mage afraid too much sun will sap his mystery."

"It's restful, which is more than I could say for the meeting of Elders this morning," he replied. "You'd have heard them wrangling if you hadn't gone shopping."

"Wrangling?" That seemed—odd. "Over what?"

"We have an unprecedented surplus, because some bright thing realized that there was a Crown bounty in Ruvan on the heads of Karsite demon-priests. So I sent someone out to the ambush site and had him collect enough bones from your burn pit for seven very handsome rewards. That, in addition to our other commissions, has led to a surfeit of actual money." He sounded more amused than annoyed. "And each of the Elders has a different idea of what to do with it."

"We're saving it, of course. . . ." She let her voice trail off, because while saving coin seemed like a very good idea, it might not be the *best* idea.

"Most of it. But I pointed out that you were responsible for all of those kills, and thus you were due the Sleepgiver's portion, and I allocated that on your behalf." She walked over to the seat and could finally see his amused expression. "I trust I am assuming correctly that all you really wanted for yourself was that colossal sheepskin and the black bearskin for your bed that you've been talking about every time you go to the second-level market?"

Now she knew why they had been missing! She'd noted their absence and felt a pang of jealousy of whoever had gotten them! And it turned out to be her! "I get cold," she said. "And I really like bearskin. But no, I cannot think of anything else I want or need."

"Good, because the Sleepgiver's Portion was enough to buy us a full grove of those drought-hardy jujube trees and another of cactus pears." He grinned, his teeth showing whitely in the gloom, and why not? This had been a goal of his for as long as she could remember, and there had never been enough money to accomplish it. "We'll have fruit from the cactus pears in a year or two at most, and from the trees soon enough. It's just the right time of year to transplant them, too. Plus, once they start to really spread, cactus-pear pads are very good roasted, so we get a vegetable *and* fruit out of them."

"Since I am going to get the benefit of cactus-pear jam, I fully approve of this," she agreed happily. She didn't bother to ask where he was going to have them planted or who he was going to hire to tend them; that had been settled long ago. It had only required the money to be able to purchase the saplings and rooted cuttings.

"And when the Elders heard what I planned for your money, they graciously allotted enough for several hives of bees to be bought in the spring to be placed in the new orchards." He looked very well satisfied with himself, and so he should be.

"Well, now, that brings me to a question of my own," she said. "Assuming those wretched Karsites will *at least* stop sending priests for the winter."

She explained about the odd Talismans and took off the necklace to give him to examine while she went on with her request to consult with other Mages about them. He handed the necklace back to her, nodding. "I'll consider it," he said. "My only concern is that you've never been outside of Ruvan; in fact, you haven't been many places *inside* Ruvan. It's a strange old world out there, with stranger people in it."

"Like what?" she asked.

He got up from his seat, pulled out the longer of his two daggers, and smirked at her. "Knife practice."

She nodded; she knew very well what this meant. It was part of standard Sleepgiver training; fight all-out while discussing something. Real weapons, not wooden practice ones; a Sleepgiver at her level—or her father's—had to be able to pull his blow so accurately that you could barely get a hair between the blade's edge and the target's skin.

She pulled her own long dagger, and they began to circle each other. "You know about the Karsites already," he said, avoiding her jab at his gut as she dodged his cut at her wrist. "Theocracy. That's perilous stuff." She lunged, he jumped up backward onto the stone table to avoid it. "I don't know if their god ever did speak to them directly, but he doesn't now. My little birds tell me all the 'Appearances' are pure magic."

She followed him up onto the table and sucked in her gut to avoid his lunge. "So they make sure all the Mageborn get pulled into the priesthood?"

He saluted her with his knife, then turned it into a neck strike, which she parried. "Or declared heretics and burned. That's what they do to *everyone* with Mind-magic, too. Not just people that manifest it and can't control or hide it."

Her eyes widened, as at the same time she slashed for his wrist. "*Everyone?* But that means—" She parried a double-feint strike. "—they're burning *children* as soon as the power manifests at all!"

"Exactly." He rolled off the table. But she was not taken in by the fact that he seemed to be retreating. "Another good reason to hate them, if we didn't already have one. If—" she took an oblique jump off the table, putting her several arm's-lengths away from him "—oh, good move! If I'd been in charge when they made that contract offer, I'd have done plenty of investigating before I took it." He was forced to come to her, as she took an advantageous position where he could only come at her directly. "But your great-uncle didn't, and no one has his memories, so we'll never know why."

"That's probably *why* he ordered no Talismans made of him at the end," she suggested, parrying his quick succession of cuts easily. "He was ashamed. He'd made a terrible mistake, it got worse when we broke the contract, and in the end, he lost his grandson anyway."

"Reasonable assumption." He dodged as she made a dive-roll, slashing at the backs of his legs as she passed. "And that brings us to Cousin Mags and those crazy Valdemarans. They're ruled by horses—" He went for her as she rolled to her feet, but she had the momentum to easily evade him. "—well, sort of. I got to know two of them. The horses, I mean, not the Valdemarans. I got to know several of them besides Mags. They're not really horses. Not sure what they are. Spirits incarnated, I would guess, maybe ancestral ones."

She went for his eyes and he parried at literally the last second before she was going to pull. "There are worse things," she said after she had thought about it for a while.

"There are," he agreed, "But anyway, no one can be King or Queen who isn't partnered with one of them. And they overrule their riders all the time. So . . ."

She spun out of the way of the next strike. "So, ruled by horses. You've told me what else the riders do, which all seems sensible enough."

"They don't allow magic either, which is how our Sleepgivers ran into trouble," This time he shoulder-rolled right over the table to give himself some breathing space. "Somehow—and don't ask me how—they've tamed an entire country full of air spirits to find and surround every Mage that passes the border and stare at him."

She held up both hands, signaling a brief halt, so she could give him a look of utter incredulity. "Stare? Just *stare?* How is *that* supposed to keep a Mage out?"

"Think about it, you're a Mage," he countered. "You've got dozens, maybe a hundred of these things, surrounding you at all times. Staring at you. You can see them. You can sense them even with your eyes closed. Sleeping or waking, they're *there.* You can't chase them away. You can't wall them out. You can't persuade them to leave. You can't destroy them." He waited while she thought about it.

She tried to imagine it for herself, and after letting her imagination run for a while, found herself shuddering. "See?" he said. "That interfered with the old-style Talismans the Sleepgivers wore, making those personality fragments even *more* unhinged than they were before, and that in turn affected the Sleepgivers wearing the Talismans. Game on?"

She nodded, and he slid across the table at her.

"But you weren't wearing one of those," she pointed out, going for him instead of trying to dodge, which sent him in turn writhing out of the way.

"I was not. So that's why I could see what had to be done. And, regrettably, had to end a few of our own people in the process." He rushed her, she stepped aside at the last moment and scored his back with the flat of her blade. "Ah, good one! Point to you! To be honest, by that point they'd all been inside Valdemar long enough that they weren't capable of thinking *at all* anymore, and the personality fragments had completely taken over."

"Mercy kills," she agreed, and started to feel the beginnings of an ache in her side. "Do you want to continue this and get your point back?"

He sheathed his knife. "No. Let's get some water."

She sheathed hers as well, and followed him into the home, where there was always a terracotta jar of fresh water waiting beside the door. "So, the Valdemarans are ruled, or co-ruled anyway, by spirit horses, and Mages can't get in there. What happens to people born Mages?"

He dipped out a pottery cup of water for her and then one for himself. "As far as Mags could tell me, they're fine as long as they don't actually *do* any magic. It's active use of magic that brings the tormentors out to play. And there's no one to teach them, so I suppose it lies dormant." He shrugged. "Not my business, nor that of the Nation."

She nodded. That was eminently sensible. Let the Nation tend to the Nation's business; Cousin Mags was no part of it, so let him and his kingdom do what they liked. But that made her think of something else.

"What do we do if someone else offers a contract to us to go into Valdemar?" she asked. "I doubt Cousin Mags will sit back and allow that to happen."

Her father shrugged and sat down on a sculpted bench, patting the feather-stuffed cushions beside him. She took the offered seat. "Well, I'm not going to *tell* him about it, obviously. And he doesn't have a Mind-magic ability to see the future, nor to see anything at a distance. So I'd just take care that we operated in such a way that he never found out. And I'd just send the best of the best—*without* Talismans. It's not as if Sleepgivers now can't work just as well without them as with them. How often do *you* use yours?"

"Not often," she admitted.

"So, problem solved." He set down his cup out of the way, on the stone ledge behind the bench. "Besides, the only people likely to want contracts against the Valdemaran leaders are Karsites. That's likely to be the only people Cousin Mags would *really* care about. No one else could afford us."

And then, astonishingly, he started to laugh.

"What's so funny?" she asked.

"Oh, there was *one* lackwit who sent an inquiry a while ago. Some idiot merchant who'd gotten himself exiled. Rump? Grump? Ah, I remember. *Remp.* It never got farther than our broker in Menmellith, because he wouldn't agree to pay the fee up front. Kept insisting *that's not how you do business.* Our broker kindly informed him that *was* how *we* did business, and if he didn't like it, he could find someone else." Her father wiped his eyes, he had been laughing so hard. "And then the dolt had a full-blown temper tantrum and got himself thrown into the street for his pains."

She found herself staring at him with incredulity. "When is the last time *that* happened?"

"A century at least." He shook his head. "Last I heard of him, he was trying to hire a mercenary army 'to be paid on victory.' You can imagine how well that's going."

"Less well than dealing with our broker," she suggested, knowing that mercenary captains not only did not suffer fools gladly, they did not suffer them at all.

"Remind me to tell you another time about all the bickering among the Great Clans of Rethwellan," he said, getting up. "It makes for some interesting contracts. In the meantime . . . I've thought about it, and yes, I think you should consult with other Mages about those trinkets of yours. If they're as old as you think, they could be both powerful and dangerous. If there's a mystical catastrophe, I'd rather it happened somewhere other than the Mountain."

All her spent energy came back at that. Not that she was worried about some sort of 'catastrophe'—but if her speculations were right, and there was some kind of elemental spirit confined to these Talismans, it had been a *very* long time since they had first been bound, and if they were released, they were likely to be disoriented and possibly annoyed. It would be better to have Mages about who were more acquainted with handling such spirits than the ones here in the Mountain were.

"How long before I can leave?" she asked eagerly.

He grinned. "As soon as you can persuade your mother."

She sighed. "This is going to take a lot of whiles."

———

The school, or more properly, the *enclave* of Amber Moon Mages lay to the west and north, in the finger of Rethwellan that stretched into Menmellith. It was closer to Karse than Sira liked, but then, White Winds was nearly twice as far away to the south, and she would still have to go nearer to Karse than she liked. Amber Moon seemed like a much better choice, and her father and, reluctantly, her mother, agreed.

She did not take her beloved partner Aku as a mount. The

Nation's horses had a very distinct look about them, and riding one would give her away to anyone who knew what a Sleepgiver was.

She did ride *out* on Aku, but only as far as the nearest horse dealer, where she got a serviceable desert pony and sent Aku back home without his saddle, saddlebags, and bridle. These she transferred to her unlovely but decent-tempered new mount and went on her way.

She did not bother with any manner of disguise, other than not carrying her Sleepgiver wrappings with her. The baggy trews, wide-sleeved tunic, and waist-wrappings (so useful for concealing so many things!) were not so distinct from the sort of things that most of the people of Ruvan outside the Nation wore that she thought there would be any problems. Indeed, the trews were *so* baggy that unless she was riding, they could pass for skirts, so she very much doubted she was going to outrage any sensibilities about a female's "proper" attire.

This was still dry country, most of it given over to herds of goats allowed to roam free, so she camped every night. That was really her preferred option; there was no shortage of desert hares, and by noon she had usually bagged at least one, which took care of dinner that night as well as breakfast and lunch the next day. Her only complaint was that the pony was ploddingly slow. Except for the few small villages she passed through, she saw almost nothing.

This was, in fact, the most boring journey she had ever taken.

The *only* thing that bothered her was that this was flat land; there wasn't anywhere to sleep at night that was as hidden as she would have liked, and there was no one to share a night watch with. It occurred to her more than once that she should have brought one of her siblings along . . . but it was too late now.

So she compromised by making "camp" at sunset, staying in

place just long enough to cook her supper and eat it, douse the fire, and pretend to go to bed. Then she'd pack everything up and slip back to a spot with better cover (much to the discontent of the nameless pony), and go bed down there, usually at the base of bushes that would disguise the outline of the pony and provide a momentary deterrent if a red wolf or desert cat made a try for her.

Tonight, however, had been the exception to that.

Just at sunset, when she stopped for her false camp, she saw a storm on the horizon. She had just enough time to hurriedly build a fire and cook her hare when it swept in.

She was no stranger to desert storms and knew their power. She made sure the pony was tied securely to a stout bush, then she wrapped herself up and threw her oiled groundcloth over herself and her gear literally the moment that the first drops turned into a deluge.

Without even the scant shelter of a bush, the ground under her was soaked in moments, and she huddled beneath her inadequate shelter, rain literally pounding her. This was probably the most miserable she had ever been in her life; her hands, nose, and rump froze, the rest of her was cold, and all she could do was sit there and endure it.

When the storm finally passed, she was too numb for a moment to realize that the constant pounding on her head and back were gone. She shook her head to clear it, threw off her groundcloth and—

—froze—

She was, literally, surrounded by Karsite demons, all too easy to see because they glowed an ugly, sickly yellow.

She leaped to her feet, allowing rage to fill her, and determined to kill as many of the unholy things as she could before they dragged her down.

6

After a day, Tory's initial alarm had passed. He went on about his business while Kee made sure none of *his* relatives were the ones that had given them that alarming gut punch, and they met, as usual in this weather (which was much too nasty for a wall-run), after supper in the Royal Library.

Drizzle pattered on the library window as they entered; Tory had waited for Kee after spotting him hurrying up the hall toward the door.

It was a fine room to lounge in; almost no one ever came there, and there was always a good fire burning. It smelled of applewood smoke, old leather, and the unique scent of old paper. "I've got nothing," Kee told Tory, as Tory settled into a comfortable chair next to the fire. "I just came back from talking with Father. We've had Heralds check on every last distant cousin we can find, and no one's hurt, no one's been attacked, and the only thing I can think of is the obvious."

Tory nodded. Kee was right, by process of elimination. "It's *got* to be on my side, and my mother's relatives are all accounted for too. Which means it's the Black Sheep."

Kee snickered as the fire popped. "Actually, considering they are in the majority where they come from, your grandfather and his sweetheart are the ones that ran off, and your father refused the family invitation to come home and sit on the throne, it's more like your father is the Black Sheep of the family." Then he sobered. "Well, what are we going to do?"

"Do?" Tory shrugged. "Nothing. They're *professional assassins*, Kee. They murder people. They live a dangerous lifestyle. I wouldn't think any of them live too long. And we don't even know what country they live in, much less where this happened and who it happened to!"

"But. . . ." Kee frowned. "This was personal. Like a cry for help."

"To go *where* and help *who*, Kee?" Tory shook his head. "And for all we know the person in trouble is in trouble because he tried killing someone better than he is—and it's probably someone who didn't *deserve* to be murdered. Their only consideration when they kill people is whether or not they are going to get paid for it. Father's cousin Bey might sound romantic in the stories, but he's a killer-for-hire, Kee, and so is everyone in his family, and so is everyone in his clan, or tribe, or cult, or whatever they call it." Tory had given the experience he and Kee had shared a lot of thought over the last twenty-four hours, and he was not at all inclined to let himself get all emotionally entangled in a situation he knew literally nothing about.

"But he saved your father!" Kee said desperately, and Tory suppressed his own frustration and annoyance at his friend, who clearly had been listening to too many Bardic tales. There was *nothing* romantic about people who killed for money. *Besides, Bey hadn't done badly out of the deal, now, had he? He got to be their "Prince," and then their "King," because Papa didn't want any part of the people or the title.*

The popping and crackling of the fire punctuated his words.

"And Bey also got himself the throne because Father wasn't there to claim it," he replied steadily, saying what he had been thinking out loud. "See what I mean? It wasn't noble altruism. Bey got quite a lot out of the situation. Much, *much* more than he would have if he'd followed orders. Honestly, I have to wonder if the truth was that Cousin Bey went looking for father to kill him himself, if father'd shown any inclination that he'd changed his mind about returning with the Sleepgivers that last time."

Kee finally subsided, although Tory was fairly certain he wasn't going to hear the last on the subject.

But he had made up his mind. It served no purpose to go haring off in a random direction to "save" someone he didn't know, who might not even deserve saving, and who, in fact, was probably already dead.

And there was an end to it. He changed the subject and got Kee's mind off the whole thing. Once and for all, he hoped.

———

Except . . . it wasn't the end of it.

So far as Tory was concerned, everything was going spectacularly well. False summer had descended with its lying promise that autumn was moons distant, with dry, sunny weather and warm, balmy nights. Kat was back, having successfully solved yet another problem that had involved stupid, stubborn highborn people making claims Tory would rather not hear about. Abi was back, but only to negotiate for more money for those walls, which, as Tory had correctly guessed, were going to have to be double stone walls with rammed earth between them, because the quality of the local stone was so low. But there was absolutely no point in going any further with the project at this time of the year; the town was going to have to rely on its old log palisade for another winter. So at least Abi would get to celebrate Midwinter in the comfort and luxury of the Palace.

She'd be turning down invitations to fetes and would-be suitors right and left, if Tory was any judge. She wasn't *remarkably* good-looking, at least not to his brotherly eye, but she wasn't unpleasant to look at either, and impecunious second and third sons with nothing of their own to fall back on would look at her and see a highly successful, Master Artificer with as many Crown Commissions as she cared to take. They'd know for a fact that she was a prize for someone like them, and they'd find all that outweighed beauty any day.

Abi, of course, was more than wise to that sort of wooer and would take their invitations if she cared to, turn them down if she didn't, and, either way, leave them disappointed in the end. Well, she would if the last several years were anything to go by, and he didn't think any of those would-be suitors had suddenly bloomed with desirable attributes in the last year.

There might be women who found her equally attractive, but . . . well, that sort of wooing tended to be a lot more circumspect, and he had a notion he didn't know enough about it to spot it.

Though he thought Abi probably would have said *something* if she found someone else attractive enough to consider for more than a season or so. Tory wasn't sure what, if anything, she was looking for in a mate, but he knew one thing for sure: it wasn't a pretty parasite.

Meanwhile it was good just to all be together at once for a change.

Their parents obviously felt the same and were taking advantage of having all their offspring home at once for some old-fashioned family fun that did not involve looking for foreign agents or other bad actors.

Tonight was one of those nights. And for the first time in a very long time, Amily had taken a night off from her duties as King's Own, and they'd all gone down into Haven to see a play. They even took Larral, who'd quite enjoyed himself and, from the many and varied expressions on Perry's face, was making his opinions on the antics known to his partner. It was almost more fun watching Perry than the play.

The play itself had been exactly the sort of thing Tory liked: a comedy, a romantic farce, just bawdy enough to be hilarious, with lots of acrobatics and slapstick humor and a plot as shallow as a Midsummer puddle. It was given in one of the largest inns in Haven, one with a huge common room and a purpose-built stage. They were all actually quite familiar with this particular inn; Mags had a hidden changing room in the stables where he and Perry and sometimes Tory could change from disguises into their normal garb and back again.

Decent wine flowed (though not enough to impair any of them), there had been much laughter, no one in the audience got obnoxious, the players had been good, and there had been absolutely nothing to mar the event.

They were walking back up to the Palace in the balmy evening—no one in his right mind was going to accost a group containing *two* Heralds plus two muscular, armed young men and a "dog" almost the size of a small pony. And they were just about out of one of the neighborhoods of small merchants—

when out of an alley behind a candle shop came a sharp *"Hissst!"*

They all stopped and, as one, drew weapons. No hesitation, no pause for thought. Suddenly the peaceful family party bristled with cold steel.

Nothing happened.

"Who's there and whatdye want?" Mags asked suspiciously.

"Hissst!" came the whisper again. *"Cousin Mags! It is Ahkhan! The son of your cousin Beshat! I must speak with you most urgently!"*

"What in the seven hells——" muttered Perry, but Mags waved at him to be quiet.

"Then come out where we can see you," Mags said. "Yer gonna have to forgive me for bein' suspicious, but th' last time I tangled with your kin, aside from Bey, it didn't go so well."

"Understood," said the whisperer, and he . . . well, one moment there wasn't anyone there, and the next moment there was a fellow in mottled black and gray wrappings standing in the moonlight on the cobbled streets, holding out empty hands. "So you see," he said, pulling the wrappings down off his face, tilting it so they could get a good look at him in the light of the full moon, and showing that, indeed, there was no doubt that he and Mags had some relatives in common. "Please, may we go somewhere that is not so public? My father sends me to you, he says, to ask for the repayment of the debt."

Mags cast a glance over at Tory, and Tory sighed, knowing exactly what Mags was thinking right now. That this could not be coincidence. That this had *everything* to do with what Tory and Kee had experienced at Harvest Fair. And that, of course, Mags *did* owe Bey a life-debt, and it had been too much to expect that such a debt would never be called in.

And that they were going to have to at least hear this cousin out.

But it also occurred to Tory that the only real question in his mind was . . . it had barely been two weeks since he and Kee had felt that unknown person under some sort of deadly attack. If that. So how in *hell* had this young man crossed half the length of Valdemar and beyond in the course of a fortnight?

———

There was no question of allowing an *assassin* into the Palace, of course, so they had all gone down to the pawn shop, slipped in the back way, one and two at a time, and sent the two employees home, closing it for the night. Once they had all crowded into the back room, they listened to Ahkhan tell his tale.

When they were all settled, each of them using some box or barrel or crate as a seat, with Ahkhan standing in the middle, the young Sleepgiver gave Mags a low bow.

"You will please to be putting the magic of Truth upon me, so that you will know all I tell is so," the fellow said. "The one that forces Truth, so you will know also that I hold nothing back."

Mags exchanged a look with Amily—and they *both* closed their eyes for a moment, then stared fixedly at Ahkhan, their lips moving silently, until a strong blue glow surrounded the Sleepgiver.

He sighed as it settled, as if he actually felt it. Maybe he did? Tory knew nothing about Sleepgivers, but they had to be extraordinarily sensitive and aware of all sorts of things in order to be as effective as they were.

"You must know that when we canceled the contract with the Karsites, the Karsites did not accept this thing," he said, as if choosing his words very carefully. "They took it ill. But rather than the civilized answer of demanding their fee back, they elected to take their repayment in our blood. Or rather, they *tried* to. It did not go well for them."

Mags snorted. "I c'n imagine."

"I tell you what is not much known; the Nation lives in the center of Ruvan. The Karsites knew roughly where. So they sent their demon-summoners to strike at us in our heart." A faint smile flickered across his face. "As I said, this did not go well. They have only been *permitted* to go within striking range of the Nation because we allowed it. They were blinded by arrogance and anger and were easy to ambush. It is my sister Siratai who has been charged with these ambushes since she was old enough to take missions."

"Alone?" Amily asked incredulously.

Ahkhan shrugged. "There were never more than one or two at a time. Of course, alone."

Tory was actually impressed; impressed that the Sleepgivers had been waging a very one-sided war against the Karsite demon-summoning priests all this time. Impressed that Ahkhan had not just readily agreed to have Truth Spell cast on him at the outset, but insisted on it.

"After the last such incursion, they appeared to accept their defeat. There was a long pause, then a longer pause, and . . . something occurred that required Siratai take a journey outside the Nation's bounds."

Finally, he got to the point. The story ended up being a very simple one—that Ahkhan's sister (also an assassin) was supposed to go to some experts to consult with them and had never arrived. That Ahkhan himself had traced her path and found a dead pony and some of her belongings, but not her—and the very certain signs that she had somehow been caught unawares by more of the Karsite demon-summoners than she could fight off. And that she had been taken alive. During the course of this explanation, it was clear that he was trying to talk about real magic—but the difficulty *anyone* in Valdemar had in giving voice to that subject was making it impossible for him to do so. They were all getting the gist of it, however. He had taken to calling *Mages,* "experts," which at least had made his narration less strained.

"We have consulted those same experts of Amber Moon, and our own, and they cannot find her. It was the experts of Amber Moon who suggested that the Mind-Mages of Valdemar might be able to succeed where they could not. And my father remembered that you are a powerful Mind-magician." The fellow—who looked to be exactly Perry's age—now turned his gaze on Mags with hope. "Can you? Can you help us?"

"Ah, hell," Mags groaned. "Ye've put me in a awful position, lad. *I* cain't. But I'm pretty damn sure I know who can. Problem is. . . . one uv 'em's a Prince."

Ahkhan drew himself up, suddenly looking years older. "Then take me to the King," he said, with dignity. "I am empowered to negotiate for a prize he could never otherwise win. The pledge of all the Nation that never shall a Sleepgiver lift a hand against any in Valdemar for as long as the Nation shall endure."

Tory had no idea his father knew that many obscene words. . . .

———

They *didn't* take Ahkhan to the King, of course. With what they had learned at first hand, and what Mags' memories told him, if this *had* all been a ruse and was a suicide strike against Valdemar's Monarch, there was very little anyone could do to stop it if Ahkhan and the King were in the same room. But they left Ahkhan cooling his heels in a very secure Guardpost outside the walls of the Palace while Mags and Amily consulted with the King and the Privy Council.

Tory and a very excited Kee were left outside of these negotiations, much to the latter's chagrin; they were left cooling *their* heels in the Royal Library. Kee was all for this "adventure," as he persisted in calling it. Tory . . . Tory was very much of two minds about it. On the one hand, he'd literally never been out of Haven in his life, and this was beginning to sound not unlike the "adventures" that Perry and Abi had had, experiences that turned him many shades of envious green every time he thought about them. On the other hand, this was going up against *Karsite demon-summoners*, and even if all they did was pinpoint where the Princess (as Kee insisted on calling her) was being held, they would almost certainly have to go inside Karse's border to do so. Which was very likely to lead to a most unhappy ending to the "adventure." He remembered only too well the harrowing tale Abi had told of her own fight with demon-summoners, and those hadn't even been Karsites.

On the third hand . . . there was no doubt his father *owed* cousin Bey. Being in debt to the King of a tribe of assassins was not a comfortable position to be in.

And on fourth hand (there were two of them, after all, so there were four hands between them) . . . Truth Spell didn't allow for the least shading of lies, not in his father's hands. Ahkhan really *was* empowered to offer what was an absolutely extraordinary concession. While Karse was Valdemar's only open enemy, allies could turn foe, and there were always internal enemies to reckon with.

And that only covered the danger to the Royal Family. There were feuding families, criminals, and others who might be able to muster the high price a Sleepgiver could command to take out a rival or rivals. To be able to purchase the safety, not only of the current Monarch and his family, not only *every* ruler of Valdemar forever, but *every single citizen of Valdemar in perpetuity*. . . .

Tory couldn't see how the King could possibly turn this down.

Even though it meant his own son was going to be put into danger.

Kee knew better than to babble out what *he* was feeling as they waited, but it was all clear enough on his face. This was his chance: his chance for adventure, his chance to leave the shadow of his father and brothers, and on top of everything else, his chance to *do something* for his Kingdom. Kee might not be a Herald, but he was raised by Heralds and with Heralds, and that was what Heralds *did*.

The debate started in the earliest hours of the morning and lasted long into the night, as the two of them waited to hear what the King would decide. Kee declared himself too excited to eat, but eventually Tory made him go down to the Royal kitchens and do so anyway, because excitement coupled with not eating was going to make both of them sick.

And at last, just before midnight, they were summoned by Amily to come up to the King's private chambers, where he had retired after making his decision.

And as soon as Tory saw the King's face, looking suddenly much older in the firelight as he sat in his favorite chair, waiting for them to come before him, Tory knew what the answer was going to be.

"You're going. I'm told Mags' cousin has a mount that has the speed and endurance of a Companion," he said without preamble, as Kee managed to contain his excitement. "I don't even know how that's possible, but since time and speed are of the essence, Rolan has asked two Companions to take you as far as the Menmellith Border, where . . . well, the Sleepgiver wasn't able to tell us how he was going to get you across two entire countries, but it was clear he could do so, and you'll find out when you get there."

Kee drew himself up and summoned all his dignity. "Thank you, Your Majesty," he said formally. "Tory and I will not fail you."

"Just don't fail to come back," said his father, his voice a little choked. "Your mother would never forgive me."

"Well, we haven't been training in those assassin tricks all this time for nothing, Majesty," Tory put in. "We may not be as good as my cousin, but we're pretty damn good at not being seen, even better at keeping ourselves alive, and that's how I intend to keep things. In, out, and done and no one the wiser. That's my plan."

Kee gave him a *look*, but in the next moment he clearly realized that it was the absolute wrong time to voice any disagreement with such a plan. Instead he nodded vigorously, and echoed. "In, out, and done. Definitely."

That was when Tory decided it was time for him to gracefully withdraw and let the King be a father.

And deal with his own father.

Who likely would have half a night's worth of admonitions about keeping the Prince safe.

At least, Tory thought, as he headed toward the family's suite, *he's already been through two sets of hair-raising situations with Perry and Abi. I hope he's used to it by now. Because otherwise it's going to be a damned long night.*

They met Ahkhan outside the walls of the city by arrangement. Rolan had, via Mags, introduced them to the two Companions who had agreed to be their transportation as far as the Border. Tory and Kee knew both Companions well, from frequent visits to Companion's Field and the grooming sessions that unpartnered Companions enjoyed from anyone who would grant them. A strapping young mare named Tariday was Kee's mount, and a slightly smaller mare named Elissa was Tory's. Ahkhan had assured them again that "transportation" would be waiting at the Border, and from the difficulty he had in getting the words out, Tory surmised that the "transportation" was going to be magical in nature.

Now *that*, in all of this mess, was something he was actually looking forward to. Perry and Abi had *both* gotten to see real magic in action, and a lot of it. His only brush with real magic was the firebird feather Perry had brought back to him as a souvenir from his adventures . . . and while it had seemed very magical to him as a child, the truth was that a firebird was a very natural creature without—to his knowledge— any magic about it. At least no more magic than Companions.

It was a pity they couldn't Mindspeak with their mounts, but . . . he reckoned that mime could probably go a long way. And there was always "nod for yes."

Ahkhan was already waiting for them outside the city walls, where he had left his own mount stabled. Interestingly, that implied he had money with him that would be accepted in Valdemar . . . but then again, the Sleepgivers that had been in the pay of Karse had, too, so perhaps, Tory thought, that meant *they* had agents here that were actual Valdemarans. Or maybe they had contact with Rethwellan or Menmellith agents. Or . . . well, simplest of all, maybe he'd just exchanged money with a merchant.

Not everything has to be complicated and devious, Tory, he reminded himself. *Not even with Sleepgivers.*

They had left in the predawn, moving swiftly, but Tory looked at Ahkhan's horse askance in the pearly gray light. It was a rough-looking thing, just larger than a pony, and he was afraid there was no chance the three of them would make any real speed.

But the Sleepgiver mounted and looked back over his shoulder at them. "Try to keep up," he said, and away he and that "pony" went—

At a canter that looked extremely painful for the rider, who had to stand in the stirrups to keep from losing his spine, a pace so astonishing that Ahkhan and his mount were almost out of sight before the Companions got over their shock and raced after him.

They caught up, of course, but Tory simply could not believe this rough-coated creature could keep up such a blistering pace for long. Surely this was just Ahkhan showing off.

Surely they'd slow within a few furlongs. . . .

A candlemark later, he was thinking, *Surely they'll slow within a few leagues . . .*

At noon, he was thinking, *Surely they'll stop for a rest!* But no; Ahkhan ate in the saddle—although his horse slowed to a lope that allowed him to *sit* in the saddle for as long as it took him to eat and drink—and they perforce did the same.

Only as the sun was going down did Ahkhan finally speak. And they had neither slowed nor stopped in all that time except to relieve themselves and gulp some water. "Do we camp or take to an inn? Natya will do well either way, but grain tonight will keep her running well tomorrow."

Tory caught Kee's eye. "We have permission to use the Waystations," Kee called. "And there's one not far."

"Is this private? Is there grain?" Ahkhan wanted to know.

"Yes to both."

"So be it. Pray take the lead," the Sleepgiver replied, and Tariday moved past him and took over the lead. Ahkhan's mount didn't seem to like this, as she demonstrated with some head tosses, but she settled and kept within an arm's length of Tariday's tail.

The next village was the size of a toy in the distance, gilded by the rays of the setting sun, when Tariday moved off the road and onto the path that led to the Waystation. Tory was of two minds about using the place; it was going to be small, meant for two Heralds at a time at the most, and they'd be crowded, but there was also no telling what kind of inn was in the village, and they could very well have ended up sleeping on the floor there. Or worse, packed into a bed with a couple of strangers and Ahkhan, and what the Sleepgiver would make of that he had no idea.

Like all Waystations, this one was a sturdily built hut—constructed of stone with a thatched roof—just big enough for two or three people if one of them slept on the floor. There was a shelter attached for the Companions and Ahkhan's horse, and plenty of provisions. There was also a well; all Waystations were either on a pond, stream, or river or had a well. When they reached it, Kee dismounted first and headed to the Waystation to open it; Tory took the hint and followed both the Companions to the shelter, where he took off their saddles and tack, gave them a good rubdown, and left them with hay in one manger while he grabbed the bucket hanging inside off its hook and went to get water. When he returned with the first bucketful, Kee was bringing measures of grain out of the Waystation, and Ahkhan had settled his mare next to the Companions. She seemed extremely mannerly. She was not fighting the others for the hay, and when Kee poured the grain into the second manger, she just put her nose in and ate like a civilized creature, not gulping down the grain as fast as she could manage to keep the others from having any.

Tory was astonished all over again.

Nor did Ahkhan tie her up. "Stay, Natya," he told her; her ears flicked back to acknowledge that she had heard him.

Kee stood there with his mouth open, then closed it with a snap. "That's not a horse," he said, flatly.

"It is a horse bred for thousands of years for endurance, intelligence, and strength, not looks or size," Ahkhan corrected him. "She and her kind are not unlike the Shin'a'in war steeds. The ones they *keep*, not the ones they cull." He patted her rump. She munched, more slowly now, and then turned her attention back to the hay. "There, she has had enough. If yours leave any grain, she may come back to it later tonight. And now that I have ordered her to stay, she will stay. Where do I sleep?"

"In here," Kee said, gesturing toward the door of the Waystation. "There's two beds and the floor, which do you want?"

Tory took one last look to be certain that Natya was as mannerly as Ahkhan claimed, but she was standing hipshot and completely relaxed, slowly chewing a few blades of hay, and looked as if she found herself quite at home. He followed the other two into the Station.

There were, as Kee said, two bedboxes built onto the wall and plenty of floorspace in front of the fireplace for a third bedroll. Kee had started a fire and lit the Waystation's sole lamp. Ahkhan surveyed the area with a glance. "The floor will suffice," he said. "Do you have provisions, or shall we eat cooked oats?"

"We've got plenty, we don't need to go that far," Kee told him. And he raised an eyebrow.

"But I enjoy cooked oats. Shall I make a pot to break our fast in the morning?"

Kee looked at Tory, who shrugged. "Might as well. We're in a hurry, after all."

Ahkhan nodded. "Indeed, we are. Might you try to find my sister before we seek sleep?"

"We'll *try*, but no guarantees," Tory warned him. "I've got the feeling that first time was a fluke because your sister was surprised and enraged. If her emotions aren't ramped up to a fever pitch, we probably aren't going to be able to touch her until we're physically closer."

Ahkhan grimaced. "She will not be. She controls her feelings well, that one. A Sleepgiver *does*, but she is extraordinarily good at it. Will you try before or after food?"

"Right after we put some padding between us and the bottom of the bedboxes," Tory told him, and the two Valdemarans went out and fetched big armloads of hay. The sun was already down and the stars starting to appear in the east—and the night air gave no warning hints that things were about to turn either cold or stormy. If this weather lasted, they'd make *astonishing* time to the Border.

Roughly a candlemark later, he and Kee emerged from their trance to find Ahkhan sitting on the floor with them, watching them intently. Tory hadn't exactly gotten an image or even a hint of emotion, but he *had* gotten . . . something. A sense of something very distant that was not any of his relatives he was familiar with. And yet, it was familiar, as if he had sensed it before, so it probably wasn't Bey or any of Bey's other children.

"Well, she's alive," said Kee before Tory could say anything, as they unclasped wrists. "That's all I can tell you. I know it's her, though; I couldn't mistake that . . . whatever it was I got from her . . . for anyone else."

Ahkhan looked to Tory for confirmation, and Tory nodded. The Sleepgiver didn't say anything, and he certainly didn't make any great demonstrations of relief, but Tory somehow knew without any doubt that he *was* relieved.

"This is excellent to hear," he said. "Now we eat and rest."

"So we do," Kee agreed.

Tory and Kee were both carrying hard bread, dried meat, and hard cheese. Ahkhan contributed . . . something. A bar of something that tasted of both meat and something sweet—dried berries?—that he cut slivers from with a knife that appeared from somewhere on his person. It tasted a lot better than Tory would have thought, a very little like a roast with cherry sauce.

Tory tried not to think where that knife might have been and what it had done in the past as Ahkhan casually whittled bits of supper with it.

Ahkhan also contributed the leaves of some spicy-smelling shrub that he brewed into a tea that somehow also tasted sweet. "This is excellent!" Kee exclaimed after the first sip. "What is it?"

"Something we call spicebush, and the leaves of a plant we call *tava*, that lends sweetness," Ahkhan replied. "It will aid in sleep. In the morning, a second brew, from ground beans, that will make you dance like a kid in springtime."

Beans? Seemed unlikely, but . . . so did Ahkhan's horse.

"I'm sorry we couldn't sense more," Kee said apologetically, alternating bits of Ahkhan's contribution with bits of their own.

For the first time, Tory's cousin actually smiled a little.

"You gave to me more than you know," he said. "Sira is alive. You do not know our Sira. If she is alive, she is alert and thinking. If she is thinking, she is planning, and if she has not already made the lives of her captors a misery. . . ."

He paused.

". . . she very soon will."

7

Sira woke, as a Sleepgiver must after being drugged, all at once. She took a careful assessment of her surroundings and of herself while giving no hint that she was conscious. She judged that she had been unconscious for roughly three days, perhaps more, but not much more. She'd been stripped to the skin, and reclothed in some shapeless baglike garment made of what felt like the coarse material grain sacks were made of. Well, that meant all her overt weapons were gone . . .

She cursed herself for not realizing she'd been followed, that she'd been identified. After all, she'd stared in that dying priest's face and told his masters what Bey wanted them to hear. To be sure, she'd been completely masked, but it was always possible they'd had some magical way of knowing who she was, and that had been a mistake.

Or perhaps they had merely been scrying the perimeter of the

Nation's borders and tracking anyone coming in or out? In that case, she should have been more careful and left at night. And she should never have allowed that storm to change her camping plans. Stupid, stupid, stupid. Arrogant, and too sure of herself; well, now she had to fix what she'd broken.

Interestingly, they'd left her Talisman and the necklace of smaller Talismans. Had they been afraid to touch the things? Or did they not recognize them for what they were? She smiled internally, for at least this proved they were anything but infallible. Well, things could be much, much worse. Her father had wanted to send the Karsites a message; perhaps she might be able to finally deliver it in a way that would make some impact.

No sounds of anyone else in the room; she lay on a stone floor, which implied stone walls, and if anyone had even been *breathing* in here, however quietly, she'd have heard it.

She slitted her eyes open. Yes indeed, four stone walls, ceiling with wooden beams, stone laid over them. And it was cold, though that had not been the first thing on her mind when she had been taking stock of herself. Part of her training had involved inuring herself to cold; like all Sleepgivers of her proficiency, she had sat outside in the dead of winter clothed only in a wet swath of fabric and dried it with the heat of her body. This chill was nothing. There were small windows with iron bars inset in them on two of the walls, and a brisk wind was blowing through them.

So, so, so. It seemed that instead of dungeons, the Karsites built their prisons above ground. Or this one, at least.

Having learned all she could from where she lay, she got up, went over to the window, and looked out.

An impressive vista. It appeared that the Karsites built their prisons *up.* There was nothing but scrubby not-quite-desert all around, with mountains in the distance. Not her mountains, of course. She had been too far from home for that. She reckoned she knew where she was by map: east of Menmellith, east and north of where she had been going.

Well, now she knew where she was. The next thing to learn was what they knew of her.

A quick guess put her about five stories above the ground, so she was at the top of the tower. Probably the exact top of the tower; they would likely put the prisoners they were the most nervous about at the top, with four floors-worth of guards and barriers between her and the bottom. Assuming, of course, she went out *through* the tower, which was not necessarily what she would ultimately do when she escaped.

Because she *would* escape. There was no question of if. The only questions were how and when.

Right now she did not have enough information to figure a way out.

The cell was bare except for a bucket with water in it. There was a hole in the floor that, given the stains around it, served as a jakes. She wrinkled her nose at that. Unsanitary *and* a waste. Well, that told her one thing she didn't know before; these Karsites had no idea of the kind of people they were dealing with in the form of the Nation.

Yes, they had good homes, sufficient food, and comforts now. But they had gone through centuries of privation, and they had never forgotten this. The Karsites only *thought* they were hard. The Nation trained its children in deprivation and how to survive it. *All* of them, not just the Sleepgivers.

And this was why she already knew she would escape. Unless they had a dozen of their demon-summoning priests here. If her adversaries were only human, they stood no chance against what she could bring to bear.

And even if they did . . . her necklace of small bronze Talismans might just hold the answer to that.

She went to the corner of the room farthest from the door, sat down and arranged the bag-like garment for maximum coverage, closed her eyes, and extended her magic senses. She immediately noticed the shields on all the walls; shields that walled things in *and* out. They had not thought this through. Yes, such shields prevented anyone from scrying her and might hold off some magical attacks—and yes, they prevented her from getting a message out. But they also confined anything she turned loose within the four walls, at least until the shields were broken from within, or brought down.

They had truly not thought this through. She was not trapped in here with them. *They were trapped in here with her.*

Her main reason for visiting Amber Moon had been that she had not wanted to inadvertently wake something in the heart of the Nation that she could not put back to sleep again, and she had the impression that the Amber Moon Mages had more experience with the sort of Talisman represented by the ones around her neck.

But now that she thought about it . . . they did not have experience in the peculiar magics of her people. These couldn't have come from outside the Nation, even if they dated all the way back to when her people had first come to the Mountain. And the reason she knew this was these odd Talismans were things that her people had used and thought important.

She had suspected there was something sleeping, but powerful, bound in these little things. Now would be a good time to find out what was in there, even if she inadvertently woke it up. And she wasn't in the least worried about unleashing something she could not control *here*.

A tiny smile flashed across her face for just one brief moment.

Had there been any Karsite guards looking through the window in the door at that moment, their blood would likely have frozen in their veins.

The sounds of footsteps laboring up the stair, then of a key in the door alerted her, and she abandoned her investigations in time to greet the guard who opened the door to place a bowl just inside with a face as unreadable as a slab of obsidian.

He did not venture into the cell, and the door was only open for a few moments, but she had noted that he wasn't watching her as he put the bowl down, he was watching the bowl. She could have been across the room in half that time, and in the other half, she could have slammed the door into his chest, shattering the ribs, pulled him *through* the door, breaking his skull on the floor, or gotten her hands on his head, snapping his neck.

So they still had no idea what, exactly, they had prisoner. Otherwise they'd never have sent one man to deliver a meal. More information. Was it possible they didn't know she was a Sleepgiver? Or did they really not understand how dangerous a Sleepgiver was?

She waited until the sounds of footsteps faded, counting them this time, to give her an idea of how many floors there were, exactly. A door slammed shut somewhere beneath, and her total told her that her guess had been correct; there were five stories to this place.

Only then did she get up and look at the bowl, mindful of the fact that although there was no way of being spied upon physically that she would have been able to see, they could be scrying her. She had no intention of letting these Karsites know she was also a Mage, so although she *could* have taken steps to detect scrying, she had not done so. It was no great hardship to present an image that suggested she was cowed, even frightened by finding herself a prisoner.

The bowl was wood—a wise choice, since a pottery bowl could have been broken and turned into sharp-edged shards. The contents were some sort of grain porridge. She picked up the bowl and took it to her corner. It was gummy and bland, most of it overcooked, a few grains almost raw, and it didn't even have any salt in it, but it was fuel and she ate it slowly.

And while she ate, she was casting a spell, telling the porridge to replenish itself from its source. So until she felt sated, the level in the bowl never really dropped below half.

There were many spells involving bringing food to the caster, but this was the simplest, and the only one she knew. As a Mage, she was nowhere near the level of the ones at Amber Moon. Most of her expertise lay in knowing everything there was to know about the magic of the Talismans. How to make them, how to break them. Still, she had a few skills that were going to come in handy now, like the one that could keep her fed even if they decided to try starving her out.

I'm not going to do anything against them until they leave me no choice, she decided. She would put off revealing that she was a Sleepgiver until the last possible moment . . . and when they did find out, it wouldn't be by her *telling* them.

So once she finished her meal, she extracted a single uncooked grain from the bottom of the bowl and wedged it between two stones in the wall. Now if they tried to starve her, she'd still be able to magically apport the porridge from the kettle of this stuff kept perpetually cooking somewhere—out there. A kitchen on the bottom floor probably, with raw grain added to it as it was emptied into prisoners' bowls. The gummy overcooked paste combined with half-cooked grains told her that much.

It also told her that there might be other prisoners here, otherwise she'd probably have been given scraps from the guards' table, not stuff that was only cheaper than scraps by virtue of it being produced constantly.

Other prisoners. No point in even thinking about them. They couldn't help her, and even if they could, they probably wouldn't.

She put the bowl by the door and went back to her corner, huddling up in feigned distress. In actual fact she was studying her bronze Talismans with the same ferocity she brought to bear when sharpening a new physical skill.

The thing about spells was that as processes, they were *always working* once cast, unless there was a way built into them to stop and start them. Like the sun shining, or the grass growing. Unless you built an end to them, or at least a way to pause them just as the onset of frost ended growing grass, they kept going as long as there was energy for them.

And the difference between lesser Mages, like Sira herself, and the great Mages, was that the great Mages had ways to tap into sources of magical energy other than themselves to keep their spells going long past their deaths.

Most of those energy sources were limited too . . . only the greatest Mages had ways of tapping into sources that were like natural springs of water, virtually eternal and self-renewing.

Like the Mages her people had brought with them when they escaped that great conflict of long ago.

Now there were ways of breaking those spells. Destroying the object they were cast on was one. The problem with that was you had a not-insignificant chance of releasing very physical energy when you did so, something she hadn't wanted to risk at the Mountain. Plus, in this case, there was something bound to the Talisman, and if you released it that way, besides not knowing *what* you had released, you could do so in a way that injured it and made it angry. Or, angrier.

Now that she had been imprisoned, destroying the Talismans was not an option. That left her with the need to stop the process of the spell in other ways.

One could break it with magical force. . . .

But she wasn't strong enough to do that.

Which left unraveling it or making it break itself.

There was always a place in a working spell where the thing had been "tied off," where the Mage who had made it put the last piece in place and sealed it, and the sealing of it had set the spell in motion. If you could see that place and break the seal, or interrupt the spell just before the sealed-off spot, the spell would immediately begin to unravel under its own momentum, like a ball of yarn unraveling as it rolled away from you, or a sweater unraveling as its wearer walked away while you held the end in your hand.

That was one option.

The second was to spot a place in the spell where you could insert a small magical construct that would jam it—like inserting a bar of iron into the moving wheel on a wagon. Eventually, the bar would jam against the body of the wagon, and the spokes would start to break, the wheel would disintegrate, and the corner of the wagon would collapse as the wheel fell off, at which point the wagon would be going nowhere anymore.

That was actually a lot easier with a spell as old as these were. "All" she had to do was study one for long enough that she'd see the recurring "hole" where she could insert her "iron bar."

But this was why they called ancient spells like this "tightly woven." There weren't many holes, and they were hard to spot.

Still, what did she have at this point besides time?

So she sat with her eyes closed, huddled in the corner, and watched with the concentration and patience of the practiced Sleepgiver that she was.

Looking for the place where she could begin unraveling, looking for the "hole" she could use to make it break itself.

Eventually she got up to use the hole in the floor for waste, using part of the water in her bucket to rinse the area clean—because why not? She could use the entire bucketful and refill it at her leisure. This prison had the advantage of being above ground, so insects were at a minimum, and she'd been given no bedding, so there were no bedbugs or fleas, but buzzing flies would certainly interrupt her concentration. Not to mention she didn't like any part of her cell being filthy.

She refilled the bucket, took a moment to drink—this was dry land, and there was no point in getting dehydrated—and went back to work.

The guard returned just at dusk, took the old wooden bowl, and replaced it with another. This time he left a roll of bread with it. Once again, he failed to watch her as he set his burdens inside the door.

Once again, she feigned being afraid of him and waited until he was long gone before getting her food.

At least this time all the grain was cooked, if not cooked properly.

The bread was welcome, and she ate it slowly as she *apported* two more rolls under the cover of her garment, to keep anyone that was scrying her from seeing what she could do. She saved a bit of the last one in the corner behind her so she could apport more, later. The brown crust blended very nicely with the brown stone; if you didn't know it was there, you wouldn't see it.

Darkness came rapidly, as it always did in dry lands. She composed herself as best she could for sleep, spending a little bit more of her energies on a short-lived spell of her own that would keep the stone in her corner warmed until dawn.

And that ended her first conscious day in captivity.

She expected that, whether or not someone was watching her, her captors would lose patience around about the third day. And when she showed no sign of doing anything other than huddling in the corner, right after her morning meal on that third day, it appeared that was exactly what had happened.

The door slammed open. First two guards came in, one of them carrying a padded stool, the other with both a sword and a dagger out. The latter glowered at her as the first put the stool in the middle of the floor and left. She smiled inwardly at that; they much underestimated her if they thought that would place the occupant out of her reach.

With much rustling of black robes and ponderous steps, a Karsite priest entered the cell and sat down on the stool. He was a tall man, bearded, balding, and of late middle age. His features proclaimed him to be a hard and inflexible man, which was not at all unexpected.

She could have put up shields, but she did not. She did not want him to know she was a Mage—and her father had said that the Karsites burned every child they found with Mind-magic in their sacrificial fires, so he wouldn't be able to read her thoughts. Instead, she watched him with narrowed eyes in absolute silence. Let him speak first. Let him speak a very great deal. She intended to learn much from him while telling him nothing.

"What is your name, girl?" the Karsite asked, in tones that suggested that the mere fact of her being a female made her beneath him. He spoke in Ruvan, and there was a suggestion in the raspy tone of his voice that the dry desert air did not suit him. She answered him in the same tongue.

Of course, even if he had known the language of her people, she wouldn't have answered him in it.

"Sira en Anhita," she said truthfully, for he might have a truth-telling spell on her. She would answer everything with the truth . . . just not all, or even most, of it. Just in case he knew her father's name—unlikely, but possible—she called herself "the daughter of her mother," which designation was equally used among the Nation.

He frowned, as if he did not like that answer. "What are you, and why were you traveling from the stronghold of the Sleepgivers?"

"I am a hunter," she said. "And I journeyed to consult with the Mages of Amber Moon, in Rethwellan on the border of Menmellith."

He snorted with derision. "Do you think me a fool?" he demanded. "Women are not hunters."

"This woman is," which was true, after all, though what she hunted was mostly Karsite priests. . . . But already he had told her that he did not know she was a Sleepgiver, and he did not think Sleepgivers could be women.

And yes, at this point, she thought him a fool.

"Not possible," he stated flatly, visibly irritated.

"Have it your way," she said, and shrugged. "Then animals must impale themselves upon arrows they find and come to die at my feet." She gave him the blankest stare she could manage, then added, "In the breeding season, I also keep pigeons and chickens."

Also true; she took it in her turn to feed the family flocks.

"You came from the mountains that hold the Sleepgivers," he accused.

"Many people live there," she said indifferently. More truth. The Sleepgivers had no problem with other peoples sharing their territory, so long as the Nation got its due portion for the privilege.

"What do you know of them?" he pounced upon that with triumph.

"That they are dangerous to know and more dangerous to cross, and that is enough."

"And yet you wear their Talisman!" he all but shouted.

"This?" She touched the stone Talisman at her throat. "This is the memory of my mother. She gave it to me."

As she had hoped, he was not fluent enough in Ruvan to tell the difference between *in memory of my mother,* and *is the memory of my mother.* Thwarted, he glowered at her.

"You are impudent."

She shrugged.

"You know more of the Sleepgivers than you have said," he stated.

"I know I am more afraid of them than of you," she retorted.

He grew red in the face. "I am a great and powerful priest of Vkandis Sunlord!" he roared. "I can have you locked here until you starve!"

"And you'll still get no more from me than water from a stone. My people have a saying: *Do not expect clever speech from a dog; you will wait forever and be no wiser at the end of days.*" This was, indeed, a common saying in Ruvan. The Sleepgivers had adopted it.

What she was hoping for now was that this fat fool would give up on her and turn her loose. Even if all they released her with was what she stood up in, keeping her weapons and her clothing out of sheer spite, she could still make her way back home. Turn her loose in the desert and she'd have food, clothing and weapons in three days. They wouldn't be *good*, but they would do until she could get better.

But the fool cooled his wrath and glared at her. "You were taken wearing far too many weapons for a chicken farmer," he stated. *"Concealed* weapons."

She had hoped he hade forgotten that. Worse luck.

"I told you, I am a hunter," she informed him, grateful now that she had not been wearing more than a dozen knives, and none of the specialist tools of a Sleepgiver. "Such things are the tools of a hunter." Perhaps she could have explained the fine wire garrote as a snare, but some of the other things? Unlikely. "As for concealing my tools, I was alone, and when one travels alone, it does not do to advertise what one owns."

He continued to glower. "There is more to you than you are saying."

She sighed with exasperation. "And you keep saying I am merely a girl. You cannot have it both ways. I am a hunter. Nothing more, nothing less. So either you accept my being armed as the proof of that, or I am merely a girl who farms chickens and you have no reason to keep me here."

"You are altogether too clever for a chicken girl," he growled, and he heaved himself up off his stool. The flunkey hastened to retrieve it.

"And you have no grandmother's tales of clever chicken girls?" she mocked, figuring at this point she had nothing to lose by angering him further. "What a singularly dull people you Karsites are! *We* have dozens. Also, tales of clever hunters. And half of them are about *girls.*"

For answer, he flounced out of the cell, turning back only to say, "We shall see how three days without food or water loosens your tongue, wench," before the flunky threw open the door and allowed him to exit, slamming the door behind him.

Three days with plenty of bread and water suited her just fine. She made sure to eat and drink in the dark, being fairly certain that there was not a scrying spell known anywhere that allowed someone to see what was going on in darkness. But it was autumn, and the nights were long; it was no great hardship to stuff herself full just before dawn, waking herself automatically to do so, and do so again after sunset. She could easily sleep out the night, and wait out the day.

And in the daylight, she studied her Talismans and surreptitiously exercised. It would not do to be caught at her usual exercises, but there were many ways to make them look like a girl who was half-mad and dancing. Particularly when she hummed loudly as she moved.

At the end of three days, she heard the sound of labored steps on the staircase; she had been listening for just that, of course. She took her seat in the corner, and waited.

The entire charade with the stool was played again. This time she paid closer attention to the flunkies than to the priest. They were either too terrified of their master to react properly, or they were singularly careless. If she had wanted to (she didn't, not yet), she could have had the long dagger off the one playing guard in an instant, gutted him, slit his master's throat, and driven it through the eye of the one minding the stool before the latter had more than a glimmering hint that all was not well.

But that would leave her having to fight her way out of this tower, and after that possibly a much larger building, with only two short swords and two long daggers. And by the time she looted and adapted the clothing on the bodies, the entire tower would be alerted and ready to stop her.

Not ideal.

The priest's expression was somewhere between a glower and a sullen frown. "What are you, wench?" he growled, when he had settled himself.

"I told you. I'm a hunter," she repeated patiently. "I was on my way to consult with the Amber Moon magicians when you people decided to attack me with demons for some reason. I can only guess it's because I was coming out of those mountains the Sleepgivers call their own. The Sleepgivers actually don't *care* if other people live in their mountains as long as nothing the others do interferes with them. And as long as you give them a tenth of what you grow or catch for the privilege of living there."

"Have you seen any?" the priest asked.

"Of course. They approach anyone who enters peacefully to warn them what not to do. As long as you obey those rules, they leave you alone, except to collect their tenth once a year." Once again, all true.

The priest stared at her for a very long time. "You seem remarkably fit for someone who has done without food and water for three days," he growled.

"I'm a hunter. In the desert. I'm used to doing without food and water. I'm also used to skinning and gutting an animal, small or large, using every part of it, wasting nothing, and curing the skin with sand and its own brains. Would you like to see me demonstrate?" She said the last to antagonize him as much as to try to persuade him to let her go. "I've skinned, gutted, and eaten mice and lizards. I've gotten by eating insects. And you forget that dew collects on stone, and this cell is made of stone. That's water enough for me."

All of these were true. They had been part of her survival training. She'd been ten at the time.

Just then she heard considerable activity outside the cell door; it opened again, and another priest with a trailing set of two guards came in, one, as before, with a stool.

This priest, also garbed in black, but sporting a huge gold necklace with a sun-disk around his neck, was very old; to someone not used to reading faces and posture as well as Sira was, he would have looked kindly. But the wrinkles in his face told her of far more frowns in his life than smiles, even if he was smiling now. And she already knew what was coming.

I cannot believe they are actually resorting to "good interrogator/bad interrogator."

If the situation had been less annoying, this would have been amusing. It was, at the moment, only annoying, because they had not yet threatened her with physical harm.

But unless she could persuade them to free her now, that was just a matter of time. By this point she was losing her confidence in her ability to get out of here on her own.

In fact, I'm beginning to think I might be in trouble. . . .

"Now, now, my brother," said the second priest to the first. "I believe we need to reassure this girl, not frighten her."

"She's not frightened," the first growled. "She's impudent."

The second pretended to ignore him, and leaned toward her, still smiling. "So, girl, what is your name and why were you traveling from the land of the Sleepgivers?"

"My name is Sira, I am a hunter, and I was on my way to the Amber Moon magicians to consult with them about my mother's Talisman," she repeated, deadpan.

"A hunter? That is a strange thing for a girl to claim," said the second, with a false smile.

"Not among the people of the desert of Ruvan," she countered. "It does not require great strength to be a hunter, especially of small game. It takes endurance, patience, and skill, the former two of which females have in abundance."

"Indeed?" His chuckle was as false as his smile. "And how is it you come from Sleepgiver lands if you are not a Sleepgiver yourself?"

"Because the Sleepgivers allow any able to sustain themselves and produce goods for trade to dwell within the mountains the King of Ruvan has granted them, provided that they keep a respectful distance from the Sleepgiver strongholds and pay them a tenth of what they make in tribute." She shrugged. "No one sane flauts this rule. They are dangerous."

"So you say. And yet they have not harmed you." The first interjected himself into the conversation.

"They have no need, for I do not break the Sleepgiver rules." She had no difficulty keeping her expression as bland and wooden as a carved figure's. And before she answered, she always made sure she was phrasing things so that she would not trigger a Truth Spell. "It is safer for women in the Sleepgiver mountains anyway, and there are several such as I who take advantage of that. They have laws against interfering with a woman. Or anyone, actually," she added.

"Indeed?" The single word invited elaboration. She didn't give it. She did think about adding "Why don't you try it and find out?" but that would be giving them insolence and she didn't intend to give them anything.

"You know, girl. . . ."

You're still not using my name.

"We could just let you go on your way. If you would just cooperate with us." He beamed at her, as if he had just offered something extraordinary.

She gave him the blankest look she could manage. "I am a desert hunter. My name is Sira. I was on my way to consult with the Amber Moon Mages about my mother's Talisman," she repeated. "No one who lives on sufferance in Sleepgiver lands is allowed near enough to them to learn anything. Now, if you want a long talk about the habits of desert hares, sand deer, hopper rats, topknot quail, and silky goats, I will be happy to cooperate and tell you all about them."

The first priest pounced. "That Talisman! The Sleepgivers wear them!"

"The Sleepgivers may very well wear Talismans. Not like this one," she corrected. "Many people wear Talismans. You yourself wear one about your neck."

"But why were you going to the Mages of Amber Moon about yours?" purred the second priest.

"Because sometimes I think I can hear my mother giving me instructions when I need guidance," she said, with absolute truth. It took some tricky thinking and deliberate pauses to make sure she was concentrating on the *right* Talisman when answering a question about them, but this was, in fact, the absolute truth. That the Talisman *also* gave her muscle-memory of how to perform some very impressive feats of fighting and agility—

Well, they hadn't asked about that, and she wasn't going to volunteer it.

This time both priests frowned, as if this answer puzzled both of them. It certainly wasn't the one they expected.

"Perhaps we could—" the old priest began.

"It doesn't happen all the time, and for anyone else it's just a dead piece of stone," she said flatly, and started to take her own Talisman off. "But if you want to risk it. I don't know what will happen if you start mucking about with it. Mother-magic is very powerful, if it is indeed magic and not my own good sense talking to me."

The first priest started to reach for it. The second stopped him. "Better not," he cautioned. "I've never heard of something like this before."

The first pulled his hand back, grumbling under his breath.

They both studied her for a long, silent time, while she just sat there, expressionless, not doing anything to encourage them, but obviously not cooperating in the way they wanted either.

The silence got so oppressive that she finally decided to break it herself. "The desert hare," she said, in bored tones, "Makes its warren in the roots of the thita bush. It only emerges at sunset and remains out until a few glass-turns after sunrise. It gets most of its water by licking the dew from the leaves of the thita, where dew collects. It gets the rest by eating the dead-man's-hand cactus. You'd be poisoned if you tried that, but the hare somehow isn't; those cacti are its main source of food. You can catch them by setting a snare in the runs it makes through patches of these—"

"Enough!" snapped the first priest.

"Would you rather hear about the top-knot quail?" she asked, innocently.

"No!" His face was getting very red.

"What about the sand deer? Did you know it's actually possible to train a brown-wing desert hawk to help you kill them?" She resisted the urge to bat her eyes at him.

"I said enough!" he spat, and he rose from his stool. "It's obvious you have no intention of cooperating. We'll have to resort to other ways of making you talk."

The older priest got up without a single word, his face settling into the disagreeable expression that was probably his normal one. All four guards and both priests left the cell, leaving her alone once more.

Obviously, they were not going to let her go.

And obviously, that last sentence had been the threat of physical measures.

Well, damn, she thought. There was no hope for it. It wouldn't be long now before she was forced to give them evidence that she was, in fact, a Sleepgiver.

And she still had no plans for getting out of here.

I am definitely in some difficulty now.

8

Tory was very impressed. The three of them had, indeed, made *astonishing* time to the Border.

It certainly helped that they began each day's journey in the dim light of predawn and ended it at twilight. And the fact that they paused during the day only for brief intervals and made use of what they carried and what was in the Waystations for food rather than relying on inns and taverns sped things up considerably.

But there was absolutely no doubt, whatsoever, that Ahkhan's sturdy little horse had every bit of the speed and stamina of a Companion, and Tory would not have believed that if he had not personally witnessed it.

"This is nothing," Ahkhan said dismissively, when Tory said as much on the third night of their journey. "You have good roads, we have not encountered bad weather, and there is still plenty of rich forage *as well as* hay and grain. My Natya can do this in the desert, and be ready for a battle at the end of it, so long as she has grain once a day." He chuckled. "Though, if she were to live in your pastures, she would soon become as round as a pampered pony."

And long before Tory expected to, they had reached the Border with Menmellith, just after noon on a glorious autumn day. There was a Guard station there, but it was more of a courtesy than a hindrance to anyone crossing into Valdemar.

It was a station with a full garrison of twelve, a proper stone building with a stone stable attached, capable not only of holding the garrison, but providing rooms for Valdemaran officials or Heralds, should any come this way. There were two Guards on duty at the roadside as they rode up, and they looked with surprise at two non Heralds riding what were obviously Companions but going in the wrong direction to have been newly Chosen. They recognized Ahkhan though, and registered shock that he had traveled from this very station to Haven and back in so short a time. "Does that nag of yours sprout gryphon-wings when no one is looking?" asked one of the half-dozen Guards who emerged to eye this extraordinary beast.

"She is of her kind, as the Shin'a'in war steeds are of their kind," Ahkhan replied with a faint showing of pride. "And a member of one's family, as theirs are of the Clans."

One of the Guards looked very disappointed at that. Tory wondered if he had been on the verge of making an offer for the horse. Tory wouldn't blame him for disappointment if that was what had been on his mind.

There was a little palaver that needed to happen—they needed to state their business ("Crown orders," with papers to match) and their names (though Kee made no mention of the fact that he was a Prince). And that was all, presumably because they were leaving Valdemar, rather than entering. Ahkhan's name got crossed off a list as someone who had entered and exited properly without making any trouble while he was there, and they were wished good luck with their business.

Oddly enough, there were no corresponding guards on the Menmellith side of the Border. Tory wondered about that—did they just not care who came and went? Or was this more a reflection that the Border here was more . . . fluid than the Valdemar border was?

Didn't Abi say something about that when she was down here? Maybe that was it; if the inhabitants of this part of Menmellith had been perfectly free to decide whether or not to join Valdemar, that could mean that there wasn't nearly as much control over the outlying regions of Menmellith as there was in Valdemar.

Which was rather worrying, because that left these people open to be annexed by Karse, which would not be good for Valdemar.

Then again, they really loathe Karse here . . . and perhaps they have their own militias to deal with any problems.

He decided that he'd talk about this with his father and mother when he got back home. All he could really do was report on the situation; it wasn't as if he could actually *do* anything about it.

They crossed without any more fuss than that, and then it was Ahkhan's turn to take the lead. He had pledged last night that the promised "transportation" would be no farther than three candlemarks from the Border, and he seemed completely confident that this "transportation" was going to get them wherever it was he intended to take them. Where that was, Tory had no idea. Probably not the Sleepgiver stronghold, though. Despite the fact that Bey had sent his father several missives over the years, the leader of the Sleepgivers had yet to divulge just *where* the Sleepgivers lived, and all Ahkhan had said was that it was "in Ruvan."

So Tory had no expectation of what they were going to see when Ahkhan led them off the main road down a side path that ran through the hills that were so typical of this part of the world. That path took them deep into a forested area to a walled enclave much too large to be a farm. The walls themselves were brown stone, and very old and tall, with imposing wooden gates that must have taken three men to open and close. It looked like some manner of religious holding rather than that of a noble; but the gates *were* guarded, and the guards returned Ahkhan's salute as if they knew him before they moved to open those gates.

Ahkhan dismounted. "Here, you may leave your Companions," he told them. "You will not need them again, this side of the Border."

They both dismounted and removed their packs; Tariday and Elissa could easily find their way back to Haven from here. Tory was rather sorry to see Elissa go. Although they couldn't Mindspeak, he'd found her to be rather eloquent with voice and gestures, to the point where they could have something of a conversation. She seemed just as sorry to part from him; she gave him an affectionate nuzzle and a low whicker before turning her back on him and following Tariday back down the path they had come at a brisk canter. They'd be safe enough on the way back.

As for him and Kee, well . . . this was where the adventure and the journey into the unknown began.

Tory shouldered his pack and followed Kee in through the gates.

He was not extraordinarily Empathic, but he did sense things about those guards that "felt" very like Ahkhan—and quite unlike the Valdemaran Guards he had known all his life. A sense that beneath their calm exteriors, these were exceptionally dangerous men, and a sort of affinity with Ahkhan himself. *Curious.* As the gates closed behind them, he saw that Ahkhan was already talking with a group of three, two men and a woman, wearing short robes over wide-legged trews, all in mismatched browns and grays. One man was tall, balding, and bearded, one middling, ginger-haired and bearded, the woman was square-jawed and blond, and they all looked nearer to sixty than thirty. He felt a bit of a thrill as he noticed that although the colors of their clothing did not match enough that the outfits could have been called a "uniform," they each had what looked like some manner of arcane symbol embroidered on the right breast of each robe. So this *was* some kind of organization, but probably not religious in nature. *Could this possibly be some sort of magicians' stronghold?* His heart beat faster at the thought.

One of the two men turned toward them, and beckoned them to join the little group, smiling. "Welcome to the Northern School of the Amber Moon Mages," he said cheerfully. "You are just in time."

In time for what?

"I am Bertolome. I am the Chief Mage, here," the man said, accelerating Tory's heart-rate. "I'd give you a warmer welcome and show you the School, but time is of the essence. We're to supply your transportation to the Southern School, in Rethwellan, near the Karsite Border, and we'll need to hurry in order to accomplish that."

He was speaking Valdemaran, with a decided accent. At this, Ahkhan pursed his lips. "My thanks for your reminder, Bertolome.

I had nearly forgotten something very important," he said, in tones that suggested reproach had been earned for his own forgetfulness. He turned to the female magician. "Would you have those amulets I bespoke from you?" he asked politely.

"Of course," she chuckled. "I was just waiting for you to ask." She reached into a belt-pouch and took out two clear crystals strung on leather cords, handing one each to Tory and Kee. They both took them, dubiously.

"What's this for?" Kee asked. Perhaps he was just now recalling Mags' descriptions of those Sleepgiver Talismans that were intended to take over the wills and personalities of their wearers.

"Languages," said Ahkhan, succinctly, as the three Mages watched them closely to see their reactions. "These will give you the ability to speak and understand the languages of Menmellith, Rethwellan, Ruvan, Karse, and the Nation."

"But—how?" asked Kee, as Tory now looked at the crystal in his hand with growing excitement. Magic! This was *real* magic! In his hand! He couldn't wait to try it! He pulled the leather cord over his head even as Kee blinked at his own crystal incredulously.

"You will need these tongues," Ahkhan told him, smiling slightly, as he heard the words in what sounded like perfect Valdemaran— and yet, he heard something else, faintly, that was nothing at all like Valdemaran, which he understood to be the Sleepgiver language. "If you wear them long enough, all five of those languages will seep into your mind and take hold as if you had learned them naturally."

"This is amazing!" Tory responded in the same language, as Kee looked at him as if he had grown a second head. Probably because to Kee it sounded like both of them were babbling.

Then Kee shrugged, and pulled the cord of his crystal over his own head, as Ahkhan motioned to him to do so impatiently. "All is in readiness," said the second man, who had been silently watching until now. This was in the language of Menmellith, and Kee gaped at him. "You were only just in time, for we were about to close the way soon. Come."

He didn't wait for an answer, but turned and headed into the large brown stone building behind them all, a plain building as big as the Heralds' and Healers' Collegia combined, that filled the walled enclosure. Tory hastened to catch up to him, as Ahkhan strode after him, Kee and the other two Mages bringing up the rear. Inexplicably, Ahkhan was leading his horse. Surely they were not going to allow a horse into the building—

But it appeared that they were!

"All *what* is in readiness?" Tory asked, as they entered through a side door and began crossing a series of interconnected rooms— it appeared these people did not have hallways. He didn't get a chance for more than a glimpse of what was in any of them, but one was full of books and reading stands, one was what looked like a stillroom full of faint scents that made him want to sneeze, in the next, several people appeared to be engraving something on stones and metal pendants, and in the last, people were diligently copying down a complicated diagram that an old man had drawn in chalk on a slate surface set into the wall. In all of them, every wall and floor was constructed of stone, and the ceilings appeared to be stone laid over close-set beams. Tory wished desperately that they weren't hurrying through these rooms so quickly, and equally he wished that Abi was here to explain what he was seeing to him.

They certainly didn't build like this in Valdemar, or at least, not in any part of it that he'd been in.

And in all of these rooms the people wore the same robes-and-trews in various shades of browns and grays that the first three Mages wore, with the same symbol embroidered on the breast.

"Our transportation is in readiness," Ahkhan told him, which actually told him nothing. Were they heading for a stable full of the kind of horse that Ahkhan's Natya was? Was it something more exotic than that? Magic carriages? Gryphons?

Finally they came to a set of double doors made of hammered copper. The man—magician!—who was leading them there threw the doors open, to show that the room contained nothing except a free-standing black stone arch at the end of it, and a great many people.

But the arch was filled with what *looked* like glimmering water, if a sheet of water could be made to stand upright, and the people were coming and going *through* it.

"You're just in time," said the magician who had brought them here. "If you hadn't arrived today, you'd have had to wait at least a full moon, if not more."

Ahkhan smiled. "I told you we'd be here today. You should know you can trust the word of a Sleepgiver by now." He turned to Tory and Kee. "Get in line with the rest," he instructed. "When your turn comes, step through the archway." He gave Tory a little shove to get him going; there were only three people ahead of him.

"But—" Tory objected.

"Just *go!*" Ahkhan said impatiently. "They can't keep the Portal open forever! We're probably the last ones that will go through today!"

"You are," the female Mage confirmed. "So don't dawdle. This takes the energy of most of the School."

There were only two people ahead of him now. Then one. And then none, and before Tory could object, Ahkhan stepped behind him and gave him a shove, and he went stumbling toward that weird substance that looked like vertical water before he could stop himself.

There was a moment of terrifying darkness, and complete disorientation.

And then he was stumbling into a room that appeared to be the mirror-image of the one he had just left. "Move!" someone snapped at him, and reflexively, he obeyed and cleared the area in front of the arch, as Kee stumbled across the threshold behind him, then Ahkhan, looking as if he was emerging from a bath, leading his horse who looked entirely unruffled by the entire experience. The horse honestly looked as if she had weathered things better than Kee and Tory put together.

And the moment Ahkhan appeared, the entire surface of the stuff filling the arch shivered, turned black, and vanished. Now there was nothing but a black stone archway, showing the brown stone wall behind it.

"Now we're in Rethwellan, near the South Menmellith Border," Ahkhan said, before Tory could say anything. "This is the Southern School of the Amber Moon Mages, and what you just went through was a magic Portal."

Still feeling disoriented, Tory struggled to remember his maps, and then gasped when he realized just how great a distance they had traveled in what was barely the blink of an eye. Why, this was at least as far as it was from the Northernmost Border of

Valdemar to the Southernmost! But—how?

—but it was *magic*, of course. Real magic! A portal was a door . . . so somehow, that arch had been a magical door, and it had taken them hundreds of leagues away in the blink of an eye.

"This was where my sister was heading when she disappeared." Ahkhan told them, as the room emptied of people, leaving them alone. "The Sleepgivers have a contract with Amber Moon. We supply them with Primary Guards and Trainers; when we need magical expertise we can't manage on our own, they supply that. And when we need to move from south to north quickly, they give us transportation between the two schools."

"Why would you—" Kee asked. He was pale, and looked as if he was more shaken by the experience than Tory was. "—why would you supply them with people?"

"Because not everyone who undergoes Sleepgiver training has the stomach to serve the Nation as a Sleepgiver," Ahkhan replied quietly. "So they elect to go into long service to serve the needs of the Nation in other ways, such as here. We have a similar contract with two other Schools of Magecraft, but the one with Amber Moon is the oldest."

Tory raised his eyebrow at the Prince. "It makes sense," he observed. "Who better to plan and carry out defenses than an assassin?"

Ahkhan nodded. "It serves us well. Now, we are near where my sister disappeared. Do you think you may be able to sense her now?"

"Once my stomach stops trying to crawl up my throat, yes," Kee told him.

"Then I will arrange for a small quiet room. And some mint tea." Ahkhan hurried off, giving no indication that they should follow.

So, after looking around and seeing nothing like furniture, Tory sat straight down on the floor. Kee joined him a moment later, moving in a way that suggested that if he moved any faster, the results would be regrettable.

"I think I'm going to lie down now," Kee said, putting his packs down and using them as a pillow. He looked quite green at this point. Tory didn't feel quite as sick as Kee looked, but a wave of dizziness suggested it might be a good idea if he followed Kee's example.

Once down, he stared up at the polished beams of the ceiling and the neatly laid stones above them, and he wondered again how the building of this place had been accomplished. And *why?* Why so much stone? Did it serve some special purpose for these Mages? Or did they build in stone for defensive purposes?

Maybe it was to prevent people from setting fire to it. Certainly you wouldn't be able to set fire to a building that was made almost entirely of stone.

Or were Mages likely to set things on fire by accident?

He realized as he lay there on the stone that part of his dizziness was due to being drastically overheated, which probably accounted for some of Kee's illness as well. As the cold stone of the floor drained the heat from his body, he began to feel better—and then to feel exhausted, as if he had run a very long distance. It felt very good to just lie there on the cool floor, staring up. Under the circumstances, in fact, the floor felt just as good as a mattress.

After a while he noticed that things even *smelled* different here. Drier, dustier, a hint of some sort of bitter herbal scent. Not unpleasant, but very different from Valdemar.

Ahkhan took his time about returning, and when he did, it was without his horse. He moved so silently by himself that to Tory it seemed as if he had performed another feat of magic and just *appeared* at their side, looking down at them with very faint sympathy. "My first transition through a Portal was equally fraught," he said, looking at Kee, and Kee jumped a little when he spoke. "I should have remembered that, and warned you of it. Come, I have cots and mint tea arranged. Both will make you feel better."

Tory rolled up to his feet; Kee did the same, with a little more effort. "Are we going to have to do this again any time soon?" the Prince asked plaintively.

"Not until your return journey," Ahkhan promised him. "Though . . . whether that will be soon or late, only you can tell me."

This time, he led them through only two of the linked rooms— although the building looked nearly identical to the one they had just left—before taking them up a stone staircase where, at long last, there was a hallway, with dozens of doors leading off it. This must be something like the dormitories in the three Collegia, Tory surmised. Or maybe guest quarters? In either case—given that Ahkhan had promised cots, they were probably bedrooms.

And that was what it proved to be; the narrow rooms they were led to were quite comfortable for something made entirely of stone; there were low beds, a couple of chests, a wooden wardrobe, and somehow shelves fastened securely to the stone walls. There was no glass in the small windows; instead, there were heavy wooden shutters, which were currently open to catch a breeze much warmer than he had felt in Valdemar.

There was also a small table beside the bed in each room, with a glazed pottery pitcher and cup. Kee immediately poured a cupful and drank it down. "That's better," he said heavily. "I need to lie down—"

"And sleep," admonished Ahkhan. "You clearly took the transition hard. You may well be Mage-blooded. I am impatient to learn if you can touch my sister, but not so impatient that I wish you to be ill. Drink another cup, and sleep. You too," he added, looking gravely at Tory. "You may not be Mage-blooded, but the transition was not easy for you."

Tory was not at all inclined to argue with the Sleepgiver. He went next door to the room he had been given, dropped his packs on the floor, drank down two cups full of the mint-and-honey tea, and all but fell into the bed.

His final thought before exhaustion overpowered him was to wonder—if Kee was Mage-blooded, where on earth had that come from?

Well, it's a Gift like any other, I suppose, he thought. *It could come from anywhere. . . .*

The next thing he knew, Ahkhan was shaking him awake, and the golden quality and slant of the light coming in the windows suggested it was very late in the afternoon. "Kyril is awake and prepared to try if you are," the Sleepgiver said, as Tory knuckled his eyes.

"This is generally better not done on a full stomach," he replied by way of agreement, and stood up. He was pleased to feel no dizziness, nor that drained feeling. "Let's see what we can do."

Kee sat cross-legged on the foot of his bed and gestured to Tory to sit at the head. He did so, and they clasped wrists. It took no time at all to fall into that familiar trance.

And suddenly his darkness lit up with a cluster of new "presences."

One was very near, but it was one he was used to by now; that was Ahkhan, sitting at the window and watching them gravely. Six of them were near-ish—as near as, say, Abi would be on one of her very distant missions to build something, and these were all new to him.

He strove to "see" them all, and sense what was going on in their minds. Ahkhan was easy; Tory had known for some time now that the Sleepgiver's calm and confident exterior masked a storm of worry for his sister. There was nothing new there, except a heightened anxiety that he and Kee would be able to make contact with her.

He moved to the five, distant 'beacons' and concentrated on the first, a presence that seemed to attract him the most powerfully. He found himself observing an older man, about his father's age, alone in a room that appeared to be carved out of the living rock of a mountain, in grave conference with a group of even older men and women. He looked uncannily like Mags. The family resemblance was unmistakable. *Is this father's cousin Bey?* It must be, because he was the one that "attracted" Tory the strongest, probably since he was the nearer relation.

All right. Let me see if I can "read" anything from him. If we manage to find Sira, it will help if I can get a sense of how she's holding up, even if I can't Mindspeak with her. He concentrated for a moment, and got the distinct impression that although this man was putting on a "normal" face for the benefit of those with him, he was deeply worried about his missing daughter.

Not far from him, perhaps no more than a few rooms away, was a boy on the verge of manhood, and another a little older diligently doing something in a still-room. And again . . . there was no doubt that they, too, were worried about Sira, and they were using this task as a way to keep themselves distracted.

The next two were physically farther from the first two. A young man about Perry's age and a much younger woman, were engaged in running and climbing all over a course that was built on and next to a mountain slope, a course that made his own roof-running look like a child playing in a back garden. And again, it was very clear that all this was a distraction.

And last of all, he found a young man maybe a year younger than Abi, training dogs—his rapport with them was second only to Perry's, and he was teaching them how to dodge thrown weapons and blunted arrows as they ran in to attack men wearing so much padding to protect themselves they could scarcely waddle. He, at least, was succeeding in distracting himself with his task as he coordinated the pack of six dogs to come in to attack and retreat as if they were teasing a bear, never letting the men get a moment to gather their wits, evading the weapons, weaving around like a pack of ferrets.

Their mother must be there *somewhere*, but since she wasn't related to Tory at all, he wouldn't see her unless she was literally standing next to one of his distant cousins. And even then, he would be unable to sense what she was feeling.

Right. At least I've established that I can reach the other cousins from here. So . . . Sira, let's hope you are within my range.

So . . . there it was. A very distant seventh. Farther than the six, and in an entirely different direction; they were east and south, this was east and north. In the south of Karse, if all this in his mind lined up with maps.

With glacial slowness, a picture began to form in his mind. First, he saw a girl about Kee's age, her hair cut at about chin-length, wearing a sort of shapeless bag for a garment. She seemed to be meditating, wedged into a corner. Gradually, he made out a stone floor, walls, ceiling. A cell, with nothing in it but the girl and a bucket. Try as he might, he couldn't manage to extend his view past the walls of the cell, so eventually he gave up, and fell to examining the girl herself.

She looked unharmed. No wounds, no bruises, no sign of mistreatment. He did his best to figure out what she was feeling, but all he could get was a combination of *worry*, and exasperation at herself.

Well, if she was feeling annoyed at herself—for falling into this trap?—surely that meant she didn't have anything more serious to concentrate on.

At least . . . he hoped not.

The family resemblance to his father was startling, more so than in any other of the cousins. Her youth, when compared to his father, didn't make a great deal of difference either; she had a very "hard," refined face, and like Mags, she was so good at controlling her expression even when alone that it was unreadable. The only real difference between them was that Mags' "resting face" was one of affable stupidity—he'd told Tory that it made people consistently underestimate him. Whereas Sira's resting face was a complete blank, not merely like a statue, but like a statue that has been deliberately carved to look impassive.

This, combined with the general lack of information he was able to get merely by observing her, had the effect of making him feel immensely frustrated. Most of the time he was perfectly all right with not being a Mindspeaker of any kind, but at this moment in time he definitely wished he had his father along on this little "excursion." No one had ever really tested the limits of Mags' Mindspeaking ability, and it would have been awfully useful to have been able to discover what the blasted girl was thinking!

It was that frustration that broke his concentration and dropped him out of the trance—dragging Kee along with him. He opened his eyes to see with some shock that Kee was absolutely *furious*.

"I wasn't done yet!" Kee hissed, in a show of emotion that startled him.

"What did you see?" Ahkhan demanded, eyes alight, interrupting whatever remonstrance Kee had been about to deliver.

Tory spoke first. "Well . . . we found her, all right. It looks like she's in a prison cell. They've taken her clothes, and presumably everything else she had on her. She's not hurt, not even bruised, so I guess she hasn't been mistreated. Yet," he added, because surely Ahkhan understood *that* was only a matter of time. He thought about adding what he'd felt . . . but he wasn't altogether sure about that, so he decided to leave it out. "I couldn't see anything that wasn't in her immediate vicinity, so I don't know where she is, although there was normal daylight coming in through the windows, so she's not underground."

"She's angry," Kee interrupted. "And frustrated. And starting to be afraid. She's at the top of a tower, in something like desert, but I didn't get a chance to see more before I got dragged out." He glared at Tory a moment, then turned his attention back to Ahkhan. "She's definitely in Karse, as you thought. I'm pretty sure they don't actually know she's a Sleepgiver, or they'd have her in chains at the very least, and she's not."

"I'm certain you're correct," Ahkhan agreed. "But it won't be long before they find out. Because sooner or later, they're going to try something unpleasant, and she will not tolerate that. Hopefully it will be later, much later. Hopefully she is clever enough to keep them frustrated, but not so frustrated that they feel reduced to brutality."

That certainly sounded odd, coming from the mouth of an assassin . . . but then again, didn't the Sleepgivers pride themselves on doing their work quickly, so quickly the victim didn't even have time to feel fear?

Well, mostly. I suppose they haven't been treating the Karsite priests they've been killing that way.

"Well, can you two still sense the direction she's in?" Ahkhan asked.

They both nodded. Tory felt it in his breastbone now, as if he was pulled in that direction by a cord. Presumably Kee felt the same way.

Ahkhan spread out a map on the floor and instructed Tory to kneel on a spot marked *Amber Moon South*. It was a big map, and Tory's jaw dropped a little when he saw how far *Amber Moon South* was from *Amber Moon North*. It was . . . impossible. But Ahkhan wasn't inclined to give him time to think about that just now.

"Close your eyes, extend your arm, and point to her," Ahkhan ordered, as if he perfectly well understood that Tory *could*, in fact, do this. Tory obeyed, and felt Ahkhan doing something at the tip of his finger.

"Now open your eyes and move to the bed. Prince, if you would do the same?" Ahkhan said politely, and Kee scrambled to oblige. Now Tory could see that Ahkhan simply put the end of a weighted cord at the end of Kee's finger and marked the place on the map where the cord dropped.

When they were both on the bed, Ahkhan took something out of a pocket that proved to be a short stick that unfolded into a whiplike baton. Using this as a straight-edge, he drew a line with a wax crayon between the dot that represented where they were now, to the dots where the line had fallen, then extended it beyond. Then he sat back on his heels and contemplated it.

"Well," he said, finally. "She is somewhere on that line between the western Karsite Border and the north-eastern Karsite Border. Given that the Prince saw that she was in a desert . . . and this map is reasonably accurate. . . . I would say she is somewhere in here."

He made a circle with the crayon on the map in an area that seemed to be mostly surrounded by high hills or low mountains.

Tory eyed it dubiously. "That's a lot of territory to search."

"Not so much. I know she will be *on* that line. I merely need to look for a fortified place with a tower." He began to fold up the map. "I could wish that we had tried this trick back at the northern school of Amber Moon, because now I must backtrack. Cousin, Prince, you have been of inestimable value to us in our search. Consider the bargain sealed. I will send word to my father to that effect before I leave."

"Wait—you mean you're leaving? *Now?*" Kee demanded. "Without us?"

"Putting you in danger from Karsites was in no way part of the bargain," Ahkhan replied calmly. "You will be fine here at Amber Moon for the next moon or so when they again open the Portal. Or if you would rather not wait that long, I am sure they will find you mounts and an escort back to your Border—"

"We're *not* going back!" Kee said firmly, and with great passion. "Our job is *not* done! The closer we can get to Sira, the more we can see around her, and the better we can prepare you for what's going on! And the closer we get, the more accurate we can be in figuring out exactly where she is, instead of you wandering around in hostile territory trying to find exactly the right stronghold she's held in! And on top of that, we can help you! We can help you get her out! We *have* to help you!"

This outburst took Tory entirely by surprise, not the least because of the heat with which it had been delivered. He knew, without a shadow of a doubt, that Kee meant every word, and that he was actually restraining himself from throwing himself on Ahkhan and not just demanding to go along, but begging.

He also had no idea *why* Kee felt this way.

But that didn't matter. Kee was his best friend. And Kee *never* did anything impulsively. He might be the almost-youngest Prince, but he had been trained as a Prince, and Princes cannot act on mere impulse.

So if Kee felt that strongly—Tory was going to have his back.

"He's right," he said, looking right in Ahkhan's eyes. "You need us. Our job isn't done yet."

Ahkhan went very still for a moment, and Tory was afraid he was going to refuse their help.

But "As you wish," he said.

9

The Karsites left her alone for another day, another day in which she was (presumably) without food or water, which would (presumably) weaken her resolve—or at least, her "impudence." She still had no idea if the Karsites believed her imposture or not.

And what did they expect to get out of a roaming hunter if they *did* believe her? She knew quite a bit about the nomadic hunters that roamed the edges of the Nation, being acquaintances of several, and those hunters really did not know much about the People at all. Nor did they care, to be honest, as long as they had free access to the game and a market for what they killed.

Certainly they knew nothing about the Mountain stronghold; not where it was, not what it looked like, not how many people lived there—nothing that would be at all useful to the Karsites. Exchanges of carcasses—and bones for the lammergeyers—for money were made at remote sentry points; that was the closest anyone not of the People was allowed to get.

So what did these Karsite lunatics expect to get out of "Sira, the lone hunter?" Were they *that* deluded that they thought the People gave access to their stronghold to just anyone who happened to live within the lands they claimed?

Well . . . they might be.

Certainly the Karsites had proven themselves to be remarkably ignorant of the ways of the Nation before.

In which case, she could shortly expect brutality when mere deprivation did not gain the information the Karsites wanted.

And when they tried brutality, they would *certainly* discover that she was not a mere hunter. Because, if she looked at things dispassionately, the simple ability to endure brutality would probably convince them she was a Sleepgiver, so why endure it passively? And while in theory she could pretend to break and give them false information, *that* would convince them that she was a Sleepgiver as well, and then, well, she could imagine a lot of fates they'd consign her to and none of them were good.

No, allowing them to do what they wanted to her was not an option she'd have taken even if she thought that doing so would allow her to escape. Which it definitely would not.

So her best course of action was to go ahead and reveal herself while she still had an advantage; she had that advantage right now because she could use this cell as her high ground. It was the best she could do, under the circumstances. Access to the cell was limited to the door. They were unlikely to unleash any of their demons on her inside this structure—if she had been informed correctly, they couldn't do it by day in the first place, and in the second place, the creatures were known to be indiscriminate, and would attack anything, friend or foe, that was in their immediate vicinity. And that was assuming that either of the Karsite priests was able to summon their demons at all. She was under the impression that this was an elite ability, limited to a fraction of the priests, and she couldn't see such elites being wasted on a desert prison.

Even if they did think she was a Sleepgiver.

All things being equal . . . when (not if) they made their move, she thought she was ready for them. What she *hoped* was that they would simply allow the guards free access to her, to do as they pleased. If that happened . . . that would be the best possible thing for her. Not *good*, but the best possible course out of many that were much worse.

At least she thought she had found the right place in the binding spell on the first of the bronze talismans to stick a proverbial "spike." And if whatever was in there did not immediately turn on her—

Her head went up, thoughts interrupted, as she heard a single set of boots on the stone outside the door, and the key turning in the lock.

One Karsite, one of the guards she was familiar with by now, entered the cell and locked the door behind himself. Big, muscular, bearded. Clearly thought himself to be quite the man. She pretended to shrink back into the corner as he strolled toward her. "Well, little rabbit," he said, smirking. "They gave me some orders about you. Said they'd give me a turn of the glass with you all alone and see if I couldn't persuade you to be more cooperative."

She was coiled up as tightly as a spring. He had moved to within a hands-breadth of her feet. He pulled off his belt with its weapons and pouches, dropped it to the floor, and took his eyes off her for a half a breath to loosen his trews.

And that was when she uncoiled, lashing out and up with both feet together, smashing both of them into his crotch with all the considerable power of her legs.

His mouth gaped, he gasped for breath and *started* to double over. *Started*, because she'd already pulled her legs under her and launched her head at his chin, lashing out with the heel of her right hand at the same time to smash his larynx. Her hand connected first, her head second, as he was already starting to topple backward.

He collapsed, choking, eyes bulged, and the back of his head hit the floor with a solid—and wet—*thud*.

He immediately went into spasms.

But she was already moving again.

She wasted no time, pulling his trews down around his ankles before he fouled them, pulling his tunic up to his armpits a moment later. And predictably, he voided his bowels and bladder moments later, but by that time she had gotten his boots and trews off, saving them as well as the tunic.

Working quickly, she stripped him of everything but his soiled breeks, found the keys, dragged him over to the door and out onto the landing, then retreated to her cell to make the most of her time with her loot. By the time that "turn of the glass" was done, and his fellows came up to see what he'd done with her (and maybe get a turn with her themselves), she'd turned part of that sack they'd given her into a comfortable breechcloth and breast-wrap, used the rest to bind the bottoms of the trews tight around her calves, pulled on the tunic and shortened the arms, stuffing the excess into the toes of the boots, and belted the lot tight. She waited for them with a smile on her face and knives in both hands, standing where they could see her from the door.

But of course, the first thing they saw was their very dead comrade, stripped of everything but his shitty, soaked underwear. Their eyes followed the wet red streak on the floor from his head to where he'd died in the cell. And *then* their eyes tracked up to see her.

"Hello, boys," she said in Karsite. "Want to play a game? Your friend did, and lost."

"Vkandis' Cock!" choked one, and slammed and locked the door. Which didn't matter, she had the keys anyway.

There was a lot of movement, then quiet. She reckoned they'd decided to retreat, probably carrying the dead body of their comrade with them. She took a moment to use a scrap of cloth to clean up the piss and shit from the floor and pitched the rag down the latrine-hole. When no one appeared immediately, she kept one ear tuned for the sounds of footsteps in the stairwell while she took stock of her loot.

Besides the clothing and the two fighting knives, she had a pouch with a horn spoon and a small eating knife in it, another with some extremely welcome dried meat, a third with a set of knucklebones and some coppers and a couple of silvers. There had been some extra rawhide thongs laced to the belt that would come in handy as well. The belt was a single piece of leather long enough to go around the waist twice, then pull tight through a set of double iron rings. The boots were strong, soft, and well-made; either the Karsites issued their guards with extremely good boots, or he'd done the sensible thing and invested good money in a pair himself.

When she finally heard shouting and babbling at the foot of the stairs, she readied herself, moved a little closer to the door, and ran over her plan in her mind as many times as they gave her, while the guards decided what they were going to do. She listened closely to the boots on the stairs, visualizing who was coming up, and in what order, and how many.

A very big man in the front, followed by two more, trailed by a third. So, just four. She stepped to one side of the door; it crashed open, and the first man charged through with a roar—

Only to land flat on his face as she tripped him. At the same time, she plunged her right-hand knife into the throat of the second man as he got all tangled up with the third, both of them trying to get through the door at the same time. He dropped his sword to bring his right hand to his throat, she grabbed the sword before it had fallen more than a finger-breadth and slashed up and back across the inside wrist of the third man's sword-hand, cutting it down to the bone, slashing arteries and tendons. They both staggered backward, blundering into the fourth man, giving her just enough time to stab the man on the floor in the back before the second man dropped to the floor outside the cell, gurgling and choking on his own blood. The sword dropped from the hand of the man with the severed wrist, and he began screaming, clutching at his wrist as blood poured from it. The fourth man stared at her in total shock, then she got him in the eye with her left-hand dagger. Then she finished the third by half-decapitating him with the sword.

They were all still in the process of dying as she stripped them of everything, throwing it all into the cell, taking the tunics and partial armor by simply cutting it off them. She dragged the first man out onto the landing and left him with the others, then slammed the door shut again, panting.

And she stood there, still as a stone, listening. She was certain that if the Karsite priests were able to scry, they'd been watching the whole thing—so she painted a feral, half-mad grin on her face as she listened.

And as she listened, once again, she took mental inventory. Four belts with pouches, daggers and sheathes, and sword sheaths. A metal breastplate from the first man through the door—which hadn't done him much good since she'd stabbed him in the back. Four swords. Four half-helms. Four sliced-up and blood-soaked tunics—which was all right, since she had a decent set of clothing now, and had other plans for the tunics as well as for the belts. It was a pity she hadn't had time to get the trews, but . . . oh well.

Now they knew exactly what they were up against, so far as sheer fighting ability was concerned. They knew they'd never be able to pry her from this cell, because the very construction of it meant no more than one man at a time could come at her through that door, and that was suicide.

Their next move would probably be to catch her sleeping. They already knew they couldn't starve her out, nor make her go mad with thirst, though she doubted they had any idea yet how she was managing to do "without food and water." So their only chance at taking her would be to wait until she fell asleep from sheer exhaustion.

But they didn't know Sleepgivers.

They didn't know she could get enough rest packed into short stints; that she could divide a good night's sleep into small packets spaced throughout the day and night. They also didn't know that she could set a little spell to jar her awake the moment something as small as a mouse moved in that stairwell.

They already feared her now, but their masters would probably force them to make one more try, tonight, when they thought she was asleep. And when that foray was over, the guards, at least, would be gibbering in terror at the idea of going up against her, and not even the threat of a demon would make them move.

Finally, when there was not so much as a whisper of sound in the stairwell, she turned her attention to the pouches on the belts. More of the same; dried meat, money, a couple of amulets that obviously had not done their owners any good, a whetstone (that was useful!), more thongs, a pot of hair pomade (someone had been a dandy), a firestarter.

Having made her inventory, she sat down in her corner and cut up the tunics into careful, even strips, winding some of the cleanest around her feet until she had crude stockings that made her feet fit the boots properly, and laying the rest aside. Then she waited until night, then apported a loaf of bread, did the same with the dried meat, and had herself the best meal she'd eaten since she came here. *Then* she took off the boots and unwrapped her feet. What she would do next required bare toes.

She put herself into short-sleep.

The alarm spell jarred her awake immediately. She had arranged all but two of the daggers on her belt before she went to sleep; now she put one between her teeth, held the other in her left hand, the best of the swords in her right, and scrambled, lizardlike, up the wall to end up perched on the stone lintel above the door. They probably had no idea when they'd constructed their prison door that they were basically giving someone like a Sleepgiver a perch as comfortable as a full window ledge. She waited there, in the dark, as four more men crept up the stairs, probably thinking they were as silent as owls.

Beneath her, the door swung slowly open. And light poured in from the torches they had brought with them.

Because of course they did. Idiots.

She immediately slitted her eyes to keep from being blinded by the light. And as the first man crossed the threshold, she dropped on his shoulders.

Since he was hunched over, she drove him to the ground, hitting the stone with his chin, and she rolled away to stand up against the wall beside the door, as the torch he'd carried in his off-hand fell into the cell and lay there guttering. The second man—they'd learned not to crowd the door at least—waved his torch wildly about inside, completely blinding himself as to where she was until she stabbed him under his arm quillons-deep with her sword. She left the sword in him as he fell, spun out of the way as the third man flailed at her, and the first man got to his feet just in time to get hit by his own man as he flailed with his sword. The first man screamed when the sword caught him across the bicep, and she got him in the throat with her dagger, got the dagger out of her teeth with her right hand, bound the third man's sword with her right-hand dagger, and punched him in the throat with her left hand. He fell back against the fourth man as she snatched sword and torch out of the third man's hands, thrust the torch into the fourth man's eyes, and kicked him down the stairs. He landed on his back with a sickening *crack* about halfway down, and didn't move.

Once again, she stripped what she could from the three men she could reach, shoved their bodies out of the cell, and slammed the door.

Inventory could wait until morning.

Three times that alarm spell jogged her awake. Each time she called out something mocking, like, "You're not as stealthy as you think you are," or, "Are you really sure you want an early grave?" Each time she heard hasty retreats down the stairs, then went back to her special Sleepgiver doze.

She woke with the dawn and took inventory, then wrapped her feet again and put the boots back on. She'd taken a big risk by going barefoot the last time, but it had been the only way she could have climbed that wall. They wouldn't fall for that trick again— although she very much doubted the Karsites would be able to convince their men to make a third attempt on her—so there was no point in risking her feet in a fight. If any of them were smart enough to concentrate on stomping hard on a bare foot with their hard-soled boots, they'd break every bone in it and disable her. And at that point she could easily be overrun.

The loot this time was three more breastplates, three half-helms, three tunics, six daggers, three swords. Quite the embarrassment of riches when it came to weapons, even if they were dead average work. Also three torches. No more personal goods; these men had properly prepared for a fight. In their minds, they weren't guards anymore, they were soldiers confronting an armed and dangerous enemy, and they were preparing themselves accordingly.

The breastplates were fundamentally useless to her, unless she wanted to use one as a shield, which she didn't. That wasn't a style Sleepgivers trained in. But having them meant that her enemies *didn't*, and that had been reason enough to take them. Most prison guards didn't go armored; there was no reason to. So it might just be she currently held most of the armor in the building in her cell.

Maybe.

If she was lucky.

Well, the breastplates and the half-helms were useful for one thing at least. She piled them up against the door, where anyone rushing in would have to stumble over them. So if for some reason her alarm spell didn't wake her, the clamor of people stumbling over loose hunks of metal would.

I'd give a great deal to have that ability Cousin Mags has, to see the thoughts of others. She would love to know what the Karsite priests were thinking.

Well, if wishes were fishes, she could feast for a year.

She turned her attention to the belts.

They were all alike; long leather straps with twin rings on the end; no buckles, no holes. . . . ideal for her purposes. But she would have to be very careful with them; she couldn't risk ruining a single finger-length of them.

If she actually *thought* about what she'd just been through, things would be very bad . . . but she'd been trained to keep her emotions under tight control until the moment it was safe to let go of them. So instead of reacting, she went on with the next logical thing: putting a good edge on every single one of the weapons she had. Water and the whetstone; an exercise that was as calming as it was useful. And if the Karsites were scrying her, they'd see her sitting there apparently at her ease, calmly sharpening steel, as if contemplating all the throats she intended to cut.

What she was actually contemplating was if eight leather belts was going to give her the length she needed to climb down from this cell on the outside of the tower. If she cut them in half lengthwise and spliced them together, she was pretty certain she'd get within dropping distance of the ground, even if she didn't get all the way there. For her purposes that was quite near enough. She had no idea how she was going to get out of that cell window, but one thing at a time. Make her leather "rope," attach one of those helms to it to hold it across the bars, that was the first thing to be done. No, the second thing. The first thing was to get a good enough edge on one of these daggers to be able to slice the belts in a controlled manner.

And she was going to need time to do that, and more time to slice the belts. Preferably without anyone observing her.

So. It was just after noon. Now was the moment to see if there was anything to these ancient Talismans, or if whatever had been bound to them was too weak to do anything when released.

She paused long enough to take off her necklace, as if to adjust it, and removed the Talisman she'd been studying the longest. She put the necklace back on, and surreptitiously tossed the Talisman halfway into the cell. Then she created her little magical "spike," a kind of "immovable object," waited for the binding spell to cycle around to the right "place," and drove the "spike" in the "hole."

Then she put up the best magical shields she knew how to create and waited, sharpening a dagger the entire time.

Disrupting a magic spell in this manner was not instantaneous. And since she was behind her shield, she really couldn't "see" the tension building up as the spell strained against the thing that was blocking it. All she could do was wait. But eventually, things would build to the breaking point and the spell would shatter, and when it did. . . .

She had finished one edge of the first dagger and was working on the opposite edge when the spell broke.

For someone who did not have the ability to see magic, there was just a little glint of light on the floor where the Talisman lay, as if the sun had reflected from it for a moment. But for someone who did—the cell filled with a blinding flash. And her ears popped. And her shields bowed, and nearly broke.

But you didn't have to be able to see magic to see what rose up out of the floor, uncoiling and unfolding out of nothingness. *That* was visible to anyone who had the eyes to see it.

And with a shock to the heart, she knew what it was immediately.

A water *afrinn,* a creature of spirit with an affinity for water.

It was transparent, made of living water, faintly tinged green. It looked like a finned serpent with the needle-toothed, multi-antennaed, spike-spined, blind-eyed head of a nightmare.

And it was staring straight at *her.*

If I don't drop my shields, she realized, *it will think I am an enemy. But if I do drop my shields, it can tear me to shreds before I can blink if it so chooses.*

On the other hand, you can't bind an afrinn *without its consent. So maybe it didn't think it was going to be bound for centuries, but it volunteered to be bound in the first place . . .*

She stood up and dropped her shields.

The *afrinn* flashed across the space between them instantly and hovered there, its teeth so close to her face you could barely have inserted a piece of paper between them, staring into her eyes with its blank, featureless orbs.

"I did not bind you," she said softly, in the language of the Nation. "But I did release you, and I am sorry it has been so long that you have been bound. I am sure whoever did bind you in the past never intended that. Your Talisman was lost, and I only recently found it and discovered how to break the binding spell."

It continued to stare, saying nothing, unmoving and apparently unmoved.

Oh, of course.

"Take your freedom," she said. "But be wary, there are magic walls about this place, and everyone inside it but me is your enemy. And if you feel any gratitude to me, you will take out your ire at having been bound for so long on them. They certainly deserve it, for I am as surely their prisoner as you were imprisoned in that Talisman."

For one more moment, it stared at her, as if it had not heard a word she had said.

Then in the next moment, it uncoiled and flashed across the cell with a splash, forcing itself under the cell door.

Then the faint screams began.

She went back to sharpening her dagger, and when it was finished, braced it between her feet, and began slowly slicing the first leather belt.

It took some turns of the glass before she felt the shields around the building suddenly drop, then come back up again. By that time, she had sliced all the belts into two equal pieces and had attempted to apport a loaf of bread.

But what had come up was soaked and inedible. And a second attempt just brought up a mound of raw dough.

She knew what must have happened at that point; the *afrinn* had been racing through the building, putting out every fire it could find, before it turned its attention to the humans and their goods. So every fire in the kitchen was dead. Every torch, out and soaked through. Every lamp, extinguished. Every fire in every fireplace, also soaked. If there was a forge and a blacksmith, those fires were out too.

And, very probably, everything in the prison that could be ruined with water, had been. All the clothing. All the bedding. All the weapons would have to be dried immediately, or they would start to rust. Herbs had surely been soaked, so seasonings and medicines and spell components had been ruined.

Which means it was thinking, *and thinking only of escape, so rather than attacking people, it was just terrifying them with the way it looks and making an utter nuisance of itself so the priests would drop the shields and let it out.*

And eventually, the priests must have gotten the idea—or resorted to dropping the shields in sheer desperation—and let it go.

The fact that the shields came right back up again was proof that the *afrinn* had merely taken the opportunity offered and sped away, probably in search of the nearest body of water in which to renew its powers and itself.

Meanwhile . . . well, the Karsites could initially have had no idea where it had come from, but they'd probably decide before very long that it had somehow been her doing. They'd probably consider it some new form of demon; so far as Sira knew, her Nation was the only one that knew about *afrinns*, which were rarely found in the mountains of their territory and were generally left alone unless the *afrinn* approached a Mage with a bargain or out of curiosity. Amber Moon certainly did not deal with them, and they were physically the closest Mage School to the Mountain. And mostly, all that the People knew of *afrinns* these days were tales and legends and those rare sightings, because the Mages of the People rarely left the safety of the Mountain.

So why had seven *afrinns* agreed to be bound into Talismans? And for what purpose? There had to have been some reason why it was advantageous for the *afrinns*.

Maybe in the long-ago past they were being hunted, and this was a way for them to be safe? Or maybe there was some other danger to them. And in return . . . there may have been an actual release to the spell, as opposed to breaking it, that would allow them to come out and help their wearer.

Speculation for another time. Right now, not only were the Karsites possessed of a "guest" who had proven to be far more dangerous than any of them had reckoned on, but now they were faced with a cold building that was getting colder, ruined food, and no way to cook it.

Hrmm. So am I.

She contemplated the stack of three torches she had set off to the side. She had a firestarter. And she had a mound of raw dough. And one of the breastplates could serve as an adequate grill to make flatbread. If only she had more wood.

She went over and picked up one of the torches, and discovered that it was nothing more than a stick of wood wrapped in oily rags. Well. . . .

She unwrapped the partially burned rags; they'd serve as kindling. Meanwhile, provided the wood for this torch had come from a common woodpile . . .

It had, and in a half turn of the glass, she'd apported enough to make a decent fire. In another half turn she had patted the dough into circles that were merrily grilling on the breastplate. By the time the dough was gone, she had a very nice pile of grilled flatbreads of the sort the People commonly made; she had extinguished the fire but had poured a half-helm worth of water from her bucket into the shallow dish of the breastplate and dropped some of the dried meat in. In the last of the twilight she feasted on bread dunked in hot broth, and hot stewed meat.

The meal tasted even better knowing that at that same moment the prison was full of miserable Karsites whose every possession had been soaked clear through and who were probably chewing soggy, cold trail biscuits instead of their usual hot dinner.

She sat down in her corner on a padding of torn tunics, knowing that, although her circumstances were far from ideal, tonight she was the most comfortable person in the prison.

———

She woke only once, alerted by the alarm spell, heard two sets of footsteps on the stairs, and called out into the darkness, "Did you enjoy the attentions of my friend? Would you like him to come back and visit you again?"

There was no answer, of course, but she had no doubt that her message would be taken straight to the priests. They might have entertained the thought that the appearance of the *afrinn* in their midst was the result of some coincidence; she had just made sure they knew exactly where it had come from. And she had planted the idea that she could call it back, even through the shields. Of course, even if she'd known how to do that, she couldn't; she didn't have the power to break through those shields to get a summons out.

But she did have six more Talismans to choose from.

I'll try Air next. Keep them guessing.

She heard footsteps—one pair—retreating down the staircase. So they'd left a guard on the door. Not that this was going to impact her in the least, since by this time she was absolutely certain there was nothing the priests could threaten their guards with to make them enter her cell. But it did suggest something more interesting.

That for some reason, they were now unable to scry her. If they had ever been able to at all. It was possible they were not Mages.

It wasn't the shields she had put up on herself—she'd never put them back up after she had taken them off to confront the *afrinn*. But the Karsites were not trained in deprivation as the Sleepgivers were, and that was doubly so for their priests. So . . . down there in the bowels of the prison were two priests wearing cold, wet, clothing, possibly sitting in front of a guttering fire that was producing more smoke than heat, too uncomfortable to do any magic at all. So they'd resorted to an ordinary pair of eyes to at least make sure she didn't creep out of the cell in the dead of night and start slaughtering them.

A delightful thought. I certainly would, if I could.

Of course, without knowing the exact layout of the place, she couldn't actually do that. But they didn't know that.

This is probably the worst night of their entire lives.

The thought made her grin with savage pleasure.

Well then, before I sleep, I wonder if I can think of any other ways to increase their misery.

10

Now that their little party was within reasonable striking distance of wherever Sira was being held, the first order of business was transportation. Sadly, there were no magical portals that would get Tory, Kee, and Ahkhan to the other side of the Karsite Border. Or, rather, if there was such a thing, it would be in Karsite hands, so, obviously, using one was not an option even if Amber Moon had had access to it. Tory and Kee had come well supplied with money by the Crown, however, and because of their parsimonious ways on the trip through Valdemar, they still had most of it left, so they put some of it in Ahkhan's hands and sent him off to get two more horses.

Or rather, Ahkhan had volunteered himself, when they had suggested the idea.

"Your pardon," he had said dryly, "But even understanding the language, I think you are neither good judges of horseflesh suitable for these parts nor good bargainers. I shall get the horses."

Tory refrained from telling the Sleepgiver that he'd had *plenty* of experience in bargaining as one of his father's agents. Because Ahkhan was right on his first point. He didn't know the first thing about horses, other than how to ride them. All the horses he and Kee had ridden back home had been the best in the kingdom, well-bred beauties from the Royal Stables. And he especially didn't know how to choose a horse for desert conditions.

Besides, while Ahkhan went off and did that, one of the Amber Moon apprentices volunteered to help get them garbed in something that wasn't going to get them shot on sight in Karse. This seemed like an excellent plan to Tory.

She took them into the little village that was attached to the school; Tory was dubious that they'd find anything in a place so small, but she brought them to a cottage that turned out to be literally *crammed* with used clothing of every description. The main room was full of stacks and stacks of neatly folded garments, with paths running among them. Tory had never seen so much clothing in one place at one time, not even in the used-clothing shops in Haven. And it was all *clean,* too; no musty smell, no scent of things left unwashed, and not even a hint of mouse. He couldn't imagine how the owner managed that.

Well, this was right near Amber Moon. A spell to repel pests and mildew, perhaps?

"This is May," the apprentice said, introducing them to the little old gray-clad woman who lived here amid the maze of clothing. "She has been outfitting travelers going through our portal for as long as she's been alive."

"And my father before me, and my grandparents before him, and back as long as Amber Moon has been here," May agreed, smiling, a smile which transformed her wrinkled face into a web of friendliness. "You're not the first to want to go somewhere without standing out, and you won't be the last. Where are you going?"

"Karse," said Tory, anticipating trouble already.

"Pfft. Pick something harder," she scoffed. "Wait right here."

She vanished into the heaps of clothing and returned with a towering armload of earth- and sand-colored fabric, which she dropped at their feet. "You'll be able to use most of the clothing you've got," she informed them. "But with Karse, at least here in the south, it's all about the wrappings and the layers. I'll show you."

And so she did. "In the desert, you have to use layers," she explained, as she fitted both Valdemarans with long, open robes of very light linen to go over their existing shirts, tunics, and breeches. "Light layers by day, heavy by night. To keep the sun off you in the day, and keep you warm in the cold desert night. To keep the sand out of the inside of your clothing. To muffle your face in during a dust storm." As she spoke, she bound the robes around their waists with long sashes, then took another such sash and wrapped it around their heads, and a third around their necks, loosely. "Wrappings to keep the sun directly off your head, wrappings to keep it off your neck; it might seem ridiculous at this moment, you might think this will make your head hotter, but I promise you, it won't. There. Now you look like proper Karsite travelers."

Tory looked at Kee, who in turn was examining him, and was astonished how much difference a little rearrangement of clothing made. To his eyes, Kee looked quite exotic, despite the fact that the difference amounted to one robe and three sashes. Surely he looked the same to Kee.

"Now, pay attention," May continued. "I'm going to show you how to do the headwrap yourself. Don't think to have it stitched together so you can take it on and off like a hat. No true Karsite would do that, and you'll give yourself away in an instant. Now, let's replace those boots with sandals. *Keep* the boots, you'll need them to ride, but if you end up going afoot for any length of time, you'll want sandals. Sand will collect in your boots and rub your feet raw; it will pour right through sandals and just leave your feet a bit dusty."

It took a couple of candlemarks of instruction and practice before May was confident they knew exactly what they were doing. She sent them off a bit poorer in the pocket but infinitely richer in knowing how to wear and move in their new outfits.

By the time they got back to Amber Moon, Ahkhan had returned with two horses. Where he had gotten them, Tory had no idea, although given that this tiny village had a person who *specialized* in clothing to make you blend in with the people down here, there was probably a farmer nearby who bred horses good for desert travel.

They encountered him, with the two new horses, just inside the gate, where they all paused so the Valdemarans could admire their new mounts.

These beasts were rather finer looking than Ahkhan's scrubby little mare, although they were small and slender compared to Valdemaran horses, with big foreheads, huge eyes, delicate muzzles, wide nostrils, arched necks and deep chests. They were gentle too; they both took to Kee immediately and lipped him delicately as a sign of their favor.

"Good stock," Ahkhan said approvingly. "If we live through this adventure, I may take them home to run with our herds. They don't have the endurance of Natya, but they have more speed in a race, and a bit of new blood will do our herds good. I am told the bay is called Aly and the chestnut is called Vesa."

At the sound of her name, Vesa transferred her attention to Tory. He scratched her forehead, and she snorted in approval, then rubbed her head against him vigorously.

"The lady has made her choice," Ahkhan observed. "Best not to try to change her mind."

"I have no intention of doing that," Tory assured him. In truth, he was very taken with the mare. She wasn't the golden palfrey he had dreamed of having as a child, but she was a charming creature.

"I have obtained provisions," Ahkhan continued. "We can leave in the morning. Crossing the Border will be . . . interesting. But if you two think you can pass yourselves off as mercenaries, there may be a way that will expose us to little more than tedium and perhaps a few bandits."

"We're decent fighters, if that's what you mean," Kee replied. "We've both trained most of our lives."

"Don't forget, my father had one of those Talismans of yours forced on him, and he absorbed a lot of your Sleepgiver tricks," Tory reminded his cousin. "And he's been training both of us in those, as well as the conventional weapon training we got from our Weaponsmaster."

"Good, good, then we will see if fortune favors us as we near the Border. For tonight, let us join the Mages for dinner, then start before daybreak." Only then did he smile slightly. "I see May has given you lessons. Come, this will be our last civilized meal. Let us enjoy it."

Tory raised an eyebrow at Kee, who nodded, and rather than going to the main building, they took the reins of their new horses from Ahkhan and followed him to the stables, where they put Aly and Vesa into stalls on either side of Natya so the horses could get used to each other. Then they removed the tack, gave the beasts a rubdown, and measured out grain and water for them under Ahkhan's approving eye. *"Now* we go eat," said Tory.

Actually, they washed up first; Amber Moon had a washing station with a long elevated trough of a sink, and pitchers of water and bars of hard soap at intervals, just outside the place where everyone ate. You had to wash up before you were allowed to enter the dining hall, which was not unlike the ones at the Collegia.

Like in the Collegia dining halls, the meal was communal, with bowls and platters of food set along the table that people passed around. The food was quite unfamiliar; instead of sliced loaves of bread, there were round, flat, grilled bread-things that served the same purpose. Not like pancakes, but like bread that had been fried like a pancake. There was a very tasty pastelike substance you were supposed to eat on the bread, barley cooked in broth with shreds of meat (mutton, Tory thought) and chopped vegetables, and some other things in smaller bowls he couldn't recognize at all but ate anyway. For drink there was a faintly astringent cold tea of some sort and honeyed fruits at the end.

Through all of this he picked up an underlying tension and impatience from Kee. He had a good idea why—Kee seemed to be taking this job of running off into Karse to rescue Ahkhan's sister very personally. And that was puzzling him, because usually he and Kee were of one mind on most things. He just didn't *understand* why Kee would feel this way. They'd done the job they'd agreed to. Ahkhan himself had said as much. The bargain was made, and the Sleepgivers would never trouble Valdemar or the Royal Family again.

So why this desire to throw both of them headlong into danger and uncertainty? Kee had never shown this sort of impetuous behavior before.

I could just ask him. . . .

I should just ask him.

He pondered that all through the meal, then waited to see if Ahkhan was going to ask them to check on his sister before they all went to bed, but he did not. Instead, he said, "They have given us those rooms we used before. Our things are all there. I will lead the way. I advise early sleep, for it will still be dark when I awaken you."

And sure enough, Ahkhan led them up to the same corridor they had been in before, except now curious lanterns that produced no heat, only light, hung on the wall all along it. Tory paused at the one just outside "his" room and peered at it. It appeared to be a glowing golden orb, merrily floating in midair inside the glass ball that held it. The ball itself hung on a bracket coming out of the wall that he hadn't noticed earlier, but when he examined the whole rig more closely, he understood why. The bracket was hinged, and had probably been folded against the wall when they had first come through here. And someone must have come along here during dinner, hanging up the glass balls with their little glowing orbs inside.

More magic! he thought, with a flush of wonder. *Well, this is a school for it. I wonder if this is something they have the beginning Mages create for practice?*

Ahkhan was already in his room and had shut the door; Tory followed Kee into his, and Kee turned to look at him in surprise.

"I just want to ask you a question," he said, before Kee could say anything. "Why did you decide without even asking me about it that we were going to help Ahkhan rescue his sister?"

"I didn't—" Kee began, indignantly. Tory interrupted him with a look.

"You did. You spoke before I had a chance to say anything, and at that point, I didn't have any choice but to back you up," he said, sternly. "And be honest, now, Kee. You spoke completely without considering what you were promising. *You* might think the fact that you're a Prince isn't all that important, but it *is* important. We're about to go barging right into the homeland of Valdemar's worst enemy, and if we're captured and the Karsites find out who you are, it's going to cause all kinds of problems. And you put me in a bad position, because you gave your word, the word of a Prince, before asking me what I thought. That left me with no choice but to agree at that point. So the least you can do is tell me *why* you are so insistent about this, when Ahkhan himself said we'd discharged our obligations."

"I—" Kee began, then deflated, and sat down heavily on his cot. He looked up at Tory woefully. "I just *have* to, is all. I don't know why. I just know I do. The idea of running back to Valdemar makes me physically ill. The idea of not doing everything we can to get Sira free makes me want to throw myself off a bridge." He sucked on his lower lip. "And before you ask, I am pretty sure nobody put any magic spells on me to make me feel this way. I don't know why anyone would—Ahkhan might welcome us along, but *he* is a Sleepgiver and we aren't, and he could probably manage just fine without us. And if he wanted us bewitched, he'd have done both of us, so neither of us would be asking any awkward questions."

Huh. "Well, all right then. That's a reason," Tory said reassuringly. "We neither of us understand it, but it's a *reason,* and that's good enough for me. Maybe we need to get closer so we can give Ahkhan an exact location for him to succeed. Or maybe we'll be needed to get him and his sister out of Karse. For all I know, you've got a touch of Foresight, just enough to know that things will go badly if we're not there. So we'll go."

Kee looked up at him with gratitude. "I should have known you'd back me up," he said gratefully. "I should have talked to you first."

Tory knuckled the side of Kee's head. "Yes, you should have, and don't do that again. Now get to sleep. I'll be doing the same. Don't snore!"

"I never—" Kee began indignantly, but Tory closed his door, cutting off his protest.

———

Ahkhan was as good as his word; he woke them at an unholy time of the morning, even before false dawn. There wasn't anyone else awake in the entire school except the kitchen staff, who stuffed them full of fresh, hot bread, fried eggs, and fresh milk before sending them on their way to the stables.

It was *cold.* Granted, it was late fall, but the day before had been warm. Now he was very grateful for the long robe, and the woolen cloak to wear over it all. *Layers.* May was right. All these layers were warmer than one single thick cloak of fur.

They saddled their horses, and Ahkhan distributed the supplies he had bought into packs he tied on behind all three of their saddles. "Wear your weapons openly," he said. "We are mercenaries now. We escorted a party here to Amber Moon, and now we are looking for another party or caravan to hire us."

Tory nodded; it was a simple story, one that they could count on Amber Moon to verify, one that their well-worn weapons would back up at a glance. The gate guards let them out and closed the gates of the Mage-School behind them. Tory looked back with regret. If Ahkhan's quest were not so urgent—or if Kee hadn't volunteered them both to help—he'd have stayed a few more days before returning to Valdemar, hoping to see more magic. Not that the Portal wasn't impressive all by itself! It was! But . . . it would have been nice to see some more wonders.

Ahkhan took them due east, rather than east and north, which was the direction he and Kee had indicated. Tory had no idea why, but Ahkhan had mentioned finding a caravan, so perhaps this was a trade road, where you'd expect to find such things.

The horses didn't much like traveling in the dark, but perked up considerably when false dawn gave them enough light to see by. They picked up their pace, then, and Tory was relieved to discover that his mare, at least, had a smooth, pleasant gait. He had not been looking forward to mastering the punishing style of Ahkhan's Natya.

But, as when they had traveled through Valdemar, Ahkhan was determined to drive an unrelenting pace. They only stopped at noon—when the air had warmed enough that he'd removed his cloak, rolled it up, and tied it on the packs behind him—and that was just to water the horses at a well with an attendant dressed almost exactly as they were, whom they paid for the privilege. The traveler's rations Ahkhan had gotten were semi-familiar; hard traveler's biscuit, dried meat, hard cheese that would keep well without spoiling, not like his bars of whatever-it-was, and they ate while the horses slowly drank, Slowly, because Ahkhan directed them to pull the horses' heads up frequently to keep them from drinking too quickly. When the horses had drunk, Ahkhan directed them to drink their fill and refill their water bottles at the well. The attendant just watched them like a hawk, as if he thought they were going to drink more water than they had paid for.

Then they were off again. And sunset brought them into strange country indeed.

They had been winding their way through very dry hills, covered in scrub bushes of unfamiliar varieties and strange plants that Tory did not recognize at all. The road now took them through a narrow, deep, dry canyon of red-streaked rocks worn smooth in a way that suggested they had been cut by running water, although there was not a drop of water to be seen. *Could it be wind instead? Could the wind have done this? Or is it just that these rocks are so old that the water that did this was . . . millennia ago?*

The canyon wound and turned like a snake, making it impossible to see very far ahead of them or much more than a slit of sky overhead. It was weird and beautiful and like nothing Tory had ever seen before. The wind sang in the curves and whistled overhead. It felt like an adventure, at last.

Eventually the canyon let them out onto a flat plain covered with the most amazing rock formations that Tory had ever seen in his life.

Like the canyon, they were streaked and layered in red, orange, and yellow. And they looked for all the world like towers of pebbles carefully cemented together by some mad artist. There were other formations, too, but those were the ones Tory couldn't take his eyes off.

All he could think was . . . *oooh.*

Ahkhan noticed his wonder. "We call these rocks *hoodoos,*" he said. "There are all manner of legends about them. Some say they were made by the gods when the gods were children, playing a game to see how high they could stack pebbles. Some say they are all that is left of an army of demons, turned to stone by a great hero Mage. Some say they are the remains of a clan of evil people who were turned to stone by the gods for their misdeeds. And some say they are the chimneys of creatures that dwell in a labyrinth beneath our feet."

"What do *you* think?" Tory asked, finally managing to get some actual words out.

Ahkhan laughed. "I think that one need look no further than water, wind, and sand. All of this around us is sandstone, easily cut by water, easily scoured by windblown sand. Some layers are harder than others. And I think the gods have other things to do than play with pebbles, even gods that are children."

"What about turning evil people to stone?" Kee asked.

"Possible but unlikely," Ahkhan said dismissively. "If such things were likely, there would be more pillars of stone in the world than people."

I can't argue with that, Tory thought. "Well, where do we go from here?" he asked aloud.

"There is a watered place with grazing and a spring not far from here, still on the right side of the Border. It is the final stopping place for most caravans going into Karse. We will camp there tonight, you will try to see my sister, and we will see if we are in luck and there is already a caravan there. Most caravans are always willing to take on another few guards, as so few mercenaries are willing to go into Karse."

Looking around him, Tory was exceptionally skeptical that there could be any water at all, much less the sort of haven Ahkhan had described, anywhere in this arid land. And yet, a half a candlemark later, the road brought them to a box canyon so lush and inviting he would have thought it was in Valdemar, not out in the middle of the desert. There was ankle-high grass, verdant bushes, even real trees, with a tiny stream cutting through it all and meandering out among the hoodoos. And at the back of the canyon, a clear, deep pond, deep enough that the water was a lovely blue, and wide enough for fifty horses to drink without jostling each other. Birds sang in the trees and flitted among the bushes. Tory thought he had never seen anything so peaceful.

And, to Ahkhan's disappointment, it was completely empty of humans. "Ah, well, we will see what the morrow brings," he said. "Meanwhile, we have our choice of resting places. Do you know how to picket horses?"

"Not at all," Kee confessed.

"Then I will show you, and we will make camp, and you will see what you may see."

It turned out that there were a lot of rules about this place, which Ahkhan explained as they set up camp. The horses were allowed to eat their fill of the grass but could not touch the bushes. Humans were not allowed to pull up armloads of grass to make a soft bed; if you wanted a soft bed, you could flatten the grass, or you could find a sandy patch and make a sort of dish for yourself. They were not allowed to hunt anything within the canyon. "Out there, yes," Ahkhan told them, waving at the desert beyond the canyon walls. "Not here. This is a refuge for all things, and that includes wild ones. This is water-peace, and it is near sacred. No fighting, no stealing, and certainly no killing."

"Just who enforces this?" Kee wanted to know.

"A desert tribe that lays claim to this place. They are even more secretive than the Sleepgivers. There are three of them watching us now."

"What?" said Kee, looking wildly all around.

Ahkhan shook his head. "Give over. You will never see them. But they certainly see you. They are also masters of magic. They might not be able to turn someone into a stone for violating water-peace, but anyone who dares to be so foolish as to break the peace will find they have many ways of making their displeasure known. Not even a Sleepgiver would take a target here. But that means we need not set a guard tonight and may sleep as soundly as in one of your Waystations. And when we leave, we will leave a tribute of money for them to take."

Kee kept peering up at the tops of the canyon walls around them, trying to spot the watchers. Tory saw no reason to doubt his cousin and didn't try.

They watered the horses first, then moved them to a patch of ground with knee-high, rather than ankle-high, grass, and Ahkhan showed them both how to tie the beasts up so that they could graze freely without getting loose and running if they were spooked. "And my Natya will be lead mare and will keep them calm regardless," he added matter-of-factly.

They made their beds up nearby. Ahkhan cautioned them again not to tear up armfuls of grass merely to make their sleeping spot softer, nor break off branches from the bushes to do the same. "And we will not have a fire," he added. "There is no need, and fuel is scarce in the desert. Unless," he added, "You have no objection to hunting for dried dung to make a fire with."

"What?" Kee exclaimed. "You do that?"

"All desert peoples do."

"We don't really have anything to cook, and we should be warm enough without a fire," Kee finally said after a moment of thought.

"Good." Ahkhan sat down on his bed and nodded approvingly. "This is how you prosper in the desert. Waste nothing." He opened his pack and took out his waterskin. "Oh, it is permitted to swim, but take some water, go far enough away from the pond that you will not contaminate it, and make yourself clean first."

"That sounds like a good idea, without the swimming part. It's already getting chilly." Tory suited his words to actions, got a leather bucket and a tiny sliver of soap, went off to the back of the canyon, and cleaned himself up. It was . . . a bit uncomfortable, knowing that *someone* was certainly watching him, but if that was the price of sleeping undisturbed, he'd pay it. He made sure to take his bucket bath where some trees would get the benefit of the water.

When he got back to their little encampment, Kee and Ahkhan's damp hair suggested that they'd followed his example.

They ate, and watched the light dim—quickly, a lot faster than he was used to—and the stars come out. And the stars were amazing. They seemed so bright and so near that Tory fancied if he climbed up one of those cliffs, he could touch them.

And that was when they heard it. A long, low whistle, off to the right. It was followed by another to the left. Then a third, behind them.

By this time it was too dark to see each other except as shadows, but

Tory looked over at Ahkhan anyway. "That's not a bird," he stated.

"No, it's our watchers," his cousin agreed. "They are making themselves known to us, which means they now trust us to behave ourselves and keep the water-peace."

"That's . . . reassuring. I guess," said Kee, and yawned. "Are we getting up before dawn is even a thought again?"

"No need. We'll wait one day for a caravan. If one doesn't find us here, we'll look ahead on the road. And if we still don't find one, we will chance crossing the Border on our own." Ahkhan paused. "Can you look to see anything of my sister now?"

"We'll look." Kee sounded as if the prospect had shaken all thoughts of sleep out of his head.

It took almost no time to locate her tonight—although "locate" was about all he could do. It was as dark in her cell as it was out here in the desert; she was tucked in a corner and apparently sleeping sitting up. The one big change was that--as far as he could tell in the dark—she was wearing actual clothing instead of that sack she'd been in before. And she seemed to have things piled around her.

He said as much when he emerged from the trance. "Do you suppose this means the Karsites are treating her better?" he asked, as Ahkhan's silence on being told this stretched into uncomfortable territory.

"I do not know what to think," he said, finally. "It could mean that they are treating her better. It could also mean that she took the clothing from one of her guards, in which case they now know she is fully capable of killing an armed man while she is fundamentally naked."

Tory didn't say *She can do that?* because he knew very well his father probably could, and there was no reason why Sira couldn't do the same.

And he wasn't naive. He knew very well what would make an imprisoned woman decide it was worth revealing what she was and kill one of her guards.

"Do you think they realize she's a Sleepgiver?" he asked.

"Well. Since I believe she was ambushed precisely because she was coming from our stronghold and they were already thinking she at least knew something about us, I am fairly confident that yes, they know." Ahkhan went silent again. "She has the high ground. She is in a stone cell, and they can only come at her, one at a time, through the door. So the only way she will leave that cell is if she wills it."

Kee's voice rose with alarm. "Can't they starve her out? And she can't have access to water—"

"Ah, but she does," Ahkhan assured him. "She is a Mage as well as a Sleepgiver. All she needs is to have a bit of food or water and she can use that to *apport* more from the source. No, she is secure enough. "

"Then why are we bothering to go rescue her?" Tory demanded, a bit angrily. In fact, he was of more than half a mind to saddle up the horses and ride right straight back to Valdemar the hard way if he had to!

"Tory—" interjected Kee.

"If she can do *everything*, why does she even need us?"

"Tory—" Kee repeated more urgently.

He was just getting started. "I mean—"

"Peace," said Ahkhan, holding up his hand. "I understand you. And no, she cannot do *everything.* She can hold her own, but if she could have escaped, she would have by now. Yes, she is a Mage, but . . . she is a sort of *bag of tricks* Mage, if you take my meaning. She knows how to do a few things that serve her well, and she has deeply studied our Talismans, but even an apprentice of Amber Moon could best her in a magical confrontation. I am certain that should they unleash enough of their demons on her, she could not survive. And yes, she is a Sleepgiver, but you know yourself that our abilities are suited to ambush and murder, not actual combat. We— *I*—am going to help her, because even if she somehow escapes the prison, she will not escape pursuit, and because she is no match for a single heavily armed man in the open, much less a group of them, and still less so an armed force backed by demons."

Tory subsided, all his anger running out of him. "Oh . . . "

"And if you wish to turn back at this moment, I will not prevent you," Ahkhan continued. "We *are* going into an enemy land, your enemy as well as mine. This is not your cause. A few drops of shared blood does not make it so."

"We're staying," Kee said firmly before Tory could reply.

"I am . . . relieved," said Ahkhan. "I am but one man, and a Sleepgiver. Like Sira, my training is not for direct confrontation."

Tory rolled his eyes, but . . . to be honest, now that Ahkhan had explained things a little more, he was beginning to feel like Kee. Not because he felt the pressing need to rescue Sira, but because he was beginning to like Ahkhan very much, and he didn't want to think of him going out there to rescue Sira alone. And now he understood his father's ambivalence about Ahkhan's own father, Beshat. Ahkhan was honest, reliable, *trustworthy*, and charming.

And a cold-blooded murderer for money.

Which was used to support the needs of his people.

But nevertheless—

Argh.

"I thank you both, for Sira's sake," Ahkhan said simply. "And I thank you for relieving my mind about her this evening. Good night."

And with that, he lay down and rolled up in his blankets, for all the world as if this were a peaceful camping excursion.

Tory, however, stared up at the stars for a very long time, trying, and failing, to sort out his own confused mind.

———

In the light of predawn, he half-woke, saw someone squatting in the grass at his feet, and came completely awake with a yell of alarm that awoke both his companions.

"Peace!" Ahkhan said immediately, putting out a restraining hand as Tory fumbled for his dagger. "This is one of our hosts." The Sleepgiver managed a half-bow from the tangle of his bedroll, which the figure returned.

Tory shivered in the cold air of predawn, which did not seem to affect their host in the least, even though the man was naked to the waist, wearing only a pair of leather trews and a breechcloth of leather. His head was shaved, and his body had been painted in irregular stripes of red and ocher. He held a sort of spear in one hand, and he had a bow across his back and a quiver of arrows at his side.

"Greetings, guests," the man replied, in the tongue of Menmellith, but with an odd, lyrical accent. "I come to invite you to break your fast with us. There is hare and fruit."

Fruit? At this time of the year? Tory was eager to find out more, and equally eager to eat something besides traveler's biscuits, so he was glad when Ahkhan accepted for all three of them.

They simply got up and left their blankets and possessions where they lay and followed the man to the front of the canyon, where a small fire burned and the bodies of several hares roasted on spits above and around it, making efficient use of every bit of heat and flame. Along with the four men who awaited them there, there were four unhooded hawks of a kind Tory had never seen before, jessed and on perches stuck into the ground. They were handsome birds, lean, mostly a very dark brown, with lighter brown on their shoulders and black-tipped white tailfeathers. Tory was intrigued that they were not trying to attack one another, even though they were completely unhooded.

All four men were dressed like the first, except for one who had a small deer pelt as a kind of cape fastened over one shoulder and under the opposite arm.

"Peace to you," said Ahkhan. "And thanks for your hospitality."

"You and your friends are mannered, Sleepgiver, and we had more hare than we needed," said the first man. "Better to share than to waste."

Tory was shocked at first that they knew what Ahkhan was—then he realized that if they were the night guards, they had probably been able to hear every word spoken from their hiding places on the cliffs.

"Sit, eat. There will likely be a caravan; this afternoon, tonight at the latest," said the man wearing the deer pelt. "May you prosper against the demon-priests," he added, and spat off to one side, ceremoniously.

They took a seat and accepted portions of hare and some odd, reddish fruits that looked nothing like anything Tory had ever seen before, red-skinned, green-fleshed, a kind of oval lump with spines here and there which the others were snapping off with the flats of their blades. He watched the others cut off the ends, slit the side, and peel off a thick rind before eating the core. He did the same. It tasted like slightly sweet cucumber. Or maybe melon. It went very well with the gamey hare.

They all ate in silence, but it wasn't an uncomfortable silence—more like the silence of men who are accustomed to saying few words and keeping their own counsel. Tory would have liked, very much, to ask them about their lives, but their manner made it clear that such questions would be impolite. It was enough that they had been given this brief time with their hosts.

When the last of the hare had been eaten, and the guts and heads fed to the hawks, who ate until their crops bulged, the first man stood up while the others quickly cleaned up the area until it was pristine again and took up their hawks on their leather-guarded wrists. "It is time for us to go. At about noon, go you there—" he pointed to something that was broader than a hoodoo but looked to have been shaped in the same way, that stood opposite them at the mouth of the canyon. "Climb it, and let yourself be seen. If the caravan master needs you, he will hail you down. If he does not, do not importune him; either remain in your camp or go on your way."

Ahkhan bowed to him, and he returned the salutation. "For the food, for the hearth, for the words, our thanks."

"By your words and your manners, be welcome," said the man, and the five of them turned and walked away.

"They didn't even ask us our names!" Tory said, astonished.

"It's not their way," replied Ahkhan. "And not one traveler in a hundred who stops here will ever see them. We're lucky. This is my second time to share hearth and food with them. I think they respect

Sleepgivers as being not unlike them, a fellow desert people."

He motioned to the two of them with his head, and they all moved back to their campsite. "I hope one of you two can climb," he said. "We'll need to be up on that rock up there at noon."

Tory just smiled. He had the feeling that he and Kee were finally going to impress Ahkhan with something.

II

Sira stood nose-to-nose with what she could only assume was an *afrinn* of air.

It barely fit in the cell with her; it was a winged and feathered creature with a long tail of two elaborate, curved plumes, an equally long neck that was bowed in an absurd curve to put the creature's reptilian head on the same level as hers, and it looked as if it were made of blue glass.

She had waited quite a while before breaking the binding spell on the second Talisman; she wanted to make the most of every bit of advantage she got from each creature she released. It was only when she'd awakened to hear cautious whispering down at the bottom of the staircase that she decided to release the second *afrinn* rather than take the chance that she might not be able to handle a third invasion of her cell.

This time she'd dropped her shields as soon as the initial energy of the release was gone and stood up to meet the creature on its own terms. Now it regarded her with the same blank stare as its predecessor had.

Which was, of course, much better than being attacked outright.

"I am very, very sorry you were imprisoned for so long," she said softly. "I am sure it was due to mere human forgetfulness rather than malice, but nevertheless, I apologize deeply for the neglect. Now I give you your freedom—" she paused, and steeled her nerves, because this next could go *very* wrong "—but I myself am imprisoned here at the will of an enemy of your kind and mine. And if you should choose to work out some of your entirely understandable anger on them, even past the point where they drop the shields holding you in here, I would be very grateful."

The glassy eyes stared into hers for a very long time indeed. But it didn't seem to take offense at anything she had said, which was promising.

Then, when the silence had gone on for so long that she wondered if the creature had understood her at all, it dipped its head a little to her. She bowed to it—and then, in a rush of wind that nearly knocked her off her feet, it was gone.

And screams erupted from the stairwell, screams that, this time, did not fade as if the screamers were running, but rather, were cut off abruptly, as if something quite bad had happened to them.

One can only hope, she thought with grim satisfaction. After all, there were children's tales that suggested that the *afrinns* of air could suck the breath right out of your body and keep it from returning.

Well, whether it did that or not, she suspected the garrison of this prison, and the priests in it, were in for a lively time.

As for her, she occupied herself with apporting a couple of loaves of fresh bread before the *afrinn* blew out the fires in the kitchen. Or blew *on* them, making them much hotter, and burning the bread that was in the ovens to cinders, and rendering anything else that was cooking inedible.

At this moment, oddly enough, with the *afrinn* fully occupying the Karsites, the worst thing she faced as long as it was raging around the prison was . . . worry. She had adequate food and water, and she was clothed properly now. Her limited number of spells useful in this situation was pretty much spent. She couldn't see much out of her windows. And she still hadn't come up with a way to get past the bars on the windows and let herself down with her leather "rope." Nor did she have a good idea of how to get away from here without being run down by guards on horseback. It was impossible to say how large the garrison here was, and coming at her mounted would be a good way for them to wear her down and take minimal damage themselves. She was secure for the moment, but *she* could think of one way they could eliminate her, if they gave up on getting information from her. All they had to do was clear the garrison out and turn their demons loose in here after darkness fell. Problem solved.

I hope they don't think of that.

To add to her concerns, for the last week or so, at least, she would have been willing to stake money on the fact that *someone* was trying to make mental contact with her. Mental, as in mind-to-mind, and Mind-magic rather than the sort of magic she was familiar with. And that was . . . strange. The Sleepgivers were not given to such powers and honestly had no way to train anyone in them, so it wasn't someone from home. The only nonworrying aspect of this was that the Karsites *absolutely* did not have anyone with those powers; her father had told her that they would identify children with mental and magical abilities in early childhood, murder the former, and train the latter in the priesthood.

And truth to be told, every time she did feel that brush of another mind, the contact wasn't threatening. In fact, it was reassuring. It felt as though someone was desperately worried for her and trying to reassure her.

And curiously enough, the contact left the image of a handsome young man lingering in her thoughts. And not one whom she had ever seen before.

So it wasn't from home and it wasn't the Karsites, which begged the question—what, or who, was it? And why? If it was a hallucination of some sort, why did it only come just after dark and linger for only a little while? And why did she feel no other effects? Was it a combination of wishful thinking and exhaustion? Was it just a dream? That was certainly possible; given her erratic sleeping of late, she could easily slip into a dream-state without realizing it.

Wishful thinking combined with dreaming, probably, she thought. Because much as she hated to admit it, she welcomed "him" when he arrived and felt bereft when he was gone, and that was a combination both unnerving and embarrassing. As if she were some village maiden mooning over an imaginary dream-lover. *At least I'm not getting so soft as to hallucinate him in daylight.*

For one moment she entertained the possibility that her father had somehow enlisted the aid of his Valdemaran cousin—for his cousin most certainly *did* have mental powers, and quite formidable ones according to Beshat.

But no, that was highly unlikely. What could her father offer his cousin that would entice him to try to find her? And besides, what good could he do from within Valdemar? He certainly wouldn't *leave* Valdemar; he had a family, as well as duties there. Besides, she got the distinct impression of someone her own age, not the age of her father.

But . . . one of the cousin's children, perhaps? That might account for the feeling of kinship.

But no, again, what possible enticement could her father have offered that would suffice? And besides, the family resemblance ran strong in Beshat's bloodline. All of his children looked powerfully like him, and not at all like their mother, and it was reasonable to assume it did in the cousin's line as well. And this young man she saw in her mind's eye looked nothing at all like any of her kin.

I just hope this doesn't mean I'm going mad, or that the Karsites are somehow playing a trick on me.

She listened as hard as she could for any signs of what the *afrinn* was doing out there in the prison stronghold, but she heard nothing. She had already run through her usual exercises three times today, and truth to tell, she was tired. And she would have liked very much to have a real bath. And she really wished that she had her own clothing again—

Wait . . . maybe I can do something about that.

She was able to apport bread (or dough) and dried beef and water because the bread and dried beef and water she was using as her apportation anchors had come from a larger supply and thus were connected, magically.

But *she* was connected to her clothing and weapons. Maybe

she could use that connection to apport those here!

It was certainly worth a try!

By late afternoon, she was absolutely exhausted, and it was a good thing that the *afrinn* was fully occupying the attentions of the Karsites, because if she'd had to fight off another attempt to take her down, she'd have lost. She'd eaten every bit of bread and had apported more (evidently either the *afrinn* hadn't blown out the fire or the oven had been hot enough to bake in before it did, because there actually was bread to apport) and more dried beef. And she was back in her *own* clothing, with her *own* weapons and possessions around her again, not the least of which were her exquisitely made boots that fit her feet like no others. And thanks to the blankets and warm woolen cloak, she didn't need to expend any energy keeping herself from freezing.

She still wasn't anywhere near free, but at least she was comfortable again. And she had a much better arsenal to defend herself with.

She tried not to regret all of the clever Sleepgiver weapons she *hadn't* brought with her. The caltrops she could have spread in front of the door that would have pierced even the stoutest of boots. The poisons she could have used on her weapons. The garrotes that could slice off a man's head—or be strung across the door to slice him off at the ankles. The wire saw she could have used to cut through the bars on the window. Or the acids she could have used to eat through bar or stone. The smoke she could have used to fill the cell so no one could see her. If she'd had her usual bag of tricks, she could have made a dummy out of the clothing she had discarded, cut through the bars, climbed down the tower, stolen a horse and been halfway home before they realized she was gone.

Well . . . if she could just get something to take a single bar out, she could still do that. But she didn't have anything, and careful examination had proven that the bars were too tough for anything she could improvise, even now that she had her things with her again.

Watch and wait, and who knows? Maybe one of the other afrinns in the Talismans will be able to do something.

Even as she thought that, *something* roared in through the window, spun up a wind-devil in the middle of the room that sucked everything loose into it, sending dust flying all around her as she held down her belongings with her body.

And then the *something* resolved itself into the *afrinn* she had released, and the wind died down to nothing. She got to her feet, bowed a little, and approached it as it hovered in midair.

"Are you having fun?" she asked it, dryly. She hadn't really expected an answer, but she got one. The thing opened its jaws in a toothy grin. A very, *very* toothy grin.

"Are you making their lives miserable?" she continued, encouraged.

The creature nodded once.

"Are they afraid of you?"

A very emphatic nod.

Then, a brief moment of hope. "Can you do anything about getting me out of that window?" she asked.

The *afrinn* turned its monstrous head to look at the barred window. Or at least, she thought that was what it was doing. It was hard to tell, since, like its predecessor, the water *afrinn*, it had completely blank eyes.

It cocked its head sideways for a moment, and she let herself hope a little more.

Then it turned back to her and shook its head.

She sighed. *Well, it's only air. There's only so much it can do.* "Thank you for considering it," she said, politely, trying not to show her disappointment. Then something else occurred to her; this thing had had time to go all over the prison. Maybe she could get some information out of it. "How many humans are there within these walls?" she asked.

The creature stared for a moment, then began to nod. It had reached ten when she realized that it was counting for her, and she held up a hand. "More than twenty?" she asked.

An emphatic nod.

"Fifty?"

Another. Her heart sank. She'd hoped she had taken out a substantial percentage of the potential guards here when she'd killed eight. It appeared not.

"A hundred?"

Another emphatic nod.

"Two hundred?" This was not good.

This time the nod was not so emphatic. In a few moments she had established that there were two hundred and fourteen humans within these walls. A number that did not give her sanguine thoughts.

Now, at least ten of those would be tied up—the Karsite priests certainly each had a retinue of five apiece, and those servants would be utterly useless for fighting. And some of the others would be cooks and stable hands and a blacksmith, and the like. But that left at least a hundred seventy-five fighting men she was going to have to put into her calculations, one way or another.

And it meant this prison was a lot bigger than she had thought.

It meant that there wouldn't be a few men pursuing her if she escaped, there would be a small army.

And it meant that unless she could keep them occupied with *afrinns*, they could just keep sending men up here to try to take her and wear her out. And if these Karsite priests couldn't conjure demons, they could send for ones who *could*.

"Have they tried to let you out yet?" she asked.

The *afrinn* grinned again and nodded. She got the distinct impression that it was getting a great deal of enjoyment out of tormenting the Karsites. But—

"Are their barriers still down?" she asked. It nodded again.

Huh. "Would you stay here overnight? Long enough I can get a real sleep?" Right now, aside from escape, that was the one thing she wanted the most. A good sound sleep that lasted the entire night all wrapped up in her warm woolen cloak. . . . More than a dinner of something other than bread and dried meat. More than . . . well, about the same as a real bath.

The *afrinn* nodded, again, emphatically.

"Can you keep the priests busy for—a while?" she asked, unable to think of a way to ask "for about a turn of the glass" in a way the *afrinn* would understand. "Then come watch up here at sunset while I sleep?"

The *afrinn* grinned and nodded, twisted in midair, and flew out the window.

She gave it a good long wait, then stripped down to her skin and gave herself as good a bath as she could with just a rag and clean water. It wasn't the best bath she'd had, but at least she got the first layer of filth off, and her own clothing was still reasonably clean, so she didn't feel bad putting it back on.

At least I've got the blood off me. That stuff got everywhere. It had been so long since she'd killed anyone the way she'd slaughtered her guards that she'd forgotten how it would get into her hair, behind her ears, caked under her fingernails. *Ugh.*

By the time the *afrinn* got back, she had eaten and was rolled up in her cloak, with her blanket and the torn clothing between her and the cold stone of the floor. It stationed itself in the middle of the cell, just hanging in midair, the plumes of its tail swaying back and forth, lazily. And for the first time since she had left home, she allowed herself to relax and was asleep immediately.

She awoke at dawn, with confused memories of something that didn't feel like a dream. That young man again, clearer this time. He kept staring at her earnestly, as if he were trying to tell her something, but he didn't speak. His lips didn't even move, which would have been useful, since she could read lips perfectly well. It should have been annoying, but when he finally faded away, she was disappointed. And found herself wishing he'd come back, even if he wasn't much better company than the *afrinn*.

Maybe he *was* the *afrinn?*

But no, no, she'd had him plaguing her thoughts since before she released the *afrinn*.

When she woke at last, she felt better than she had since all this began. But the first thing she noticed was that the *afrinn*, although it had not changed position, had a little more restlessness in its posture.

"I'm awake," she said immediately, and it rotated to face her. "Do you want to go?"

It nodded.

"Then go, with my thanks," she said, and without any hesitation it whisked out the window and was gone.

She didn't even stop to think; she pulled the next Talisman off her necklace—another she thought represented water—and cradled it in her hand, studying it. No giving the Karsites any breathing room this time.

Satisfied that it worked like the other two, she tossed it into the center of the room, "spiked" the spell, put up her shields for the third time, and waited for the flash, then dropped them.

But nothing seemed to happen.

She stared at the spot where the Talisman lay, puzzled. The binding spell was certainly broken. The flash of released energy had been correct, and the spell was no longer in effect. Had the Talisman been empty, for some reason? But why was the binding spell still active? Had the *afrinn* somehow . . . died? Or gone irrevocably asleep?

She had just gotten to her feet when she noticed that the Talisman had suddenly disappeared.

No! It hadn't disappeared! It was buried under a little heap of sand! A little heap that doubled in size with every heartbeat, until it wasn't a "little" heap at all, it was a mound, then a pile, then, as she backed up in alarm, a big pile—an *enormous* pile!—a pile that filled the cell!

And then the pile of sand began to move. It somehow managed to *writhe*, like a live thing, and as her heart accelerated, it took on . . . shapes. A flattened sphere. A series of fat disks. Then a spiral—

And then, a spiral mound whose upper end terminated in the enormous head of a serpent. A Horned Viper, but one made of continuously moving grains of sand, one whose coiled body was as tall as she was, and whose head was bigger than her entire body.

Its tongue—made of sand—flickered out and touched her face. And for all her control and training, she winced. She couldn't help it.

I—must have grabbed the wrong Talisman. . . .

This was certainly an earth *afrinn.*

The tongue touched her face again. Like the others, this *afrinn* had featureless, blind-looking eyes, but she had no doubt it saw her perfectly well. As an involuntary shudder came over her, she took a deep breath, straightened her spine, reminded herself that the first two *afrinns* had been disinclined to kill her, and spoke her little speech.

The sand-serpent, which seemed to be constantly rebuilding itself, simply lay in its coils while she stammered through her speech, betraying nothing. She held her breath, waiting for some sort of response, because even if the other two *afrinns* had been friendly, there was no guarantee that this one would be.

Finally, with a hiss of shifting sand, the *afrinn* raised its triangular head above its coils. Then it turned its head away from her.

And waited.

For a moment, she couldn't imagine what was going on, but then it dawned on her, as it shoved its nose forward, in a gesture that seemed impatient. The door! It wanted her to open the door! Of course—unlike the water *afrinn,* which had been able to pour itself under the crack beneath the door, or the air *afrinn,* which could go wherever the wind could, this creature needed an actual egress.

She edged around it, grabbed the handle, and shoved the door open, backing quickly out of the way. It moved much faster than anything that big had any right to, pouring itself out of the door and down the stairs with an accompanying *ssshhhh* of the shifting sands of which it was made.

And then it was gone.

But the screams coming up from below were, if anything, more horrified than she had heard before.

Well . . . it's a giant snake. She couldn't imagine anything more terrifying to see coming down those stairs, other than an equally large spider. The other two *afrinns* had been somewhat monstrous, but that was the thing about a monster, it was something you didn't have an instinctive reaction to. But a giant snake? An entirely different story. *Everything* about a snake made every creature she had ever seen react in fear, and humans were no exception.

I'd better get some bread before the kitchens are abandoned, and the bread burns to coals.

The *afrinn* announced its return in late afternoon by bumping the door with its nose. At least, that was what it sounded like. Since human guards would certainly not have bothered to knock, she assumed it was the *afrinn* and went to open the door to let it in. It still looked like a giant horned viper, and she wondered if that was its natural form, as the fish thing and bird thing appeared to have been the natural forms of the water and air *afrinns.* She thought about asking it if it could take any other shape, but before she got a chance, it filled up the center of the cell again, and then . . .

. . . collapsed.

Panic hit her; had she done something to kill it? Had the Karsite priests figured out a weapon to use against it? Had she just lost the only thing that stood between her and them but her own skill?

But then, before she could do more than utter an inarticulate groan, the sand started moving again. And before her amazed eyes, it took on an entirely new shape.

The shape of a building.

And not just any building. This one was a square structure with a single, tall tower rising from one corner, as perfectly formed as if it had been cut from (somehow moving) sandstone by a master sculptor. Every little detail was there, from windows, to tiny figures of humans and horses in the center of the structure, in front of what she assumed were stables. But why—

And then it hit her.

This was her prison.

As she realized this, she filled with an excitement as powerful as her panic had been moments before, and she paced around the "sand castle," drinking in every detail.

The outer walls, judging by the thickness and the little windows on the inside walls, weren't just defenses, they were living and storage places. The inside of the square structure was a big courtyard with a well, a stable, and what she thought might be a smithy. There were other, smaller structures there too, but they probably weren't important for her purposes. Privies, probably, and storage sheds. As she watched, the roofs of everything inside the courtyard melted away, and showed her the details of what was in them. There were stalls for no more than twenty horses, so most of the troops here must be foot soldiers. So this was a garrison, not just a prison.

Now the interior buildings melted away, and she transferred her gaze to the tower. As she had guessed, it was five stories tall. The walls and roof melted, and there were the walls of her cell with a little sand-figure in it that stood for her, and a stair up to where the roof had been. So besides being her prison, this was a watchtower.

Presumably there was no watch up there now. The *afrinn* had almost certainly terrified them into flight.

The fifth story dissolved, revealing an empty fourth story, then the third, all empty. So she was the only prisoner here, after all.

And now the roof of the entire complex melted away.

She bent over the sand castle with furious concentration, burning every room, every door into her mind. There were no corridors here. Rooms led directly into one another, and there were only four entrances into the building itself, all on the courtyard. And only one way out, a passage all the way through the first story next to the stable. If she was going to escape, it was going to have to be either by climbing down out of the tower or by getting to one of those doors out into the courtyard. Either way was fraught with danger. Climbing down the wall, all the Karsites would have to do would be to get archers out into desert outside the garrison, and she'd be an easy target. But to get out the other way—she'd have to make her way through half a dozen rooms that might or might not be occupied—

Then the second story melted away, and she saw that it was worse than that. She'd have to make her way to the *end* of this wall, go down a set of stairs, and then get back through half a dozen rooms to get to the door into the courtyard.

Then across the courtyard and out through the passage into the desert. And the passage almost certainly was protected by gates at both ends.

The sand mounded up again, rearranged itself for a bit, and sluggishly settled into the form of the enormous Horned Viper again. But something about the way it moved suggested to Sira that it was . . . tired?

"Are you all right?" she asked, with real concern. After all, this *afrinn* had apparently just spent the last several turns of the glass crawling all over this benighted place, just so that it could show her a map of the thing. She hadn't even asked it to!

The thing lifted its head from its coils, slowly, and just as slowly shook it, back and forth, twice.

"Are you tired?" A sudden thought struck her. "Do you need magical energy?"

It raised its head a little higher, nodded, then sank back into a heap. That's when she saw that even the ever-moving sand particles were flowing much more slowly than before.

Well . . . the other Mages had taught her how she could share her own energies with them when a task needed more than they could summon on their own. That should work with the *afrinn*. She should at least try.

There was just one slight problem.

"I'll try to help," she told it. "But you need to stop moving the sand around. You'll take my skin off, otherwise."

She hadn't realized how ubiquitous the sound of the hissing sands had become until they suddenly stopped, and the *afrinn* turned literally into a statue made of sandstone in front of her.

She placed one hand on either side of the blind-eyed head, gazed fixedly at the nostrils, and concentrated. She gathered her power from deep inside herself, and moved it up and out into her hands, projecting it with all her strength into the statue. Except, of course, it wasn't a statue, it was a living thing, and the moment her power touched its power, she sensed *and* saw the dim "light" of it take on strength. She fed that "light" as long as she possibly could, until sheer exhaustion made her break the connection, and her leaden arms dropped away.

She staggered back a couple of paces and dropped to her sleeping pallet. It even took her a while to get back the energy to wipe her eyes.

But as soon as she had broken the bond, the *afrinn* came back to life, its sands virtually dancing with renewed power. It shifted its coils and slithered over to the window, examining it speculatively.

"Do you think you can eat through the bars or the stone holding them?" she asked, hope renewing *her* strength.

A horned viper didn't have shoulders to shrug, but as it pivoted its head to look at her, she got the impression of one, as if it had said, "I don't know."

"Will you try?" she begged.

For answer, it thinned down, and wrapped its sinuous body in and around all of the bars, several times. Then the sands themselves sped up, moving so fast they were a blur.

The Viper held that position for what felt like half a turn of the glass, before unwinding itself and returning to the center of the room.

But . . . alas. All it had been able to accomplish was to polish the bars to a soft matte shine and the stone in which they were set to gloss.

The *afrinn* looked at her, then hung its head.

"Please do not feel bad. It's not your fault they built so well," she said, soothingly. "You have done far more for me than I could ever have imagined by showing me how this place is built." She smiled at it. "Though I wish I could have seen them run from you like mice in a tunnel."

The *afrinn* raised its head again, and flicked her check with its tongue. This time she didn't flinch.

"If you are inclined to stay for a while, I can grant you more power once my own reserves recover," she suggested. "You can leave whenever you feel ready to go."

It nodded and settled into its resting, coiled position, spreading out to block the entrance to the cell.

She ate, and drank, and settled herself for another good, solid night of sleep, because surely nothing and no one was going to dare coming up here with *that* waiting for them.

The sound of the hissing sands was curiously relaxing, now that she was used to it. But she found herself wishing, as the light faded from her cell, that she was able to communicate better with the creature. There were so many questions she had—why were the *afrinns* bound to the Talismans in the first place? What had that long-ago Mage—or Mages—expected to accomplish? Why had they *stopped* doing such bindings? Was it because they had learned to make the sort of Talisman she was used to? Why was this *afrinn* so exhausted, when the other two had not been?

So many questions. They rushed around in her head like the circling sand that made up the earth *afrinn*, until she chased answers that eluded her even in her dreams.

12

Ahkhan had swarmed up the rock formation like a lizard, with Tory and Kee right behind him. Tory had left his cloak and long robe behind—though Ahkhan had not—because he was not used to climbing in them, and this was definitely not the time or place to learn. Especially not since this was a very new sort of stone for Tory—and Kee—and this would be a bad place to make a stupid mistake.

The worst part about the formation was its fragility; the surface tended to crumble, like aged brick, when you pressed on it. He didn't have any slips on the way up, but there were a couple of uneasy moments. Once they were up there, Ahkhan took up a position like a formal lookout on a watchtower—highly visible from any direction except directly behind them—and braced himself in place, clearly prepared to spend candlemarks waiting if he had to. Tory got himself a more comfortable spot he could more-or-less sit down in, just below him. Kee had the best luck; he had a spot just as comfortable as a chair, positioned well below Tory.

And so they waited, each of them alone with his thoughts. Tory's were pretty tranquil; he wasn't going to buy trouble by worrying about what was going to happen when they crossed into Karse because he had absolutely no control over that. So he admired the very strange view and tried to identify the few moving specks he saw in the distance. Kee's clearly were not tranquil; Tory could see his face from here, and he had that eaten-up-with-worry look. *And I bet it's about the girl.* Kee had clearly fallen, and fallen hard, which was strange, since he'd never actually met her, but not completely unheard of, especially in a romantic like Kee. Not that Kee would ever admit to being a romantic, but Tory knew that compared to Mags' offspring, he'd had a very, very sheltered life, and one exposed to a lot of romantic stories, especially in his own family. He wondered what it was that had been the trigger. Was it that she was in danger? Was it that she herself was probably more than his match? Was it that she was exotic? Tory hoped it wasn't the last. She might take that as an insult. *And I'm getting way ahead of myself again.*

Then he spotted something against the hard, bright, blue sky. A bit of rising cloud that wasn't actually a cloud.

It turned out, the keepers of the waters were right. There *was* a caravan on the way. From their high perch, they could see it leagues away.

At first it was just a tiny puff of dust in the distance, a bit of thin yellow against the hard blue sky, but even at that, Tory could tell it was far more dust than would have been kicked up by two or three riders. But despite having brought his waterskin, he was hot and thirsty long before the caravan was even visible under that plume of dust, and by the time they got close enough that the leaders would be able to see *them*, he was more than ready to come down.

Meanwhile, Ahkhan was up there, posing like a statue and just about as impassive, looking as if the sun and heat had absolutely no effect on him. It was a little irritating, to tell the truth, but Tory told himself that this was just what the Sleepgiver *did;* when he wasn't actively involved in something, he turned into this passionless rock. *And the discipline is probably what keeps him from a lot of boredom.*

Finally the caravan got within shouting distance, though the fact that the leader really wanted to address them had been apparent long before that. He kept shading his eyes with his hands, and gazing up at them, but in an eager, rather than apprehensive, way.

Now, Tory didn't know anything about caravans in practice, but he had a good idea in theory, and it looked to him as if this lot was seriously undermanned so far as their protection went. There should have been a half-dozen more guards than there were, if he was any judge. So if he was right, it was no wonder the leader was looking up at them as if he couldn't wait to recruit them.

"Hail!" the leader shouted, as soon as it was even remotely possible for them to have heard him. "Looking for work?"

"Aye!" Tory called, before Ahkhan could clear his throat and answer.

"Meet at the entrance to Willow Vale!" the leader shouted back. "I need to try your paces, but I'd rather not break water-peace doing it!"

"Coming down!" Ahkhan replied, and gave Tory a look that said *what do you think you're doing?*

"I know what I'm doing," Tory replied to the look, and grinned. "I've been a merc before. Let me handle this one."

"Oh. Well, you are full of surprises," was all Ahkhan could

manage, as Tory stretched out his leg and nudged Kee with a toe to get him moving.

The caravan was waiting at the entrance to the valley—Tory had taken the time to splash some water from the pond over his head and get enough of a drink that he wasn't dying of thirst anymore. Kee and Ahkhan followed his example before they all walked out to meet the caravan.

The leader sported a mighty black mustache and bristling eyebrows, and he was dressed as they were; the sole difference in his garb was that instead of fabric forming the crown of his headwrap, the wrap had been formed around a conical helmet. Tory immediately wanted one of those; it was a brilliant idea, a cut at the head would slide off the helmet and the sword would get fouled in the fabric long enough you could gut your man while he struggled with it. *I hope they have spares.*

The leader, who looked as if he could have been a fighting man himself, brown skin showing signs of decades out in the weather, eyed them all appraisingly and evidently liked what he saw. "Experience?" he asked, all business. Perfect. Just the way Tory wanted things.

"More than it looks like. Worked at our fathers' sides since we were old enough to use a knife and a sling," said Tory confidently. "The old men told us to go see the world while we still could; been working our way down from Northern Rethwellan. Banked most of our pay at Bourde the Goldsmith up North at Harvest Moon and came down here to get winter work."

As he had expected, the mention of Bourde, who did a brisk business in managing the finances of really successful mercs, made the leader's eyes light up. Bourde and his fourteen sons from three wives had a web of goldsmiths from southern Valdemar to the Dhorisha Plains to south of Rethwellan. There were even Valdemaran Guards, former mercs, who banked their fortunes with Bourde. Having an account with the family gave you a lot of instant reputation—it meant that you were honest, and it meant that you were prosperous (and smart enough) to have enough money put by that the goldsmiths were willing to hold it for you.

"Good, good," the leader said. "Are you mounted?"

"Two Erdars and a Kalitt," said Ahkhan.

"You know your horseflesh. How d'ye want to be tested?"

"One at a time," Tory told him. "Practice sticks; I don't want anyone worse than bruised, least of all us. All of your men against each of one of us, we fight in the middle of them, until we defeat all of them or they defeat us." He grinned. "Don't worry, they won't be working long enough to get tired. Then we'll talk pay."

One bushy black eyebrow went up, but the leader simply told one of his guards, "Bring all the practice sticks, you and the lads stay here while we try these fellows. Ismal, take the caravan in and set up camp according to the laws."

The guard he had addressed tapped one of his fellows on the shoulder, and the two of them went to the rearmost wagon and came back with armloads of practice sticks, each the length of a sword or a dagger. The caravan continued on into the valley under the eye of a younger man whose face boasted a slightly smaller version of the leader's formidable moustache. Tory dropped his belt with its weapons on the ground and accepted a short and a long stick from one of the two guards carrying them. "I'll go first," he said, glad he was wearing his boots and not the sandals. He wasn't at all sure about his footing in those yet.

"Are you the best of the three of you?" the leader asked, still with that eyebrow raised.

Tory laughed. "If I say 'yes,' you'll think I'm boasting, and if I say 'no,' you'll think I'm trying to pull something over on you. The truth is that we're all good in different ways. Though Ahkhan is a better marksman than Kee and I are."

He figured that was probably the truth, since Sleepgivers preferred to do their killing at a distance if they could.

"This is true," Ahkhan said, modestly, looking utterly unruffled. Tory hoped he was unruffled, although he was pretty certain, given how he and Kee had trained, that they could, indeed, each best all five of the mercs without too much trouble.

Meanwhile, Tory had checked the weight and balance of his two practice sticks, and he stepped into the middle of the informal ring the caravan guards had made. The mercs were all in good shape and handled their sticks with confidence, but not overconfidence. Seemed fair to Tory.

"Remember," he cautioned them. "No point in any of us getting hurt. If you take what would have been a mortal cut, you drop out. I'll try to hit you just hard enough to let you know you've been hit."

The oldest of the guards smirked at that. "Worry about yourself, boy," he said.

"Go!" ordered the caravan leader.

The five guards lay on the ground around Tory, in various states of chagrin, though Tory was dead certain none of them were worse than bruised, except in spirit. Tory had taken three of them out in the first rush, and the other two shortly thereafter. He went to the oldest guard and offered a hand up. The guard stared at the outstretched hand for a moment then shrugged, and took it.

"I guess you really didn't need to worry," he said with chagrin. "I'm Kerk."

"Tory. You'll get another chance in a moment," Tory told him, helping him to his feet. "Kee's next."

Kee bounced on the balls of his feet, eager to get started, as the five guards once again arranged themselves around a rough circle. Kee took a bit longer than Tory had to take them out, partly because now they were warier and didn't just rush him as they had rushed Tory, but partly because Kee *wanted* to take each of them individually and maneuvered them so he could.

Then it was Ahkhan's turn; he took about as long as Tory had, although he hardly seemed to move at all, just slid out of the way of attacks and returned each with a devastating response.

The poor guards got to their feet for the third time, looking as if they felt utterly humiliated—but the caravan leader clearly knew fighting men, because he called out in a booming voice, "That's the finest work I've ever seen in my life . . . and no shame in being defeated by it. Tell Ismal to break out the wine, you've earned it."

That cheered them up considerably, and they collected their practice sticks and trotted into the valley, as Tory, Ahkhan, and Kee gathered around the caravan leader before following them in.

"I'm Hakshen Tiron, and I'm taking this caravan into Karse to trade spices," he said. "I trust you have no problem with my destination?"

Tory shrugged. "As long as the Karse priests have no problem with us."

"Well . . ." Tiron smiled grimly. "That's where I'm pleased to have you. The Border patrols are little more than bandits. With five guards, they were sure to shake me down for goods or gold. With eight—they probably won't."

"What happens if they try anyway?" Tory wanted to know. "Are we supposed to fight them off?" He paused. "I'll be disappointed if you say no."

"You won't be disappointed," Tiron replied, the smile turning feral. "The desert can hide a lot of bodies. Patrols vanish all the time. I'll explain more later."

Tory clapped the man on the back. "A man after my own heart," he declared. "Let's talk pay."

By now Tory could read Ahkhan's expressions reasonably well, and as he haggled with Tiron, he watched the Sleepgiver go from skeptical, to surprised, to admiring. But Tory really *had* played the part of a mercenary, and more than once, even as young as he was. While Valdemar didn't employ any mercenary companies to fight for them, there were plenty of jobs for single sell-swords, as anything from guard work on the stock at a jeweler or goldsmith to the personal retinue and guard troops of the wealthy or highborn that were not unlike small personal armies. Mags had first had Tory observe agents of his who were mercs, then later required Tory to act exactly as a real merc would when working as an agent within a noble household or at the establishment of a rich merchant. He had managed everything from negotiating his own pay to tending his own arms and armor. Mags had required the same of Perry; he'd offered the training to Abi, who'd refused on the grounds she was unlikely to need it. And even though those had been trials and not actual jobs, the brothers had both *worked* as mercs, for at least a couple of moons. Kee hadn't had the benefit of any of that because it was likely his father the King would have had quite a few objections—but Kee had the good sense to keep his mouth shut and follow Tory's lead.

By the time the small group had gotten to the pond—where some of the caravan were respectfully setting up a latrine area far from the water and some were hauling buckets well away from the pond and stream so they could bathe—he and Tiron were very close to a deal. Finally, he sucked on his lower lip a moment and said, "I'll tell you what. I'll take your last offer if you throw in three of those pointed helms on top of it."

"Done!" crowed the caravan master, with the glee of someone who is sure he has gotten a bargain. Tory was reasonably sure that Tiron had been planning to give them—or at least lend them—the helms anyway. But that was fine. He'd given the impression of driving a hard bargain, but not one that Tiron was feeling any pain over, and he was now someone Tiron respected. After all, the money was not the real object here. Getting into Karse without alerting anyone was the real goal, although the helms were going to be a useful bonus.

Once the bargain had been struck and some initial money had changed hands, the three of them moved their horses to where the caravan horses were picketed and their bedrolls to the area where the rest of their new companions in the desert were settling down. They introduced themselves to their fellow fighters—the merchants, aside from Tiron and Ismal, didn't seem interested in much besides their dinner and bed—and Ismal began passing out dinner to everyone.

Since there wasn't a fire to sit around, and it seemed that no one had managed to kill any game on the way in, dinner was pretty much exactly the same trail rations they had already been packing—but at least it was someone *else's* rations, which didn't make inroads on their own.

Except for wine. True to his promise, each of the guards, including the three of them, got wine. It wasn't *good* wine, but at least it wasn't so bad it peeled the skin off your tongue.

"How is it you ended up short of men?" Ahkhan asked, when the first frantic inroads into the food had subsided. The heat of the day had subsided as well—here inside the shelter of the rock walls of the canyon, the air was positively pleasant. There was even a faint sweet scent, though Tory couldn't see anything blooming.

The eldest of the guards snorted. "Some of those damned demon-priests crossed over into Ruvan about a fortnight ago, and their demons shredded up a village east of the Amber Moon school. Dunno what they were looking for. Guess they found it, because they kited right back across the Border before anyone could catch 'em or any survivors could get to the next village for help, but you know how it is when these things happen."

Ahkhan's head tilt invited elaboration, and Birk was perfectly happy to provide it. "Some damned fools got it into their heads that the Karsites were bringing priests down south to make a try to push into Ruvan or Rethwellan, and anyone trying to cross over was going to end up as demon fodder. Next thing you know, it's not a damn-fool rumor, it's the gods' own truth, and most of the sell-swords had cleared out of town."

"Some people will believe anything," Ahkhan murmured. Tory

knew exactly what he was thinking. *That must have been the raid that got his sister. And once the priests had her, since the demons weren't going to be sated by killing one poor horse, they just turned their pets loose on the nearest village.* That would be absolutely typical behavior for the demon-priests; to their minds, anyone who didn't worship their god was a heretic and deserved killing.

"*That's* the truth, brother," Birk agreed. "Me, I've been across this Border more times than I want to think about. Demon-priests don't bother our kind, and they don't bother the caravans we guard. If they did, their trade would dry right up, and they need the trade as much as we do. If the rich want their spices and the Healer-priests want their medicines, they have to put up with us heretics, because they don't trust their *own* people not to make a run for it once they cross the Border."

"Border works both ways," Tiron agreed. "Keeps things in as much as it keeps things out. But it keeps me in business, so there it is."

"Surprised they don't put a wall around the whole damned country," opined one of the others.

Tiron snorted. "Any sane man knows that walls don't work. You can't guard every furlong, it would bankrupt you, and you still wouldn't have enough people to do it if you put everyone you could call a fighter in the country up on it with a spear. And what good's a wall with no one on it? Anyone can go over or under it. A wall's useless except around a city, and even then, it'll only defend you for about a month in a siege. The best thing a wall can do is keep beasts and bandits out, not armies or people determined to cross. Not that anyone would go into Karse for less than what we're getting. Ah, and that reminds me—there's rules about Karse."

"Serve 'em up," said Tory, steadily. "We aren't going to buy trouble, there's enough as it is."

"First rule; you don't start *nothing.* Karsite insults you, bullies you, shoves you around, you eat it. Common folk won't do that, they're no braver than rabbits, but the soldiers and their version of highborn nobles and absolutely the priests will. Eyes down, yessir, nossir, thankew very much sir. You eat it, with one exception. Out in the desert, if its a patrol, you eat it until *they* draw weapons or start helping themselves to the caravan—that means the goods, or the stores, our beasts, or our gear. Then you can do what you want."

Tory nodded, but had a question. "Why's that? I mean, why's it fine to defend ourselves in the desert as long as they start it?"

"Because Karse pays their army shit. So they get shit for soldiers. They're allowed to rough up the common folk to get what they want, but sometimes some of them take a notion into their heads to aim for higher loot. And the ones in charge know exactly what's wearing their colors." Tiron smiled grimly. "Remember what I said about Karse needing us traders. That's why, when patrols go missing, nobody asks any questions. What they don't officially know about, nobody has to get punished for. It's all very neat and tidy."

"The smart ones know where to stop and who with," Birk put in. "And if they ain't smart enough to stick to the fair game, then Karse don't cry when they disappear. They know they've got shit for soldiers, but they don't cry if the *stupid* shits eliminate themselves."

Kee was smart enough to keep his face impassive, but Tory could feel his dismay. The idea that the fighters of the Karsite army, the people that the common folk were supposed to be able to depend on to protect them, were actually preying on them, was utterly revolting to him. *And more revolting than the Sleepgivers murdering people for money?*

"Surely they're not all like that," Kee ventured.

Tiron shrugged. "Prob'ly not. Most of the units are supposed to be garrisoned where the men in each unit all come from—supposed to give them incentive to protect that's more potent than just money, since they're protecting people they know. But the Border patrols down here are scum. I've *heard* that one of the punishments they give criminals is to assign them to ride the Border, though I don't know if that's true. I do know they've got no reason to protect anything but their own hides, and every reason to do what they can to add to their crap pay."

Silence. Evening insects began to sing, softly.

"That's crazy," said Kee.

"That's Karse," the leader and all the mercs said in a chorus, looked at each other, and laughed. They fell quiet for a while, sipping the last of their wine. The sky overhead was still blue, but here in the canyon shadows gathered, and the light dimmed. It would be quite dark soon, and with no fire, there was no reason to stay awake other than starwatching. And Tory didn't think these fellows had any interest in the heavens.

Tiron wiped his mouth with the back of his hand. "The other rule is, if a priest tells you to fall in with everyone else and do the dance for Vkandis, you do it, to prove you love the god. Common folk don't have to do anything but stand there like a lot of sheep while the priest blathers anyway, so it's not as if they'll catch you out on not being one of the sheep." Tiron pulled off his headwrap and helmet and ruffled his hand through his abundant, short black hair. "Just stand there, keep your eyes down, fall in and fall out with everybody else. Makes them think they've got us all properly under their thumb, does us no harm. It all may be stupid, but it works to keep the money coming."

"If it's stupid but works, it isn't stupid," said Tory.

"Keep thinking that way and you'll go far, boy," Tiron chuckled.

The sun touched the horizon, and Ismal poured out another round before stoppering the wine-cask and putting it up in the wagon again. The six merchant drivers were already bedding down under their wagons. "Normally, we'd draw lots for night guard now," said Birk. Tory had been wondering about that. "No point, here, with the guardians keeping water-peace, so enjoy a restful night."

He and the others were sipping the last of their wine slowly, as if it were a fine vintage. *Well, it's wine, anyway.* They had all arranged their bedrolls in a rough circle around where a fire would have been if there had been a fire.

"How many more of these do you think you'll be doing, Master Tiron?" asked one of the others. He sounded a little nervous.

"Plenty, Derdan, plenty," Tiron chuckled. "Don't let those rumors spook you. The only Karsite Border anyone needs to worry about is the one up north, with Valdemar. As long as they've got the Ghost Riders to worry about, Karse isn't going to give two shits about the rest of the world."

Ghost Riders? Huh. Not too bad a descriptive for Heralds and Companions, actually.

"And when I decide my bones are too old for sleeping on the ground, Ismal is taking over," Tiron continued, slapping his son on the back. Ismal laughed.

"I may take over before you decide to retire, old man, so you can drive the wagon while I ride," the younger trader said. "Or we could run two caravans for a while instead of one, and double our profit."

"Listen to the young pup!" his father said with admiration. "Just like the old dog! Anyway, Derdan, don't worry; you'll have work with me for as long as you want it."

"I just want to save up enough to open my wineshop," Derdan sighed. "And get myself a nice wife."

"Now why is it that every other merc I meet wants to open up a wineshop or a tavern?" Kee asked, speaking up for the first time this evening.

"Well, we know booze, we know drunks, and we know how to handle both," Derdan replied, logically. "What do *you* want to do, if you don't want to open a tavern?"

"I haven't found it yet." Tory heard the ring of truth in those words as his friend spoke them. "So I'm doing this until I figure out what it is."

"And if you don't?" Ahkhan prompted.

"I guess I'll keep doing this." Kee grinned in the twilight. "What about you, Ahkhan?" There was just a tiny bit of challenge in those words; Tory doubted anyone but he and the Sleepgiver heard it, but it was definitely there.

Ahkhan smirked. "Staying in the family business." He glanced over at Tory. "I'm fairly sure Tory would say the same."

"Tory can speak for himself, thanks, and yes, I'll probably stay in the family business." He raised an eyebrow at Ahkhan, then realized Ahkhan couldn't see it in the growing darkness. "Have you got a wife picked out, Derdan?"

"Don't know what anyone needs a wife for," scoffed Birk.

"Shows what you know," Derdan replied. He held up a hand—which was barely visible in the thick twilight at this point—and counted off fingers, oblivious to the fact that no one could see him counting. "Wineshop needs a cook. Wineshop needs two people at least to serve. Man needs someone to tend his home. And having a wife means someone in his bed and breeding kids to help with the wineshop."

"Man can hire all that done," Birk drawled. "Well, maybe not the kids part, but if you picked up a couple orphans, you could hire that too."

Derdan snorted. "Not for as cheap as a wife."

"He's right," Tiron seconded. "Marriage should be a good, sound business decision. That worked for my pa, and my pa's pa, and for every other man—and woman!—that I know."

Ismal made a very slight sound, as if he objected, at least in principle, but he didn't say anything, and his father evidently didn't notice.

"What about love?" Kee countered.

"What about it?" challenged Tiron. "Are you going to base a marriage on something that springs up out of nowhere, irrationally, and *absolutely is going to change* because you can't sustain an emotion that strong for very long? Or are you going to find a woman you get along with, a woman you can work beside, and brings either skills or property of her own to the table?" He snorted. *"Love.* That's fine for fancy songs and theater and the nobly born, but people like us need to be practical."

Tory thought of all the highborn parents at Court jockeying for advantageous marriages for their children and felt impelled to add, "Even the nobly born and the rich feel the same way,

Master Tiron. At least, the parents do."

"Not that I'd ever force a youngster to wed someone he couldn't stand," Tiron continued. "That's just asking for trouble. Trouble and people in beds they shouldn't be in and every manner of mischief, and the next thing you know, feuds! No, nor someone too old or too young, neither."

This time the sound from Ismal was a sigh, and it sounded relieved.

"I'd marry an older woman," Derdan said. "Long as she's brisk enough to work the shop and the house and brings some money of her own to the arrangement. She's bound to be grateful, see, especially if she's an old maid, and if she's too old for children, like Birk said, I can always adopt a couple useful foundlings to take my name and work the shop just like blood-born. I'd marry an ugly woman, too, if she's nice-tempered, smart, and good to be around and a good cook," he continued stoutly. "Same reason. Bound to be grateful, and no worrying about her canoodling either. Man eats a lot more often than he beds a woman. And it ain't a face I'm thinking about in bed, anyway, cause by the time you close up a wineshop, it's too dark to see a face."

"You make some powerful points," Birk replied, sounding surprised.

"Old head on young shoulders," Tiron proclaimed, sounding pleased. "If I had more men like you, I wouldn't have to replace *any.*"

"You won't have to replace me, Master Tiron. It'll be a long while before I have the money for that wineshop, and by then it'll be Ismal in charge, and you—you may be ordering your wine from me, sitting back in your fine home and enjoying grandkiddies."

This was not the first time Tory had listened in on conversations like this one. Most people looked at marriage as a business arrangement, and not just the parents. He'd overheard plenty of highborn, parents *and* children, scheming about advantageous marriages. In fact, it might have shocked these men if they knew how often he'd overheard pretty young ladies or handsome young men *planning* on marrying people old enough to be their grandparents, with the express intent of betraying them behind their backs while enjoying a higher status or greater wealth and a lot more freedom than they had while mere unwedded children.

Or maybe not. There probably was a fair share of that in every class, in every country. It certainly formed the backbone of many ribald theatrical farces.

He wondered how they did things among the Sleepgivers. The few stories that Ahkhan had dropped painted it as a surprisingly egalitarian society. And certainly Tory's grandfather had married for love. For that matter, so had Ahkhan's father, Bey.

But the conversation had moved on to other things—or *thing:* the sort of wine that Derdan intended to serve and sell. ". . . . and I'll have the cheap red and the hard cider in the taproom, see," Derdan said lovingly. "That'll be what's in the barrels, and that'll be all I ever serve in the taproom. But I'll keep my eye out for good vintages in bottles and stick them down in cellar. And I'll have a cellar if I have to dig it m'self. And I'll make it known to the people with money in town that I have better stuff in the cellar for 'em. Shirka reds, Amusa blush, Dulan Temple honey mead, Quirun whites. Charlot rosewine if I can get it. And . . ."

At this point Tory just rolled himself up in his blankets and let Derdan go on about wines. It was clear he knew a lot about them, and it was clear that he was passionate about them, and it seemed that he'd never gone on about them like this to his fellow mercs before, because they all seemed fascinated. If not by the wines themselves, about Derdan's level of expertise and his enthusiasm.

Tory just let his mind drift, and only at that point did he realize that he and Kee were *not* going to be able to "look in" on Ahkhan's sister tonight—or, indeed, most nights—because sitting there in the middle of their fellow mercs clasping wrists would look . . . odd. And sneaking off together would just make for assumptions, assumptions he had *no* idea how the others would react to. Maybe they'd be fine with it. Maybe they wouldn't. They couldn't take the chance.

Then again, this had been Ahkhan's idea in the first place, so presumably Ahkhan had known this was going to happen.

He fell into sleep, still half-listening to Derdan, who was now describing what food went best with what wine.

He didn't dream, not that he remembered, but he woke feeling as if he *should* have been dreaming, as if something . . . had happened that he hadn't experienced. It was a decidedly unsettling feeling, but no one else seemed to be disturbed, so he put it down to falling asleep listening to someone else talk.

Meanwhile, the morning was clear, cool, and made you glad you were alive, and he was more than ready to get on with the day and travel farther down the road. He wasn't sure what they were going to do when they had to part company with the caravan, but presumably Ahkhan had a plan.

He'd never been on a caravan before, but things went pretty much as he had expected from his reading. All of them made up their packs and bedrolls and threw them in the back of one of the wagons. Then the mercs ate first while the merchants got their horses in harness—and the merchants ate while the mercs got their horses saddled. Everyone made sure that every single vessel that could hold water was filled and had no leaks. Then Tiron mounted his horse and took the lead with Birk beside him, directed the three of them to cover the rear, and the caravan moved out with the rest of the mercs arrayed on either side of the line of wagons.

Once they were out of the canyon, Kee kneed his horse to bring her briefly to Ahkhan's side. "Sira's still all right," he said. "She had . . . something with her, something big and powerful, not an animal or a human. I couldn't figure out what it was, but it seemed like it was protecting her."

"Really!" Ahkhan was taken aback. "That—seems unlikely."

Kee shrugged. "Without touching Tory, I couldn't make out much."

"But you could make out something. Huh." Tory scratched his head. "This is unexpected."

"But welcome," Ahkhan said. "All right, I want you both to keep your eyes on the horizon to either side of us. I'll watch the rear. You're looking for—"

"Anything," Tory interrupted him. "Movement of birds particularly. Dust. The quick glint of sun on metal."

"Exactly." Ahkhan nodded, relieved. "All right then, you know what to do, so do it."

The morning passed uneventfully. Except that it got steadily hotter, they were eating a lot of dust in the rear, and Tory found that the headwrap kept his head a lot cooler than even a hat. They paused just before the Border to water the horses, eat, and give the horses a rest. Kee and Tory took Birk's place at the front, and Birk took theirs at the rear. Ahkhan went to take up a position on the right side.

There was no sign just when they passed the Border, but Tiron assured them that they had and that now they had to keep their senses sharp for both would-be bandits and Karsite patrols.

"I have all the proper papers," he said, "But as I said, that won't stop stupid patrols from being stupid."

"Exceedingly stupid," Ismal added sourly, from his seat driving the lead wagon. "Even if they succeeded in killing us all and taking our goods, *they can't sell any of it.* They don't know where, or to whom, and that's all information Father keeps in his head. Spices and medicines are not like cloth or gemstones; you can't sell them to just anyone."

"Especially in Karse. Some of this stuff you have to have a special license for." Tiron shook his head. "Well, let's—"

But Kee, who had been watching the horizon, whistled sharply at the same time that Birk did, both of them pointing at a mere whisper of dust hanging in the air. The caravan stopped. After a moment it became obvious that whatever was making the dust was coming toward them.

Tiron sighed. "Not bandits, not moving that slowly. Well, now we find out what kind of Karsite bastards we'll have to deal with. Let's just hope they're not complete idiots."

13

The earth *afrinn* took a little journey down the tower and back up again in the morning. When it returned, it moved briefly over to the corner farthest from the one where Sira slept, and then coiled up in the center of the room and looked at her expectantly.

Curious now, she walked around it to see that it had deposited a pile of brightly polished arrowheads in that corner. A little confused, she picked one up and looked at it. The wooden end of the shaft was still in the arrowhead, but it looked as if it had been sanded flat to the socket.

"What—" she said, and then it struck her, and she chuckled. She turned to the *afrinn,* which had shifted its sand so that now its head was pointing at her. "They shot at you, didn't they?" she asked.

The *afrinn* nodded.

Of course they had. And since the *afrinn* was just a giant pile of constant and swiftly moving sand, the wooden shafts of the arrows lost in it had been abraded away to nothing, leaving behind the metal arrowheads.

"They really are unobservant." She sighed and looked into its eyes. Did it see out of them, or did it just see with all of itself, and the shape of the serpent was just a convenience? Earth *afrinns* were mostly rumor and deduction to the Mages of the People. No one had ever seen one that she knew of—other than the highly dangerous and legendary Stone Man, and this certainly wasn't one of those. They just knew that since air, water, and fire *afrinns* existed, there must certainly be earth *afrinns.*

"I wish you could talk," she told it. "I wish I knew what it was you were seeing. And how."

Abruptly the sand stopped moving, and the *afrinn* went from a serpent made of dancing sands to a vaguely sand-shaped pile. For a moment, she feared she had somehow offended it—but then, as close to her as possible, two vaguely hand-shaped depressions formed, then filled in again.

So—it wanted her to put her hands on, or in, it again? The way she had when she'd given magic to it? Well, why not? If it had wanted to harm her, the easiest thing for it to have done would have been to leave.

So she knelt down next to the sand and put her hands in it.

Nothing happened for a while, so she closed her eyes experimentally.

And suddenly she was engulfed on all sides by sight. It was as if she had eyes everywhere; she saw herself kneeling in front of herself (and *that* was disorienting), but she was equally aware of the door behind her, the window to one side, the floor and the ceiling.

But then her "vision" expanded.

There was no adequate way to explain it, but she "saw" the four floors of the prison beneath her, then the wings to either side, the next two corner towers (much smaller than the prison tower), the other two wings, forming the second two sides of the square, and the final small tower opposite the prison tower.

And that was the moment she understood exactly how the *afrinn* had mapped out the entire prison in its sands for her. Not by crawling all over every bit of it, as she had assumed, but because it could *see* the structure and was aware of every nook, every storage place. In fact, she got the distinct impression it had only gone physically as far as the base of the prison tower.

And she soon was aware of more, because as she concentrated on any one area, she sensed the lives in it, from the horses down to the mice and beetles. More than sense . . . if they were making a noise, she sensed that too, as a vibration. And when the life was a human, if it was talking, she could understand it.

I can scry without scrying! she realized with excitement.

She sensed the *afrinn's* approval.

Now she moved her area of concentration slowly, from room to room, determining by the sounds what was going on in them. Nearest the prison were the armory on one side—tenanted only by someone mending his armor and grumbling about it under his breath—and the kitchen, or at least, *a* kitchen on the other. And that made sense, actually; it meant the shortest route to get food to the prisoners, and the kitchen would never, ever be empty. In most garrisons she had ever seen, there would be one or two specialist cooks, but the rest of the staff would be soldiers, often assigned there as punishment. Anyone trying to escape that way would be going through a room full of soldiers who weren't happy about being there in the first place as well as things that could be used as weapons.

She found nothing of any interest in the wings nearest the prison tower, but in the corner tower opposite the prison she found what she was looking for: a large, luxurious suite of rooms with its own small kitchen and one room that absolutely reeked of power and prestige.

And two humans in it.

". . . . and how should I know?" said a querulous voice as she sharpened her focus. "I've never heard of one of those sand things either! The men tried shooting it with the arrows I put Vkandis' Blessing on, then they used the ones with the poisoned heads, and they might as well have been shooting it with sugar candy for all the effect it had!"

Without words, the *afrinn* conveyed its contempt of these creatures and that the reason they had never seen *afrinns* before, even though the *afrinns* had dwelt here for longer than the humans, was that the *afrinns* took great care never to be seen by these god-botherers.

She almost choked at that "description." But it was certainly apt.

"Well, I've sent for the High Brotherhood," said the second voice, in tones of barely suppressed rage. "They should be here soon enough. And when they arrive, the de—I mean, the Terrible Swords of Vkandis will make short work of that thing and will overcome the Sleepgiver. Assuming the High Brothers don't just want her finished off, which I would say is a fate too good for her."

"She should be debased and tortured and bound with every means we have in our disposal and taken to Sunhame and burned alive in the Holy Fires!" the querulous one said, and he spat. "When will they arrive?"

"However long it takes to get back from the Northern Border. That's where they went after they captured her in the first place. You know the priority is to keep the Swords on the border as much as possible. They told me they had gotten my request and were on their way this morning, that's all I know."

Sira shivered. *This is what I had been afraid of.*

She felt the *afrinn* nudge her mind. *You should withdraw,* was the feeling, with the sense that while the *afrinn* knew it could observe these Mages safely alone, it was not certain it could do so linked so intimately with Sira.

She withdrew her presence, but not her hands, and she opened her eyes, seeking not the surroundings but the *afrinn* itself; she probed delicately at the creature's physical self.

"You still need sustenance," she declared to the pile of sand, and once again she poured her magic into it. After all, how could she do less, given what it had just shared with her?

Two more attempts by the *afrinn* to eat through the bars or the stone of the window resulted only in metal and stone polished to a mirror gloss. Either the prison tower was reinforced somehow with magic she could not see, which was possible but not likely, or it was made of something much harder than anything she had ever come into contact with. She was beginning to think it was both, that special magic had been used to reinforce the window but that the window itself was extremely robust. Now that it was polished, it revealed a structure that didn't look like any rock she knew. And the metal of the bars was certainly not the relatively brittle cast iron it would have been if the Sleepgivers had made it.

There was a hard, cold spot deep inside her now, and she was not ashamed to admit that it was fear.

She *should* have been a lot more terrified. She probably would have been, except that every night when she closed her eyes and drifted off to sleep, there was someone there reassuring her. Telling her that she could get out of there. Promising that she was strong enough and smart enough to do so. It wasn't the promise of some nebulous rescue, which she would not have believed, but rather the surety—from someone unknown—that she would find a way. Was it just her mother's wisdom in her Talisman? No, not possible. Was it something or someone in the last four bronze Talismans? She didn't think so. It was all bound up with that nebulous dream personage, the young man she could not identify, yet felt she could trust.

Which was ridiculous. Things like that only happened in tales other people told each other, not in the lore of the Sleepgivers, who were practical and hard-headed and knew there was no such thing as lovers you first saw in dreams.

So when the *afrinn* showed signs of being restless and anxious to leave, she sent it on its way and decided to try something different. She would release two of the *afrinns* at once, one water, and one air, and see what happened.

The earth *afrinn* nudged her once, quickly (to avoid abrading her), and left through the prison rather than through the window, leaving behind the impression that it intended to terrify as many of her captors as it could on its way out. And as soon as it was gone, she took two of the Talismans, laid them side-by-side, and spiked the spells.

But this time the result was not as impressive.

The air Talisman gave barely a shimmer as it released its captor, and the creature that emerged was a mere ghost of the first air *afrinn*. Literally a ghost; it was scarcely a sketch of a little winged lizard hanging in midair, listlessly. And the water *afrinn* was not in a much better state, a sort of finned hound composed less of water and more of fog.

And neither of them moved after she made her little speech; instead, they looked at her mournfully, as if trying to say, "You've given us our freedom, but we're too weak to take it."

A wave of bitter disappointment crested and crashed over her. But she did her best not to show it. After all, it wasn't *their* fault they were too weak to help. Besides . . . she should probably be able to do something about that.

She cupped both hands around the place in the air where the air *afrinn* hovered, scarcely visible, and poured magic into it, closing her eyes to concentrate. It wasn't until she felt her knees buckling that she stopped and opened her eyes to see if her work had had any effect.

She *did* let her legs collapse under her when she saw that it had. The winged lizard was larger now and more "present," and not just a sketch in the air but a delicate, detailed thing like a sculpture of blown glass. And she was not at all mistaken, she was *sure*—it was looking at her with a real expression on its reptilian face, and that expression was gratitude and even adoration.

The water *afrinn* also had an expression, much easier to read on a face that was not at all unlike a delicate gaze-hound's—it was hope.

"I need to rest," she told it. "But yes. I'll help you, too."

It looked as if it was too tired to do anything at all but very much wanted to express itself with enthusiasm.

She rested and ate, and by midafternoon she was ready to try to help the water *afrinn*.

Meanwhile, the air creature had left—but not, she sensed, deserted her. After she opened her eyes for the second time that day, with the water *afrinn* in much the same state of "repair" as the air *afrinn,* the air creature returned. She had no idea what it had been doing . . . but there was a definite aura of satisfaction about it.

By this point she was truly ready to drop and was very glad she had a stockpile of food and water, because she certainly would not have been able to *apport* a drop or a crumb. She was so tired her jaws were sore, and she was barely able to chew. In fact, she fell asleep with a half-finished chunk of bread in her hand, conscious only of the fact that the air *afrinn* had taken up a station between her and the door, and the water *afrinn* was nowhere to be seen.

———

The first thing she did in the morning, after cleaning herself as best she could, was to strengthen the two *afrinns* again. This time wasn't nearly as draining; it seemed that besides gaining power from her, the two were finally regaining it on their own. And it was just after lunch that two new and surprising things happened.

The first was when the water *afrinn* literally herded her over to the latrine hole and then, without warning, unleashed a literal torrent of pleasantly warm water on her, drenching her and her clothing.

She spluttered, standing there paralyzed with confounded surprise, and with the sense that she shouldn't react until she figured out what was going on. It increased the temperature of the water somehow and continued to drench her while looking at her expectantly.

It took her several moments to realize—the *afrinn* was actually cleaning her! Or trying to, anyway.

Well, she was no stranger to bathing or washing clothing without the aid of soap, so she stripped down, used her wrappings to scrub herself off, then, while the water continued to cascade over her, scrubbed all of her clothing against the stone of the floor, scrubbed all of her purloined clothing and rags, and finally gave her short hair as much of a scrubbing as she could. And meanwhile, apparently unlimited warm water (in a desert!) continued to pour over her in a glorious stream.

I wish we could get this at home, she thought, a bit giddy with how good it felt. Nor was that all—when she finally (with regret) signaled to the *afrinn* that she was in no more need of its services, the air *afrinn* immediately took its place and began blowing hot, very dry air over her. In no time, she was dry, her clothing was dry, and she was the cleanest she had been since the time she'd stayed at the Amber Moon enclave, where they had a hot spring one could soak in for blissful ages.

"Thank you," she told them both, when she was dressed again, and smiled wryly. "Well, I may be about to die, but at least I'll die clean." The *afrinns* didn't react to that; she assumed it was because they simply didn't comprehend her. What they understood seemed to be very hit and miss.

"I wonder if they've moved men back up into the prison tower," she mused. "After all, you two aren't all that impos—"

She stopped, because the air *afrinn* was . . . shimmering. The other *afrinn* hadn't done that, at least not in front of her.

The shimmering became a blur, and the blur, a mist that expanded into a sphere, and then the mist cleared—and she was looking at herself. But this was a version of herself that would have struck terror into the heart of the most hardened demon-summoning Karsite priest or the most foolhardy and brave Karsite soldier.

Just to begin with, "she" was two heads taller, had three-inch-long fangs, and was wreathed in fire. She was armored from head to toe in what looked like the same sort of black chitin that armored scorpions, she had an actual *scorpion tail* complete with sting, and in her hands were matched great swords.

She gaped at the vision, which stared at her out of expressionless eyes. Then the figure shimmered and blurred, the mist rose and cleared, and the air *afrinn* was back.

"Did you just transform?" she gasped. It shook its head. Well, that left—"Illusion!" she cried. "You can create illusions!"

It nodded.

So *that* was why the Karsite guards were staying away from the prison. One look at that demonic version of her, which probably matched what they thought she looked like anyway, and they wouldn't venture up the stairs for anything the priests could offer them.

But that wouldn't last once the demon-summoners got here. The best it bought her was time. She still needed to get out of here.

"I'm going to release the second earth *afrinn*," she told the other two. "There's no point in staying up here any longer. I can't get out the window, so let's at least get farther down the tower if we can. The closer we are to the ground, the nearer we are to escape."

The two *afrinns* pulled back into the corner with her, and she put the shield up around all three of them. She tossed the first of her last two bronze Talismans on the floor and spiked the spell.

This one took longer to break itself apart; it took so long that she was afraid that the eventual release was going to be as anticlimactic as the last two.

But when the spell broke . . . it was spectacular.

The release of power brought with it a release of real light and heat the equivalent of suddenly splashing oil on a fire. She threw up a hand reflexively, but she did not look away in time and found herself blinking tears out of dazzled eyes, unable to see what was in the room with her for a long while. The only thing she did do was drop the shield, to show that she was not an enemy.

And when at last she was able to see, she found herself staring at the thing she had released, mouth going dry with fear.

Of all the *afrinns* that the Mages of the Mountain spoke of, the one they warned never to approach, never to bother, and above all never to anger was . . . exactly this.

The Stone Man.

It stood unmoving in the center of the cell. It looked nothing like a stone statue, as might be assumed from its name. What it looked like was a roughly man-shaped rock formation. There was no discernable face in the lump of rock that was its "head," certainly nothing like eyes or a mouth. In fact, she couldn't even tell if she was looking at the front or the back of it. She couldn't tell what sort of stone it was made from; it was a uniform gray-brown, with fissures where ankles, knees, elbows, and hip and shoulder joints would have been.

And it most certainly did *not* need power from her.

She stood frozen in place, afraid to move lest she attract its attention and wrath. She wished she hadn't dropped the shield.

Not that it was very likely the shield would have done her much good, but—at least it would have been something.

There was no fighting a Stone Man. Not if you were a mere human. Only the most powerful Mages had a chance. Someone like her would be turned into a red smear on the floor in mere moments.

But the two *afrinns* with her swarmed the thing.

She held out a hand to try to stop them, afraid of what it could do to the delicate little things, even though they were themselves creatures of magic—but a moment later, she realized that they were not swarming it to attack it.

They were swarming it to greet it.

———

She sat on the floor, unable to stand anymore, her knees gone weak with relief. Whatever was going on, this much was clear at least. The Stone Man had no intention of attacking her. Instead, it and the other two *afrinns* were in some sort of silent conference, three points of a little triangle of intense concentration.

The Stone Man *did* turn its head to—presumably—look at her from time to time. And she assumed that, like the other earth *afrinn*, it had the ability to "read" the entire prison complex and that it understood what it was and what was in it. But she longed with all her being to be able to talk to it directly, to warn it about the Karsite priests that were coming, and to beg it for protection. She was long past the arrogance and hubris that had made her think she was a match for anything here and that it was only a matter of time before she broke out and got away. This prison had been made to hold tougher creatures than she was, and she had no doubt at all that the Karsite priest had meant every word that he had said about torturing and abasing her and sending her to be burned alive at their capital.

But the Stone Man—if legends were true, and she had no reason to think that they were not—was the one magical creature she could think of that was more than a match for the Karsite demons. And they should not be able to do much more than scratch its stony surface.

If it would help her. . . .

The utterly silent conference went on for so long that she finally gave in to her growling stomach and ate and drank, never taking her eyes off the creature.

The longer this goes on, the better for me, right? she thought with growing hope. *After all, those two afrinns know I'm not the one responsible for binding them all to the Talismans, and I'm not the one responsible for losing the Talismans in storage for so long. And I helped them! They know I didn't need to do that, and I did it without being asked. Surely that has to count for something . . .*

The Sleepgivers did not pray to any gods. It was their creed that the gods had set the world in motion, then gone off to do god things, utterly forgetting their creation as they moved on to something else. But as someone who had gone outside the Mountain and had seen and heard of gods that had done more than that (even if the Karsite miracles were nothing more than sham and magic), Sira dared to breathe a hint of a prayer.

Gods of law and . . . and kindness . . . if you can hear me . . . please believe that if you help me survive this, I will dedicate my life to Father's plan of turning the Sleepgivers from the path of murder to the path of protection. Please persuade the Stone Man to help me. Please get me out of here.

She knew that it would only take her urging for her brothers to give their whole hearts to this project, in defiance of whatever the Elders thought. Her father had already set his plan in motion, and with her brothers behind it, once it had reached the third generation of *their* children, it would no longer be a *plan*, it would be accomplished.

As the light outside the prison turned to a mellow orange-gold, in token of the sun going down, the Stone Man turned away from the other two *afrinns* and, with ponderous footfalls that vibrated the floor, came to within an arm's-length of her.

She stood up.

The other two *afrinns* moved to stand at her side, a gesture that gave her some hope.

"I-I-I am Sira," she stammered. "I released you, and I beg your forgiveness for you being imprisoned for far too long in that Talisman. I know I have no right to ask it of you, but please, I beg you, I need your help."

A strange, grating sound emerged from the top of the Stone Man; the sound was like a stone mill wheel grinding dryly against the bedstone, without any grain between them.

The sound made her shudder with terror, and she braced herself, hope lost, expecting to be struck down at any moment.

But the sound went on . . . and nothing happened.

And finally, she realized, with relief that nearly made her faint, what the sound was.

It was laughter.

14

The patrol turned out to be a lot of nothing; as Tiron had predicted, the Karsites took one look at the eight well-armed guards—and second glances at Ahkhan's smile—and merely checked to make sure Tiron had all the proper paperwork and permissions from the Karsite rulers. Then they hastily went on their way. The mercs waited until they were out of earshot, then the ribald remarks began.

The mercifully brief interruption over with, the caravan set off northward, at a hard pace that took them out of desert lands and into something that was more like dry grasslands and rugged hills, with thin patches of forest and brushland, where the land was not cultivated. This area was more populous, although nothing like Valdemar's lush farmlands. There were many small villages and what looked like farms large enough to hold several generations of extended families. The grazing herds were mostly goats, with some herds of donkeys, horses, and mules, rather than cattle or sheep. Tiron told him that the primary grain crops here were barley with a little wheat, rather than wheat and oats. It was impossible to tell from the stubble exactly what had been standing there before the harvest.

But there were orchards, although it was too late for fruit, and too late to tell what fruit trees were out there. And vineyards!

When they stopped briefly at a small town—which they did only because part of their cargo had been ordered by an herbalist there—they augmented their provisions with some fresh food, and aside from apples, what was on offer was a monotonous selection of cabbages and several kinds of beans. They also got flour and raisins, which would certainly be welcome.

And that was their sole stop in four days of travel. Tiron was extremely anxious to get to their destination, and he pushed them all as hard as he dared.

"Here's the problem," he said over a welcome change of pace of goat-and-vegetable stew, the night after they'd stopped to offload the spices and medicines that had been bespoken. They were camped just off the road, in a spot that was obviously used heavily for just that purpose, in a little cul-de-sac cut out of the side of a hill. That way they had earth on three sides of them and needed to keep watch only from the top of the hill. "There's no good way to get to where we're going from where we left. Road building isn't the Karsites' strength. Or interest, either, to tell the truth. They prefer that their people stay put where they were born for their entire lives."

"Easier to control what they see and hear," Ismal said sourly.

Tiron nodded. "So we're going to have to go north, parallel to the Menmellith border, then go due east again, because that's where the roads are. Then we'll hit the Sunserpent River, and there's a road that runs alongside it that will take us to Son's Springs, where we leave the main part of the goods. That's a lot more leagues than if we'd been able to drive as the crow flies—but you just can't get there from here."

"The one good thing is that we're going to be within running distance of either the Menmellith or Valdemar Border for most of the way," his son added, brows creased and looking worried in the flickering firelight. "If something bad happens, we can cut our losses and head west; if things go really badly, we'll cut the horses loose from the wagons and make a run for it. The Karsites will be so busy looting the wagons that we'll get enough of a head start we'll make it to safety."

Tory cast Ismal a doubtful look. "Do you know something you haven't told me?" he asked.

Ismal shrugged. "I just don't like the fact that those demon-summoning priests had the balls to tear up a village in Ruvan," he said. "I've had a bad feeling ever since it happened."

"They were probably chasing one of their own renegades who took shelter there," his father suggested, patting his son on the shoulder. "If it was someone with Mind-magic who somehow escaped their Fires as a child, you *know* they'd have gone to the ends of the earth to destroy him. And the Karsites have never cared if innocents get killed as long as they get their quarry. You ask them! They'll tell you that if someone who gets cut down is truly innocent, he'll go straight to the arms of the Sunlord. And then they'll give you the side-eye and point out that is much more desirable than living a long and miserable life on earth."

Ismal snorted. "Yeah, that's what they say about the kids they send to the Fires. They go straight to Vkandis, because they never get the chance to use those sinful powers and soil their souls."

"But the people in that village weren't Karsites!" Kee pointed out. "So they won't go to Vkandis!"

"Then the Karsites will tell you they deserved to be killed as heretics. Trust me, they have every possible excuse for being murdering bastards," Ismal growled. "I hate it every time we take a caravan in here. I'd rather find another market."

Tory bit his tongue to keep from blurting out that he could probably arrange that, since from what he'd seen, nearly everything in those wagons would find plenty of buyers at good prices in Valdemar. But he made a mental note of it. Something to bring up later, if, after all this was over, he could catch up with Ismal and his father again.

But his father laughed. "You worry too much," he said fondly. "You're like your mother. The Karsites have too much to lose by interfering with us. Too many important people want what we bring to them."

Personally, Tory would not have been willing to bet his safety on that presumption, and from Ismal's face, neither was he. But it was not Ismal's caravan, nor his business, and he would have to continue to follow his father's orders—however misguided he thought them to be.

They all went to bed—there was wood enough here that a nighttime fire was both possible and welcome. And Tory had pulled the first watch. So he set himself up above the camp on the top of the hill with a cup of that spicebush tea he'd come to enjoy, put his back to the fire so his eyes would adjust to the dark, and allowed his thoughts to drift while his eyes did the work. It was cold up here, but all the layers of his clothing kept everything but his nose warm, once he pulled his headwrap down around his ears. Silence reigned; so much silence that the crackling of the dying fire was the loudest thing he heard—that and the occasional grunt as someone below tried to find a more comfortable sleeping position.

For the past two nights, even though he and Kee had been at least an arm's-length away from each other, they'd still been able to see Sira when they searched for her as they pretended to sleep. That had to mean that they weren't that far from her now.

Kee had probably been able to see her much more clearly than Tory could, given the level of anxiety Tory was getting in waves from the Prince. So far, Sira was holding the Karsites off and doing reasonably well, at least so far as Tory could tell.

But of course, that was a temporary state of affairs. The longer she could keep her captors' at arm's-length, the more certain it was that the Karsites holding her had called for help. He suspected that the Karsites were walking a knife-edge at the moment. They were expected to get results by themselves, and calling in help would mean they were failures. Failure tended to get treated harshly in Karse. But the longer they went with Sira holding them off, the more their superiors would grow impatient, wondering what was taking them so long to break her. And eventually, the amount of trouble they'd get into for not breaking her would be outweighed by the amount of trouble they'd get into for not calling in help, and they'd send for reinforcements.

And that help would almost certainly involve the demon-summoners. Tory knew that, Ahkhan knew that, and Kee had probably figured that out for himself.

Which partly explained Kee's level of anxiety.

But not all of it.

Surely, surely Kee and Sira could not be Lifebonded. . . . They hadn't even met! Tory didn't much care for the idea of Lifebonding in the first place—it seemed to him to be more horrible than romantic to find yourself tied for life to someone else so intimately that if one of you died, the other one didn't want to live anymore. And having their Prince life-bonded to a foreign *assassin* was going to be a pretty tough thing to persuade even the most broad-minded person in Valdemar to accept. What the King would think about it, well, Tory didn't even want to contemplate what kind of reaction the *King* would have.

And yet . . . if it was a Lifebond, and not just infatuation with some imaginary creature Kee *thought* Sira was, the King was pragmatic. And if no one ever made reference to exactly *where* Sira was from . . . if she was just introduced as "a foreign highborn from a desert clan". . . .

There have been stranger spouses in the history of Valdemar's royals.

It helped that Kee was pretty far down in the line for the throne, which should make his choice of mate of interest to no one but himself—and perhaps any foreign princesses whose diplomats had been thinking of alliance marriages. *I don't know of any of those, but there's no telling what's going on in foreign courts.*

And what better person could you have standing secret bodyguard on the King and his family than a trained assassin?

But Sira is also a Mage. Would she be willing to give that up? There was no way a practicing Mage could live in Valdemar for long without going insane. And for that matter, Tory had no notion if a *non*-practicing Mage could live in Valdemar without going insane. And what about her Talisman? Would wearing it make her vulnerable? Would she give it up?

And maybe my imagination is running away with me. All of this could merely be the result of Kee fancying himself in the role of a gallant rescuer. This . . . infatuation could all be based on some picture the Prince had in his head which had little, if any, resemblance to reality. After all, what did they *know* about Sira in the first place? Next to nothing about the kind of person she was like to live with.

True, they knew she was brave. They knew she was smart. They knew—because Tory had seen her face, and he was dead certain Kee had too—that she was not unattractive. But did she have a temper? How did she really feel about people who were not of her Nation? Was she kind to animals? Was she cruel to children? There were all manner of traits she could have that would be too much for Kee to deal with. And right now, Kee could be painting himself a mental portrait that was at odds with the reality.

And he was all too ready to forget that she was an assassin. That she probably had no intention of leaving the Sleepgivers, and if Ahkhan was anything to judge by, had absolutely no guilt over being a multiple murderer.

Mind, if I were murdering Karsite priests . . . I wouldn't have any guilt either.

So when Kee met the reality and found it at odds with his vision, the problem of the Prince's feelings just might solve itself.

All right. I'm going to let sleeping dogs alone, as the saying is. The one thing I could do to drive him straight into a commitment to her would be to criticize her or his feelings, because he's going to feel he has to justify them. No point in getting into a fight with him about the girl, when, odds are, the minute they lay eyes on one another, he's going to get a rather rude awakening.

Especially if she has absolutely no interest in him.

That made him feel a good bit better. Because why should she?

He's a total stranger and a foreigner, and the only reason he got involved in this is because he had a dream in his head that, no matter what, is not going to match up with reality, now, is it? I just hope she doesn't break his heart too badly when she turns him down.

At least we're not likely to be in any sort of situation where she's going to laugh at him. Things are going to be pretty damn frantic when we finally get to her. We're all going to be too busy trying to survive to worry about feelings.

Well, now that brought up the horse in the solar; they were going to try to break this girl out of a Karsite prison. Presumably an extremely secure one. He and Kee would probably be able to help, but the fundamental planning and work were all going to be on Ahkhan. So far, neither he nor Kee had been able to see outside that cell to understand what the conditions were. They had no idea how many guards there were, where her cell was, or anything other than that the cell was above ground. And neither of them had any experience at all in breaking into or out of something as fortified as a prison.

We probably had better all have a conversation about that.

Sooner, rather than later.

The farmers and herdsmen of Karse avoided them as if they were infected with plague. The town- and village-folk interacted with them only when they were forced to sell things to them. So even though these hills were inhabited, they were just as isolated as they'd been in the desert. And there were absolutely no road signs either; they only knew they were going the right way by frequently consulting a heavily annotated map that had served Tiron for decades, because there was literally no way of telling whether the "road"—more like a faint track—they were following was the right one or was one that had diverged from the proper road a few leagues ago.

Tory, of course, had absolutely no idea of where they were. All he knew was that the hills had gotten steep enough that they effectively shielded the farms behind them from the road. *These people really don't want to have anything to do with strangers.*

Of course, if they were the least little bit helpful to strangers, particularly nonKarsite strangers, they ran the risk of accusations of being tainted by heresy. Or worse, of being heretics themselves.

I don't imagine they want anything to do with their own troopers either. So, another good reason to keep hidden too.

The road wound in and around the hills, effectively muffling sound and hiding anything that was more than a few furlongs ahead of them.

So it came as a complete and utter surprise to everyone when the road made a sudden turning out onto a flat plain—and there was a barricade across it, manned by. . . .

. . . . far, far too many armed troops. *Way* more than they could handle.

These looked nothing at all like the Border Patrol troops. Their armor, their uniforms, were all matching and in good repair. They weren't milling about, even though they looked just as surprised to see the caravan as Tiron's people were to see them. And the moment these troops realized they were not alone, they formed up, both in front of and behind the barricade.

Kee, Ahkhan, and Tory were at the rear, so they couldn't hear Tiron, but Tory imagined that he was cursing under his breath. Nevertheless, he directed the caravan to continue, only signaling for them to stop when he and Birk were face to face with what looked like the commanding officer of this troop.

"Turn yourself right around and go back the way you came," the officer commanded, his voice sounding strained. "No traffic on this road until further notice!"

Now that they were closer, it was clear to Tory that every single one of these men was under some tremendous stress. Clenched jaws, furrowed brows, white knuckles as they clutched their weapons, and the telltale signs of faint trembling that showed they had been under this stress for far too long told Tory—and, without a doubt, also told Tiron and Ahkhan—that these men were not too far from breaking.

So it was with no surprise that he heard Tiron speaking in soothing tones, rather than impatient ones—or worse, barking out a challenge. "Troop Leader, we're simple merchants. We're conveying a cargo of some import to the High Priests Durchloss, Entschmitt, and Gurether. They want it—they are expecting it—rather urgently."

The troop leader winced visibly at those names, but he shook his head vehemently. "I'm sorry. No one passes. No one at all. That's my orders. Now, you can turn around and go back the way you came, or you can go straight east around that hill behind you, where you'll find a track that will take you into Menmellith, and from there you can make your way into Hardorn, cross the border there, and travel down again along the Sunserpent River. But you can't pass here."

"But the High Priests—" Tiron persisted.

The troop leader swallowed visibly, but he remained firm. "I will take personal responsibility for the delay. I'll even send a message to that effect, if you can write it."

"I can," Tiron said steadily, and motioned to Ismal, who jumped down off the wagon seat and took the reins of his horse. Tiron rummaged around in the back of the leading wagon and returned with a sealed note, which he handed to the troop leader. "Will you pledge by your faith in the Sunlord that you will see that message delivered to the three High Priests at Son's Landing?" he asked.

"I pledge this," the troop leader said. "Now, you must turn around. And be across the border or far, far down the road as soon as you can, or I cannot guarantee your further safety."

That was when Tory managed to angle himself so he could see into the plain beyond the barricade—a plain ringed by hills—

In the center of which stood what looked to be a very large structure. With a high tower.

And he had no doubt at that moment that they had found where Sira was imprisoned.

Rather than going back the way they had come, Tiron directed the caravan to take the alternative route, the one that the troop leader had said would take them into Menmellith. And for a while no one said a word as they guided horses and wagons over rough, rocky terrain that threatened to break wagon wheels and horse ankles until they finally got to an even fainter track leading west that at least had the virtue of being smooth.

And that was where Tiron held up a hand, halting them all. At his signal, all the guards and the merchants dismounted from wagons and horses and gathered around him.

"What the actual seven *hells?"* he exploded, and then he fell silent, unable to get words past his outrage.

All the others exchanged looks, except for Ahkhan, Tory, and Kee. Tory held his tongue; this was not his secret to give away. Kee also wisely remained quiet. Finally Ahkhan spoke, reluctantly.

"The structure in the middle of the plain behind the barricade. . . ."

"What about it?" Tiron demanded. "We've gone past it two dozen times or more with no problems. The road doesn't go anywhere near it—the road skirts the edges of the hills."

"It's a prison," Ahkhan replied.

"*And?*"

"There is . . . someone in it. Someone dangerous to the Karsites. Someone who has unexpectedly given them trouble."

Tory held his breath, and he sensed that everyone else except Tiron and Ahkhan was doing the same.

Tiron took three, slow, measured breaths. "And I am guessing you have something to do with this prisoner?" he said at last.

Ahkhan nodded.

"And the reason the troop leader told us to get the hell out is because the demon-summoners are on the way to deal with this prisoner."

Ahkhan inclined his head. "Very probably."

"And now you're going to leave us, because you three are either foolhardy, gallant idiots, or you're even more dangerous than that prisoner, and you intend to get the prisoner out before the demon-summoners arrive."

Ahkhan sighed. "We are probably both," he admitted.

Tory had no idea Tiron knew how to curse so fluently.

But when the caravan leader had finished, he fell silent again.

It was Ahkhan who broke that silence. "If I may have access to your writing supplies, I may have a solution to your dilemma that will result in, at most, a small loss to you, as opposed to a total loss. I can give you an introduction to Amber Moon North and entreat them to purchase the whole of your cargo."

"And if you'd prefer to make a bigger profit, I can guarantee that in Valdemar," Kee said. "I just need access to those same supplies."

Tiron stared at him, rage draining out of him to be replaced by utter astonishment. "And just who are you that you can guarantee anything in Valdemar?" he demanded, then shook his head. "Never mind. I'm better off not knowing. Ismal, take them to the writing chest."

In the end, all three of them wrote letters. Ahkhan wrote to the head of Amber Moon North, enclosed another letter inside it, and sealed it all with his Talisman. And Kee wrote to the ranking officer at the Guard Post on the Border, enclosed a letter to his father in that, and sealed it all with his signet ring.

And Tory wrote to his father via his father's closest agent just over the Border and sealed his with nothing at all, since the letter was in code and it didn't matter who saw it.

It was a difficult letter to write because there was at least a fifty percent chance that by the time his father and mother saw it—well, he and Kee would be dead. In it, he took full responsibility for letting Kee get away with this crazy, stupid idea of rescuing his cousin. He begged their forgiveness for allowing any of this to happen. But he reminded them that at least the two of them had bought absolute security for Valdemar *forever,* at least from the Sleepgivers, and that, all things considered, was probably worth their lives.

That's my judgment anyway, Father, and you said I was old enough to trust my own judgment.

And, heyla, maybe by the time you get this letter we'll all be laughing about it.

That was all he could manage; he was already feeling sick.

He didn't know what Kee had written, but the Prince was white-lipped and determined-looking as he handed over his letter to Tiron.

"I should try to dissuade you three," the older man said heavily. "But I can see there's no point in trying. I'll be praying for your success to all the gods I can think of."

"I would like you to take our horses," said Ahkhan, shocking Tory. "They will be of no use to us if we succeed, and they will be a handicap as we cross that open plain. If you go into Valdemar, the border guard with the ginger moustache and beard expressed an admiration for my Natya. I would like you to sell her to him. He has a good eye for horseflesh and will care for her well."

Natya is like a clan member to him . . .

He either thinks we're going to fail, or he is stripping down to essentials so we can get in and out before the demon-summoners get here. In either case . . .

Bloody hell.

———

They had only trail rations, water, and weapons. No extra clothing, no bedding. Moving with great caution, making sure they could not be detected, they had made their way through the hills up north past the road and the barricade on it. Out there in the plain, when there were breaks between the hills, the structure loomed, like a dark fist extended skyward.

Tory was glad of the concentration it was taking to keep under cover, scuttling from spot to spot. It meant he wasn't thinking about anything else.

Finally Ahkhan reckoned they were far enough away from the barricade that they could pick a place overlooking the valley directly, and he chose the top of a low hill to aim for.

Once they had a spot where they could see the tower clearly and had made certain they were out of sight of the guards on the road,

Ahkhan had all three of them settle down under the cover of some bushes to wait until dark. The only way they were going to get across that empty expanse was under cover of darkness.

But, ironically, Tory saw that once they could get across most of it, there *was* some cover in the form of scrubby trees and more bushes, probably marking where a seasonal waterway flowed. So once they got there, they could take cover again and study the walls and the tower itself at their leisure.

They all lay down on their stomachs, careful to make sure nothing showed outside the protection of the sprawling bushes. Tory wasn't sure what kind of bushes these were--some kind of scraggly evergreen, perhaps, with very short, stubby needles. He was glad it was winter. At least they didn't have to worry about insects getting into their clothing.

"It might seem counterintuitive," Ahkhan said quietly, as Tory studied the ground immediately in front of them, plotting the best route from scant bit of cover to bit of cover, "But our best chance to penetrate the tower, once we are across the valley, might come by daylight. And in the meantime, perhaps the two of you can look in on Sira once again and at least get a sense of which floor she is on. That will narrow our target area considerably."

"I can do that without looking," said Kee, unexpectedly. "I can *tell*. She's on the top floor of the tower."

They were all lying side-by-side on their stomachs under the cover of the bushes, with Kee between Tory and Ahkhan—and both of them turned their heads simultaneously to stare at him.

"How—" Tory said, "—exactly?"

"It's—" Kee fumbled for the words. "It's like I can see heat, except it's not heat. But this close to her, even without touching Tory, if I look out there sort of sideways, it's as if I'm *right next* to the tower, and I can see a kind of glowing silhouette of her, right through the wall. There're three other things in there too, with her. One's shaped like a man, one's shaped like a dog, and one's a weird shape sort of floating in midair."

Tory's first thought was, *Oh, thank the gods, it's not a Lifebond!* But his next was, *Then what in the seven hells is it?*

For the first time in their acquaintance, Tory saw Ahkhan's mouth drop open in surprise and shock. And it took him a moment to recover.

And when the Sleepgiver *did* recover, what he said made *Tory's* jaw drop.

"Why didn't you tell me you were a Mage?"

"I'm a Mage?" Kee spluttered. Now *his* jaw sagged.

"You must be," Ahkhan asserted. "That is the only explanation for what you are seeing. We have Mages in the Nation. This is how some of them describe seeing other Mages when they are not shielded. And I have suspected that those 'not human' things you have been talking about that were with her, and apparently helping or guarding her, were some manner of magical creature."

"I can't be a Mage! Mages can't be in Valdemar without going insane! There haven't been any Mages since Vanyel!" Kee protested—but weakly.

"As long as nothing triggered your Mage Gift, yes, you would be fine in Valdemar," Tory reminded him, thinking out loud. "And I imagine the same power that keeps Mages *out* of Valdemar also prevents the Mage Gift from manifesting. It would be intolerably cruel, otherwise. But there's no reason to believe that the Mage Gift itself has died out since Vanyel's time. It's most probably just been kept dormant."

"I—uh—"

The ramifications of this were probably just now dawning on Kee. They certainly were on Tory.

Because, at the worst, Kee could never go home again. Not without risking losing his sanity.

But Tory was . . . to say envious was minimizing how he felt. He could *already* picture what he would do in Kee's position. Ask Amber Moon North for training, just for a *start.* Then become his father's agent outside of Valdemar. And a Mage Spy! How incredible would that be?

"We will discuss this further if we survive all this," said Ahkhan, bringing everything right back to the present moment. "Meanwhile, *tell* me if you see something unusual. And if you feel power rising in you to do something, then *do it.* Even untrained, it will be a weapon, and weapons are something we sorely need at this moment."

"Uh—right." Kee squinted his eyes in the direction of the tower. "I think they're all talking."

"Can you see anything else in that prison glowing with Mage Power?" Ahkhan asked, as practical as ever.

Kee stared out over the plain, his eyes practically crossing with effort. "No," he said, finally.

"Would he, if they were shielded, the way Heralds can shield themselves with Mind-magic?" Tory asked him.

"I do not know," Ahkhan admitted. "But I do not think they would have any reason to do so and waste the energy. And that is good. That means there are no demon-summoners among them."

"Yet," Tory reminded them all. "Yet."

15

Sira stared at the Stone Man, too stunned even to think. Why—was it laughing?

But the other two *afrinns* were not in the least alarmed by this. So, presumably, whatever it was laughing about had no sinister overtones.

The laughter went on for a very long time, more than long enough for her nerves to calm. More than long enough for her to wish the *afrinn* would make some attempt to communicate with her. But she reminded herself that of all the *afrinns*, the creatures of earth were the most inclined to take their own good time about things.

Some people would say "the slowest," in fact.

And there was no point in being anything other than patient with them. The earth snake *afrinn*, in fact, had probably been an exception to that rule, but, then, it was made not of stone but of swiftly moving sand. So that probably explained its "hasty" behavior.

She wanted badly to sit down after a while, but the Stone Man might take that as disrespect, so she remained standing until, at long last, it gave a last grating grunt of a chuckle and reached out toward her.

She froze again. *Now what?*

And it slowly, with extreme care, patted her left shoulder. Three heavy, but gentle, pats.

"*Aaalll . . .*" it said, "*. . . lllllyyyyy.*"

Ally! So it *had* agreed to be bound to the Talisman! And it evidently had found the fact that she was so apologetic to be extremely amusing.

But it's a Stone Man. And maybe for a Stone Man being bound in a Talisman for a couple of millennia is like being left in a room alone for a couple of days to a human. Who knows, it might have been peaceful for him. Like a meditative retreat.

At least she finally had something she could talk to! Or rather, something that could answer back. "May I sit?" she asked, politely. "Humans get tired."

It nodded, slowly, and she put her back to the wall and slid down it. And as she did that, the Stone Man slowly rearranged the boulders that made up his body so that he was "sitting" across from her.

"*Teeeeeeellll,*" it urged.

So, assuming that the creature knew nothing past the earliest days of the Nation at the Mountain, she recited as brief a history as she could—essentially the "child's history" that she told over to herself when she needed to pass the time. When she got thirsty, she took a drink of water; when hungry, she ate. And just about at sundown, she finished that and began the much shorter story of how she had ended up here.

By this time she could only see the Stone Man as a darker blot of shadow unless she used Mage Sight—and then, he and the other two *afrinns* lit up from within as if they were lanterns. She didn't use Mage Sight often—it was effortless for some but exhausting for her—but tonight, being able to see her allies was very comforting. The air *afrinn* glowed like a drawing made in the air in pale blue dust. The water *afrinn* was like a green glass sculpture with a glowing core.

And the Stone Man radiated a soft yellow light, all over, as if something had heated the rock from which he was made until it gave off light as well as heat.

They all sat there quietly in the dark until the air *afrinn* moved out into the staircase—presumably making sure none of the Karsites tried anything. Watching with Mage Sight, for the first time, she *saw* how it did that—flattening itself and slipping under the door.

For some reason . . . the longer Sira sat with the Stone Man, the more some of the strain she had been under eased. It was as if he were radiating peace and certainty.

Maybe he was actually doing that. Maybe that was part of his power. Wasn't there supposed to be a Mind-magic power that worked on the emotions? It might make sense for an earth *afrinn* to have that.

Or maybe it was something else. For the first time, one of these *afrinns* had recognized her as an ally—and didn't seem inclined to run off on her.

Finally, the *afrinn* spoke.

"Caaallllll fffffiiiiiiirrrrrrre."

Her hand went to the necklace, which now only had a single bronze disk woven into it.

The *afrinn* nodded ponderously. *"Caaaaalllll fffffiiiiiiiirrrrre,"* he repeated.

Well, what did she have to lose? Of all of the *afrinn* she had released so far, this one was by far the most conversational. The least she could do would be to do what it asked.

When she got to her feet, so did the Stone Man. It moved out of her way as she paced off the number of steps to the center of the cell, put the bronze Talisman on the floor, and went back to the wall. "You'll want to shield yourself," she warned the Stone Man— or trying to, because she wasn't sure how much it understood. "I don't know how to take the spell off, so I have to break it."

The thing just made a sound like two bricks scraping together, so she mentally shrugged, spiked the spell, and put up her shields.

And waited.

And waited.

In fact, she waited for so long, she began to fear she hadn't done the job properly and was about to lower her shields and check on it, when there was a huge flash of real light, and a blinding flash of Mage energy; she *felt* the impact on her shields and lost both real and Mage Sight for what felt like forever. In fact, she was still rubbing her running eyes when she saw a sort of glowing man-shaped blur bending over her, and she yelped.

"Aren't you supposed to be making a polite speech at me instead of shrieking in my ears? And I do have ears, you know."

The voice sounded amused—and also odd. As if it were coming from deep inside a well, or across an echoing canyon. And there was a hissing and crackling component to it as well, like the hissing of flames.

She knuckled both her eyes, then dropped her shields as the Stone Man let out another one of his rumbling, gravel-grating chuckles.

It was perfectly easy to see *this afrinn* in the dark. He glowed like the coals of a slow-burning fire, and he looked as if he were made of those same coals, too. And the air in the cell was definitely warmer, and it smelled pleasantly of scented smoke, mingled cedar and sage. "Do you want to hear the speech?" she asked.

"To be honest? Not really. I've heard it six times before, after all. Greetings, Sira! I am Eakkashet, and may I say, I am very glad you found a way to release us." Then the creature bowed slightly. The *afrinn* certainly sounded pleased. But the wonder was that he was talking at all!

"Why is it that you can talk to me and the others couldn't?" she asked before she thought. And then berated herself for being both rude and stupid. *You don't go demanding things of an afrinn!* she reminded herself.

But Eakkashet did not seem to mind. *"Borkase and I are much more powerful than the other five,"* the fire *afrinn* said, modestly. *"At least at the moment. The amount of energy it takes to remain on the physical plane with you and communicate in a way you can understand is more than any of the others could manage."*

"Caaaaan taaaaaalllk," the Stone Man objected. *"Juuuuuuuusssssst ssssssssllllloooooooooowww."*

"Yes, yes, Borkase, and it would take you three turns of the glass to say a single sentence," Eakkashet replied, and he patted the Stone Man's shoulder. *"That's one reason why he told you to release me. The other is that he can sense the demon-summoners coming. It's time for you to escape."*

"What?" It was a good thing she was already sitting down, or her legs probably would have given out under her. "How? And why are you helping me so much? What am I going to owe you after this?"

Eakkashet didn't answer her directly; instead he looked at the

Stone Man, who went rigid for a moment, then rumbled something.

"All right, I expect we can take a little time for explanation," said Eakkashet. *"First, Borkase can sense the demon-summoners coming because the earth itself rejects them as unclean. He knows where every single one of them is, and he feels many of them heading in this direction."*

"And why are you helping me? What am I going to owe you?"

"You'll owe us nothing, Sira. When your ancestors took that Portal and arrived where they did, we that you call afrinns *were curious about them and made some tentative alliances with the Mages among them. Now, I won't go into a long description about politics and warfare among the creatures of other planes—just take it as a given that we do have such things, and a couple of generations later, when your people were making quite a name for yourselves as assassins, some of us found ourselves with an acute need to hide among you. Now, this was the point in time when your Mages were trying to find a way to store the memories of the most skilled of you in Talismans so that those memories could be passed down directly. Some of us volunteered to hold those memories and be bound to the Talismans so we could hide more efficiently, and that's what happened. And then your Mages found a better way, forgot we could also be called out of the Talismans to help out when we were needed, and we got buried in storage. Until you came along."*

A big half-circle of glowing white appeared in the glowing red of Eakkashet's head. If it was supposed to be a smile, it didn't succeed in looking anything like one—but Sira found it reassuring, anyway.

The air *afrinn* whistled like a wind among the rocks.

"Now, enough chatter. You need to escape before the demon-summoners arrive. We're going to help you, but first you need to lend power to my friends, and then eat and sleep, so that we are all as ready as we can be."

The Stone Man made a small noise that indicated his agreement.

"So, it is my feeling this would better be done in daylight," Eakkashet continued.

"I agree. You'll be providing more than enough to occupy everyone's attention, and I haven't had a chance to study the ground." This was going to be hard. But if the *afrinns* could keep up their rampages for long enough, she could probably put enough distance between her and the prison that when they realized she was gone, they wouldn't be able to spot her. "Are—you and Borkase or just the others going to need a boost of power from me?" she added, hesitantly.

"Just air and water."

She was very relieved to hear that. "Uh—forgive me for asking something that is probably obvious, but—can you set things on fire?"

The *afrinn* roared with laughter. It sounded like a roaring fire. *"Oh, I am going to be setting everything on fire that does not run away from me, Sleepgiver. So eat and drink and sleep while you can, tonight, Sleepgiver. Tomorrow we will be in a race against foes and time."*

Sira beckoned the air and water *afrinns* to come to her, and she lent them every bit of her magic energies that she could muster. Then she ate and drank, eating up all the bread she had, since it wouldn't keep and was bulky to carry. But she didn't go to sleep immediately.

Instead, she packed as much as she thought she dared carry. Her weapons, her waterskin, the dried beef. When the breakout began tomorrow, she wanted to be able to sling everything on her back and go. The water *afrinn* obligingly filled the waterskin until it was tight with fresh water.

Only when she was certain that she had packed everything useful in the most efficient manner possible did she lie down. And somehow . . . she fell asleep.

There was more cover than Tory would have thought from the view from the hill. Ahkhan had a knack for finding places that held deep pools of shadow that covered all three of them.

But mostly they worked their way in a zig-zagging course one at a time, with Ahkhan in the lead and the smell of dust and dead leaves in their nostrils. Ahkhan would pick a new bit of cover and scuttle into it. That was the signal for Tory to take the cover he'd just been in, and Kee to follow into Tory's cover. Kee would give the soft whistle of the top-knot quail (something Ahkhan had taught them all) when he was safe, which was Ahkhan's signal to find the next spot and move into it.

When they were about halfway across, Ahkhan uttered a soft hoot. Tory collapsed into his pool of shadow, got a good long drink from his waterskin, and tried to relax for a moment. From where he lay, he could see the torches of the Karsite troops manning that barricade across the road. They were tiny pinpricks of light in the far distance, visible only because there was no other light out here but thin moonlight. He was pretty confident that if (when!) they came back this way during the day, no one from the barricade would be able to see them from this far away.

Unless, of course, they were all on their feet and running.

Which would be suicidal. Obviously.

While they were resting, and Tory was looking directly at the tower, the window he was watching, trying in vain to see whatever it was that Kee could see, suddenly lit up with a brief flash of light.

"What was *that?*" he hissed.

"I wasn't looking," said Kee, alarmed.

"There was a flash of light in Sira's cell." Ahkhan sounded remarkably calm, but maybe that was just a thing that Sleepgivers could do—push all their emotions aside for as long as it took them to get a job done.

"There are four creatures with her now," Kee said, instantly. "And the new one is really strong. If being lit up more than the others means power, that is."

"She must have decided to try to escape, then," Ahkhan mused aloud. "I cannot think of any other reason why she would have released . . . never mind. I will explain later. She must have learned that the demon-summoners are on the way."

"Or she just guessed, given that she must have been holding them off for a good long while, and she knew they wouldn't stand for it much longer," Tory murmured.

"We had luck on our side getting here when we did. We cannot expect to have it for much longer," Ahkhan sighed. "Well, we shall have to assist luck. Let's get to the foot of the tower, or as near as we dare."

They got in place, undetected, sooner than Tory would have expected, and once they were all well-hidden in that strip of brush and trees they'd been aiming for, Ahkhan put both hands to his mouth and hooted—an owl call, but one that Tory didn't recognize.

He waited a long moment and hooted again.

When there was no answer, he uttered a quiet oath. "She must be asleep. Which means she intends to escape by day, which suits our plans."

Kee looked at him incredulously. "Asleep? How could she possibly *sleep?*"

"Training," Ahkhan said. "And we should do the same."

"Well, I can't sleep," Kee told him stubbornly.

"Then you may take the first watch, and wake me when you find you can sleep, after all." And with that, Ahkhan pulled his cloak around him and turned into a ball of fabric.

That left the two of them alone in the shadows and the darkness. Sounds traveled a long way in the desert stillness, and there were very faint whispers that could be the men on the barricades talking to one another, off in the far distance.

It was a reminder that *they* needed to be as quiet as possible. "Let's look in on her," Tory urged. "It's the first chance we've had to do this properly since we joined the caravan. We can at least see what these four *things* with her are."

Kee nodded wordlessly, and they locked hands and went hunting.

This was the clearest sight he'd gotten of this room yet. Sira was a ball of fabric in one corner of the floor, looking rather like her brother. But this time, rather than just getting a sense of *something is there*, Tory got perfectly clear looks at all four of the creatures.

There was one at the door, hovering in midair, a pale blue-winged lizard, transparent, as if it were made of glass. There was another curled pensively next to it, also transparent, but green, a doglike thing with finned feet, like fish fins, and fins for ears. Sitting together in the middle of the room, still between Sira and the door, were two very different creatures. They looked . . . only vaguely like humans. The first looked exactly as if someone had constructed a statue out of boulders—as if one of the hoodoos back behind them had come to life.

But the fourth—

This *must* be the thing that caused the flash of light. It looked like another roughly human-shaped statue but made of glowing coals instead of boulders, coals from which the occasional flame licked.

And it opened white-hot "eyes" and looked straight at him.

"Dawn," it said, in a voice like a hissing, crackling fire. *"Be ready."* And it closed its "eyes" again.

Tory sensed Kee "tugging" at him to pull back. He broke contact and opened his eyes and was, of course, unable to see anything of Kee but a darker shadow in the darkness.

"What—what was that?" Kee gasped.

"A friend." Tory was absolutely certain of that. And inside, despite the danger, despite the fact that the odds stacked against them were terrible, he smiled. Because he had just seen four creatures that were, without a shadow of a doubt, *made of magic.* He didn't know what they were other than that, but the mere fact that they were something other than creatures of the material world made him want to jump to his feet and shout with excitement.

"Look," he continued. "With those four things guarding her, she's perfectly safe until morning. I'm going to get some sleep, and I assume if there's any night left when Ahkhan gets too tired I'll be taking the third watch. Are you sure you'll be all right taking the first watch?"

"I'm sure I couldn't possibly sleep, and I don't know how you can," Kee retorted, resentfully.

Tory was about to snap back at him when Kee put his hand on Tory's arm.

"I'm sorry," he said, sounding it. "I'm all nerves. I shouldn't take it out on you. I'm the one who dragged you into this in the first place."

"That's what friends are for—being dragged into things," Tory countered, and steadied his own nerves. *We've got—whatever it is that is up there helping Sira. That's way more help than I thought we'd have. We just might get through this.* "As long as you'll be all right, I'm going to see if I can copy Ahkhan."

He honestly didn't think he'd actually be able to get any sleep. But the next thing he knew, he was startled wide awake. The faint, predawn light gave him a better view of his surroundings than he would have thought, and beside him Ahkhan and Kee crouched in postures of tense readiness. Then the sound that had awakened him came again, from the tower.

A bird call.

———

Sira came awake instantly as something nudged her toe. It was the Stone Man, and it wasn't quite dawn, judging by the faint gray rectangles that were her windows. The Stone Man shrugged, as if in apology, and gestured to Eakkashet.

"You have allies," the *afrinn* whispered. He gestured at the window. *"Out there. I sensed someone using Mage Sight to look upon us. If there is some way you can communicate with them without alerting your foes here . . ."*

Not daring to hope, Sira jumped to her feet and ran to the window, cupping her hands around her mouth and uttering the quiet call of the cactus owl.

She waited, then gave it again.

And this time, she was answered! And not merely "answered," but answered with the peculiar lilt at the end of the call that told her someone in her immediate family was out there! Her heart raced. She had help out there! She *just* might make it through this!

She responded, this time with the flocking whistle of the top-knot quail, the one that the females would call to summon her chicks. She was asking whoever it was "how many of you are there?"

Three peeps came back. So there were three! Her heart rose further, until she almost felt intoxicated. Now there was real hope!

She replied with the warning call of the same quail, telling whoever was there to stay where they were until her signal—which in this case was going to be her, climbing down the side of the tower. At least, that was what she thought it was going to be . . . she turned to Eakkashet. "Do we have a plan?" she asked him.

He shrugged. *"I do not,"* he admitted.

She thought quickly. "You and—" she had to think a moment to remember the Stone Man's name "—Borkase go down into the prison and wreak as much havoc as you can. You go to the left at the base of the tower, and Borkase, you go to the right. Anything and anyone that can be smashed and burned should be. When you meet, I should be out of the prison and running."

The Stone Man nodded.

"We don't particularly enjoy killing . . ." Eakkashet replied plaintively.

"Well, every one of these bastards has the blood of plenty of innocent children on his hands, one way or another," she retorted, and she grimly detailed how the Karsites sought out children with Mind-magic and burned them alive, did the same to anyone they considered a heretic, and enforced their cruel regime with demons. The four *afrinns* listened silently until she was finished.

"And every one of these wretches that you eliminate means one that won't be able to go after us," she concluded.

"You make a good argument." The *afrinn* sighed, then (visibly) brightened. *"But if we just hurt them too much to chase you, then we not*

only eliminate that danger, we also stop those who will have to look after them from pursuing you as well!"

Personally, Sira was fairly dubious that any of the Karsite guards were likely to care about anyone other than themselves . . .

But I'm prejudiced. And they're soldiers. Logically, they should have some *sort of bond that keeps them from abandoning each other every time they fight something. And I've seen them drag off their injured or dead comrades. So . . . maybe he's right.*

"All right," she agreed. And then got a grim sort of satisfaction out of the fact that, if Borkase and Eakkashet actually *did* hurt the Karsites enough to put them out of the action, that would certainly mean broken bones and hideous burns, and the Karsites might well wish they were dead before it was all over. "If you see two men in robes, though, those two are certainly *directly* responsible for the deaths of children. They're priests, and absolutely no one is going to weep if they are dead."

"We'll keep that in mind," said the fire *afrinn.*

Now she looked at the other two. "Can you stay with me? With us? Are you willing to help us escape this miserable land?" she asked.

They both nodded. She sighed, relieved. The illusion-creating ability of the air *afrinn* was likely to come in handy . . . and as for the water *afrinn,* they were going into the desert. Whoever was out there waiting for her certainly had food provisions but probably not much water. She had nothing but the dried beef and her water bottle from her kit. Food, they could do without for quite some time. But water? No. And it would be foolhardy to try to hunt for it in a near-desert while running for safety. But the water *afrinn* would solve that problem.

"Thank you," she told them, and she turned back to Eakkashet. "What about you two?" she asked. " Can you catch up with me?"

The Stone Man regretfully shook his head. *"Tooooo slooooooow,"* he said.

"And Borkase would just make a very visible thing to follow, so he would lead the enemy right to you. Well, I am not too slow, and I can keep them from noticing me, so I will certainly go with you." Eakkashet was silent for a moment. *"Borkase, when I leave this place with the Sleepgiver, see if you can contact the other three afrinns she released and send them after us. Or if they cannot find us, ask them to set upon any of these* Karsites *they think are pursuing us."*

The Stone Man nodded. *"Caaaan't prooomiisssssse."*

"We know that," Eakkashet said soothingly. *"Just try. And now . . . how do you propose to make a hole in this wall?"* He pointed to the one with the window that Sira had just called out of.

Borkase got ponderously to his feet and approached the window. He studied it for so long that Sira began to fear this was all going to be for *nothing,* that the wall was so enchanted that not even an *afrinn* could get through it.

But then the *afrinn* turned slightly and put both "hands" on the wall next to the window.

And then . . . just stood there.

The light outside strengthened. Sira's heart pounded, and her throat closed with anxiety. She wanted to weep. Nothing was happening! The *afrinn* couldn't get through it! All this was for *nothing!*

But then she noticed something strange.

Most of the *afrinn* was made of sand-colored "boulders," with some ochre and rust-colored streaks through them. But now—the "hands" were gray.

Gray, like the stone of the walls.

They hadn't been that color before.

And as she watched, she saw that gray color creep up the "hands" to the "wrists."

And the "hands" sunk deeper into the walls.

The *afrinn* was absorbing the stone of the walls into itself!

So she kept her impatience to herself, until the *afrinn* was up to the "elbows" in the wall; then he slowly withdrew, leaving behind a hole roughly shaped like an hourglass on its side with a very fat middle. It was, if Sira was any judge, just big enough for her to squirm through, carrying her gear.

They must have enchanted just the window and the stone around it, not the wall itself. That was smart—much as Sira hated these Karsites, she had to admire them for that. Enchanting the entire tower would have been ruinously hard on their Mages, but if they hadn't done *something,* any prisoner with magic abilities would make short work of the bars on the windows or the stone into which they had been set. So they concentrated on fortifying the barred window, because not one prisoner in a hundred would have thought of going through the wall rather than the window. Well, *she* hadn't! And neither had the first earth *afrinn* she had released.

The Stone Man admired his handiwork for a moment, uttering that grating stone-on-stone sound that passed for a laugh, then moved out of the way. Sira passed her leather-strap "rope" with the helm fastened to the end through the bars of the window nearest the hole, then reached out through the hole and was *just* able to catch the rope in one hand and bring it back into the cell. The helm would anchor the rope in place so she could climb down it. If it was strong enough to stave off the blows of an ax or a warhammer it was certainly strong enough to hold her weight.

"Are we ready?" Eakkashet asked.

"Just about," she replied. Thanks to her preparations of the night before, it was a matter of moments to get her belongings slung on her back and tied down, and all her weapons distributed where she could get them in a hurry. Then she nodded at Eakkashet, opened the door to the cell, then got the rope bighted around her waist and in both hands.

The earth and fire *afrinns* headed down the staircase, making as much noise as possible. It sounded like a combination of a forest fire and an avalanche. With some strange and inarticulate howling and grinding thrown in.

When the sounds had diminished to the point where more noise was coming in through the windows than from the stairwell, she headed for the hole. The air and water *afrinns* darted past her and got out first.

The hole was bigger now than it had been before; part of the wall had crumbled away after the *afrinn* had finished his work, and she was able to climb out with no trouble at all. She tried to ignore the prickling feeling between her shoulder blades as she rappelled down the wall, bit by bit; leather straps did not make the best of "ropes," but at least there were the splices and rings at intervals to keep her from sliding too much.

And then she came to the end of the leather.

She looked down.

Still at least two man-heights to go, down onto very rough and rocky ground.

No help for it.

She looked back up, concentrating on her hands and her grip, then slipped down, little by little, until she was dangling by her outstretched arms from the very end of the strap.

Then she let go.

———

Tory had scarcely known what to think when he saw a hole forming in the wall next to the window. How?

Never mind that, he told himself. *That's the signal. We need to be ready.*

But Kee was not going to wait. Before Tory realized what he was up to, the Prince had already wriggled through the brush at the edge of their shelter and was eeling his way through the scrub grass, heading for the tower.

"What does that idiot—" Ahkhan hissed in astonishment, then broke into another cascade of curses. But he made no move to join the Prince out there in the danger zone between the shelter and the base of the tower.

Tory, however, did not hesitate. With a curse of his own, he set off on a course parallel to Kee, rather than in Kee's wake. Using absolutely everything that Mags had taught him, he squirmed over rocks and under branches that threatened to lacerate him if he made one wrong move, trusting to his ears to tell him where the Prince was. After a while, that got a lot more difficult, since it seemed that a large riot was taking place inside the prison, and the noise penetrated to the outside.

That actually made him feel a lot better. Those creatures, whatever they were, must be running rampant through the prison. And that would be taking every bit of attention of any human being in the place off of anything but the rampaging creatures themselves—and possibly escape routes for themselves. There weren't any openings on this side of the prison, so they were safe from would-be escapees.

And when he finally reached the area of rocks at the base of the tower, rather than raising himself up to look for Kee, he looked straight up at the hole in the wall—

—just in time to see a pair of boots coming out of it, followed by the rest of the girl.

She's good, he thought, as she eased her way down the side of the building, using what looked like leather straps tied together somehow. *Not* the best material for a rope, but she was making it work. She moved swiftly and surely, and when she got to the end of her tether and found herself *still* an uncomfortable drop from the ground, she somehow managed the arm strength to let herself down until she was dangling from the very end of the leather by her fully extended arms—

—and then she dropped.

Right into Kee's embrace.

Tory had no idea how the Prince had gotten there that fast— Kee reached up as high as he could, caught her as she fell, and simultaneously made a leap to the side that carried them both onto a hummock of grass rather than the rocks she was heading for.

Something pale and blue flashed by him, heading for Sira and Kee, and something pale and green slithered down the wall to join it, both things moving too fast for him to make out what they were.

Tory just scrambled to his feet and dashed over to where he had seen all four disappear.

He found Kee and Sira, still caught in an embrace, staring into one another's eyes as if entranced. *"Hey!"* he hissed, startling both of them out of it. They let go of each other and scrambled to their feet.

Sira looked over at the blue thing, which looked like a flying lizard sketched in the air in blue smoke. "Can you make us disappear? I mean, not totally, just make it look like the four of us are desert hares or something?" She looked back over at Tory. "You've got one of my kin with you, right?"

"Ahkhan," he replied shortly, since Kee seemed too breathless to reply.

She looked back over at the blue thing, which was nodding. "All right," she said. *"Run."*

16

Sira had not expected to fall into the arms of anyone. Especially not the young man she'd been seeing in her dreams.

The breath was knocked right out of her, and not from the fall. She found herself staring deeply into a pair of silver eyes that caught and held hers in a way that made her chest tight and her skin tingle and her thoughts turn to powder.

It was only when someone else hissed *"Hey!"* that she came back to herself again, and all the peril of their situation struck home with the force of a body blow.

But strangely, the effect of that entrancing stranger—presumably one of the three people who had come to help her—was to make her wits *sharper.*

As she scrambled to her feet again, she looked to the air *afrinn.* "Can you make us disappear? I mean, not totally, just make it look like the four of us are desert hares or something?"

Then, while it was thinking, she looked back over at the fellow who had startled her out of her trance. "You've got one of my kin with you, right?"

"Ahkhan," the stranger said, which was the best news she could have heard right now. She looked back over at the *afrinn*, who was nodding.

"All right," she said to both of them, and she reached out without thinking and seized the silver-eyed stranger's hands. *"Run."*

And to make sure they did just that, she launched into a sprint. She thought she'd have to drag her stranger behind her, but no, he not only kept up with her, he waved briefly with his free hand, and the most beautiful sight in the world—her brother Ahkhan—burst out of cover and gestured for them to follow him.

She was absolutely ready to do just that. *She* had no idea where she was, after all, and they did. After all, they'd gotten here, hadn't they?

They were heading north, at least by her reckoning. *Deeper into Karse? Or did those bastards drag me farther north than I thought?* Never mind. Either way, when the Karsites figured out she had escaped, they'd assume she'd be heading home, which was south. North was a much safer direction to go.

Ahkhan lagged enough on the other side of the line of shrubs and trees that they managed to catch up with him. "We need to get as much space between us and this prison as we can, as fast as we can," he said—needlessly, since that was obvious, but she was saving her breath for running.

The air *afrinn* had changed its shape to something like a huge umbrella or bubble that managed to cover all of them. "Brilliant to see you, too, brother," she replied. "Stay under the *afrinn*. He makes illusions."

There was not a lot of sign of the water *afrinn* except for a pale-green flash in the spaces between the clumps of grass ahead of them, but that was enough to tell her that he was keeping his promise and staying with them. She wondered what these strangers would make of the creatures.

And who are they? How did Ahkhan find them? And how did he persuade them to come with him. And how did they all find me?

She glanced over at the one whose hand she was not holding, just as he glanced over at her. There was a definite family resemblance there.

To *her* family. She'd looked into features like those for far too long not to recognize them even in a stranger.

But he seemed much too young to be her father's contemporary.

He must have read the recognition and confusion in her eyes, before he looked away again and concentrated on running on the rough ground. "Cousin Tory," he said briefly. "You're with Kee. Not a cousin."

She looked back over at "Kee," whose face lit up with a smile that left her dazzled—but still clearheaded. "Explain later," he said, wisely. "Run now."

So run they did. And she still kept hold of his hand.

They had to slow to a lope about halfway across the plain, but behind them smoke arose in several places from the distant gray shape that was the prison. Eakkashet was certainly keeping his promise to set things on fire.

She finally let go of the silver-eyed stranger's hand when they slowed; she didn't *want* to, but she felt the pressure of her brother's gaze on her. She still wasn't sure where all these odd sensations of utter *familiarity* with him were coming from. It was as if she had known him all her life, and yet she'd never seen him before he'd popped up in her dreams—

"Were you scrying me all this time?" she asked him abruptly. He didn't seem at all confused by her question as he loped along, easily keeping up with her and Ahkhan.

"Well, Tory and I can Farsee anyone who's related to either of us," he said. "I guess that's what you'd call *scrying* if it was done by a Mage?" He looked up briefly, to make sure they were still under the "umbrella" of the air *afrinn*. "And near as the three of us can figure, you sent out a kind of powerful shock along those kinship lines the night you were attacked by the demons. Maybe because you're a Mage. And the two of us got hit with it, maybe because of our Gift. Then your brother turned up to ask for Herald Mags' help, and Mags told him we'd be better suited for his needs than Mags would be. So here we are, and we've been trying to get glimpses of what was happening to you ever since we knew it was you who sent out that shock."

"Less talking," Ahkhan said. "More running."

She and the stranger—Kee—exchanged a look of amusement despite the peril of their situation. She was pretty sure he was thinking the same thing she was. *Brothers . . . I can eviscerate anyone who is the least bit of a threat to me, but Ahkhan thinks he needs to protect me!* If they lived to get to the border, this would be very, very funny. And even now, it was funny enough.

"If we can keep up this pace, we'll get to the hills before sundown," the other stranger—Cousin Tory—observed. "Do we go on through the night or hunt for a place to hole up and rest?"

"We make the most of daylight, but if we can find a shelter, we should make use of it." Ahkhan stared ahead, chin set grimly. "Once the demon-summoners know of Sira's escape, the night will not be safe."

She shuddered, remembering the last time she had fought the things—and that was when they'd had orders not to harm her! The Karsite priests would surely not hold them back this time.

"Is it even possible to hide from them?" Tory asked.

"I do not know," Ahkhan confessed.

"Nor I," said Sira, "But I can create magical shields, and the air *afrinn* can create illusions, and perhaps between the two we can conceal ourselves from them." Then Ahkhan increased his pace a little, and she had to leave off talking to save her breath for running.

Which was probably his intention.

What was not his intention, of course, was that she would set her mind to analyzing what had just happened between herself and Kee to keep herself from thinking about the grueling run, at least until she could get into that state where the run became a blur and she forgot about the sweat running down her back and the ache in her legs.

That would come eventually. Thinking about Kee would make it come sooner.

"Are you a Mage?" she asked him directly, after thinking about Mage-magic and Mind-magic for a while. Because it didn't seem to *her* that a Mind-magic power could have alerted Eakkashet to Kee's presence outside the tower.

"I don't know," Kee said, panting a little, and then taking a quick drink from his water bottle. "Ahkhan says I am. But Mages can't live in Valdemar—"

"So clearly his power was repressed in Valdemar, probably by the same things that drive Mages insane there," Ahkhan said impatiently. "Is there a point to this?"

"Yes, *brother,*" she replied. "Kee, you may be untrained, but there is power in you, and you may be able to tap into yet more power from the world around you. And although you can only wield it clumsily, in our case, that is much better than not at all. If something occurs to you to do, then *do it,* and do not think about it. A clumsy blow can still remove an enemy, and I am not a powerful Mage, I merely use what power I have very cleverly."

Kee definitely brightened up a bit at the encouragement. And as she smiled at him, she felt that intoxication she had been hoping for come over her, and she let herself open to it.

There was no more talk, then, until they did reach the hills, where they paused on the top of one—

Just in time to see a swift form come darting down out of the sun and through the "umbrella" of the air *afrinn,* who squeaked in protest. Accustomed to having Windhover land on her forearm, Sira automatically brought her left arm up, and the creature alighted on it for a moment, before hopping to the ground and taking the form of Eakkashet.

"*I have good news and bad news,*" the *afrinn* said without a greeting. "*The good news is that most, if not all, of the Karsites in the prison are either disabled or tending the injured. The bad news is that they sent out riders to all the ones guarding the roads into the plain before we could stop them. It will take time for them to assemble at the prison and more time for them to get on the hunt, but they will come, and Borkase cannot accomplish much against mounted men in the open. I told him to do what he could, then see if he could contact the others. Do you want me to go back and join him? I do not want to set fire to the plain, so please do not ask that of me."*

"I don't want you to set fire to the plain either, Eakkashet," Ahkhan replied, before Sira could say anything. "That would be so wasteful that it would shame us for the rest of our lives. And it could prove to be as much a danger to us as to them. Please stay with us. I am Ahkhan, Sira's brother."

"Then we should go. I will scout ahead for hiding places." The *afrinn* transformed again; this time Sira saw plainly what form he had taken—a firehawk, appropriately enough, a bird that was known to fearlessly hunt the edges of wildfires, preying on the creatures the flames drove from their burrows and hiding places.

Eakkashet dove under the air *afrinn's* bubble this time and winged away to the north.

"We must concentrate on leaving little to no trace now, not on speed," Ahkhan said, looking severely at Kee and Tory. Kee flushed, but Tory just shrugged.

"Good thing we both got Sleepgiver training in doing just that," her cousin replied, in what was not *quite* a mocking voice, and not *quite* something Ahkhan could take exception to.

So they resumed their trek, this time being careful to walk on loose sand, which would hold no trace of discernable footprints, or rock, which would hold nothing at all, picking their way across the valleys between the hills, still heading north and now west as well, as the sun sank behind them and cast long shadows that they tried to remain in. And when they *had* to venture into the sun, it was where nothing was going to see the long shadows that *they* cast. The air *afrinn's* illusion could do nothing about the sun, which now betrayed that they were very much larger than a family of desert hares or even a small herd of prong-deer.

The sun had dropped down behind the hills, the sky aflame, and Sira was very much afraid they were going to have to make do with sheltering under brush, when Eakkashet came winging back.

Taking his two-legged form, but a version in which the fires of his being were so subdued that his surface was gray ash, he waved to them to follow.

On the other side of the hill was a deeply cut dry wash. And Eakkashet leaped down into it—a distance that would have broken her legs, but, then, he *was* an *afrinn*. She and the others took the chance while there was still light to see and free-climbed down the rocks; and there, just where Eakkashet was standing, was the water *afrinn* and a deeply carved cave in the cliff.

But this was a wash . . . and the presence of that cave alone—

"Don't worry," Eakkashet said. *"Atheser will keep you safe if there is a storm and water comes down. And Merirat will make an illusion of stone over the mouth of the cave once we are in."*

Sira was not inclined to argue with him. She was the first to duck inside, to discover that the cave was deep enough that all six of them could stretch out comfortably and high enough that they weren't going to crack their heads on the overhang if they sat up. And it seemed to have a floor of nice, deep sand—possibly washed in from floods. She tucked herself into the back with a suppressed groan as her leg muscles reminded her that she had not done running exercises in a while.

Kee was right behind her and took a spot at her left, between her and the entrance. Tory followed, cast them both a quizzical look, and picked a spot opposite them. Ahkhan was last, and—well, if it hadn't been Ahkhan, she'd have said he *plonked* himself down next to her on her right in a disapproving huff.

Actually—she gave him a sidelong glance and took a moment to read his expression in the gloom—that was exactly what he'd done.

Eakkashet and the water *afrinn* followed. Eakkashet planted himself right at the entrance, and the air *afrinn* bubbled the entrance over, faintly distorting the view to the outside.

Oh . . . I do not want to move . . . but I really must do this. She groaned again as she got to her knees and eased past the fire *afrinn* to a point where she could reach the air creature. "I'm going to feed you more power," she told it and was rewarded with the brief appearance of the lizard-head in the midst of the bubble and a faint creak that sounded like gratitude.

"Can I help?" Kee asked instantly, causing her to mentally bless him.

"I should think so," she told him, as Ahkhan frowned. "Feeding power to another is one of the first things our Mages learn to do. Just use Mage Sight, watch what I do, and try to do it yourself."

Kee crawled on his hands and knees to get beside her and watch as she gathered power, gently put her hands into the air *afrinn*, and began feeding it.

"I—think I feel some of that same energy flowing nearby, and I think I can reach it," Kee said uncertainly. "It's like a little river. Should I try?"

Sira felt both startled and pleased. If Kee had found a ley-line, and if he could tap into it—he was a much better Mage, even untaught, than she was! "If you feel something the *least* wrong pull back—but try it!"

Kee closed his eyes to concentrate and tentatively reached out one hand to the *afrinn*. And to Sira's Mage Sight, he was like a river of power flowing into the creature, as opposed to her trickle.

The air *afrinn* gave a little shiver, and he pulled back, opening his eyes again. "Did I do that right?" he asked anxiously.

"I think you filled him up!" she replied. The reptile head appeared again (which was an extremely odd effect) and hissed vigorously. "Do you want to try for the water *afrinn*, and Eakkashet as well?"

"I would not reject this notion," Eakkashet spoke up. *"And if our friend is to supply you with water, he should be fed as well."*

Looking much more sure of himself this time, Kee closed his eyes and gently laid his hands on the water *afrinn*. And when he pulled back, the creature wagged the fin it had instead of a tail and burbled.

Kee turned his attention to Eakkashet and then hesitated. Sira didn't blame him in the least. Putting your hands on something that looked like a pile of burning coals was . . . daunting to say the least.

"Don't touch me," the *afrinn* said. *"Just hold up your hands, palms toward me, and let me do the rest."*

An expression of relief washed over Kee's face before he closed his eyes and did as Eakkashet had asked.

Behind her, Tory gasped. She didn't blame him. The power flowing between them was *so* strong it was actually visible, like a ray of sun shining through the clouds, except that it went from Kee's hands to the *afrinn's* body.

By this point, the sun had set completely, and the little cave was lit by the *afrinn's* glow and the power flowing between them.

At length, the *afrinn* sighed with content and said, *"That is sufficient,"* and made a little gesture. The light from Kee's hands went out.

"Are you sure?" Kee asked. "Because I feel as if I could keep that up for candlemarks."

"As certain as you are that you are replete when you have eaten a fine dinner," the *afrinn* replied. Sira glanced over at Ahkhan. He looked impressed in spite of himself. She scooted back to the place she had left, and Kee took his place beside her again.

Ahkhan seemed to be keeping a very wary eye on him, but when Kee made no move to touch Sira, not even to hold her hand again, he relaxed.

And that was when they heard voices.

All the humans froze, and Sira strained as hard as she could to hear more clearly. But all she got were fragments coming from above, up on the edge of the wash.

It was all in Karsite, though, so it was obvious that the hunt for them was up. Mostly it seemed to be men calling to one another to report that they had found nothing.

Which is monumentally stupid, since they're just telling us where they are!

Eakkashet somehow dimmed himself to nothing, which was probably a good precaution. And the temperature in their little cave plummeted. Sira hugged her cloak around herself and wished she had more layers.

Peering past the black shape that was Eakkashet, up through the wavering view through the air *afrinn,* Sira got a glimpse of torchlight as someone looked down into the dry wash. "Nothing down here!" he called, his voice echoing off the rocks, up and down the wash. Other voices answered him in the distance, as all of them froze.

They didn't dare move, and Sira was certain all of them

understood that without saying. The illusion of rock over their hiding place might hold, but not if they made any sound at all.

She was just glad she'd gotten into a comfortable position before the Karsites overran their hiding place.

She did wonder, however, how the idiots expected to actually see anything down in this wash when they were half-blinded by their own torches.

But maybe it didn't matter. Maybe they didn't care about that.

Maybe, in fact, most of them didn't actually *want* to find her. Maybe after seeing whatever carnage Eakkashet and Borkase had wrought on the prison, they were just going through the motions. And as long as it was night, their commanders wouldn't be able to tell whether or not they were really doing their jobs.

But don't count on that, she reminded herself. *Never count on anything with the Karsites.* She'd learned her lesson of being overconfident, and she did not intend to repeat that mistake. Ever.

They all waited, breathlessly, until the voices died away in the distance. And then they waited a while longer before Ahkhan broke the silence by whispering, "Is anyone hungry?"

"I have dried beef," Sira whispered back. Eakkashet increased his light and the warmth coming from him. By Eakkashet's dim glow, they exchanged food.

"Wait a moment! Don't eat the meat! I have an idea!" Kee exclaimed—also in a whisper. He took off his helm, filled it with water and had Eakkashet hold it while he dumped his share of the dried meat into it. Immediately after that, Tory, Sira, and Ahkhan did the same. That gave them broth to dip their trail biscuit into to soften it, which was a vast improvement over the otherwise tasteless things. And when the helm cooled down again—which Eakkashet was somehow able to make happen quickly—they all had warm cooked beef.

"How did you make the helm—I mean, pot—get cool so fast?" Tory marveled in a low voice. "I know you must have done it, Eakkashet."

"I am fire. I can do anything with heat and flame," the *afrinn* replied, with that strange half-circle of light showing in his "head" again. The water *afrinn* burbled, though whether that was a laugh or in agreement, Sira couldn't tell. *"Especially thanks to all the help from your outlander friend."*

Had she introduced them to the *afrinn?* She couldn't remember. She was so tired, and now that she wasn't moving, her legs were really heavy and sore, and it was hard to think of anything else. "I'm probably repeating myself," she said, and even if the others didn't notice, she could tell she had begun to slur her words a little with fatigue. "Eakkashet, this is Kee, and this is Tory. Tory is distantly related to me. Kee is not. They are both from the Kingdom of Valdemar. This is my brother Ahkhan. There is a long and probably complicated story about how they came to help me. Do you want to hear it?"

"I am very fond of stories," the *afrinn* said with interest.

"Then I'll tell it," Tory volunteered.

He began, and Sira listened at first, but eventually her eyes grew too heavy to keep open, her head too heavy to remain sitting, and the warmth of Eakkashet's power too soporific to allow her to remain awake.

So she curled up on her side with her head pillowed on her arm and drifted off to the sound of Tory's soothing whisper.

Tory finished the story. The fire-creature did that unsettling thing that passed for a smile. And Ahkhan looked over at Kee and glowered, because at some point between when Sira had fallen asleep and now, Sira's head had ended up in Kee's lap.

Tory sighed. "Enough, Ahkhan."

"Enough *what?*" Ahkhan growled, turning on him.

"We both get it. You don't approve of Kee being attracted to your sister, or her to him. You've made that abundantly clear to all of us, including her. I thought you trusted her."

"I do!" Ahkhan spat. Tory sighed. This might take a while.

"I thought you trusted her judgment," he said, patiently, and in as nonjudgmental a tone as he could manage. "Everything you've said about her was to assure us she could take care of herself. So either *you don't* and she *can't*, or you're doing what every single brother in the history of the world has done and decided there is no man good enough for her without bothering to consult her on *her* feelings. So which is it?"

Tory had decided to go straight onto this aggressive stance here and now for several reasons. First, they were all stuck here until morning, or the Karsites moved on, or both. So Ahkhan couldn't go storming out. Second, Sira was out cold; he was more than empathic enough to tell that. So she wouldn't be embarrassed. Third, if he didn't get this out in the open now, it was only going to get worse. And it was likely to get worse at the worst possible time.

"I wasn't—I'm not—" Ahkhan began indignantly, and then he deflated, abruptly. He stayed quiet for a very long time, long enough that Tory wondered whether he had just made things worse all by himself. "You two came all the way out here with me for no good reason," he admitted. "And there is a very good chance that we are all going to die at the hands of the Karsites. We should not argue. You're right."

"Well, what are you going to do about it?" Tory asked sensibly. *Well, that worked out better than I thought. This was the time to do this. Ambushed him, he can't get away, and we have death tromping around up above us, which gives a fellow a lot of incentive to be honest.* He was a good bit unhappy that Ahkhan seemed to be of the opinion that they were all going to die, of course . . .

. . . but *he* was going to try not to think of that right now.

"What are *your* intentions?" Ahkhan growled, turning to Kee.

"I—I don't know," Kee said honestly. "I'd have to know how Sira feels. All I know is it feels like I've known her all of my life. Maybe more than all of my life. Like we've been friends and more forever. I'd like to go on—or start—being friends and more forever. But I don't know if she feels that way."

"If she does?" Ahkhan demanded.

"Then I'll find a way for us to be together, and we'll do whatever you people do about getting married." Kee seemed very sure of that.

"And if she *doesn't?*"

Kee's voice faltered a little, but only a little. "Then when we get somewhere safe, we'll say goodbye as friends and I'll—I'll go do something, I guess." He sighed. "I hadn't thought that far. I mean, I'm a Mage now, and if I were to go back home, I'd have to learn how to not be a Mage again. I guess I'll do that, and if that doesn't work, maybe Father can make me the ambassador to Hardorn or Rethwellan or Menmellith or even the Shin'a'in, where being a Mage will be an advantage."

And when Kee said that, an enormous weight was lifted off of Tory's shoulders. *No one* who was Lifebonded would have said something like that. No one who was Lifebonded *could.* Whatever this was between Kee and Sira, it was something reasonable and sane, not terrifying and inexplicable.

"So you wouldn't pressure her to—"

"No," Kee said steadily.

"You wouldn't *stalk* her and pursue us back to the Moun—"

"*NO!*" he said indignantly. "Seriously, Ahkhan, you Sleepgivers have some kind of twisted idea about—about love and—and whatever if you think that! I just . . . between what I've been feeling from her all this time we've been looking in on her, and what you told me about her, I think she's amazing and I want to be her partner even if she does going on murdering people for a living. I mean, as long as it's just Karsite demon-priests, that's all right, and I'd help . . . "

His voice trailed off. Tory wasn't sure whether to laugh or cry. Poor Kee . . . what must he be feeling now? Like he'd just been given everything, but it could all be snatched away in a moment, and without warning, maybe? And, of course, to find yourself in love with a Sleepgiver . . .

"I'm not sure whether to laugh or cry," Ahkhan said dryly. "Strangely enough, the tale my father tells about the first time he set eyes on my mother is not at all dissimilar. Without the hesitancy about our heritage, of course. I believe her body count exceeded his at the time."

Kee made a strangled little noise.

"All right. If we live through this, and if she feels the same, you have my blessing, for what it's worth." Ahkhan sighed. "And don't worry about getting Father's. It's not him you need to be concerned about."

". . . it's your mother."

"More than likely. But you're a pretty thing, and evidently a powerful Mage. Both will go a long way toward mollifying her."

There was a long, long pause.

"Thank you. I think," said Kee.

Silence settled over them all. Eakkashet seemed disinclined to comment—probably none of this made any sense to a creature that was literally made of fire and probably reproduced by splitting, or merging with another of its kind and dividing into four, or some other insane (by human standards) thing. Ahkhan had said his piece and, having said it, was obviously satisfied.

Kee? Well, Kee probably had a head full of Sira right now since he'd finally gotten Ahkhan to stop glaring at him, and between that and the very urgent need to get across a border--any border-- before the demon-summoners got on their trail, that was more than enough to occupy his mind.

That left Tory wondering what the *hell* he was going to tell the King. Because he, with his limited empathy and being pretty good at reading girls, was absolutely certain Sira felt exactly the same way about Kee that he felt about her. Which meant that one way or another, Kee and Sira were going to be a couple. So how to tell the King that his son was going to marry a Sleepgiver?

And there was one other thing.

If they lived through this, it was pretty obvious that whether Kee and Sira managed to live in Valdemar, had to go to the Sleepgivers' Mountain, or went to live somewhere in between, there was one phase of both his and Kee's lives that was over. They would still be best friends . . . but they would be best friends apart. He could not compete with Sira, and he did not want to.

So he and Kee would never be quite the same again. In fact, there was a good chance that he'd never even see Kee again once they escaped.

Kee would be fine. He had Sira.

But what do I do?

The darkness had no answers.

17

They all woke at dawn; nearly simultaneously as far as Sira could tell. Eakkashet radiated a comforting warmth, but the cold breeze from outside the cave told them that without him they'd have spent a profoundly uncomfortable night. She woke first, to discover that somehow during the night she and Kee had ended up supporting each other.

Despite the danger they were in, that invoked a cascade of feelings in her that had absolutely nothing to do with harsh reality. All of them were wonderful. Some of them she had no names for yet. And when he woke up a moment later and smiled at her, it gave her the most irrational feeling that everything was *just fine*, even better than fine, and nothing bad could possibly happen as long as the two of them were together. She allowed herself to give in to that feeling for just a moment or two, because she knew it was not going to last.

But that bit of silent communion between them was quickly

interrupted when Tory and Ahkhan stirred and grumbled, and she and Kee separated, sitting up carefully, before the other two opened their eyes. She discovered she didn't feel nearly as sore as she had been afraid she would. Either the gentle warmth Eakkashet had supplied all night had something to do with that, or she wasn't in as bad shape as she had thought.

The water *afrinn* burbled at Tory, who held out his empty waterskin. Atheser filled the skin, the rest of them followed suit, and the *afrinn* then burbled at Eakkashet and slipped out of the shelter, beneath the air *afrinn's* illusion bubble.

"He is going to see if there are Karsites about," the fire-creature explained. *"What is our plan?"*

Ahkhan took out his map. "I think we're here, roughly," he said, putting his finger on a spot. "I'd like to get over the Border into Menmellith. That's not *ideal,* because a mere border isn't going to stop the Karsites from crossing it, but they might hesitate, and that will give us a chance to get far enough ahead of them to buy some merc help, or summon some help from the troops guarding the Border."

Sira nodded, sucking in her lower lip when she saw how much farther north the Karsites had taken her than she had thought. How had they done that, in so short a period of time?

Maybe by riding their horses to death and having new mounts ready when the old ones were about to drop. They seem to think anything is disposable except themselves.

They all gnawed on trail biscuits and drank water while they considered the limited view the map gave them. "Essentially," Ahkhan said, finally, "all we know for certain is that if we go north, we'll be going from hills into mountains, we'll likely be limited to traveling in the valleys, which will make it easier for the Karsites to ambush us. But if we go west, it will still be hills."

"Easier terrain for us, but easier for them, too," Tory pointed out.

"I can help," Eakkashet said. *"Since Kee can replenish me, I can shapeshift into a firehawk and scout from above. I very much doubt that the Karsites will pay any attention at all to a bird."*

"That would be of *immense* help," Sira said gratefully. "And you don't have to do any of this."

Eakkashet laughed. *"This is highly interesting for me—for all three of us afrinns, so far as that goes. We were idle for so long that it is a pleasure to be doing things. It is not as if we are in any danger from those fools."*

"I wouldn't be so sure of that," Sira cautioned. "You haven't yet encountered those priest-Mages or their demons."

"Nor have they encountered us. But—very well, we will take precautions." Eakkashet sounded as if he were trying to conciliate her. Well—fine. She didn't mind him being a bit arrogant, as long as he was as good as his word and was *careful* as well.

The water *afrinn* darted back, squeezing under the edge of the bubble, and burbled at Eakkashet.

"For as far as he went, he found no humans," Eakkashet said with satisfaction. *"Perhaps they have moved southward, since they did not find us here last night. That would be the logical next step. Our home is south, after all, it would be logical to assume that was where we were going. They would want to catch us before we reached that Border."*

Sira was not at all sure of that . . . but if Eakkashet and the air *afrinn* were both prepared to scout from above—well, they would at least have some warning of any Karsites between them and the Border with Menmellith.

Through this entire discussion, she was acutely aware of Kee, sitting quietly at her side without contributing anything. Somehow it wasn't a distraction; she still found herself able to focus perfectly well. His presence was more like a bulwark than anything, as if she knew she could be certain that if she missed anything, he would see it.

And sure enough, he spoke up, just as she thought that.

"We need to have more than one plan in place," he pointed out quietly. "What if we find a physical barrier, like a river or a canyon, that we can't cross that's not on the map? What if the Karsites *don't* do what we think they are going to do? We have limited supplies and limited options. I don't think we can afford to make things up as we go along. And yes, I *know* we need to get moving, but a candlemark of planning now could save us a day or more later if we get into trouble."

Eakkashet looked at the water *afrinn*, who burbled at him. *"He says he can part the water around each of us, one at a time, so that we can walk safely on the riverbed if there is a river."*

"Good, we didn't know that before. What about a canyon? I'm not prepared to try to climb down an unknown, raw rock wall with nothing but my fingers and toes." Kee raised an eyebrow at Sira's brother. "You may be that good, but I'm not."

"A canyon would be as much a barrier to the Karsites as to us," Ahkhan pointed out. "If we find something too deep to climb, Eakkashet can scout for a trail down, and the Karsites won't have that advantage."

"And if we find them between us and the Menmellith Border after all?" Tory asked quietly.

They fell silent. And it was Kee who spoke at last. "Then we go north. There is one thing we *do* know. There is one Border that the Karsites will not *dare* cross. And that is the border with Valdemar."

Tory was doing his level best to concentrate on the immediate moment and nothing else—because if he thought about the danger they were in, he knew he'd falter and let doubt take him down, and if he thought about Sira and Kee, he'd be too muddled with mixed emotions to pay attention to what he was doing. So he listened—there was nothing out there but the sound of the wind in the rocks. The breeze smelled of nothing, not even dead grass. And of course the only thing outside their cave was the opposite wall of the wash and a crooked slit of blue sky. Eakkashet slipped out first and shapeshifted into the firehawk while the rest of them ate and stretched.

Stretching, warming their muscles, was a must. They were going to have to start today's trek by climbing a rock wall—a short one, but still. Then they'd be moving at a pretty good pace for the rest of the day. No matter what, they still had to travel as far and fast as they could until they reached safety—

If we can.

The fire *afrinn* returned just as the air *afrinn* resumed its normal form. *"There was no sign of them close at hand, but they have thoroughly muddled up all the ground hereabouts, which is to our advantage. I will scout ahead. Merirat and Atheser will scout to the left and right. You just concentrate on running."*

Ahkhan didn't wait for an invitation to begin the trek. He shot out of the cave and began climbing the sides of the wash before Tory had even gotten to his feet. By the time the rest of them joined the Sleepgiver at the top, he was watching Eakkashet soaring ahead of them. "I've picked the best route for as far as I can see," he said, brusquely. "Let's go."

Ahkhan did not launch into a flat-out run, as they had done

yesterday, although Tory would not have been surprised if he had. He and Sira matched paces, side by side, in an identical lope made for endurance running. He and Kee followed right behind, and Tory, at least, was watching carefully to see where Ahkhan put his feet so he could match that as closely as possible.

He'd have been worried about dangerous animals, because only the gods knew what was out here, but not after all those Karsites had been tramping around all night. Probably any wild animals had been scared right across the plain, or were cowering in their dens, wondering when it would be safe to come out again.

At least with so many men all over this ground it would be impossible now for anyone to pick out their trail from the rest. Eakkashet was right. The ground was so muddled their trail would just blend right in with the rest.

Now and again, he looked up to marvel at this inhospitable wilderness. How did anyone scratch a living out here? Maybe they didn't. Maybe that was why the prison was in the middle of it. But that would bring its own set of problems, because everything but water would have to be brought in by wagon. And the fodder for the horses or mules—probably mules—that pulled the wagons would have to be brought along too, so that meant long wagon trains coming and going often. Was being a guard here considered punishment or a privilege? It should have been easy duty, after all, not like the kind of prison where there were dozens crowded into stinking cells, and the chance of a riot or a breakout was high.

Easy duty until they picked up Sira, anyway. That must have been quite a shock. She hadn't said anything about it yet. And now he found himself wondering just what had been going on all that time between when she'd been captured, and when she'd escaped. Obviously at some point she'd somehow called up these *afrinn* things, but how? She said she wasn't a very powerful Mage—and surely the Karsites had put protections against magic around their prison, because it was clearly one built to hold special prisoners. So how had they gotten in? Or had she somehow brought them with her?

The questions kept coming, and he welcomed them, because now he had plenty to think about besides Kee.

The country they were running through was showing stronger signs of transition from a desert to something more like dry grasslands. That was going to make tracking them harder, but it was also harder to run through the knee-high, dry grasses, which offered resistance that was not unlike running through water. And if it was less sandy, it was now more *dusty*, and his eyes felt sore and he kept wanting to sneeze.

His legs ached. How long had they been running? By the light of the sun, it was halfway to noon, and Tory, at least, was starting to feel the effects of running most of yesterday and all morning. *I wish we still had the horses* . . . But it would have been impossible to get them undetected across all that open plain. But, oh, his legs ached, and his side was starting to. His lungs burned. And he badly needed a drink of water.

At least it was cold. And dry, so he wasn't drenched with sweat as well. But he tasted salt whenever he licked his lips.

"All right," Ahkhan said quietly, as they mounted the crest of yet another hill. "Time for a breather. Slow down to a walk."

"I'd rather drop to my knees," Tory admitted, "But yes, I know, if we stop, we'll just stiffen up and it will be worse when we start again." Now that they weren't running, he reached for his waterskin and poured a generous amount down his throat as he walked. Well, that was one blessing; they weren't going to have to conserve water, not with Atheser, the water *afrinn,* ready to refill their skins and bottles at need.

Sira looked back over her shoulder at Kee. They exchanged the kind of smile that shut everyone else out. Tory allowed himself a moment of envy.

"Eakkashet's coming back," Ahkhan said, interrupting that moment. Tory peered up into the cloudless sky and saw the *afrinn* winging toward them—but there was something odd about that silhouette—

He's carrying some—

Tory barely got that thought out when Ahkhan ducked, and he was nearly hit in the face by a large, dead rabbit.

He had the presence of mind to catch it, and a moment later he had it stowed in his mostly empty pack.

"I didn't know he knew how to hunt," Ahkhan said, bemusedly.

"Neither did I," his sister replied.

"Beats dried beef," Tory pointed out. "He can hit me in the head with dead rabbits any time he likes."

Ahkhan held them to a walk until Tory's legs were just about feeling normal, then after they had all had a piece of rock-hard trail biscuit, he set the pace at a lope again. Eakkashet returned three times more with rabbits; judging by what Tory knew of hawks, the *afrinn* was roughly four times as good at hunting as a real hawk would have been. But maybe the trick here was that the four of them were working like drivers, starting up the rabbits in the grass well ahead of them and making them easy targets for the firehawk.

If the pace hadn't been so grueling, this could have been pleasant. It was not all that different from a day of falconry, except the hawk was flying itself. A cool, sunny day, driving game before them, with an assurance of a hot meal at the end of the day.

Highborns would be happy to do this. If they were on horses.

But the pace was brutal, they were *not* on horses, they'd be sleeping on cold hard ground tonight and for at least the next several nights, and Tory could only wonder how many more days of this they had ahead of them.

When the sun stood about its own height above the western horizon, Eakkashet came back once again, this time empty-taloned, and landed in front of them as they all staggered to a halt. He didn't transform, but somehow he managed to get recognizable words out of that beak.

"There are no caves," he said. *"What would work for shelter?"*

Ahkhan looked around the hill they were on top of. "Down there, that little valley, there's a thicket. That will have to do. At least it doesn't look like rain."

"Go there. I'll get the others," the fire *afrinn* said, and he launched himself into the air, winging off to the left.

The thicket proved to be made of some of those same evergreen bushes that had threatened to rip Tory apart, back at the prison. They were about half again as tall as a man, and were bushy right down to the ground, making the whole thicket look impenetrable. But with some careful probing, Kee found there was an opening into it, and there was some room in the middle of it where a lot of the branches had died, and they were able to break off enough of the dead wood to make a tolerably generous space. Enough to lie down in, at least. More than enough for everyone since they were all sitting at the moment. Tory was suddenly reminded of how he and Kee would hide in the bushes up against the walls of the Palace and the Collegia and pretend they were camping in the wilderness. At least, until the gardeners found them and chased them off.

All three *afrinn* arrived just as they finished cramming all the broken bits in against the bases of the bushes. They had a distinctly resinous scent, which was not unpleasant, but it suddenly made Tory think of something alarming.

"Eakkashet, you're not going to catch this place on fire, are you?" he asked with anxiety. "These things smell like pine, and pine goes up if you even *look* at it sternly!"

"I will make sure I do not," the fire *afrinn* assured them.

Tory pulled the first of the rabbits out of his pack and frowned at the stiff body. "Well, that brings the second question. How frugal are we going to be with these rabbits?"

"Frugal?" Sira asked.

"I mean . . . we can't eat the skin, but are we eating everything else?" Tory elaborated. "Because normally I'd go bury the guts but—"

"Sleepgivers waste nothing," Ahkhan said sternly. "Each of those rabbits can make three meals for a person if we waste nothing."

Tory sighed. He was afraid that was going to be the case. That was going to mean a fair amount of work. "Can either of you help me with them, then?"

"I will. And Atheser." She crooked a finger at the water *afrinn*, who wagged its tailfin. "Let's take this work out of the shelter, and into the open, since it's going to be messy."

"I can——" Kee began, getting to his knees.

"No need," Sira told him with a smile. Tory put the rabbit back in his pack and crawled on hands and knees behind Sira out into the valley itself. He glanced upward; Merirat, the air *afrinn*, was gliding in lazy circles above the thicket, keeping watch, wearing its winged-lizard shape. He looked like a bit of colored smoke.

I'm not sure we could have gotten this far without them.

Tory had learned how to skin and clean game a very long time ago, right after his brother had come back from his adventure out in the Pelagirs. So he trimmed off a big patch of grass almost even with the earth to give them a place to work, covered that bare patch with the trimmed grass laid flat, then skinned the rabbits expertly, without even a single tear in the skin, and laid the skins out, fur-side down. Then he took off his headwrap and helm, impaled the helm into the dirt by its point, and set to work butchering.

"I'll clean the guts," Sira said, instantly seeing what he was about. And as he emptied the innards into a skin, then added the head, she took up the "clean" parts—the heart, lungs, liver, kidneys, and put them in the upturned helm, cracked open the skull and added the brains, then with the help of the water *afrinn* made short work of cleaning out the stomach, intestines and bladder before adding those as well. In fact, with the help of Atheser, that cleaning went so fast that she was done about the same time as he finished quartering the rabbit. So he laid the quarters on the pelt, and she bundled it up, while he went on to gut the next.

When they were done, they had a helm full of innards, and four packages of meat. Sira took charge of the helm, he got the packets and they wormed their way back into the heart of the thicket.

There he and Kee split the innards between their two helms, Atheser added water, and Eakkashet cooked it all up into stew.

It wasn't bad. It could have used some salt and a lot of herbs and wine, it certainly had a liverish and very gamey taste to it, but it wasn't bad. And at least there was plenty of it. While they were eating, Eakkashet grilled the rabbit quarters on his hands. As Ahkhan had said, these would serve for breakfast in the morning and the midday meal on the run. Sira brought out some (hopefully clean) rags from her own makeshift pack to wrap them in, and they each took one set of quarters and stowed them in their packs.

At least it's too cold for ants. The food should be safe enough, and they wouldn't have to brush a layer of insects off it before they ate.

By the time they were finished eating and Atheser had cleaned the helms, it was full dark, with a darkened sky so thickly spangled with stars overhead that it looked like a tradesman had spilled silver beads over a swath of black velvet. "Shall we?" Kee said to Sira— who evidently understood perfectly without any further words that he meant "shall we feed the *afrinns?*" because she sidled up next to him and put her hands onto Merirat, and he put his next to hers.

And oh, how Tory envied them that perfect understanding in that moment. And something more than envy, a sadness that made his eyes sting for a moment, and he wasn't certain if it was sadness for what he didn't have or what he was losing. Maybe both.

But he choked both down. *This is life, and life isn't fair, and I know that. And I am not going to make Kee unhappy just because I am.*

Besides, depending on what was waiting for them tomorrow, the last thing he wanted on his conscience if everything went to hell was to have spoiled the last hours those two had together.

"So. . ." he said instead to Eakkashet. "What exactly was going on in that prison before we got there?"

The fire *afrinn* chuckled. *"I had a very good view of it all. Sira is . . . remarkable. Let me tell you some tales."*

———

Sira belatedly realized what Eakkashet was about to do too late to stop him.

I am never going to hear the last of this from Ahkhan, she thought, cheeks flaming, as Eakkashet began with a brief explanation of how he and his fellows had been bound into their bronze talismans, then proceeded with the moment the deluge made Sira take shelter and discover that the storm had been the cover for the demons to surround her.

As she and Kee moved to fill Atheser with power, Eakkashet had moved on to her interrogation at the hands of the Karsite priests, and Kee chuckled once or twice as the fire *afrinn* made her words sound rather funnier and much more defiant than she thought they had been at the time.

And he kept on talking as they finished with Atheser and moved on to him. Or rather, Kee did; she sat back and watched him work with admiration for his deft handling of ley-line power, something she could only dream about doing. Of course, that also left her free to listen to the fire *afrinn's* tales with chagrin.

When Eakkashet was done, she was very glad it was dark; her cheeks were so aflame it was almost painful. All she could think about was all the missteps she'd made in handling—or rather, not handling—the Karsites. And, of course, the colossal misstep she'd made that got her captured in the first place.

She sat there in the darkness with Eakkashet cheerfully radiating warmth, with her hands cradled in her lap, and wondered what to say. Or was it better just to say nothing at all? Surely now Kee was thinking she was quite the fool. And her brother! Any moment now he'd begin—

"I'd have bungled that from the beginning and probably be very dead," Ahkhan said into the stillness. "I'd have tried to jump the guard that brought me the first meal, proved by that I was a Sleepgiver, and I doubt I'd have gotten far out of the prison tower."

He cheeks cooled and she raised her head. "Surely not," she objected.

"Oh, absolutely I would," he assured her. "I wouldn't have made it past a day once I was awake."

Well, that made her feel better. She could still see all the blunders she'd made . . . but perhaps anyone would have made those same blunders. At least she had managed to string things out so long that help had arrived at the very moment of her escape!

"It would have been easier if I had been able to—" She was about to say *scry,* when a sudden idea hit her. *Kee* was a much more powerful Mage than she was, even if he was untrained. If *he* could scry, if she could manage to teach him how, that would be even more effective than the three *afrinns* scouting.

"Been able to what?" her brother prompted her.

"I just had an idea," she told them all, and she picked up one of the helms. "Atheser, can you fill this with water?"

A moment later the weight of the helm told her the *afrinn* had done just that.

"Kee, come sit knee-to-knee with me, with the helm between us," she ordered, and the rest of them all shuffled around a little to give them the space to do that. She spun up a very dim, temporary Mage-light to shine down on the water in the helm, as she directed Kee to put both his hands on it. "Now, I am going to try to teach you how to scry."

"Is that like Farsight?" he asked, "I can't Farsee anyone Tory and I aren't related to—"

"It's a bit like Farsight, but you aren't limited in what you scry except in what you know," she corrected him. "For instance, you *know* exactly what the Karsite troops look like. So you concentrate on that, lend your magic power to your thoughts, and project both into the water."

As he frowned and stared down into the helm, she coached him with everything she could remember about how the Sleepgiver Mages taught scrying, keeping her voice calm, even, and persuasive.

And when she had come to the end of what she remembered, she began again. Patient. No expectation in her voice, but at the same time, plenty of confidence. He was untaught, but he was *very* powerful. He could do this. She had faith in him. And she told him so repeatedly.

And then, gently and slowly, a picture formed in the water in the helm.

A fire, with a pot over it.

The view receded. There were men around the fire, bowls and spoons in the hands. Karsites, there was absolutely no question of it; they wore the same uniform as the guards at the prison.

The view receded again. Now they could see much more detail, and the extent of what was around the fire and the men there. This was a temporary camp: no tents, only the men, bedrolls, and horses picketed nearby.

And the view pulled back again. And her heart sank. This was not just *a* camp. This was a line of camps. As the images grew smaller, she counted three . . . five . . . seven . . .

They were about three furlongs apart, close enough that each encampment could see the ones on either side of him, easily.

And the image receded even farther, showing a very, very long line of camps, each camp with its own campfire, a line of little yellow stars across the black dark of the hills.

"That's—a lot of men," Ahkhan said quietly. "That's way more men than were quartered in that prison. That's an army. Where are they?"

The line of little yellow dots blurred and vanished as Kee moved slightly and the water stirred. Kee looked up.

"Due west of us," he said, bleakly.

———

"At least we had plenty of warning," Tory said, after all of the *How did they get there so fast?* and *Where did they all come from?* s were spoken and chewed over without any progress. "And Kee was right yesterday. We need to go North."

"They must have been scrying *us*," Sira said, coming out of her daze at last. "That's all I can think."

"But if they had someone scrying us continuously, they'd have ambushed us already," Ahkhan pointed out. "So it must have been just a glance, maybe today, long enough to know what direction we were heading."

"They also must have some way of sending messages almost instantly," Tory replied, thinking out loud. "We can do that, with a relay of Mindspeaking Heralds. Or with my father alone, he can reach to the Border and maybe beyond. So—it's probably just one

Mage, with a way to do the same thing, but he's busy with a lot of things right now, and maybe he can't tap—what was that? Ley-line power? Maybe he can't tap that, so he gets tired. So he just sees what general direction we're heading, maybe even two days ago, sends out messages, and all the men that are available go straight to intercept us before we get to the Border. But all *he* has time or strength to do is see that we're going west, so that's why they deploy in a long line, to catch us no matter where we turn up. So. What do we do about it?"

"We go north," Kee repeated immediately. "To Valdemar."

"More—" Tory prompted the two Sleepgivers. "We need more of a plan than that. I don't know anything about magic, but when we don't turn up, that Mage is going to go looking for us again. More—what more can we do?"

Sira pulled on her lower lip. "He must have been able to see through that illusion Merirat bubbled over us, somehow." She looked to the air *afrinn*. "Can you do something against scrying?"

The air *afrinn* shook its head.

But then he brightened, and hissed.

"He says he can cast the illusion of the four of you continuing to move toward the west and then turning south before you reach the line of troops," Eakkashet translated. *"He says that if the scryer looks no farther than that, and does not cast his nets wider, that will deceive him. His kind have done that before."*

"Will you have enough power to keep doing that for a while without getting more power from me?" Kee asked, anxiously.

The *afrinn* nodded vigorously.

"That will buy us a lot of time, if it works," Ahkhan said.

"Is there *any* way we can, I don't know, confuse how we look?

Some sort of illusion that will work against the scrying?" Kee asked Sira. "Or would a shield against magic work? Is there such a thing?"

She shrugged helplessly. "I don't know," she admitted. "I never got that deeply into scrying and illusions."

"Is there a way to tell if we're being scryed, at least?" Kee asked again, sounding a little desperate.

She shook her head. "I don't know," she repeated.

"We'll have to take our chances, just as we have from the beginning," Tory said, keeping his voice steady and confident. "We all knew this was a possibility and that much of what we're doing is going to depend on luck. And every league we can put between them and us is an advantage. Once we get into the mountains, we'll be better off than mounted men."

"That's true," Ahkhan agreed. "So, we have a new plan."

"North and west," Tory said. "And trust to luck."

18

Sometime between when Tory managed to fall asleep and the time he woke up, the temperature had plummeted. Drastically. When he woke, all four of them had moved in the night to snuggle up to Eakkashet, with the other two *afrinn* perched atop him. And he had turned to lie flat on his back with arms and legs outspread to give them all something to snuggle up to.

Even so, with Eakkashet's warm—well, whatever it was made of—to get his back against, Tory woke because his nose was cold . . . not quite painfully cold, but not far from it. And although his back was toasty, he was curled in a ball with his arms and legs tucked up and they were still cold. His breath made white smoke in the cold air, and when he opened his eyes, all of the tiny needles on the trees around them were white with frost.

"Winter is here," said Kee from the other side of the fire *afrinn*. "And I don't like it. It's one thing to look at frost from the inside of a warm room while it's forming on the window. It's quite another to have it forming on your nose."

"I bet the Karsites will like it even less," Tory pointed out, as the others started to stir. "I wouldn't mind some snow to slow them down at this point, except it would make our tracks really obvious."

That startled a hiss out of Merirat, followed by a series of hisses, as Tory rummaged in his pack for the cold rabbit. Eakkashet sat up and increased the heat he gave off, while the rest of them treated him like a campfire, dug out their rabbit and began eating.

"Merirat says that gives him an idea," the fire *afrinn* said. *"And he thinks he knows now how a scryer found you. By the movement of the grass as we passed. The scryer looked for you, saw nothing—then saw the grass moving and understood that was where you were. There wasn't anything he could do about that."*

"We did plow through it, and there was no way to keep it from briefly showing a wake," Ahkhan admitted ruefully. "Well, now we know. Too late for it to do us any good, since Merirat is leaving us to lay a false trail."

"Yes, but Merirat says that now he knows how to make the illusion of you running to the south more convincing. Instead of flying above the grass, he'll fly through it, to make it move as if the four of you are running through it." Eakkashet did that unnerving smile again, although Tory was slowly getting used to it. *"So everything will look as it should."*

"We should just be glad they don't seem to use tracking dogs," Tory pointed out. "If they did, we'd be cooked." He finished gnawing the last shreds of meat and tendon from the rabbit bones, sucked what little marrow there was out of them, and stuck them in among the debris at the foot of the tree behind him.

Just as he got up, so did Kee, who started stretching and warming up. The Sleepgivers exchanged an unreadable look and did the same. Eakkashet stood, and the water *afrinn* jumped to its feet. Merirat hissed.

"Merirat is going now. He wants you to know he will be waiting for you at the Mountain. He is sure once he gets past the Ruvan Border he will know the way."

Sira approached the *afrinn*, who hovered just in front of her, wings absolutely still as he looked into her face. "Merirat—I don't know how to thank you. Be careful! Don't let them hurt you! You have done so much for us, so much for *me*, I don't think I could bear it if something happened to you." There was an odd, choked quality to Sira's voice, and Tory glanced at her to see with surprise that she had tears in her eyes. The person who murdered people for a living—was getting emotional over something that wasn't even human.

Merirat hissed, and bobbed cheerfully in the air. No one needed any interpretation of that. It was clear he was saying something like "They'll have to catch me first!"

And then he wiggled through the trees, was gone. They gave him more than enough time to get far out of sight of their shelter—just in case. And then, after making sure no one was leaving anything needful behind, they wormed their way out of the thicket and began the third grueling day of running.

———

Sira would never have admitted this to anyone else, not even her brother, but the farther they got from Ruvan, the more anxious she became. Maybe this had been a terrible idea. They should have gone due south instead of west.

But . . . if they had, they still wouldn't be in Ruvan; given how far north the prison was, they'd still be running parallel to the western border of Karse. And surely long before they got to Ruvan, there'd be another army massed on the southern border waiting for them.

She was determined not to show it, but she was one big internal knot of anxiety at this point. Much more desperate than she'd been even in prison.

Now it was noon, and they were taking a brief respite from the running by walking; thank the fates and fortunes there was still no sign of pursuit, nor had they encountered any Karsites. The hills were steeper now, and bigger. Not quite mountains yet, but not far from it—and when they got to the tops of the taller hills, it was easy to see the real mountains in the distance, the ones that marked where the border with Valdemar was. Eakkashet had repeated yesterday's performance in catching prey for them to eat later, but this time catching three rabbits and two large birds that Sira didn't recognize, about the size of chickens.

At least they weren't going to starve.

But now that they weren't in high plains, and the land was exponentially better watered and more fertile, they had to be a lot more careful; they hadn't encountered any Karsite *soldiers*, but there were farmers and herdsmen here.

Thanks to Eakkashet, they'd been warned off of one village of the former well in time to avoid them. Villages, it seemed, was how the Karsite farmers here organized themselves: villages in the middle of fields, instead of individual farms in the middle of fields. It made sense, actually; given how tightly the priests controlled things here, they certainly would not want anyone living somewhere out of their sight. And control.

It was a peculiar sort of organization to her eyes; villages laid out in circles, with barns and stock-pens around the outside, houses on the inside, well and temple in the center, and fields radiating out from the central circle.

It was well after harvest, so fortunately there was no one out in the fields but livestock grazing on stubble. They had to detour through scrub forest to avoid being seen, but thanks to Eakkashet's vigilance, they didn't lose too much time. It was only after they were a good league away that Sira realized what the odd grouping had been modeled on: a sun-disk, surrounded by its rays. If every village was like this, and they probably were, then every Karsite village was literally an icon of their god.

Probably every town and city too.

It . . . was unnerving, actually. The *afrinn* laughingly referred to the Karsites as "god-botherers," but this concrete display of such fanatic devotion that it was even branded on the face of the land made her understand just how powerful that devotion was.

And potentially, how dangerous.

Because every single Karsite, not just the soldiers, was surely a danger to them. They could not take the chance that word of the manhunt had reached even these tiny villages via the resident priest. And that priest would certainly have made the god's will known to every villager old enough to understand.

Even children were potential enemies. Without a doubt, they'd been primed to watch for strangers and run to alert the priest if they got even a *glimpse* of someone unknown crossing the hills.

So they had to pass far enough from the villages that they couldn't see the villagers, because that meant, in turn, they couldn't be seen.

Now she sorely missed Merirat's illusion bubble.

Herdsmen were easier to avoid; the herds of mixed sheep and goats milled together on the hillsides like great white clouds, easy to spot in the distance, and long before they themselves were visible to their tenders. And as for the dogs minding those herds—the dogs were trained to worry about wolves and other predators, and they didn't give a damn about what some priest had said. New humans were not threats, so new humans would be ignored in favor of keeping one eye on their precious charges and the other looking for wolves.

Or at least that had been the case until this moment.

Eakkashet came winging back to them, and landed. *"There are two herds,"* he reported. *"One on each hill. And the land is not good around those hills. I do not think it wise to go between the herds, so the choice is a bog or a field of boulders."*

Ahkhan groaned, but he said, "Boulders. Even if the bog were frozen solid, which it won't be, we'd get wet, and in this weather, chilled, and we'd have to stop and hide somewhere while you dried us out and warmed us up."

Eakkashet turned into one of the large game birds he had just hunted for them. *"Follow me,"* he said. *"And when I say* down, *crawl."*

They moved forward, around and to the left of the two hills, bent over and toe-heeling at a snail's pace. All too soon for Sira's peace of mind, he said *"Down!"* and the lot of them went to their bellies.

They couldn't see the sheep, but they could certainly hear them, baa-ing, the bells on the lead goat and the bellwether clanking now and again. Eakkashet had not exaggerated when he said "field of boulders." When they rounded the base of the hill, it looked as if a giant had strewn the valley and the next hill with assorted rounded rocks without even a hint of dirt or grass between them, rocks ranging in size from a man's head or a child's ball to rocks the size of a village house.

And there was no good way to get through them.

Eakkashet would walk a path for them for several feet, then jump up onto the top of a taller rock to scratch and peck as if he were hunting for food—but in reality keeping a wary eye on the hilltop. When they had managed to inch their way on their bellies to just under where he stood, he would jump down again and find another piece of the path to get them around the hills with their flocks. Maddeningly, sometimes he had to backtrack, because the way he initially chose was too exposed, or it wasn't possible for a human to squeeze between the boulders.

It was cold. It was increasingly painful to crawl like this, straining arms and legs in ways Sira, at least, was not used to, bumping knees and elbows on unforgiving stone. And it was *agonizingly* slow. Every moment they wasted in here was a moment they were not running toward that presumably safe northern Border. And meanwhile the sun moved on blithely overhead, marking time that was passing too swiftly for how slowly they were progressing.

Finally—*finally!*—the boulders ended in the first piece of real forest they had seen in Karse; the trees gave them more than enough of a screen to shelter them from the sharp eyes of the shepherds. They crawled, one by one, into the underbrush, then into the forest proper, and finally got to their feet. Ahkhan didn't lead them in a lope down game trails that went, more or less, in the right direction, he led them in a sprint, in a desperate attempt to make up for the lost time.

Sundown found them still in the forest, in a valley between two forested ramparts Sira would have called *real* mountains. The grass here was still long, but not as long or as stiff as the grass had been in the dry plain—much easier to move over, but it did hide rocks and branches, so you had to be very careful where you put your feet.

There was a stream running through it, which would have been welcome if they hadn't had Atheser with them. But it gave Sira an idea.

"You're going to hate me," she said. "But we should all take off our boots and wade. At least a couple furlongs, while Eakkashet scouts ahead for a place to spend the night."

"That water is *freezing!*" Ahkhan protested.

"Yes, but if Tory is right and they decide to use tracking dogs, it will break our scent," she said reasonably. "I don't want to do this any more than you do—but it's not cold enough to give us frostbite, and it's a precaution we'd be stupid not to take."

Ahkhan was already at the bank of the stream and removing his boots by the time she finished speaking. He tied the laces at the tops together, slung them around his neck, rolled up his trews, and waded in.

And swore. Long and vehemently. "You do realize there is bound to be a village along here somewhere, don't you?" he asked as he started wading upstream.

"Eakkashet will see it before we need to worry about it," she replied, as Atheser burbled with joy and plunged headlong into the water, going straight to the middle and swimming enthusiastically upstream.

Then she steeled herself and stepped off the bank into the water.

It was worse than cold. It was *painful.* And the cold traveled right up her legs, up her spine, and chilled her to the bones. And the worst part was that not only was it frigid and painful, it was both at the same time; somehow the cold didn't numb her feet enough that she didn't feel the pain. And the bed of this stream was full of rocks she couldn't see, so on top of all that, she was trying not to step on anything wrong and turn an ankle, bruise her instep, or worse.

Worse would be falling in. Very much worse.

Her concentration narrowed to the stream, the streambed, and where she was putting her feet. The entire valley could have been hiding a Karsite soldier behind every tree, and she wouldn't have seen them until it was too late.

"One furlong," she gasped, finally. "One furlong is enough."

"I think you're insane for wanting that much," her brother grumbled.

"Ah, Sira?" said Tory, from behind her.

She ignored him, concentrating on placing her feet in the rushing current.

"Sira?" he repeated.

The current was definitely getting stronger. Of course it was. The stream channel had started to narrow.

"*Sira!*"

"*What?*" she snapped, turning around and nearly losing her balance.

Tory stood there, *not* in the stream, boots on, both hands full of some kind of water weed.

"*Why aren't you in the stream?*" she hissed. She wanted to scream it at him, but who knew what was in those trees or up on the sides of the mountain?

"Because this stuff I have here? It's skink cress. It kills scent. All you have to do is rub it all over your boots. It lasts for candlemarks." He held out both hands full of the stuff to her. Behind him, Kee was rubbing a handful of the greenery all over his boots, starting with the soles. Remarkably, Tory didn't look angry at her. Or smug.

"Why didn't—"

"Because you were already in the water before I spotted it," he interrupted. He whistled like a top-knot quail, and Eakkashet came winging back. "Please come out of the water and let Eakkashet warm your feet before you lose toes."

She clambered back up onto the bank and accepted the handful of weed from him, managing not to snatch it. She was angry at him, at herself—it was irrational anger, born out of panic and anxiety, and she didn't dare turn it loose, because if she did—well, there was no telling if he might not just tell her to go to hell and persuade Kee to come with him and head off to the Valdemar Border without them.

And she couldn't bear that. Oh, the *afrinn* would stay with her—but Kee would be gone. And—no. It wasn't worth losing her temper.

Ahkhan took the other handful at the same time as she grabbed hers. As soon as she got near him, her nose wrinkled at the peculiar bitter, musky, pungent aroma.

"What *is* that?" she asked.

"Skink cress," Kee repeated. "Smells like skink. Skinks are lizards nothing will eat because of that scent." Kee took one of her boots from her and began rubbing it all over with the stuff. "Tory's brother Perry taught us about this stuff, in case we were tracking someone with a dog and he refused the trail."

"Ugh," she replied, coughing, as the harsh fumes got into the back of her throat. "I don't blame them. What do you do when that happens?"

"Track some other way. The dog's ruined for at least the rest of

the day, if not several days, and may even have to be retrained."
Kee handed her the boot; she pulled on her stockings, put it on,
finished the other, and stamped her frozen feet into place inside.

"Thank you, Eakkashet," Ahkhan told the *afrinn*, "But our feet will
be all right for now. We need to find shelter for the night quickly." He
glanced up- and downstream nervously. "We still don't know where
the demon-summoners are, and we want to be someplace sheltered if
they're close enough to turn their pets loose after dark. Those creatures
can cover a great deal of ground very quickly. Summoners could be
leagues away from us, and the demons could still find us." He looked
at Tory. "I don't suppose you know a demon-repelling plant do you?"

"If I did, I'd have brought a saddlebag full of it with us," Tory
pointed out. "If your feet are really all right, let's get moving."

Tory waited until the others had gotten underway; he wanted to
make sure neither Ahkhan nor Sira were having trouble walking,
and to make certain of that, he planned to bring up the rear.

And keep an eye on their backtrail, just in case, because he had
a notion that, even as good as they were, Ahkhan and Sira were a
bit distracted just now.

So, once they were well on the trail beside the stream, he turned
to peer downstream—

And found himself staring into the eyes of a monster.

It was a winged and feathered creature, hovering right behind
him, making lazy motions with huge wings that had nothing to do
with keeping it in the air. It had a long tail of two elaborate, curved
plumes, and an equally long neck that was bowed in an absurd
curve to put the creature's reptilian head on the same level as his. It

was taller than he was, and it looked as if it was made of blue glass.

He couldn't help hinself. He screamed.

The other three turned, whipping out weapons faster than he could blink.

But then Sira uttered a crow of delight, sheathed her sword and far too many daggers, and ran back to where he stood nose-to-nose with what was certainly a Karsite demon.

Or—not.

"You found us!" she exclaimed in joy, just as Eakkashet the firehawk came winging back to them again, and threw her arms around the monster's neck. The fire *afrinn* transformed in the act of setting down, and the serpent-bird-thing greeted him with a twitter.

"Merirat found her," said the *afrinn*. *"After he reached the end of the line of Karsite troops. This is Halina, who is my old friend, and was one of the afrinn Sira freed from her talismans. It is good to see you again, my friend!"*

The—well, Tory could only suppose it was another air *afrinn*, like Merirat was—twittered back.

"Yes, yes, you are right. We must find shelter quickly. Watch our backs while I seek it." And with that, Eakkashet transformed again . . . but not into a hawk, into some sort of owl. And he winged off silently into the gloom.

Eventually, when it was fully dark and they were stumbling along with the help of moonlight, and the right-hand side of the stream had turned into a rocky cliff, they found that shelter.

Eakkashet led them across the stream—which Atheser protected them from, as he had promised he could, so they could walk dry-shod—and into a cave just above the waterline. From what Tory could see of it, it must have been cut by the stream in flood.

The water *afrinn* accomplished his tiny miracle by wrapping himself around each of them in turn, making a barrier out of himself that kept the water at bay. But he could only do this one at a time, so no one, not even Sira, chided him for not offering to keep them dry when she proposed her plan of walking up the streambed.

By this time they were all starving, cold, and exhausted. Tory wanted badly to lie up against Eakkashet's warm side, and it was literally all that he could do to force himself to go to the water's edge to gut and clean the animals Eakkashet had caught.

To her credit, Sira came to help too. He hadn't expected that. She put up a Mage-light so they both could see what they were doing. "I'm sorry I screamed," he said sheepishly.

"I'd have screamed if Halina had been up in my face so unexpectedly," she admitted. "It's just a good thing that no one was around to hear it. If there had been, I would be very annoyed with you right now."

Well, he couldn't argue with that.

"It's a damn shame," he continued, changing the subject quickly, "that we can't pluck these birds for roasting whole instead of skinning them."

"For the fat and crispy skin," she agreed, and licked her lips. "But—wait, why don't we have Eakkashet burn the feathers off?"

"And spread the stink of burning feathers far and wide?" he countered. "I thought about that, but scent, especially of burning things, spreads a long way. I'm not willing to take the chance for a bit of hot, fatty skin. Besides, it'd be pretty flat without salt."

The was a long silence. "You're better at these wilderness things than I would have thought," she admitted.

"Sometimes a spy has to skulk outside a town because he'd be really obvious *in* it," he pointed out.

"Well—that's true." She looked toward him, and smiled. "Thanks for all you are doing, Tory. We'd never have gotten this far without you."

They finished their work—Tory making sure to save as much of the fat from the bird as he could. They'd been eating trail biscuit, dried beef, and rabbit, a notoriously lean meat, for days. He was feeling a craving for fat, and he knew their bodies needed it. Bits of fat trimmed as best he could from the bird skin went into the helm with the innards. The birds had obviously been putting on weight for winter.

When they went back into the cave, they found that Eakkashet had made a sort of fireless campfire by heaping up river stones and heating them until they glowed. Sira put half the contents of the helm into Kee's and impaled them both among the stones after Atheser added water. Eakkashet took the meat to grill. Then they all sat back wearily against the water-smoothed back wall of the cave, which Eakkashet had also heated, and let the warmth sink into their bones.

The new air *afrinn* stirred restlessly as they let out equally exhausted sighs, then, all on its own, moved over to the cave entrance and bubbled it. Tory was about to suggest that wasn't necessary, then changed his mind. After all, Kee and Sira—Kee especially—could replace any power the creature spent in making its illusion.

And the illusion might confuse wolves, bears, or pards that smelled the meat and came to see where it was. Enough to give them a chance to get out their bows and discourage further investigation. Tory wasn't naive enough to think that their bows were going to be powerful enough to kill a bear or even a pard, but a shaft in the hindquarters would be painful enough to make either bolt, without enraging them enough to cause them to attack.

Finally the stew smelled done, Eakkashet took up the helms and cooled them, and they shared the food. Ahkhan and Tory shared one helm full of stew, and Kee and Sira shared the other. The addition of the fat the biscuits soaked up answered a gnawing in his stomach that the rabbit hadn't been able to assuage.

"What would have happened if the Sleepgivers had been transported here instead of to the Mountain, back in the beginning?" Kee asked, in a near whisper, as they finished the last of the innard stew, packed up the cooked quarters—one-half bird, one-half rabbit, each, wrapped in their rags and stowed in packs— and cleaned the helms in the stream. Tory got a last handful of skink cress and scrubbed the stones outside the cave. The stink was powerful enough to make his eyes water for a moment. But better safe than sorry. He and Sira had been kneeling there, and there was surely the smell of blood and body fluids all over those stones. This would keep animals away.

"This fat land?" Ahkhan laughed quietly. "There would be no Karsites, there would be no Sleepgivers, and probably there would be no Mags and his family. Because if there had been no Sleepgivers, my father's uncle would have had no cause to leave the Mountain we would have built here. And we would likely be a Nation of herdsmen and farmers, with a core of Mages and a cadre of warriors to guard the rest from threats from without, just as we were in the most ancient days. And *you*, Kee, would have had no cause to ever meet my sister."

"And that would have been a great—"

A blood-curdling howl split the night air.

It was not a wolf—no wolf born had ever made a sound like that. It was like the uncanny marriage of a wolf howl, a pard snarl, a bear bellow, and the sounds of humans shrieking in unbearable pain.

Tory tossed the weed into the stream, flinging himself back into the cave. Halina did . . . something that made the surface of her shiver and go slightly opaque. Sira extinguished the Mage-light, and Eakkashet put his hands on the campfire stones, extinguishing their glow and cooling them within a heartbeat. In the moonlight pouring down onto their side of the stream, Tory saw the air *afrinn* sealing herself down against all the external surfaces of the cave-mouth. Was she making sure no scent from in here leaked out into the night? He fervently hoped so.

The sound came again, answered by three more. The howls had the unsettling effect of sounding as if they were coming from everywhere.

"Demons." Sira hissed, needlessly.

All of them except Halina scooted as far back into the cave as they could get. Even Eakkashet. The temperature inside the cave plummeted—was that Eakkashet's doing, so that the area of the illusion didn't register to the demons as warmer than the surrounding rock? It was a good idea—but that meant they were all huddled together in near-freezing temperatures, getting colder and colder as the moments passed.

As the temperature dropped, the feeling of tension in the cave grew—and the howls got closer and closer.

With a *thud* that vibrated the stones under them, a Karsite demon leaped down from the top of the cliff above them into the stream.

Tory stuffed his hand into his mouth to keep his gasp from escaping, as the thing looked upstream and down, its nose in the air, sniffing. It got a nose full of the skink weed and sneezed, sending foul-smelling mucus into the stream.

In the moonlight was impossible to tell what color it was except that it was pale. It had a big, blocky head that was mostly mouth. The mouth didn't close all the way, because of the interlacing teeth, far too many of them, thin, and needle-sharp. Two horns like cow's horns grew from its head and another from where its nose would have been. It appeared to have no neck, just a head set on massive shoulders, arms that were far too long and ended in claws as long as Tory's forearm. Right now it had those claws curled under so it could walk on its knuckles. Its back sloped down to massive hindquarters and ridiculously small hind legs. The head had three eyes, one on either side and one in the middle. It was naked, with strange skin that looked like plates of boiled-leather armor. Tory was pretty sure if they fired an arrow at it, unless the arrow lodged between those plates, it would bounce right off.

In short, it was impossible.

It continued to sniff and sneeze, only stopping once to utter one of those howls. Tory covered his ears with his hands to keep out that sound, which was so completely terror-inducing that if he had not been sitting already, his knees would have given way.

Then, as if that weren't bad enough, the wretched thing sat right down on the bank, squarely in front of the cave entrance, continuing to look up and down the stream.

Despite the fact that he was huddled with the others, Tory felt utterly alone in his terror. He was afraid to breathe, afraid that the thing might hear it, despite the noise of the water over the rocks outside the cave. In fact, he was quite sure he had never been so terrified in his entire life.

And just when he was certain he was either going to break down or pass out from the fear—the thing stood up and roared a challenge downstream.

And it was answered by something that sounded like metal being torn in two. And it was struck by a hurtling object larger than it was, an object that was transparent, moving like a thunderbolt, and even more terrifying to look at than the demon was.

The demon was knocked off its feet and a good wagon-length upstream by the thing, which reared above the water and uttered another one of those screams. It looked like a finned serpent with the needle-toothed, multiantennaed, spike-spined, blind-eyed head of a nightmare.

And it was bigger than the demon.

The demon got to its feet again and roared back. And that was when the new creature somehow grew *larger.*

Somehow? In an instant, Tory realized he knew very well how the creature was getting bigger. He saw pulses of water moving from the stream up into the creature's body, increasing its bulk, making its teeth longer, its spines more numerous.

Tory watched, mind and body absolutely paralyzed.

It reared back and struck at the demon, which barely managed to leap backward away from teeth that snapped closed so close to the demon's face that scarcely a hair separated them.

The demon turned tail and ran, bellowing.

The creature coiled up its serpent-body, rearing half of itself above its coils, and Tory waited in terror for the thing to figure out that they were there.

And then his insides turned to water as Halina made a hole in herself.

And the serpent looked swiftly from left to right, and dove into the cave, shedding most of its bulk into the river again as it did so.

If Tory hadn't been so paralyzed, he would have screamed his lungs out.

But Sira leapt up from her spot against the wall and flung herself at the creature. For one, panic-stricken moment, Tory was afraid she was putting herself between it and them.

But no—she was flinging her arms around it and weeping softly, murmuring over and over, "You found us! You found us!" while Atheser whisked in excited circles around them both.

And that was when his mind finally emerged from paralysis, and he knew.

This was a water *afrinn*. And not just any water *afrinn*.

This was the first of the *afrinn* that Sira had released from her necklace.

And it had, indeed, found them.

19

Sira mostly just listened, still caught in the cold paralysis that the demon had sent her into. The water *afrinn's* name, it seemed, was Vela. And it was not just any water *afrinn*. She was Atheser's mate.

"But—how?" Kee asked Eakkashet, bewildered, looking from the small water dog to the enormous water serpent and back again.

"We are not humans. Or animals," Eakkashet reminded her. *"Also, the males of the water-kin are much smaller than the females."*

"I'm trying, and I still cannot not imagine it," Kee sighed, "And it makes my head hurt to try. There's one of those ley-line things really close. I'm just going to feed all of you and not think about it at all."

Sira could not bring herself to move, not even to invoke a Mage-light, but Kee seemed to understand. He reached over to her and squeezed her hand once, then fed power into all the *afrinn*. By the time he was done, Vela and Atheser quite literally glowed with the power, negating any need for a Mage-light, and Vela settled herself in the corner in a tight coil, with Atheser lying down atop her.

Slowly, thoughts seeped through that cold inertia that held her. Merirat must have found Vela as well as Halina.

"You arrived at exactly the right moment, Vela." That was Tory. "It looks like you are a match for at least one demon."

"It also looks like the demon didn't recognize that he'd been chased off from something he'd been sent to find," observed Kee.

How could they talk so *normally* after what they had just seen? The thing had been within moments of finding them, and then it would have called for help. And she very much doubted Vela could have taken on more than one of the things!

The fire *afrinn* warmed the cave to the perfect sleeping temperature, and the heat overcame her desire to stay awake, stay vigilant, because surely, *surely,* the priests would realize that Vela had been protecting something and would send *all* the demons back. She tried to fight encroaching sleep, tried to hear what the *afrinn* and Kee were murmuring to each other—she caught "your scent in the water," but not much else—but exhaustion was too much for her.

But her dreams were full of horror.

Tory woke to something that, until now, he would never have considered an agreeable aroma.

Hot fish.

His eyes flew open, and he saw that Eakkashet was grilling gutted fish on his open hands, and Kee was already enjoying one. He sat up quickly and reached out involuntarily.

Eakkashet chuckled and upturned his hand to drop one into his. He had to juggle it from hand to hand for a moment until it cooled enough to hold and bite into, but the rich taste of fat-laced smooth-skinned trout was one of the best things he'd ever eaten in his life. Moments later, all of the others were eating, and Atheser kept slipping out to dive into the stream and come back with more, until they were all sated without having to touch their meat from last night.

But Sira didn't seem to be eating, and he was pretty sure why. Seeing that demon—well, it must have brought the moment she'd been captured back to her.

And that kind of killed his appetite too. Because he knew, just as Sira knew, that the moment they all stepped out of this cave, they would be back in terrible peril. The demon-summoners were somewhere out there, and hunting for them. And yes, Vela could chase off *one* demon, but they already knew there were more, because they had all heard the demons calling to each other last night.

And if he thought about that too hard—it would be so tempting, just to stay right here. Never leave this cave. Let the *afrinn* keep them all warm and fed, and maybe in a moon or two or three or by spring, the Karsites would give up and move on.

Except he knew that they never would. Once the Karsites actually knew they had found Sira, they'd call for more conventional troops to surround the area. They'd stay behind the conventional troops for safety and keep sending the demons, until all of them were either dead or captured.

And honestly . . . dead would be preferable to what the Karsites did if they were caught.

———

Sira woke up from her nightmares mired in despair. And the longer she sat there, the worse, more despairing, she felt. And the cave ceased to be a refuge and became a trap.

When the others had finished eating, none of them made any move to pack up and prepare to leave, either. Finally, after the sun itself penetrated the valley and made the surface of the stream outside sparkle, it was Tory who said what they were all thinking out loud.

"I really, really don't want to leave here."

The words fell into the silence like leaden balls. Sira felt herself just freezing up inside again, that insidious paralysis combined with the fear, and kept her mouth clamped shut.

She glanced over at her brother. His eyes were dark and full of the same fear. She'd never seen him this way before. And if *he* was afraid—what hope did she have?

"I don't want to leave here," Tory repeated. But his tone had changed. "But I'm going to. You don't have to go with me. I wouldn't blame any of you if you stayed here until next spring hoping the Karsites would give up on finding you. I've never in my life seen anything as terrifying as that demon of theirs, and we know they have more than one." He looked soberly at Eakkashet and Vela. "I don't think even you *afrinn* would be able to beat as many as they can conjure. But I'm not going to let that stop me. And if nothing else, maybe I'll be able to pull them away from the rest of you long enough to let you escape."

Kee glanced briefly—sadly—at Sira, and then said, "I can't let you do that alone, Tory. I'm coming with you."

Eakkashet let out a sound like distant thunder. "*I cannot allow you to go alone, either, friend,*" the *afrinn* said. "*Vela and Halina can stay to protect and defend the others, but I will go with you.*"

With that, Vela and Halina began to protest in their own way, and under cover of the quiet but vehement conversation, Sira fought against the black demon of despair in her own heart. Logic was not working against it.

So she used something else.

She used emotion.

Here was Kee, beside her. Someone who was willing to *die* at the teeth of those demons in order to buy her time to get to safety. And Tory, whom she did not love as she loved Kee, but whom she had come to respect and value, equally willing to do the same so that she and Kee could escape *together,* despite the fact that his ties with Kee went back far, far longer than hers. And the *afrinns,* who really owed her nothing at all, but out of some bizarre sort of kinship and friendship were going to do their best to keep her from the Karsites, whether they went with Tory or stayed here to hide her . . .

It was a terrible battle. Perhaps the worst in her life. The black wolf of despair fought madly against the white wolf of hope in her soul.

And . . . slowly . . . the white wolf gained ground. Until the despair retreated, and only hope remained.

"No," she said aloud. "We will go on as we planned. And we will all go together, or none at all."

Kee turned and seized her hand in his, and his face was full of such emotion that it made the white wolf howl in triumph. "Yes, we will," he said quietly. "Won't we, Ahkhan?"

"As the Nation has always," came from the corner, but now Ahkhan's voice was no longer hopeless either. "Together or not at all, my brother."

"Besides," Tory said, after a long, long silence, that no one seemed to want to break, "Timing can be on our side. If we can reach the Valdemar Border before sundown, they can't summon the demons to stop us, and we've won. So let's get moving and run as fast as we possibly can."

———

With Vela providing a much more effective illusion over them than Merirat had, and with no need to hide other signs of their passage when there was a water-scoured, bare rock "path" beside the stream to run on, they pushed themselves to the limit to make up for the time they had wasted. The map gave them no real clue as to where they were or how far it was to the Valdemar Border, but at this point, since the stream was running more or less directly north, it made no sense to try for the Menmellith border and have to cut their own path through the mountains. If need be, even if cliffs rose on either side of them, they *could* run in the stream, because Vela had assured them that, unlike Atheser, she could surround all of them with a water-free zone to run dry-shod.

Tory concentrated on nothing more than the next step. He was pretty sure the rest of them were doing the same. Make each step perfect. Don't trip, don't misstep, don't be off-balance, don't strain. Make each step perfect. Breathe. Breathe. Feel the air, take in the scents of winter, every step bringing them nearer to safety, nearer to home. Each step perfect. Each one a tiny bit of art.

And imperceptibly, he moved into a place where he was nothing but a body moving through space and time, where nothing mattered but the perfection of movement, and his mind was . . . still.

In that stillness he was aware that they were *all* running at exactly the same pace now, feet hitting the trail at exactly the same moment, or so nearly that it made no difference.

Was Sira working some kind of magic? Was Kee? It didn't matter. All that mattered was the movement. Through space. Through time. Through the sunlight lancing down on them between the mountains. Through the streambed, when, at last, they did have to move into it. Then the dance became a little more intricate, as they had to weave among larger boulders worn smooth by water and time, following the path that the water itself took, moving as smoothly as the water—the poor water, which had been forced away and surged against the rock walls on either side of the cut canyon, splashing in indignation against the stone.

Then they were out into another valley and back on a path, and he wasn't even aware when they'd made the transition, only that they had.

Even hunger didn't interrupt them, only the need to smoothly reach for waterskins and bottles, smoothly drink, smoothly replace.

He had never felt like this before during a run.

He might never again.

It didn't matter. All that mattered was the path, the perfection of each step followed by the next and the next and the next. Through time. Through space.

On and on and on. And the mountains became hills, hills covered with the kind of forests that looked familiar. They could not be far now. Tory refused to consider anything but that; it was familiar, but he needed to keep running.

But in the back of his mind, he sensed . . . something. Was it magic? It had to be. It felt as though it was coming from Kee. And it had to be magic, magic binding them all together, flushing fatigue out of them, pushing more energy into them, healing weariness, lending strength. A new thing, another new thing from Kee. A wonderful new thing, born of need and desperation and pure, powerful will. The sort of will that, to be honest, he had never imagined that Kee had.

This was not the Kee he knew and had loved as a brother all his life. And this was wonderful. And this was terrible. Because even as he ran, supported by Kee's strength, he felt Kee separating from him, step by step, league by league, a little at a time. Pulling away and leaving behind an indentation, a negative of what had been there. Pulling away because Kee had grown too big to fit that mold anymore. And this was right and proper and true. And it was agony.

And none of that mattered because it was what it was, and it would be what it would be. And whether you liked it or not or were ready for it or not, everything changed. And the important thing was the next step. Always the next step. The next perfect step.

"*I feel it,*" Eakkashet said, suddenly. "*I feel them! The air spirits, ahead, sensing us, waiting for us to cross, so that they can surround us and watch us and make us go away.*"

Tory let that news put more strength into his steps. *That means . . . well, we're close enough for a powerful earth entity to sense other elemental spirits. I wish I knew how close that was.*

But it couldn't be that far. This sort of country felt so familiar, it almost felt like home. He increased his pace as the stream curved around a hill, and they followed the path around it.

And then his strength failed.

Oh, gods. Not close enough. Tory's heart dropped into his boots, and he skidded to a halt, knees going weak with fear.

The way was barred by demons. They blocked the path and

stream and ranged up and down the hill on either side, weaving
their blocky heads from side to side, hissing and growling. Twenty—
thirty? Too many. Behind them, on the right-hand hilltop, Karsite
priests in their distinctive robes. At least half a dozen.

"I thought you said they couldn't conjure the demons by
daylight!" Ahkhan exclaimed.

"Don't shout at him, that was what I was always told too," Sira
countered, slowly drawing her sword and longest knife.

"You might as well not try to hide behind your illusion," one
of the priests called down from the hill. "We know you are there.
Our Swords can scent you. Surrender and we'll be merciful and
kill you ourselves. Or fight, and we'll let our Swords cut you into
tiny pieces, slowly."

"Swords?" asked Tory, as Halina gathered herself together into
her normal form, hissing with anger.

"That's what they call the demons. *The Swords of Vkandis.* Not
very original. Back to back, everyone." Sira put her back to Kee's
even though it meant she couldn't look directly at the line of
demons. But then, she probably didn't want to. And it wasn't as
if they weren't going to see far more of the creatures than anyone
would like in a moment.

That left Tory facing the priests and the demons. He and Ahkhan
moved into position with the other two; Eakkashet dropped to the
ground in front of them, as Vela moved to guard the rear behind
them, inflating herself with water from the stream, hissing with
anger. Eakkashet bellowed, and—

—suddenly there was a pillar of fire about twice the height of a
man, standing between them and the demons. It was near enough to

leave Tory feeling slightly scorched until Eakkashet moved forward.

This new form was, frankly, almost as terrifying as the demons were. He had to remind himself that this thing was Eakkashet, who had proven himself to be their friend.

The priests did not seem impressed—but suddenly there was a distortion in the air around the priests, just as Eakkashet flung what looked like a ball made of fire straight at them.

It hit the distortion, as if there had been an invisible wall between them and it; the fire splashed like water, sending droplets into the dry grass around the priests, sparking tiny fires around them. The fireball hadn't impressed them—but the fires at their feet certainly did. Three of them moved forward to stamp the fires out. Eakkashet roared again and flung another fireball, but this time aiming for the ground in front of them. Fire sprang up all along that line of distortion, filling the air with smoke, which drifted past the shield— for it must have been a shield—and making them cough and choke before one of them invoked water to put it out.

And then the demons charged. Tory braced himself, his heart racing, and his hands clenching on the hilt of his sword and dagger.

Within moments they were surrounded by snapping jaws and clawing talons—

—that strangely, slipped and slid off a similar distortion surrounding *them*. Tory glanced over at Kee, to see his face contorted with concentration. Was *he* doing that, or was he aiding Sira? A look at Sira didn't tell him anything; her face was a blank.

Tory tried to cut at the demons and realized something else as his sword hit a slightly yielding surface but didn't get anywhere near the demon. The demons couldn't reach them—but they couldn't fight the demons either. They were at an impasse. And it was utterly terrifying to be in the middle of a circle of these ravening things. The growling sent cold down his spine, the mere sight of all those teeth made him sweat, and the stink of their breath alone was enough to choke a vulture. And he had no idea if they actually *could* claw or bite their way through that arcane protection.

And the shield—it must have been a shield like the one Abi had described in the story about the fight against the Mages Remp had hired—couldn't be kept up forever either. Magic, like Mind-magic, depended on the strength and energy of the caster, and eventually Sira or Kee was going to get tired. If they weren't already! They'd been running all day, and it was nearly sundown.

But before he could say anything, the situation changed again. Vela and Eakkashet each hit the part of the mob nearest Ahkhan with a double roar, knocking the demons away from the shield and forming a two-sided layer of protection of their own. Then they did it again, and again, forcing the demons back a good double cartlength. Then Eakkashet and Vela took up a double guard on Ahkhan's side of their circle as the demons surged back.

"Drop the shield!" Ahkhan screamed and turned to face forward, squeezing in next to Tory. "We can't do anything if we can't hit them!"

In answer, for a moment, the protection bulged in the direction away from Eakkashet and Vela, driving the demons further away for a second time, giving them room to swing their swords.

Then it vanished, and the wave of demons crashed down on them.

For the next several moments, Tory was much too busy to be aware of anything other than his own weapons and the demons he was hacking at. Sweat poured down his face and back, and every nerve felt on fire with terror. This was a lot different from all that practice he'd done back at Haven . . . there was no time to think ahead or plan the next move, only last-second reactions to something coming straight for his face. Usually teeth.

He was on the side where Vela was; she used splashes of water to blind the things, and somehow she managed to make those sharp teeth of hers solid enough to sink into demonic flesh, while he hacked at anything that got within range of his sword. Sometimes he managed to lop off a claw or slice into an eye. Mostly, his sword skidded on leathery hide and bone and made shallow cuts that didn't seem to inconvenience the demons in the least. Heat on his other side told him Eakkashet was doing something, but he couldn't tell what.

Was there no end to the things? Or were they dropping out of sight after he hacked off limbs and split heads, to crawl out of the way and heal again? He couldn't tell much from the cacophony around them. The demons shrieked and growled whether they were hurt or not, and Vela and Eakkashet had reverted to fighting silently.

He panted with effort, his sword feeling as heavy as lead, and his sleeves shredded by the many near-misses he'd had just in the last several moments. So far he was otherwise untouched. And that was mainly because the demons fought with no coordination with each other and no thought, just dumb animal slashing and biting. He knew he was lucky. And that the luck couldn't last. The only reason they hadn't gotten hurt yet was because the demons were so incredibly stupid they were hindering each other and getting in each others' way so much that even the bites and slashes that reached the humans were weak and ineffective. That was probably because the priests couldn't see into the mob well enough to direct them.

Ahkhan swore, and he almost turned, but then he realized why the Sleepgiver had cursed. The demons were pulling back.

Most of them. About five, reacting to the room they'd just been granted by the withdrawal of the others, fell on the humans with renewed fury.

He was using street-fighting techniques designed for working in close quarters; unfortunately those techniques depended on facing foes who didn't have armored hides and heads the size of a draft horse's, full of dagger-long teeth. Short, brutal blows, rather than full swings were all he could manage, and he couldn't use punches to the throat or dagger thrusts at all without risking losing a hand. The demons were doing better now that there were only five of them. His arms already stung from claw grazes, and there had been tugs at his back where his pack and cloak were; if one of those things got in a full, ripping tear, he'd be on the ground and bleeding out even from an arm wound.

"Shield up!" Sira yelled, and suddenly the creatures were shoved away from them by that invisible force. That left Vela—and especially Eakkashet—to wade into them. The demons didn't seem able to harm Vela at all; slashes to her watery sides just healed up immediately. But she seemed to have given up biting for head-butting charges, which sent the demons she connected with sailing but didn't seem to cause them any injury. Halina had immobilized one somehow—was she choking it by denying it air? But she could only manage one.

Eakkashet was having more luck. He charged the creatures too, but when he caught them, he enveloped them in flame, and although the tone and timbre of the demonic screams didn't change, when Eakkashet let the thing he'd been holding go, there wasn't anything left but a shapeless mass of char.

Unfortunately, there didn't seem to be any fewer of them.

"They're just calling up more as we cut them down!" Sira moaned.

Tory wracked his brain for an answer. If he or Kee had just had some *real* Mind-magic powers—the priests wouldn't have any defenses against something like that! But they didn't. And they couldn't get at the priests physically, not with all the demons in the way.

"They can't keep it up forever!" Ahkhan growled. "There has to be a point when they run out of things to conjure."

"Are you ready to surrender?" the lead priest called mockingly, from up on the hill. "We can keep this up much longer than you can."

With a roar, Eakkashet took that challenge, flared to a white heat, and charged up the hill toward the priests, aiming to take on their tormentors directly—only to be completely enveloped in demons.

Sira cried out as he vanished under a heap of the creatures, and cried out again as fire erupted from the middle of the heap, flinging some back and incinerating the rest.

And more sprang up to take their place, pushing Eakkashet back down the hill and to their side again, perfectly willing to turn into cinders as long as they turned his charge into a retreat. Because, apparently, there were more, many, many more, where their fallen comrades had come from.

And now the demons turned their attention, not to them, but to the barrier that protected them, turning their fury on it with redoubled fervor. Tory took a moment to spare a glance at Sira and Kee, and what he saw made his heart nearly stop. Sweat poured down their brows, their faces were contorted with effort, it was clear that they could not keep this up much longer. They were about to break. And when they did—none of them were in any shape to fend off the horde again.

A rumble, like distant thunder, but continuous, erupted from behind him, and he felt the ground tremble under his feet. Terror engulfed him as he realized that it was not just growing louder; whatever was making it was coming nearer, and at a breakneck pace. Now what?

He had only enough time to register utter and complete despair as the rumble came from under them, nearly shaking them off their feet.

And the entire hillside between them and the priests erupted in a column of sand as big around as a barn, and tall as the tower on the Palace, a column that ended in a gigantic snake head.

The priests gaped at it. The demons froze in place as their masters lost control of them for a moment.

And the column crashed down on them all in an avalanche of sand.

And then there was silence.

Tory's cheers died in his throat, for moving lumps in it proved that the priests' shields had held, and the demons were still active, though stunned, and it would be mere moments before they emerged again. This was not a rescue. This was merely an interruption.

And that was when two swift, familiar shapes of blinding white came over the top of the hill, leaped the sand, and landed beside them.

And his heart leaped again. *This* was rescue!

Neither Tory nor Kee hesitated. They dropped their weapons and hauled themselves up onto the backs of the two Companions that had so miraculously appeared. Kee grabbed Sira's arm and pulled her up behind him; Tory did the same for Ahkhan, as both Sleepgivers dropped their daggers to give themselves a free hand to hold on with.

And then they were off, with the four *afrinn* moving at top speed beside them, heading for the Border.

Tory looked over his shoulder and wished he hadn't.

Already the demons and priests had shaken themselves free of the sand of what must have been an earth *afrinn*, and were in hot pursuit. The priests were actually *riding* six of their demons, like children playing horsey with a parent, if the parent was a sickly mustard color, had a head out of a nightmare, and was knuckle-galloping over obstacles as if they didn't exist.

Ahkhan shouted in his ear. "What happens when we get to the Border? Is there some kind of shield there? Because if there isn't, I don't think the staring of a bunch of air spirits is going to stop these things."

"I don't know!" he shouted back.

The Companions streaked along the valleys between the hills, still following the stream. Was that so that Vela and Atheser could keep up? He looked back again. The two water *afrinns* streaked down the surface of the stream right on the tail of his Companion, while Eakkashet flew in his firehawk form ahead, side by side with Halina.

How far to the Border? And what do we do when we get there? Ahkhan is right, there's no magic barrier keeping these bastards on their side, so what—

And then they broke out into a flat space and saw it.

A line of glorious blue mixed with white.

An entire troop of the hardened fighters of the Border Guard Cavalry and three Heralds.

The line parted for them, and they burst through it, only skidding to a stop on the other side.

"Fire!" roared the Captain of the Guard, and all along the line,

archers raised bows with fire-arrows and let them fly, setting the ground alight for hundreds of lengths on the other side of the Border. Smoke and flames erupted from the tinder-dry grasses and brush, sending up a curtain of fire that spread only slowly in the still air.

Eakkashet did a wingover, flew straight into the flames, and transformed with a roar, three times as large as he had been before, a giant made of flame, howling with the voice of an uncontrolled wildfire, and flexing arms as bright as the sun.

The tumble of priests and demons came charging over the hill—and abruptly stopped at the sight of him amidst the wildfire, tumbling together in a milling, confused mess.

Eakkashet roared again, and stamped his foot. Flames shot up from it.

"Fire!" the Captain ordered again, and a rain of arrows fell among the demons and priests.

The priests, it seemed, had not been able to maintain their shields while in pursuit, and at least three shrieked in unaccustomed pain—and one fell from the demon he was riding, which promptly turned on him, as did two more next to it.

Bloodcurdling screams, quickly cut off, told of his fate, and that, it seemed decided the rest of them. With odd little *pops,* most of the demons vanished, leaving only the ones being ridden by priests to turn tail and vanish back the way they had come.

20

While Eakkashet and Vela put the fire out before it turned into something worse and threatened lands in Valdemar as well as Karse, Halina was doing *something*. She hung in the air, facing something he couldn't see, while they all caught their breath.

Actually, it was more than just "catching their breath." All of them slid bonelessly from the Companions' backs and just lay on the ground, cold as it was, for a while. Or at least it was cold until Eakkashet shrank back down to "normal" size and sat among them, radiating enough warmth that it felt like sunbathing.

The Guard Captain finally felt moved to say something. "It is almost dark—" he said to Kee, apparently recognizing him as the Prince. "We need to be away from here."

"I understand," the Prince groaned, and got to his feet, giving Sira a hand up, as Tory and Ahkhan did the same.

"Halina has negotiated a peace with the air spirits," Eakkashet

announced. *"They will not trouble us if you do no egregious magic."*

And what counts as "egregious" magic? Tory wondered, mounting the nearest Companion and helping Ahkhan back up behind him, even as the Guard Captain exclaimed, "The thing talks? What did it say?"

"Just a comment about how glad we were to see you," lied Tory. And with a wrench of his mind to put it back into the Sleepgiver tongue, he said to Eakkashet, "Come here and let me give you my language talisman, so the Guard can understand what you are saying."

He pulled it off his neck as the *afrinn* paced over to the side of the Companion, who snorted at him in a friendly fashion, and put the crystal talisman into the *afrinn's* outstretched hand.

"Can you all understand me, good friends?" the *afrinn* said in perfect Valdemaran. *"If so, let us move from this place before the Karsites return. I will light the way at the bridle of the lead horse."*

And with that, he turned into a firehawk. A firehawk on fire, as bright as four torches.

"How on earth did you *find* us?" Tory asked the Guard Captain as they rode at a fast canter straight to the west.

"I'd be damned interested to hear that myself," said Ahkhan at his back.

"Dunno. The Heralds knew," the Captain replied, as one of the two Heralds turned his head at the word "Herald," and his Companion began weaving through the pack of Cavalry until he reached their side.

"Herald Mikel at your service," the graying, ginger-haired Herald said with a little bow. "I assume you wanted something?"

"How did you know where to find us?" Tory asked, as Kee and Sira closed in on his other side.

"Herald Mags told us via Mindspeech. I don't know how *he* knew. But you can ask him yourself when we stop at the Border Fort tonight." The Herald grimaced in the darkening twilight. "*Nobody* wants to be out in the open longer than we have to. That was the biggest group of demons and priests anyone along the Border here has ever seen, and I wouldn't count on them not coming back once they regroup. They must have desperately wanted you."

"I think that's a fair assessment," Tory agreed, wearily, all too aware that he was exhausted, starving, his clothing was in rags, soaked in sweat, and it was completely inadequate against the winter chill. Somewhere during the fight, they'd all lost their packs and winter cloaks—though considering that this was probably because the demons had struck them and got those instead of a piece of their backs, he was going to consider it a fair trade.

"Now what I would like to know is, what in the name of all the gods are these *things* you have with you?" Herald Mikel asked.

"They are spirits of the elements," Sira spoke up. She and Kee looked even worse than Tory felt. It was hard to tell in the dim light, but they looked pale and drawn. "The fire is called Eakkashet. The water are Atheser for the small and Vela for the large. The air is Halina. It is a very long story, how they came to join us, but I assure you, they are my allies."

The Herald got round-eyed. "How is that even possible?" he asked.

Sira smiled wanly. "As I said, it is a very long story. And much of it is secrets of my people that I am not free to share."

"I completely understand," Mikel replied respectfully. "Still . . . seeing them in battle is one story I'll be sharing at the fire for a long time."

They finally reached the Border Fortress under full dark, with Eakkashet providing light for the lead horses to follow. If the Guards found following a flaming bird odd, it appeared that they did not find it disturbing enough to object to taking advantage of it. But it was obvious that everyone was glad to be within the shelter of the stout stone ramparts once they arrived there.

When the gate was firmly shut behind them, Eakkashet volunteered to go sit in the forge, Halina flew to the highest point of the fortress and wrapped herself around the flagstaff there, and Vela and Atheser settled into the horse trough. *"We will be fine,"* he assured Tory, before he followed the blacksmith to his overnight resting spot. *"I believe rest will be enough for now. I would not like to anger the air spirits by asking the Prince to feed us power tonight."*

Well, that settled that. The humans all followed the Captain into the barracks, and they soon found themselves seated at tables in the mess, with a simple soldiers' meal of bread and stew in front of them. Tory sat there for a long moment with his hands wrapped around the bowl, almost too tired to eat.

But he and the others must have done so, because the next thing he was aware of was that all four of them had been taken to an office just off the mess where four pallets had been hastily laid out. And that was the last he knew until morning.

In the morning, Herald Mikel woke them all with arms full of Guard clothing, which suited Tory just fine, since it was all winter wear and clean, and thus infinitely superior to what they were wearing. And more to the point there was hot water in the kitchen for something like a quick wash, which he, at least, felt in desperate need of.

By the time the sun had properly risen, they were back on the road, this time accompanied by only the three Heralds, which meant they could all go at a Companion's pace, which was much, much faster than anything the Guard horses could have managed. One Herald rode ahead to scout the road, one rode behind to cover their back, and Mikel rode with them.

"We discussed this last night while you were sleeping," Mikel told them. "We decided that getting you quickly out of range of the Karsites was going to be safer for you than riding with a Guard escort. We're taking you to the Menmellith crossing."

:The same one that you used the first time, son,: said a familiar, and oh-so-welcome voice in his head.

The other three started, and Sira looked about wild-eyed. "Who—what—"

"That was my father, Herald Mags. Your father's cousin, the strongest Mindspeaker in Valdemar," Tory told her, then continued aloud, "Father, how close are you?"

:Close enough to meet you there, where you can tell us everything in person.:

"Good," Tory sighed, both longing for and dreading the meeting. "There is an awful lot to tell."

———

This might not be the first time in the history of Valdemar that a King had been housed in a barn—but there probably had not been too many such incidences.

Mind, it was an extremely fine barn; really, it was nicer than many inns Tory had taken shelter in. It had been built by Lord Merdan's grandfather to house his collection of delicate racehorses; on the death of that worthy but improvident man, his son had sold off the entire collection, which had not done much but sire more of their kind and eat their heads off, according to the present Lord Merdan. The barn was much more impressive than the manor, if truth were to be told. The manor certainly was not as tightly built, nor as well-warmed, and it boasted of only a single water pump, and that one was in the kitchen and had been fitted recently. The barn, by contrast, had exquisitely carved stalls, solid wooden floors everywhere except in the stalls themselves, where the floors were pounded and oiled clay with drains in the center. It also had four water pumps, a copper boiler for heating water, a small kitchen, two huge brick fireplaces of the same design as the ones that served the Companions' stable at the Palace, and a very spacious one-room dormitory on the second floor for the small army of grooms that had attended those aristocratic horses. So far as Tory could tell, there was not a single draft in the entire building, which could not be said of the manor.

Of course, poor Lord Merdan was not actually aware he was hosting the King; if he had been, he would have been mortified at sticking the King, the Queen, and the King's Own in his barn to share a dormitory. He thought he was playing host to a group of Heralds and a handful of unspecified "others" that the Heralds needed to meet with. And monsters. The monsters made him very nervous, and he was just as happy that they were tucked away in the barn, in the stalls, well out of sight.

Tory had not expected the King. He certainly had not expected the Queen. Or his mother, the King's Own Herald. And he was exceedingly relieved that as soon as they had had the time to begin explanations, Kee had stepped up and spoken up for himself, including his reasoning about going into Karse. A short explanation, given that the relieved greetings had taken up quite a bit of time for both families.

That had been a couple of candlemarks ago, when they had first arrived here. Following that, the King had made it clear there was going to be a very private conversation between the Prince and his parents. This was one discussion that Tory had been grateful that he did not need to participate in.

The one with his father, mother, and brother Perry was going to be easier on the nerves. But first he'd given his report about everything, which Mags had noted with only mild disapproval, but understanding, when it came to Kee's insistence that they *were* going into Karse and they *were* helping to rescue Sira.

"I couldn't stop him without knocking him out, and even then, I think he would have gotten away from me and followed Ahkhan anyway," he told Mags.

"Prolly," Mags said laconically. "He didn' get the *Royal Obligations* stuff knocked into him th' way his older brothers and sister did."

With that part over, the rest was just narrative, although it was hard to contain his own excitement when describing all the real magic he had seen.

"But I don't understand how you knew to send the Heralds and the Guards," he ended.

"Well, fust of all, you cain't hev expected t'send what sounded like *goodbye t'ever'thin'* letters, the two of ye, and *not* 'spect us t'hev taken thet poorly," Mags replied, in what sounded like scolding for the first time since the Royal Party had intercepted the lot of them on the road to the Menmellith Border crossing. "As fer how, it 'pears thet your friend's llusions don't work on Farsight. For which we'd all better be grateful."

"Of course," Amily added, "we only needed a glimpse. Once we knew which stream you were following, it was logical you'd take it straight to the Border. So we had plenty of time to assemble a force to greet you. And Tariday and Elissa insisted on coming along in case you needed a rescue. Which—well, we'll never know if you could have fought free of them yourselves, I'm just glad you didn't have to."

Tory thought back on the fight and could only shudder. It was true that the huge earth *afrinn* that had come to their rescue *might* have been able to regather itself and avalanche down on the Karsites a second and even a third time—but it might not have. And he was just as glad they hadn't needed to find out.

They were gathered at the fireplace at the east end of the grooms' quarters. The Royals were at the fireplace at the west end. Sira and Ahkhan were sitting quietly in the middle, with the rest of the Heralds. Tory kept glancing over at them, feeling guilty about how uncomfortable they surely must be feeling. At least Kee seemed to be holding his own with the King and Queen. His head was up, his posture was confident, but not defiant, which made Tory think that—

—wait, the King had signaled to Herald Mikel.

Mikel came over, spoke a few words, and went back and got Sira and Ahkhan.

Oh, glory. Here it comes. Now he was doubly glad he was not part of that conversation.

Amily, Mags, and Perry had all followed his gaze and noted what had just happened. Tory turned back to his father, dreading what was coming next, but to his surprise he saw that Mags was smiling wryly.

"Bey c'n charm a broody hen off 'er eggs," Mags observed. "If'n thet runs in the family, an' I reckon it does, them two'll hev no prollem wi' th' King an' Queen. Jist wait fer it."

And in what Tory considered a shockingly short period of time, the Queen was embracing Sira, and the King was slapping Ahkhan and his own son on the back.

"There 'tis," Mags observed. " 'Course, it don't hurt thet murderous little gel's a Princess uv sorts."

"It also doesn't hurt that Kee can never come back to Valdemar," Tory said bluntly, finally putting into words what he hoped Kee had made clear to his parents. "He's not just a Mage, Father, he's a *powerful* one. There's no way the *vrondi* would leave him alone, even if he never performed another act of magic in his life. And . . . that's not likely. When you've got something that strong, it makes you want to use it."

Mags pinched the bridge of his nose. "I 'spect that has somethin' t'do with it too," he admitted. " 'S better Kee's gonna be safe in the safest place in th' world than playin' ambassador outside Valdemar. You say as a Mage, he's gonna be right in their stronghold, all the time?"

"That's what Sira said. She said their Mages can scarcely be coaxed to come out into the daylight, much less leave the Mountain."

"I want to go talk to those *afrinns* you have with you," Perry said, getting up. "Or, rather, try. I think they might be akin to that living city, and I might well be able to speak with them."

He was down the stairs before anyone could stop him, though, truthfully, no one really wanted to. It was just what Tory had just said about Kee—*when you've got something that strong, it makes you want to use it.* And Perry absolutely *could not* have seen nonhuman creatures and not tried to speak with them. Especially since they already knew his *kyree* companion, Larral, could. That had been established on the road here—and, in fact, Larral was with them right now down in the stable part of the barn where they were gathered on the downstairs, eastside hearth, probably giving them a *kyree's* view of Valdemar and all it contained. Or gossip. Or both.

Tory cast another look at Kee, and he felt such mingled happiness and sadness that he could not tell where one ended and the other began. Because Kee sat with his arm easily around Sira, and she with her arm around him, and he *felt*, like a physical tearing, the last of the Kee he had once known separating from him. It closed his throat, and he turned back to his parents with his eyes stinging.

To see them looking at him with compassion. Mags reached out and clapped him gently on the shoulder.

"Ev'thin' changes," Mags said, with deep sympathy. "An 'e's leavin' ye behind. This might be both hardest an' easiest way fer ye. 'Cause it's not like he died—but it's kinda worse this way."

He rubbed his eyes with the back of his hand. "I have a selfish reason, too," he admitted. "Kee was why I could reach so far with Farsight. Now—I got nothin'. Or at least, nothin' any of your agents haven't got. I—"

He choked up and got to his feet, turning blindly toward the stair and stumbling down it.

His parents didn't try to stop him.

Rather than join Perry and the *afrinns* at the hearth, he went out the door into the winter air. It had snowed the previous night, and a thin coat of white covered everything. This barn was in the middle of partially wooded hills that had been dedicated to pasturage for the horses, and the manor was somewhere on the other side of it, behind him. As a result, there was no sign of human hands but the wooden fences. It was beautiful. It didn't ease his heart, but the austere, sterile white and clouded skies did match his plummeting, bleak mood. The hole inside him hurt, and never mind that he was happy for Kee, for himself—he was devastated. Abi had her Master Artificer rank and her friends, Perry had his *kyree* and his Gift and his friends, and he had . . . nothing. And yes, he'd seen magic, real magic at work, and it had been thrilling. But Kee had his love *and* magic and what had he gotten out of this besides adventure? Nothing. In fact, he'd ended up with less than he'd had when he'd begun.

Something shoved him from behind.

He turned to remonstrate with whoever had been so rude—

And found himself looking into a pair of bottomless, sapphire eyes . . .

. . . . and felt that hole inside him fill with something new.

He lost all track of time for a while and only came to himself again when Elissa shoved him in the chest with her nose again, playfully.

:What . . . . : he began.

:We don't Choose people who have unfinished business. You had a lot.: She nuzzled his chest. *:We also don't Choose people who don't need us. Now, you need me.:*

:But . . . . : Something occurred to him, and he placed his right hand on her forehead and *looked* for his sister Abi.

And there she was. Back at Haven, drawing up plans for something. But . . .

. . . that was not all he could see. He sensed Trey, sitting on the Throne and listening to a petitioner. And Kat, circulating among the courtiers waiting to be heard, quietly *listening* as only she could.

And Niko, practicing swordwork in the salle, and the two youngest Royals at their lessons.

And Bey, anxiously waiting for word from his two missing children. And if he stretched a little farther. . . .

:What can I Farsee now?: he asked her in amazement.

:Quite a lot. If you've been there, we can See it. If you know the person, we can See what they're doing. And of course, if you're related . . . well, Chosen,: she said into his mind. *:I think between us we can still keep track of your entire far-flung family. Even the murdering ones.:* Then she laughed. *:And it looks as if there is going to be a true successor to your father, the King's Herald-Spy, after all.:*

Sira looked up, and felt a surge of emotion she did not even try to deny or hide. From the absolutely unmarked trail that led to the Sleepgiver stronghold, it was easy to see the Mountain itself, marked—if only you knew it—by the circling lammergeyers that made it their home.

Home! She glanced over at Kee, who stared up at the Mountain, recognizing it by the circling birds she had told him about. He looked back over at her, and smiled.

Kee and Sira were mounted on ponies they had picked up just outside of Amber Moon South. Ahkhan, however, was mounted on his beloved Natya; there had been a very emotional reunion between them when the Guard who had "bought" her brought her out of the stable for him and told him, "I was absolutely certain you were coming back. I was just taking care of her until you did."

They had met up with the earth *afrinn* that had saved them just on the other side of the Menmellith border. His name, it turned out, was Lyasho, and like the others, he fully intended to resume his former place as an ally of the Mountain.

Once into Menmellith, he and all the other *afrinns* had taken advantage of the Amber Moon Portal along with the three humans. From there, they had gone on ahead to the Mountain—all except for Eakkashet, who insisted on staying with the humans.

They had all been perfectly happy to have the *afrinn* along—just in case. If nothing else, Eakkashet had been the perfect night guard, since once Kee fed him power for the night, he didn't need to rest.

"So . . . now I get to meet *your* family. Please tell me they won't murder me," Kee said, and it sounded as if he was only half in jest.

"Actually, we do a lot less murdering than you think." That was Ahkhan, speaking before Sira could. He smiled at Kee. "Change is generational, my brother. It took my father a long time to convince the Sleepgivers to forsake their old Talismans for the still older kind, but it has been accomplished. And as the older Sleepgivers grow too old to practice the trade, the younger ones are looking past our traditions, and asking if they might, perhaps, find other means of serving the Nation than bringing death—or requesting that they bring endless sleep *only* to those who, shall we say, deserve it."

Kee blinked at him. "Are you saying—"

Ahkhan shrugged. "By the time my father decides to tend to the orchards and my brother Teychik is the Banner Bearer, I believe the Sleepgivers will no longer resemble the days of my grandfather, and they will mostly be employed as bodyguards."

But as Sira glanced over at Kee, she couldn't help but notice that he still looked uneasy.

"What's the matter?" she asked with concern.

"I—I'm walking into *your* home, to your people, and without any introduction or 'please may I' or 'by your leave,' pretty much announcing I'm marrying you and there is nothing they can do about it," he said, helplessly. "They don't know me, they don't know anything about me, they don't know anything about Valdemar—"

He was interrupted by the sound of laughter from overhead. They both looked up, to see Eakkashet in his firehawk form hovering above them.

"I can fix that, Prince," the *afrinn* said. *"Hold up your left arm."*

Clearly bewildered by the demand, Kee did as he was told. And Eakkashet dropped down to land on it.

But while it was a firehawk that began that drop, the bird that closed its talons on Kee's arm was the biggest lammergeyer that Sira had ever seen.

And it was wreathed in flame.

"There!" crowed the fire *afrinn*. *"You are riding into the stronghold with the fiery symbol of the nation on your arm. There could be no greater sign that you are one with the Nation, even though you were born elsewhere. I dare anyone to doubt you now!"*

"And when they discover what a powerful Mage you are," Sira added, "powerful enough to renew our old alliances with all four of the races of *afrinn*, they are more likely to be worried that you will leave than that you will stay."

"That," said Kee, looking happier than she had ever seen him at the moment, as he gazed into her eyes, "is going to be the least of their worries, my Princess."

ABOUT THE AUTHOR

Mercedes Lackey is a full-time writer and has published numerous novels and works of short fiction, including the bestselling *Heralds of Valdemar* series. She is also a professional lyricist and licensed wild bird rehabilitator. She lives in Oklahoma with her husband and collaborator, artist Larry Dixon, and their flock of parrots.

www.**mercedeslackey**.com

For more fantastic fiction, author events,
exclusive excerpts, competitions, limited editions and more

VISIT OUR WEBSITE
titanbooks.com

LIKE US ON FACEBOOK
facebook.com/titanbooks

FOLLOW US ON TWITTER AND INSTAGRAM
@TitanBooks

EMAIL US
readerfeedback@titanemail.com

CENTRAL 17-11-2020